The Engine Woman's Light

Laurel Anne Hill

Independent Press Association
First Award
Steampunk

© 2017 Laurel Anne Hill
Published by Sand Hill Review Press, LLC
All rights reserved
www.sandhillreviewpress.com,
P.O. Box 1275, San Mateo, CA 94401
(415) 297-3571

ISBN: 978-1-937818-47-0 Perfect bound
ISBN: 978-1-937818-48-7 eBook
ISBN: 978-1-937818-80-7 Case laminate

Library of Congress Control Number:
2016957318
Cover art by Julie Dillon,
Winner of Hugo & Chesley Awards

SHRP
Sand Hill Review Press

Dedicated to my husband, David,
Great-Grandma Hipólita Orendain de Medina,
and Engine Number 2472.

Journal of Before, Year 1878

1. Flight and Wilderness Walking

Zetta stared aghast at the caramel-colored foundling in the wicker basket beside her. The baby wore a ragged blue-and-white gown. This was the christening gown, the one she'd sewn, had buttoned on sons, grandsons and great-grandsons. What the tarnation was her precious creation—a family heirloom—doing on some foolish couple's mistake?

The train to the workhouse and asylum for the poor curved around a bend. Zetta swayed in her seat and grasped the back of an empty one. The baby, not even two months old, slept without stirring. Diego, her oldest grandson must have given the gown to that charity for unwanted children who got sent away. How could he have done such a thoughtless thing?

Tears trickled down Zetta's cheeks. Her bony hands— age spots like spattered paint on her pale skin—clasped each other in the folds of her skirt. Shameful red blotches hid underneath the blue fabric. *Leper. Unclean.* The grimy window to her left displayed the setting sun. The baby gown she'd sewn and tatted as a young woman was worth nothing to her family. She never should have volunteered to care for a foundling on the ride to South California.

Should have left the sedated thing wrapped in that old blanket. Ignorance would have been better than truth.

An old man across the aisle babbled nonsense. Zetta fumbled for a soft cotton rag and blew her nose. The baby's strumpet of a mother should have arranged an abortion. Local midwives would always unblock the menses of women in need. Neither the infant nor the gown would be here, then. A twinge of guilt hit Zetta. Diego's thoughtlessness wasn't the child's fault.

Zetta reached into her satchel, pulled out a Bible, then opened the book to a dog-eared page. *For though I should walk in the midst of the shadow of death.*

Her husband, Javier, had died five years ago, yet he'd visited her during the past several months. She wrapped herself in his old brown-and-gray serape. The valley he must have walked to return to her held both mystery and shadows. Such uncomfortable looks she'd received from her family while carrying on conversations with him. Her son's reaction to the red blotches on her thighs and chest had proven even more disconcerting. *Thou art with me.* The psalm brought solace.

She smiled at the infant, so perfectly formed and cute. Did a kind spirit watch over it? Perhaps an asylum attendant would take the little one home. No, the workers probably had trouble supporting their own children. North California paid the South California asylum only a set amount of money for each child, according to the agreement between their governments. This poor baby wouldn't even receive a smallpox vaccination, let alone love and schooling. It might even be sold to the Mendoza family—the descendants of the ruthless Gold War *bandidos.* Brown-skinned foundlings often were.

How fortunate Zetta's great-grandsons were, loved and safe within the walls of the Navarro family farm house. She touched her thigh. *Leprosy.* Her great-grandchildren would be even safer in her absence.

Zetta yawned. Today had been a long day, what with all the goodbyes. Too bad Diego hadn't been there. His job kept him traveling. She fingered the coarse wool of Javier's serape. Her eyelids closed.

•

Zetta awakened in dim light. The passenger car clicked against rails. A silvery glow shimmered above the foundling in the basket. Zetta blinked and the glow took form—Javier's face. This time, he still had all his curly, black hair—like in the early years of their marriage. She smelled his aroma of beer, sweeter than the scent of hot chocolate with cinnamon.

"I know I've not visited for a week," Javier said, his voice bitter. "Just listen and do what I ask. Our oldest grandson didn't exactly give the blue-and-white gown away to strangers. Diego's concealed a terrible truth from his wife and the rest of his living kin."

What was Javier talking about? What possible horrid secret might Diego—

"He's this baby's *padre*," Javier said.

Diego? The foundling's father? Zetta recoiled with a gasp, as though kicked in the chest and stomach by a plow mule. At this very moment, her great-grandsons were safe at home, dressed in nightshirts and listening to bedtime stories. Yet here was a reject, also her own flesh and blood, entrusted to her by some miracle of God. She stared in horror at the ghost, then at the infant. How could Diego have committed such wretched and irresponsible acts?

Something pressed against Zetta's shoulder. She jerked with surprise. A young nurse in an ankle-length dress and pinafore withdrew her hand and eyed Zetta with concern. The woman didn't appear shocked. Javier's apparition wasn't for her eyes to see.

Zetta knew she'd better smile. Not do anything to arouse suspicion or appear ill. The baby would be given to someone else to watch.

"I just had a bit of heartburn," Zetta said. "I'm fine now."

"If you need a stomach infusion," the nurse said, "the intern in the end car's got special teas." She patted Zetta's arm and turned her attention toward a beckoning passenger.

"Be more careful." Javier whistled with relief. "Right now, no one else knows you've been given charge of our great-granddaughter. Talk to me only with thoughts. I'll hear."

A great-granddaughter! Zetta had prayed for a girl child for three generations. Could this really be true?

"It's true," Javier said. "Now, better get down to business. At Thistlewood Station, you and our great-granddaughter are breaking out of here."

Thistlewood—not a town Zetta had ever heard of before. The place must have stood in the middle of nowhere. Well, the sooner they escaped, the better. Her great-granddaughter was not going to end up in any asylum.

"The other stations are patrolled." Javier chuckled. "Thistlewood's quiet as a grave. Claimed to be haunted. Nobody living hangs around there for long. There's a settlement ten miles or so away."

Zetta glanced around. A nurse from the forward car had drugged the baby on sleeping powder, then brought it to her. She'd used a key before and after passing through the double set of doors. All doors were kept locked while running, and most when not. Was escape even possible?

"Only one car between this one and the brakeman's caboose," Javier said. "Just one empty car and two sets of doors to an easy exit. Now I need a place to hide, but still be near you. Some people get agitated when ectoplasm hangs around in the air," he chuckled.

I know a good hiding place. Zetta opened her tapestry valise and lifted it into her lap. The owl face of a small copper candle lamp peered up from a nest of remnants. Beside the lamp rested her brass alarm clock. She pointed. Javier floated inside the timepiece. She wound the clock. How comforting, its new and ghostly sound. The time was five minutes before nine.

"There'll be a boarding and water stop soon," Javier said, accompanied by a tick-tock rhythm. "Thistlewood's on the schedule for one-forty. The last stop before South California."

Zetta sat straight up, a plan bubbling within her brain. Seventeen or eighteen passengers, most of them asleep, were in the car. Several more ought to board in a few miles. There was one lavatory in the car, at the front. What would the odds be of a passenger using the restroom between one and one-thirty at night and remembering to bolt the door? The clock ticked louder. Javier voiced his approval.

The engine decelerated and whistled a long night-piercing blast. The train rolled into a brightly-lit rural station. Locks released on the boarding gate of the car, producing little mechanical squeals. A deep voice called out instructions to board.

A ruddy-faced bald man, fat as a well-fed leech and close to sixty, staggered through the forward door. He spewed out more profanity than a saloon full of Mendozas. Who was this rude ungentleman? The sour reek of booze turned Zetta's stomach even seven rows of seats away. The attendant near the drunk scrunched up her face.

"He's all yours," a feminine voice shouted from the platform. "His name's Graham Locke."

"Go shit a pile," the drunkard yelled. "I'm not Mr. Locke."

"Sew that sot's mouth shut," a woman shrieked from across the aisle, her wrinkled cheeks as shriveled as two dried prunes forgotten in a pantry.

"Go sit on a cucumber," Mr. Locke—who wasn't Mr. Locke—said.

Mr. Locke tipped his derby hat, a pair of goggles covering the hatband, and belched. Odd. Goggles were a British South California style of apparel. The train hadn't reached the north-south border.

The nurse turned toward a flat metal telegraph pad mounted by the restroom and tapped a message. Minutes later, a lanky young man, dressed in a dark shirt, vest and trousers, emerged through the rear doorway, black satchel in hand. The intern? An older man with a brakeman's cap on his head followed. They both looked irritated and didn't reset the lock behind them.

The drunkard hollered a new round of obscenities. The nurse tried to usher him toward a seat. He pushed her aside. The brakeman ducked behind him and shoved the backs of his legs. The drunk wobbled like a lopsided toy top and crashed forward on his knees. The intern dove on top of him, syringe in hand. The nurse poured something onto a large handkerchief and joined the fray. By the time the departure whistle sounded, Mr. Locke had lost. His mountain of flesh slumped on the front set of seats. His left foot, wedged in an ankle-high work boot, protruded into the aisle.

"That'll keep him about three hours." The intern picked the syringe off the floor. He brushed an unruly clump of hair away from his eyes and ambled behind the brakeman toward the rear of the train. The two men likely shared the caboose.

What time is it? Zetta thought to Javier.

"Nine forty-five," Javier's spirit said from the clock.

"Pardon me, please," Zetta said to the passing nurse. "Could I move to a different car before that man starts another ruckus?"

"The next car," the nurse said, "is only for the—well, you know—the recruits to build new tracks. We'll try to keep the bloke quiet."

"Can't you get help?" Zetta needed to learn if railroad police or constables were aboard.

"The intern, brakeman and I will manage." The nurse fidgeted with her smock, as though fishing for appropriate words. "Don't you be concerned, now."

The nurse brought a lumpy pillow and a folded blanket discolored with a stain. She punched her knuckles against the pillow to fluff it. Zetta thanked her and leaned against the window. One doctor and no officers rode this train—a short staff. And the only other passenger car in use carried Chinese laborers, probably headed to build tracks to that new South California oil field she'd heard about. No wonder the nurse had asked Zetta to mind the child. Things might work out well, indeed.

Zetta retrieved a water jar and a flat burlap package from her valise. She unfolded the cloth and tore off a morsel of tortilla. Savoring the flavor of corn, she glanced at the brass clock.

"Head for the lavatory at twelve-forty," Javier said.

She smiled in agreement, glanced toward her great-granddaughter, then let the swaying train and muted ticks bring sleep.

•

Such dim illumination in the railcar. Did Juan, her youngest son, sit across the aisle? No, Zetta had just dreamed about his escape to Mexico. Nothing more.

She reached into her valise and felt the edges of the sealed envelope she'd addressed yesterday to Raúl, her middle son. The envelope contained the postcard Juan had sent her many years before, to let her know he and his friend, Billy, had reached their destination alive. Three words comprised the message—*God Bless Mexico*. Raúl had asked for the memento. She had meant to mail the card upon arrival at the asylum. The two boys had been very different, but close.

"Eleven fifty-five," Javier said from inside the alarm clock. "And don't fret. The young doc's in charge of a postal box in the caboose."

Zetta changed the sleeping baby's diaper, then organized her own belongings. The moon wasn't full tonight. A clear sky, though. With closed eyes, she practiced locating each object within the bag. Her lips formed silent words as she touched the envelope containing the postcard. *God bless Mexico.*

Her family would learn she'd left the train and worry about her safety. She should write a message on the back of the envelope going to Raúl. At the front of the car, Mr. Graham Locke, or whoever he was, snored more obnoxiously than a bear bloated on Sunday bacon. She grinned and printed a few cryptic sentences, designed for the eyes of her errant grandson, Diego.

A man behind Zetta cried out a muffled name. She flinched and turned. The man, eyes closed, thrashed his arm. She checked her clock. Twelve thirty-eight. Several other passengers stirred. What if they needed to use the lavatory? Zetta floundered into the aisle, her back stiff. She slipped past the fat bear, lunged for the lavatory, then yanked open the door. Once inside the necessary, she pushed a metal bolt to secure the door behind her.

The baby—she should have brought the child with her. Panic had affected her reasoning. It was too late then to go back and grab the basket. She needed to calm down and get her job done.

The lavatory smelled of urine, had less light than the main car and was barely wide enough to accommodate the wooden commode. A makeshift seat sat over the hole. Zetta had counted on some sort of seat being installed for the benefit of the infirm. Shadows obscured the track below.

She rolled up the sleeves of her cotton blouse and wiggled the seat, which was loose. When the bolts didn't snap, she sat and relieved herself, careful to avoid touching the splinters on the commode's topside.

The nurse might grow suspicious of a passenger staying in here for more than a few minutes in the middle of the night. She finished and stood, then wrenched the seat with all her might. The flabby skin on her thin upper arms jiggled. The seat bolts held. Her plan to create a diversion in the bathroom wasn't going to work.

"Are you all right?" the sugary voice of the nurse said from the other side of the lavatory door.

A sharp rap followed. Everything was going wrong. She needed that woman the way she needed a broken foot.

"I won't be much longer," Zetta said.

Zetta grunted with disgusting authenticity to mask the sounds of her real business. After a few minutes, she yanked the seat again. Her arms ached. One bolt pulled free. A dozen yanks later, the other bolt yielded. She

14

replaced the seat and rinsed her hands in the metal wash bowl, her muscles afire with pain. So long, she'd taken. What if the nurse had guessed her plan and was waiting? Perhaps the woman had looked in the valise and found the envelope. How foolish to write a suspicious note that the wrong eyes might see. Right then, the nurse could even be giving the baby to another passenger. Zetta never should have left the child.

Zetta unlocked the door and cracked it open. The coach was quiet, and the nurse stood halfway down the aisle. Two elderly women sat in line to use the lavatory, the one in front frail, sunken-cheeked, and holding a cane. Nothing bad had happened, after all.

"I'd be very careful to lock the door, if I were you," Zetta said. Her escape plan would work best if the next woman in line locked the door. She pointed toward the rotund drunkard. "He's due to wake up any minute now."

Zetta walked toward Mr. Locke, steadying herself with the backs of seats. She studied the position of his left leg and counted to three. With full force she kicked him in the shin and repeated the assault. One of his bleary bloodshot eyes opened. Swaying, she proceeded toward her seat, pretending to be oblivious to her deed.

A series of piercing cries emanated from the lavatory. The nurse raced down the aisle in that direction. Soon the nurse and the elderly woman exchanged frantic words. The poor lady trapped inside could not reach the door to release the lock. A splinter had stabbed her posterior, which then got stuck down the toilet hole. Her cries turned to howls, then to desperate sobbing. The nurse raced for the telegraph box. The intern and brakeman charged into the car. Graham Locke staggered to center stage, derby hat pulled down over his eyes and arms flailing.

"Get her off the pot," Mr. Locke bellowed. "I got to piss."

The drunk unbuttoned his trousers, then let go. An old woman yelled at him. He puked in the aisle.

With this stunning performance in full progress, Zetta slung the longer strap of her valise over her shoulder and carried the infant in the basket to the rear of the car. The connecting doors slid open as though freshly buttered. She passed through the vestibule into the shadowy emptiness of the next unit and finally into the caboose and pharmacy.

Javier's ethereal figure once again hovered by her side. All of him, not just his face. She shut the car door and hit a lever to activate the lock. The pharmacy was used to store opium and even stronger medicines. From the outside, the door would have to be forced with a hatchet. Zetta grinned and checked her clock. One-twenty.

Iron bars shielded the windows. She shoved the release latch to open the rear door. The night breeze burst into the car. The baby shifted, making a muted gurgling sound. Zetta discovered a ring of keys, then yanked and cajoled cabinets and drawers open. Here were the sedatives, the ones needed to subdue Mr. Locke. She flung glass bottles and syringes out the rear door and over the railing, except for those stored on a single tray. A commotion arose from the next car—banging, hollering and swearing.

The intern glared through a small steel-barred window from the vestibule between the cars. How delightful, his distorted face and frantic gestures. She pointed toward the remaining syringes and vials of sedatives on the tray. Then she gestured toward the open rear door. Zetta had won, and the young man knew it.

A long blast of the train's whistle, the signal for deceleration, drowned out the intern's chaotic sounds. Zetta reached down to grip her great-granddaughter's basket and spied the postal box bolted under a counter. She'd nearly forgotten. She deposited the envelope addressed to Raúl.

The train crawled to a halt. Zetta waved at the intern and exited via the rear door, resetting the locking mechanism. No one would pursue. With such a big fat problem on board and a small crew, who would bother with one old woman and a foundling?

As for the envelope, Raúl would receive it in a couple weeks. The family would gather and puzzle over her strange message. Diego would eventually decipher its meaning, at least in secret.

God bless Graham Locke, she had written, *who will be saved on the Day of Judgment from eternal damnation and permitted to sit on the right hand of Barabbas the Thief. This drunk, who would piss on the babe in the bulrushes, shall be made to part the Red Sea. Yet he will never realize what the shit he ever did to deserve redemption.*

•

The train pulled out with a series of steam hisses and regimented click-clacks. An odor of smoke and fuel oil remained. *So little light.*

"We'll head east." Javier's amber glow shimmered. "Fire your lamp first, and be careful not to trip."

Zetta set down both baby and satchel, then rummaged for the owl-shaped lantern. She struck a match on the rough brass. The candle's comforting glow soon protruded through the squinted eyes of the owl.

She maneuvered off the platform. Hardly enough moonlight to see past the end of her nose. She was too old to lug a baby down miles of trail in the dark.

"A hundred ten degrees by high noon," Javier said. "I hate to think of her little pink tongue all swollen from thirst."

Zetta heaved a heavy sigh and followed Javier's spirit light. Her toes felt out the suitability of the path. Shallow sand...probably all right. Deep stuff would spell trouble. Progress remained slow. She stepped with her left foot, her right foot, and then did it again.

Her pace steadied on the main road, which was overgrown with weeds but not as deeply rutted. Fine gravel crunched as she walked. Poor Juan. Was he happy or even still alive? Her arms and shoulders ached. She might die by tomorrow.

Zetta's toe stubbed against a hard object. She tripped and lunged forward. The baby basket slipped from her grasp. The candle lamp flew. A short infant cry pierced the air.

The dirt roadway met Zetta hard. Dear God, she'd fallen. Stunned, she lay still. Her long valise strap tangled around her arm. A bad feeling pulsed in her left foot.

"Move your hands," Javier said. "Then try your arms."

Her arms and hands stung. They worked, though.

"How about your legs?" His spirit light flickered.

Zetta moved her sore left foot and recoiled with pain. She'd twisted her ankle and would never be able to walk. The sun would fry her and the baby by noon.

Her great-granddaughter! What if the fall had hurt the child? Zetta let out a plaintive wail.

"Reach for our little one." Javier's translucent image provided meager light. "Giving up's the wrong choice."

Javier kept talking, his tone encouraging yet firm. Zetta did as told—not with ease. Her hand felt the rise and fall of the baby's chest. The diaper was wet. Nothing else seemed damp or sticky. Her great-granddaughter was probably unharmed. She prayed the sedatives given by the nurse would wear off soon so she could be sure.

Zetta groped for her valise. Dry fabric. The water jars hadn't broken. She dragged herself along the ground, searching for her lamp. There it was. Her fingers explored the contours of the owl lantern. The candle was missing.

"There are others in the valise," Javier said. "Remember?"

Zetta groaned. Her left shoe was so tight. Her injury was worse than a twisted ankle.

"Love of my life," Javier said. "Get up and follow me."

Rising happened in stages, to her knees before her feet. Zetta fought back tears, lit the lamp, then rigged her load. Plodding came next. Pain accompanied every step. She wanted to cry, to vomit and to scream. She staggered forward, always toward Javier, carrying the baby, lamp and valise. If only he weren't a ghost, could hold her and help her walk.

18

After a long while, the sun rose, revealing more than the hopelessness of a flat desert horizon. A glorious red-and-purple sky crowned a haven of rocky foothills several miles away. She blew out the stub of her last candle and tucked the owl into the valise. The terrain around the roadbed became rockier, the air warmer. Her calves tightened as she climbed. Pain, like sharp knives, stabbed her sides. The baby moved in the basket. The sedative was wearing off. Massive rocky outcrops loomed a mile or so ahead.

The agony of walking, intense and on the brink of unbearable, consumed Zetta. Her injured foot, swollen, looked as thick as an old oak. A rocky haven stood just off the roadway. Left foot...right foot. The ground was uneven and the outcrop of boulders hard to reach. The hot air was difficult to breathe. She braced for pain and stepped again and again.

At the resting place, Zetta dropped her valise and sheltered the baby basket from direct sun. She still wore Javier's serape. Odd, she hadn't noticed before then. The garment was difficult to pull off over her head. She kept fumbling. How many miles separated her from the settlement? She placed her clock where its brass surface might catch the glint of the sun and be seen.

She collapsed on the ground and elevated her swollen foot on her valise. Her stomach hurt—probably time to eat. Her plain tortilla tasted unappetizing and seemed to stick in her throat. The sun-warmed water didn't behave as though it intended to be swallowed. How dry her skin felt.

"She'll wake up hungry soon," Zetta said to Javier. "What if I don't hear her cry? And what'll I feed her?"

"Don't worry," Javier said. "Let yourself sleep."

Zetta smiled at the beautiful brown face, at skin richer in color than a pool of wild honey. The baby's eyelashes were so soft and long, and what a darling pug nose. A bird chirped from the branch of a scrub oak. The girl needed a name, something musical. What was the one she and Javier had never used?

"A fine great-granddaughter," Javier said. He seemed so close. "Write down her name."

"I can't think of the right one," Zetta said.

"Give it a try."

She rummaged through her valise for a pencil and her Bible, pain a distant companion. Her pencil practically printed a name on the first page without her help: Juanita Elise Jame-Navarro. She added the year and estimated month of birth for good measure.

Zetta clasped Juanita's petite fingers. There would be so many things to teach her—how to pat tortillas, stew beef with turnips, bake squash pie. How to ride, sew, read, do math and use beautiful words. She gripped the tiny hand tighter.

"Sleep, love," Javier said.

"Just for a bit." The desert blurred.

When Zetta awakened and stood, her body lay at her feet—on Javier's serape on the ground. *Gray. No breathing.* She was dead?

Baby Juanita wailed. Zetta reached out but couldn't touch her no matter how hard she tried. How would she help Juanita then? And what about all the other little ones the train had yet to take?

Journal of Promise, Year 1894

2. The Vision Wore Goggles

BRILLIANT LIGHT STRUCK me. I squeezed my
eyelids shut and shielded them with my wet hands. Gold-
and-white rays pulsed into my pupils. They shot right into
me. Oh, merciful spirits. Nothing could block the light's
path.

Words buzzed in my ears, loud as swarming bees.
"Locke Graham," the word-bees said. "Bless God. Bit a for
just." The rest of the utterances made even less sense. I
even kept forgetting most of what I'd just heard.

My eyes stung. Pain stabbed my ear drums. I spat out
the water I'd meant to swallow. I would have dropped to
my knees if I'd not already been on them beside the creek.
Blessed saints and ancestors! Only one thing could trigger
such an assault of light, sound and confusion: an important
spirit prepared to deliver a big vision—my first major
vision ever.

"Juanita Elise Jame-Navarro," a deep voice boomed
over the buzzing. "Open your eyes and see truth."

Open my eyes and see truth. A big vision always came
with commands. Wei, the old mystic traveler man in my
village, always said so. I was Promise's only other mystic.
Both Wei and the Shadow World of Spirits would expect
me to greet this ghostly visitor face-to-face.

Yet supernatural bursts of light could blind me for the
rest of my life. Wei had told me that, too. My heart
pounded. I breathed out hard. In less than three months
I'd turn sixteen—in June. A full-grown mystic traveler
ought to behave like one.

I forced open my eyes and winced. Over and over, I blinked. The bursts flared from a blurred figure of...a man. Many times since my fourteenth birthday, I'd visited passageways between life and the Shadow World. I'd never even heard of a spirit with this strong a light.

The man's features sharpened a little. He held a walking staff and wore the type of rough tunic and robe my people did—like from pictures in a Bible. The terrible eye-stabbing beams arose from something on his head. Still I managed to see his nose and the outline of his long white beard. This spirit man was a stranger, as far as I could tell.

My eyeballs ached. My temples throbbed. My muscles tensed so hard, they could have turned to stone. If this light got any worse, blindness wouldn't be an issue. My whole head would explode.

"My eyes are open," I declared. "Have mercy upon them, kind sir. Upon me." Nothing eased the spasms of blinking. At least the buzzing stopped. "What truth do you wish to show me? Please be prompt and clear."

The light softened and steadied. Thank God and the spirits. Through the man's image, I could see the bush behind him. Glowing spectacles rested against the brim of his flat-crowned hat. Goggles, that's what they were. Gear a modern traveler might wear in a dust storm.

"Before 1894 yields to 1895," the spirit man's loud voice echoed, "your people must take on a new life-saving mission."

"And our old life-saving mission?" Surely a spirit with the power of this one knew about the purpose the great hero Moses had given Promise. "Are we to end our prayers about that?"

"Your life, Juanita, was the last one saved by your people's old mission, as I recall." The man counted on his fingers. His staff stayed upright by itself, as if an invisible hand held it in place. "Over fifteen years have passed since that day, have they not?"

"You're right," I replied.

He'd sounded like he blamed me for the failure of our old mission, thought I should have prayed harder. Gravel dug into my knees. I pushed my dangling black braid back over my shoulder.

It wasn't my fault that my people could no longer give refuge to abandoned children, lepers and the elderly who escaped the asylum trains through the nearby valley. No escapees reached our village anymore. And not just because Promise lay between steep Sierra foothills in the middle of nowhere. The last train to stop within walking distance of Promise had carried the baby basket containing me, then an infant. That's what Papa always said. Regardless, no wise mystic started arguments with ghosts.

"Good sir." I bowed my head. "My people and I will do what the Shadow World wishes to help those in need. What new purpose awaits us?"

"That," the spirit man said, "is for your ancestors to decide."

"You mean I need to ask Great-Grandma Zetta and Great-Grandpa Javier?" I looked up. During my journeys to the Shadow World's approach passages, I always talked with them the most.

The spirit man, head lowered, waded into the creek. Clear water tumbled around his ankles. Through his ankles, too.

"You will learn whom to ask when the time comes," he said, still not looking at me. "Nonetheless, your assigned task, like the former one, connects with the trains. And it is dire."

Dire? A tingle arose in my shoulders, then raced down my spine, shooting to my fingertips and toes. Dear God, why did his eyes avoid mine?

"I beg you to tell me, sir," I said. "Will my ancestors summon me soon to provide guidance?"

"Of course. You will need that." He stared right at me. "If your task is not completed properly and in a timely manner, your community and all its inhabitants will cease to exist."

"You mean die?" I said. Who in the Shadow World had decreed such an unfair fate, and why? "But we number less than fifty. A group so small cannot perform huge miracles. We can only do our best."

The spirit man lifted his staff high. A beam of light flared across the creek's surface. The stream stopped flowing. Just stopped. Two walls of water formed, separated by newly exposed rocks and mud. Parted waters. Moses had done the same with a sea in my favorite Bible story. This stranger had parted the creek's waters here in my own world.

"Aiyeee." I clutched my jaws.

The great Moses—who'd once commanded Wei to found Promise here in Yankee North California—had long ago delivered God's messages to a pharaoh of ancient Egypt. Moses was too important to deliver just anybody's message. If this was him, the directive he'd brought me might also have come from God.

"Are you truly—" My voice squeaked.

"Your question, Juanita, ought to answer itself." Moses stroked his beard. "Besides, now is the time for heeding my words. Many streams and rivers await you. Some will part at the sound of your approaching footsteps. Others will laugh as they pull you toward murky depths. No matter what happens, never betray the new purpose the Shadow World will give you and your people." His gaze again turned to me. "Because a mystic traveler dies when the Shadow World decrees."

Then Moses was standing in a huge woven basket, the shape of a canoe. A ghost basket, it was. I could see right through the wicker. Above the basket hung three gigantic inflated bags—bright crimson, gold and blue—shaped like upside-down teardrops. The colorful bags, if they hadn't been ethereal, could have held thousands of leached acorns. And all the clothes in Promise could have fit into the canoe basket with room to spare. The thing had simply appeared, its wicker and bags connected by taut ropes.

Blade-like objects at one of the vessel's ends started spinning. Slowly at first, then faster and faster. The amazing contraption growled. It tipped this way and that, inched away from me and off the ground.

"One more detail," Moses shouted. "It is a bit of your own fault the train doesn't stop at Thistlewood Station anymore. More the fault of your great-grandmother, I suppose."

"What are you talking about?" I said. "Come back. I need to know more. Please."

Moses rode skyward. The vision faded, the surrounding clouds colored by the end of sunrise. Still kneeling, I looked down at the flowing creek.

"What did he mean?" I said to the water, "about Great-Grandma?"

"Listen," the water replied, as it sometimes did. "I told you earlier, but the light from Moses interfered with my magic. Your head immediately forgot most of what I said and scrambled the rest."

The water whispered a story about an old woman, a ghost and a baby—an escape from the asylum train. A journey through wilderness. A sleep leading to eternity. My foot throbbed with pain. My mouth and throat turned dry. I'd been the baby in the basket, but felt what Great-Grandma had.

Tears stung the corners of my eyes. And not just because my foot hurt and Great-Grandma had died carrying me to safety.

"I don't believe," I cried, "about my mother and father. They wanted to keep me. They must have."

I sobbed into my hands. My blood pulsed hard. Spirits of the water couldn't lie. Truths my heart knew tumbled their way to my brain. Years ago, I'd made up a story about my natural parents. How kind yet poor they were. How they searched to find me. I'd wanted to believe it, so I had. I lay down beside the stream.

"Your friend, Magdalena," the voice of the creek said, "has a sister she never knew." The water babbled more words, but they jumbled together.

Then one-by-one, two-by-two, those words separated and regathered. I closed my eyes and pictured a sixteen-year-old doe-eyed woman, heavy with child. The woman, like Magdalena, had the delicate lips, nose, and eyebrows of a painted doll.

An older man struck the young woman with his hand. She staggered and fell beside a wooden table. He dragged her across the dirt floor and out of the house.

"And stay out, you worthless slut," he hollered. "You're no longer any daughter of mine."

Fresh tears rolled down my cheeks. Another baby yet unborn was doomed to the train. Surely Magdalena—unable to have a baby of her own—would give anything to help raise her sister's child. I dug my hands into sand and gravel, sat up, then stood.

Moses, a dire mission, Magdalena's sister. So much had happened here this morning. The creek, no longer speaking, tumbled along like nothing had changed. It should have altered its course. The sun should have wept drops of blood.

"Please, dearest ancestors," I prayed, "summon me to a mystic passageway as soon as possible. Impart your wisdom. Before it's too late."

3. The Cave Laughed

I TURNED MY head away from Magdalena to peer down the steep hillside behind me toward Promise. The village lay hidden from view. I didn't need to see its boundary creek or little cluster of adobe buildings to picture this morning's encounters with Moses and the whispering water. Yet the knot in my stomach kept me glancing in the direction of home. God, I couldn't focus on the climb. How did Magdalena—ahead of me—manage? As soon as I'd returned from the creek, I'd told her all that had happened. Less than two hours had passed since then.

Will cease to exist... Moses had uttered those words. Had he referred to the death of me and my people? Or the destruction of our souls, as well? The next handhold felt secure. At least something did.

"Hurry up," Magdalena called, above me on the narrow, rugged path. "The village council meeting will start soon."

I maneuvered up a near-vertical section of the climb— my least favorite. Papa, beloved Galen and the rest of the council gathered near the mysterious Cave of Light. Just wait until Papa saw me there. Well, let him fume about my disobedience. I refused to wait until nightfall to tell him about my important vision. Besides, he worried too much about my safety. The cave wasn't any mystic's friend, but the Shadow World held dangers, too. My powers, awareness, and determination were stronger than Papa thought.

"Come on," Magdalena urged from up the hill. Gentle wind played with loose strands of hair from her long black braid. "You think too hard. If I can concentrate on climbing right now, so can you."

"A mystic traveler has to think hard." I edged up the next several feet of treacherous terrain. The hem of my tunic begged to trip my feet. "That shaman from the Yokut tribe would still be alive, if he'd thought harder about the cave ten years ago." He'd still be making that fragrant mint tea for me, too—and telling me exciting stories about the spirit world.

"You're not even going to be close to the Cave of Light today," Magdalena said.

How could she be certain?

Near the top of the path, I straddled a deep rut, then navigated the rift's center. The bark soles of my deer hide sandals slipped against loose dirt. Rocky handholds threatened to crumble in my grasp. A mystic traveler died when the Shadow World decreed. I was pretty sure my time hadn't arrived. Regardless, I wasn't ready to tumble off any hillside and break bones. Then I wouldn't be able to help my people accomplish our new purpose. Not before disaster struck.

"I need a pull," I called.

"Would I ever let you fall?"

I extended my arm upward and clasped Magdalena's waiting hand. That hand had once rescued me from a swollen stream in childhood. When a person saved the life of a friend, a sacred bond intertwined their futures. Magdalena pulled me onto the main trail. How good to find solid footing on level ground. I needed to rescue that baby for her to raise. She'd be a devoted mother to her sister's child.

"Allies forever," I said.

"Forever." Magdalena pointed to fresh sandal prints in the dirt. "I bet Cole and the others aren't far ahead of us. Wei slows them down."

Dearest Wei, my mentor, grew more unsteady on his feet with each passing week. This morning's visit to the sacred area would be his last, whether or not the Shadow World destroyed Promise. I scanned the east-west trail. A heaviness tugged at my heart. Council meetings were always held near the Cave of Light if weather permitted, the location of Wei's big vision of Moses many years ago.

Maybe Wei would consider me ready to represent him at future council meetings. Or they could move their meetings to the lower creek, where Moses had appeared to me several hours ago. Wei could still walk there.

"Let's go," Magdalena said.

"All right, I'm ready." I breathed out hard. "Show me the way." Well, I didn't know the area where the cave was hidden.

Magdalena nodded, her dark brown nose as delicate as a morning glory. Her eyebrows arched with grace. She bounded in the direction of the upper creek bridge. Soon she crossed the planks. The bridge swayed. So did her hips. Magdalena never let anyone in Promise—especially the men—forget her beauty. No wonder she could eavesdrop on council meetings and get away with it. Of course, her older husband, Cole, was a council member. That helped. Too bad spying and a request to speak at a council meeting were two different pots of beans.

I reached the bridge. Papa and Wei never permitted me to cross, although I'd done so once years ago and immediately scampered back toward home. I'd been too young to face the cave's power. These days, my vulnerability still worried Papa. The rest of my village, too. I was their future mystical mentor. Today, however, there was no turning back. I grasped the rope railings and followed my friend.

"We're almost there." Magdalena darted off the trail.

An uneven slope lay ahead. Odors of dust and warm dirt replaced those of greenery and water. I edged up a thin path, past massive gray rocks wedged into the hillside. Muffled voices reached my ears. I joined Magdalena at the crest of the hill, then peered over a boulder.

"They're saying the usual prayers for guidance," Magdalena said. "Get ready to surprise them."

Papa, Galen, Wei, Cook and Cole sat below on a stretch of level ground. The full council. Cook was the only woman member. They would discover us soon, as they must. I tensed my arms.

Forty feet or so beyond the group, at the base of a jutting incline, lay the entrance to a low cave. The Cave of Light would be higher up on that same hillside. Thick brush grew way up there. That shadowy spot could mark a concealed opening.

A blue-green light flashed twice from those shadows. I stiffened. Stories claimed such rays could enhance a mystic's magical power or bring death. Ordinary people could be blinded if they got too close. Moses had given me more than my share of strong beams. I'd survived unharmed. However, Magdalena—

"Look away from the blue-green light," I said.

"I'm not sure I saw one," Magdalena said.

"Be safe and look at Cole."

Another flash of light came. A horrid pressure filled my chest. This wasn't good.

"What are you two doing here?" Papa bellowed from below. "It's not your place to join us uninvited."

Papa stood up, his piercing eyes and crooked nose framed by unruly black whiskers and shoulder-length hair. Dearest Galen stood, as well. The top of Papa's head barely reached my love's shoulders. Papa faced me, his chin tilted upward and his back to the lower cave.

"Answer me," Papa demanded, the scowl on his face more prominent than the huge purple birthmark on Cole's forehead and left cheek.

Answer him? I could hardly breathe. I couldn't fend off the upper cave's magic and Papa's disapproval at the same time.

"Juanita had a vision," Magdalena shouted, "of Moses. This morning."

"It's about our purpose," I called. There, at least I'd said something.

"And my sister I've never met," Magdalena added, "plans to put her baby on the train."

"The voice of the creek told me that," I said.

"The creek again?" Papa motioned for me. Cook and Cole stood and moved closer to Papa. Wei remained seated on the ground.

I inched down the path toward the council. Dry twigs snapped beneath my sandals. My heart hammered. The pressure within my chest grew. Each new breath took more effort than the previous one. At the bottom of the grade, I stopped and fought for air. The Cave of Light tested me in some strange way.

"Are you all right, my love?" Galen hurried toward me. "You shouldn't have come here."

"I—I had to." I coughed. "Promise. Our lives. Our future. Magdalena's relative. They're all in danger, now."

Galen slipped his arm around my shoulders. Such warmth and strength he provided. My breaths came easier. Oh, how his black skin glistened in the morning sunlight, like polished obsidian. Those words of Moses. Would I live to wed my betrothed?

"Spirits of the cave," I said to the council, "showed me their blue-green light mere minutes ago. And yet I'm still breathing. Even they understand I must tell you about Moses."

"Ah." Wei clasped his palsied hands and rested his bony chin against them. "The cave—it does not invite you to speak. It dares you to visit."

"Well, she's not going to do that," Papa snapped. "Now, what about this supposed vision?"

Supposed vision? Already Papa didn't believe me. Nevertheless, I poured out my story of Moses, the light, and the parted water. Galen's eyes widened. Then came the part about the flying canoe-basket. Cole pressed his thumbs against his lips. Cook twisted her thin black hair into a bun. Wei squinted, as if experiencing the vision himself.

Papa's face remained solemn. Well, my next bit of information would raise his eyebrows past the top of his head.

"Did Moses wear goggles," I said to Wei, "when he visited you?" Of all people, Wei might know if the odd apparel had special significance.

"Moses wore goggles?" Cook's heavy-boned fingers fidgeted with her homespun tunic. "The great hero who chiseled the Ten Commandments in stone wears goggles? And he rides in an airship? Like people in British South California?"

"Moses would never do that." Papa turned toward Wei. "Would he?"

"I don't know," Wei replied. "But Juanita is old enough to tell reality from imagination."

"I believe she's seen and heard truth," Galen said, his voice clear and commanding. "All of you well know how I've spent over a hundred Wednesday nights at our lookout. Each Wednesday, don't we all pray with extra zeal for the passing asylum train to stop at Thistlewood Station? Pray some of the passengers will manage to run away? Well, each time the asylum train has failed to stop, I've prayed for Moses to send Juanita a vision about our purpose. Now it's come to her."

Galen had prayed so many times on my behalf? A pleasant warmth flushed my cheeks.

"Another spirit," Wei said, his body hunched, "probably talked Moses into doing strange things." He chuckled. "And that's the mischievous spirit Juanita must seek."

"Please, Papa." I sat down beside Cook on a patch of sandy soil. "Our earthly and eternal lives are in danger. Moses wants me to seek guidance from my ancestors."

"Then seek guidance only at the Shadow World's approach passage." Cole turned toward me. "Forget that our sacred cave beckoned you. Remember what happened to those seven fools who once prospected for gold in there."

I wouldn't forget that story. An old mining office report about the men's disappearance fifty years ago was stored in Promise's library. People back then had believed this part of California contained gold. The horrid blue-green light had probably blinded the unlucky miners. Made them tumble down a shaft in the cave.

"I'm pretty sure all my ancestors are in the Shadow World." I shifted my gaze from one council member to the next. "I'll visit my ancestors in the mystic passageway and ask for answers. As soon as they summon me. Send me a sign."

I tried not to glance in the direction of the cave, without much luck. What was the source of the place's terrible power? A blue-green glow shimmered. In fact, the light vibrated, as if the cavern laughed. Blessed saints and ancestors. A tingle shot across my shoulders.

A fearsome opponent, the Cave of Light was. May I never need to cross its threshold. But if I had to, I would.

"...will cease to exist," a woman's voice whispered, sounding like the voice of the creek. "Your library contains information your ancestors want you to learn."

The pressure returned to my chest. I gasped to fill my lungs with air.

4. A Magic Letter

I ENTERED PROMISE'S library, a one-room adobe, Magdalena by my side. Mid-morning sunlight streamed between the wrought iron bars covering the window, creating patterns of brightness and shadow on the red tile floor. The life-size, wind-up man sat in one corner, its rust-streaked head lowered. Metal showed through its torn leather scalp. For a moment, its amber eyes seemed to shift in my direction. Impossible. It had a faulty mainspring according to Papa—had always been totally broken, ever since the Yokut shaman had found it near the Cave of Light. How Clockman had gotten there, nobody living knew. A mysterious sign. Someone may have moved it by mule.

A shiver darted across my shoulders. Yesterday, the voice near the sacred cave had directed me here to find important information. Well, Clockman couldn't help. The task belonged to me.

Yellowed volumes and leather folders were piled along the western wall of the library. The corner opposite Clockman held a dozen Bibles, several books about religion, history, culture and languages, and a collection of wonderful poems. Community members usually read these "corner books" for relaxation, when grueling work schedules allowed. I'd read all the poems many times. Not all the Bible stories, though.

"You turn through Wei's journal," Magdalena said. "I'll work on the loose pages."

"That makes sense." I'd read Wei's book several times. Each time, I'd found new inspiration.

The room contained no furniture, not even a log. Magdalena knelt on a hemp mat next to burlap-wrapped bundles and document pouches of tooled leather. She peeled away a layer of fabric. Her slender caramel-colored finger rubbed the blue cover of Wei's scrapbook journal bound by rotting strands of rawhide.

"You better be careful," Magdalena said. Her black braid dangled over the front of her shoulder and small bosom. "I bet Wei doesn't remember what he wrote in here. It can't be replaced."

"I know, I know."

I wasn't a child. I always treated Wei's journal with respect. Like mirrors reflected images, holy words reflected spiritual truths.

"I'm sure you know." Magdalena curved her fingers and glanced down at her nails. "Cole's worried, though. He says damaging this book will bring bad luck."

"Oh." I pressed my lips together. Harming any holy writings, from Bibles to the sayings of Confucius, could bring bad luck. "Does he believe my vision was real?"

"Yes. And he wants to help raise my sister's baby."

I nodded, then bowed my head. A picture of my favorite drawing—a tiny candle illuminating the entire world—filled my mind. The spirits valued humble lights. Regardless, successful missions required boldness. Time to search for words of wisdom. I wiped my hands on my tunic and sat cross-legged on the floor.

The stained journal fit in my lap. I pried apart two brittle pages. Black dots speckled the paper, which smelled moldy. Magdalena opened a leather pouch and eased out a stack of odd-sized papers. I skimmed more journal pages. Nothing I didn't already know.

But what was this, an item I'd not noticed the other times? A sketch of a woman's face, the image of a figure in each of her pupils. And these words—blue-green light, deep blue light, the Virgin of Guadalupe. The ink looked almost new. Oh, yes, I recalled a story told by visiting healers last summer. Wei must have drawn this picture and recorded these words afterward.

The mouth of the Cave of Light emitted blue-green rays. Might a connection exist between this drawing and the treacherous cavern? But how? The holy virgin was said to be good and kind. An impulse made me glance at Clockman and its drab brown tunic. I didn't know why.

"Does Galen know you're here this morning?" Magdalena set some papers aside and smiled her fox smile.

"I didn't have a chance to tell him." I scratched my nose. The men were digging a new irrigation ditch and had risen even earlier than usual.

"No little walk with him through the blue oak grove last night?" Magdalena cradled her chin against the knuckles of one hand and pursed her lips. The curves of her temples gave her face a heart-shaped appearance. "Everyone gossips about you being alone with him after dark, and will until you're married."

I straightened. No surprise my strolls with Galen caused tongues to wag, even after all these months. The gossip would have to continue, too. Our wedding could be as long as two years away—my eighteenth birthday—unless my body finally became womanly first. According to Mama, the fasting required of a mystic delayed my development.

"No walk last night." I turned warm all of a sudden, although six weeks remained until the summer solstice. "And when we do walk together, we just hold hands."

"Oh." Magdalena nibbled on the end of her first finger, the way she often did when discussing matters of romance. "Cole told me to look in the old mail pouch." She crawled in its direction. "Just holding hands?"

"That's all. And there's no rule against it."

Well, not quite all. Galen often kissed my hand and forehead. Once so close to my lips I could have melted. But I wouldn't disclose this truth and risk soiling my reputation or Galen's.

"I think," I said, "the mail pouch holds papers from the abandoned mining camp. Most of the ink's faded or smeared. Do the best you can."

Back I went to Wei's journal. The usual two brittle pages still adhered to each other. A secret might lay between them. I teased the pages apart. The edge of one tore. Not good.

Only a single paragraph remained readable. The purpose of Promise was to be a refuge for escapees from the trains, whether those people be healthy or ill, innocent or guilty, wise or weak of mind. No surprise information. I lowered my face closer to the page. But the purpose would change someday, and the community's mystic traveler would need to confront strong magic to find a letter of power in the Cave of Light. Again, I glanced at Clockman. Dust coated its leather hands and enameled-metal arms.

"Listen to this," I said. "The Cave of Light contains a letter that holds magic. Surely written years ago. And only I can retrieve it and save Promise. Do you think this is a sign telling me to go to the cave? Not toward the Shadow World?"

"Maybe," Magdalena said. "If so, I'd better walk with you so you don't get lost."

"You know it's too dangerous," I said, "for you to enter the cave."

"And it's not dangerous for you?" Magdalena scraped dirt from underneath her thumbnail. "Friends stick together."

"I won't let you—"

"Read this." Magdalena handed me a yellowed clipping from an old newspaper. "It was hidden in the mail pouch. I almost missed it."

Such large print on the top—Baby killer gets dose of own medicine. I read a few lines of the text. An asylum worker in British South California had smothered three deformed orphans. A cleaning woman had found out and poisoned him. Had the asylum been the same one that would soon house Magdalena's niece or nephew? If so, how many other murderers had worked there?

I closed Wei's journal and wrapped the book in burlap. Magdalena returned the newspaper article to its place.

"The cave must be damp," Magdalena said. "Does the journal say anything about the letter being in a chest or box?"

"Maybe magic alone protects it."

"Cook needs you in the kitchen," Papa's voice admonished.

I turned my head toward the doorway. Sweat glistened on Papa's forehead and the unruly beard bordering his scowl. Had he heard the conversation about the Cave of Light?"

"We've been reading about history." I stood. "The past can teach us about the future."

"Did your ancestors summon you yet?" Papa said.

"No." From somewhere came squeaks of metal. I cleared my throat. Behind Papa and Magdalena, Clockman shrugged its shoulders. Oh, dear God. I cleared my throat louder. "They're trying to reach me, though."

I proceeded with Magdalena toward the kitchen. Papa walked in front, a shovel resting over the top of his shoulder. He didn't glance behind. My foster father and I hadn't walked side-by-side, holding hands, for years. Not since Wei had chosen me to be the next mystic traveler. Before then, Papa had shown me how a starving person could chew liquid from plants and find bugs to eat. I let out a sigh. Papa had grown particularly stern since Mama took sick months ago.

Two days had passed without me reading to Mama. A pang of guilt surged within me and gnawed. She'd been the one to teach me to read, even to let me see Clockman's inner workings. Or non-workings. I must have imagined that mechanical shrug a few minutes ago. Papa and Magdalena hadn't reacted.

"When we work on dinner," I whispered to Magdalena, "we shouldn't discuss the Cave of Light if others can hear us. Cook will tell Papa, and he's been so grumpy."

"As you say." Her curvaceous hips swayed.

We walked along the dusty path and by a spreading oak. Ahead, the kitchen beckoned. Daylight streamed through paneless windows and an open entry porch. Nine of my women friends squashed cooked beans and sweet pod flour into paste. Cook presented me with a stone bowl half-full of curved, roasted pods. I set to work pulverizing the pods into meal. Magdalena did likewise.

I focused on the sooty rear wall and its brick fireplaces. Coals glowed red under hanging iron pots where water bubbled. The group of women stirred, mashed, stoked and chatted, sweat dripping from their faces and arms. Death would strike all my people, if I failed to locate the letter of magic in the cave. I had to prevent that.

Should I visit the Shadow World tomorrow night, or the Cave of Light? If only mystical signs were always clear. A tingle arose between my shoulder blades. A rush of warmth flashed across the backs of my hands. A mystic died when the Shadow World decreed. A fate worse than death could await me.

I pressed and twisted my grinding stone against the sweet pods, the first harvested this year. A shadow crossed the bowl, shimmered yellow-brown, then disappeared. A shadow...the Shadow World? Was this the summons Moses had foretold? I listened for an ethereal whisper. Nothing.

5. Of Drumming and the Shadow World

GALEN STOOD FACING me at the gathering place. Pulses from his ceremonial drum—repetitive sets of three beats, each middle one accentuated—resonated through my being. My people, seated on logs around us and the evening fire, clicked their tongues against their palates to match his rhythm. Flames leapt, crouched and darted. Sounds, firelight and prayers would carry my soul, as always, to the corridor between the worlds of life and death.

"Mystic traveler girl," Galen called to me. "Are you ready to face the Guardians of the Portals?"

"I'm ready." Or as ready as I could be.

I closed my eyes and twirled in time to a slow beat, arms extended, palms cupping the night. The drumbeats quickened, as did my bare feet. My tresses fanned outward. I focused on the percussion. The call of the drum and my essence resonated as one.

The warmth of the fire faded. Time—some strange inner clock—reversed with each spin. I was ten, nine, seven, four. I was an infant riding a train to the asylum, then unborn. The heartbeats of the drum pounded as I turned around and around.

I breathed out my soul. My body collapsed while my floating spirit watched. There I was, upon the sandy soil in front of Galen's bare feet—my tousled hair like waist-length curtains of black silk threads. So strange, this always felt, the separation of my ethereal being from my flesh, bones and blood. The slightest breeze ought to have carried my spirit away or dispersed it like dandelion seeds. With freedom came new vulnerability.

Quivering flames flared from the earthly fire Papa tended. Time to confirm my body survived the ritual. Then I'd continue on my way and learn how to save my people by saving others. And how to find the letter of magic in the Cave of Light.

I floated closer to my slumped form, my emerald spirit glow tinting my homespun tunic. Papa, Galen, Magdalena and the others bowed their heads around my unconscious body. My slender chest took deep and even breaths. Praise the ancestors and God. May the rest of my dangerous journey to the Shadow World's portals tonight also go as planned. The usual sparkling mist formed between my spirit and the living people of Promise. Spring's second full moon shone through the twinkling haze. Eternal darkness soon bordered the scene like an endless frame for a window. Only spirits could see the passages connecting the worlds of life and death.

Only a mystic traveler or a shaman could hover in such a passage while still alive.

But where were my ancestors? After that vision of Moses the day before yesterday, and the shimmering shadow in the kitchen, surely they expected this visit. I turned toward the familiar river of crimson spirit lights flowing in the distance. The Guardians of the Portals patrolled the Shadow World's perimeter. Strict orders, they had, to keep most of the dead inside of the realm and all who were alive, out. In fact, living intruders soon became dead residents. A good thing Great-Grandma Zetta and other deceased relatives had ongoing permission to meet me here.

"Who goes there?" a deep voice boomed.

I'd identify myself to the guard. If I wasn't supposed to be here tonight, I'd step through the window back to life. But, wait. My people, with their long hair, bushy beards and hemp robes, blurred. The opening back to life shrank to a golden circle smaller than a finger ring. Gone. They were gone. My mystic travels had never isolated me this way. What was going on?

"Prepare for your judgment," the guard said. "And your fate."

Oh, dear ancestors. My spirit rippled, must have blazed a color. Black widow spiders had terrified me in childhood. If hourglass-red was my color of fear, I shimmered that hue.

"Declare yourself," a chorus of deep voices shouted in unison, the echoes louder than a thousand claps of thunder. "What living soul dares to approach the realm of the dead?"

"I'm a..."

The stench of roasting, rotten meat overpowered my spirit senses, as if white-hot coals seared mountains of maggots and carrion. No doubt about it, I flashed pond-scum green. Still, the voices had claimed I lived. Hope remained.

"I'm a humble mystic traveler," I said. "A link between the people of Promise and our ancestors. But I don't want to enter the Shadow World. My family always meets me right here."

"Ah," a guardian said. The stench of cooking, putrid flesh lessened. "Is your house Jame-Navarro?"

"Yes."

How did he know? Great-Grandma must have alerted him. Maybe Great-Grandma's rainbow light and aroma of chocolate would arrive any moment, joined by Great-Grandpa's yeasty odor of beer. Their love would soothe away my fear.

Instead, a stink wafted through me. Not as revolting as roasting, corrupted flesh but worse than wet greasewood smoldering in a doused fire.

"So, you and your people," a gruff male voice said, "want to hear about your new life-saving purpose."

Not a voice I recognized. Where was this spirit's light?

"I ought to make a proper introduction," the voice said. "You and me, we're shirttail relatives of sorts. Just call me Billy. My last name ain't worth skimmed piss. Been listening to your people's prayers. Arranged for that recent visit from Moses."

Billy had sent Moses? Who was he to have such influence? I stammered a greeting.

A scratched metal box appeared in front of my soul. An object with physical form shouldn't exist on this side of the life-death divide. The rather flat, rectangular tin blazed in the darkness like a star in the night sky. Painted on the lid was a wicker canoe topped with three balloons. Just like the airship Moses had used.

"Get ready for a surprise." Billy chuckled.

The box lid lifted by itself. Dun-yellow smoke spiraled out. Billy's spirit flashed the same muddy-gold hue. His disagreeable odor turned heavier than a threatened skunk's. A wise mystic would say something polite.

"The picture of Moses' airship is very nice."

"Moses's airship? Picture?" Billy's light vibrated as he laughed. "First of all, I designed the airship Moses used. And this box can turn into the real thing. Hop in. You're going to help drive it to the Black Mountain."

"Drive it where?" Until then, I'd never heard about a Black Mountain or a flying box.

"We're heading across yonder river," Billy said.

"Across the river of crimson lights? But I'm not dead."

"And you won't be as long as you do what I say," Billy replied. "You need to establish your presence in the place. Go there of your own free will. That way, I can take you to the mountain in a hurry, if need be. Without any crap from the Guardians of the Portals."

What was Billy talking about? Well, he'd made it clear I'd better obey. I floated into the tin airship box. He followed. The lid clinked shut above us. My emerald green spirit light, the shade of my earthly eyes, glowed on the nearest wall. That wall—all four of them—grew ten times higher. An odor of stinkweed blended with the earlier smoky smell. I flashed the colors of bile.

"Not accustomed to smoldering tobacco?" Billy said. "Someday you'll pray to smell it."

I'd smelled Indian pipe tobacco used by visiting healers, but hadn't found the aroma offensive. What did Billy mix with his?

43

"All right, Little Engine Woman," Billy said. "Plop your ether down on that seat and engage the throttle."

"What's a throttle?" What was an engine woman?

"Push that rod and you'll find out."

The seat looked more like an inverted bucket. The metal rod protruding from the floor of the box was dark as a cast iron pot. I nudged it a bit and felt a sensation of motion. An eerie moan, sounding like a windstorm, arose outside.

"Push it harder," Billy said.

I gave the thing a shove, and the airship tobacco tin shuddered. The container rocked, spun and hurled my ether against the box's wall.

"Jesus, not that hard," Billy said.

"You could have warned me." I bounced. The walls of the tobacco tin reflected my exasperation orange.

"Pull it back toward you. Ease off."

I ricocheted my way back to the throttle and did as told. The moan of travel faded. The airship tin came to rest, and its lid tilted up to open. The walls shrank to their original height. How strange.

"Wait here," Billy said.

He vanished into the silent void. I surveyed my surroundings for any sign of a mountain or spirit light. Nothing. Without Billy, I'd never get back to one of the Shadow World's portals and home. Venturing into the emptiness would be unwise.

A brilliant blue-green light appeared, like it came from the sacred cave, or the description in Wei's journal. A woman's voice called out a salutation in Spanish. The radiance deepened to the color of blue lupine flowers. Was this spirit friend or foe? I shrank into a corner of Billy's airship tin.

"Do not be frightened, child," the voice said in English, my first language. "You are special to us, gifted."

I'd heard this voice before.

"We are outside the gate to the Black Mountain." The blue light softened. "This is where I am when I speak to you through your creek. In your early childhood, your

Great-Grandma Zetta taught you many things from here in your dreams."

"I don't see a gate or a mountain." I peered over the edge of the airship tin. I didn't recall any childhood dreams about Great-Grandma, either.

"When the time comes for you to step through the entryway, you'll see a lot. On the other hand, if your earthly body doesn't possess the magic letter from the Cave of Light, you will die."

"Where in the cave should I look for the magic letter?"

"Bones will lead the way," the voice said. "I'll help, if I can."

My spirit tingled. Why would I ever need to stand on the Black Mountain—even take future mystic journeys to the Shadow World—if spirits could communicate with me in other ways?

"Eventually, you will understand all," the voice said, as if it knew my thoughts. "Magic abides by rules, even if they're not always obvious."

With that, the deep blue aura of the woman's spirit faded. Billy's yellow-brown glow arrived. His airship tobacco tin tilted, sliding me back into a corner.

"Time to head for Promise and get to work," Billy said. "You have a month or so to do your job. There's an asylum and workhouse for the poor to the south—the one you nearly wound up in. The place is northeast of Los Angeles. Brit territory. Yankees get paid to manage it. A new superintendent will soon arrive, one with his own ideas about cutting expenses." Billy lowered the lid on the box. "He'll quietly start overdosing the expendables on sleeping powders this summer."

"That would be murder." I sat on the seat. Only a monster would kill sick people and children on purpose. "Others would find out and arrest him."

"Trust me." Billy chuckled. "Unless you sabotage an empty asylum train on its way to load passengers—send Brit and Yankee newspaper reporters snooping around that dump—innocent people will die. Including that baby your friend wants to raise."

Cease to exist... All my own people would die, if we didn't take action.

I clutched the thing called a throttle. The moan that mimicked wind returned. The magic airship tin turned and tumbled.

"And speaking of trust," Billy said, "the day'll come when you'll curse me, curse the whole damn bunch of us. If you don't learn to trust and understand all your spirit family now, you won't cope or survive."

I loved Great-Grandma and Great-Grandpa. They'd rescued me from the train. I could never curse them. Billy didn't know everything.

"From now on," Billy said, "don't travel to us for advice. We'll come to you."

The lid to the box raised. A hazy light appeared in the distance, like fire glowing through a curtain of fog. Drumbeats beckoned. A force sucked me toward the sound and sparkling mist. Gray images swirled around me— shapes of my people and a fire circle. My own body lay on the ground. The two spirits who'd kept my mortal form breathing rose from my chest to leave. My soul slipped inside.

I opened my eyes.

Papa knelt and sponged my face with a wet rag. Behind him, Galen clasped a torch, his skin glistening with beads of sweat, his smile wide and warm. Dearest Galen. My people faded in and out, a moonlit blur.

My tongue hurt and felt thick. I must have bitten it. Regardless, I needed to tell Papa about the murderer, the train, and the magic letter. The instructions from Billy and the Voice of the Light poured from my mouth, like blood from a gaping wound.

Several of my people uttered soft gasps. Others whispered. The skin on Papa's forehead wrinkled like dried figs. He soaked the rag in a bowl of water. I sucked the wet cloth. Community members moved closer. Several appeared tense as taut ropes, round eyes brimming with fear. They didn't want to follow the directive of the dead, even though I'd told them all days ago what Moses had said.

Crickets' legs played their song, yet the night seemed so quiet. A pebble on uneven ground pressed against my back. Maybe stopping a train wasn't such a good thing to do. Halting one train might not prevent the murderer from carrying out his wretched plans. The warning from Moses repeated in my mind.

Papa crouched down on one knee. He helped me sit up and pressed me close. The odors of his man-sweat and heavy breath smelled strong. His hand stroked the back of my head.

"You mustn't enter that cave yet," Papa said. "Not without a back-up plan for your rescue. And sabotage a train that's running? Hundreds of tons of iron and steel? Wrong. The act would be wrong. Even if the train held only crew."

"But—"

"We're not a violent people," Papa replied. "Lives of those railroaders have worth to their own families. We must find a way to interrupt use of the train without committing murder or drawing the authorities to our doorstep." Papa stood and folded his arms against his chest. "We're not like the Mendozas." He spat on the ground.

Mendozas did bad things even to women and children. Nothing the people of Promise would do could ever match such evil deeds. Besides, Billy had claimed the murderer running the asylum would strike by this summer.

"This conversation has ended for now," Papa said.

Such a stern, unyielding look filled Papa's eyes. Great-Grandma Zetta had used wisdom, cleverness, courage and determination to save me. Luck and Great-Grandpa had helped.

Persuading Papa to change his mind wouldn't be easy. If I failed, an unknown disaster would destroy my community. If I succeeded, great peril could await us all. Great God and ancestors—who would survive to find and raise the child of Magdalena's sister?

6. A Breeze Shifts

THE WATER CLOUDED as I washed my hands in a pottery basin at the gathering place. Galen, Magdalena, Cole, Cook and the rest of my community digested a meager dinner and waited for Papa to serve tea. We all sat, chatting, on tree stumps, logs or cross-legged on the ground. Well, except for Mama, more jaundiced than ever, who lay curled up on a mat. Mama's head rested in Nurse's lap. The scene was so ordinary, as if the past several days had never happened.

Yet those days had come and left their mark. I needed to help Magdalena, and couldn't figure out how. And Papa insisted I use a rescue rope in the Cave of Light. Where did he plan to get that much hemp? Defying the will of the ancestors could trigger a horrific earthquake or poison Promise's stream. I had to change his mind. Tonight.

I flicked drops of wash water from my fingertips. The star-studded heavens stretched toward infinity. So beautiful. The Shadow World considered me special. Perhaps the spirits would gift me with a persuasive voice. After tea, I'd start a discussion about the asylum trains. Papa respected Cook's expertise in crop growth and food preparation. Everyone did. If I could enlist her support, Papa might listen to reason.

How chilly, the air. I tightened my shawl around my shoulders. Warmth and light emanated from the central fire, precious gifts on a mid-spring evening. I moved toward the log where Cook sat.

"Your ancestors have been dead too long." Cook looked up, the skin on her face taut and weathered with lines, like dried mud in a sunbaked creek bed. "No disrespect meant, but this train sabotage by summer plan— they're wrong. We need more time."

48

"Sabotage in spring could save many lives," I said, "more than we ever did by rescuing escapees. And it would save Magdalena's niece or nephew. Besides, my family wouldn't ask us to do anything really wrong."

"All wrongs are wrong," Cook said.

Best to let the comment pass until after tea. My stomach growled. Not enough rain had fallen this season. Stock supplies of beans, leached acorns and sweet-pod meal from last year dwindled. No one was comfortable about eating animals, a last resort unless one of the men needed a new pair of deer hide breeches. The past month had been hard.

The breeze shifted. Burning sapwood sparked and spat into the night air. Smoke curled from the fire and stung my eyes. I moved and sat near Galen. It would feel nice if he held my hand. Magdalena's husband, Cole, grinned at us, displaying his discolored teeth.

"Watch out," Cole said to Galen. "Your mystic traveler girl has a purpose."

Galen smiled. My cheeks warmed. I should have expected such a comment. Cole was perceptive, with a fine sense of humor. Missionary doctors had adopted and raised him in a huge North California city, a place with gaslights and thousands of residents. He had spent his fourteenth summer in Promise while his adoptive parents had hiked on a healer's pilgrimage. Afterwards, he'd stayed. According to Cole, the world beyond Promise considered the birthmark on his face disfiguring. How odd, when the mark clearly proclaimed his gift. Cole divined drinking water for our community when the streams ran low. Water always spoke to him from underneath the ground.

Would people outside of Promise consider me ugly? I had no birthmark, but my nose and ears were much larger than Magdalena's. One couldn't predict what strangers might think. A thin dry stick in the fire ignited and shrank to ashes. I inched closer to Galen.

"Two minds, one purpose," Galen whispered into my ear. "I have some ideas. Let's meet later tonight and talk about your ancestors' plan."

I nodded and mouthed a silent reply, entwining my hand with his. He—age twenty-three and surely the future leader of Promise—admired and supported me. Who cared about strangers' opinions?

"Magdalena showed me an article from an old newspaper," I said, my voice low. "About an asylum. Have you—"

Dry twigs snapped. I looked up. Papa approached the fire circle with hesitant strides, holding a pottery tea urn away from his body. It was a man's job to prepare the bark and leaves for tea, and a man's job to serve the beverage. Too bad he often served me stern words, as well.

The nurse woman received a cupful of tea to share with Mama. Everyone else sipped directly from the serving vessel. When my turn arrived, I grasped the urn by its handles and inhaled the aroma of mint before I sipped. The tea, tepid by then, had the delicious bitter tang I loved. Better than the tang of Billy's prediction. How could he have claimed I would curse my spirit family someday? Where? In the Cave of Light? Speaking about the cave, the Voice of the Light should have described the magic letter's location.

I took the usual second mouthful of tea. Papa frowned at me—a big, chin-to-forehead expression, as if anything smaller might disappear in his whiskers. I swallowed my tea too fast and coughed. Something gnawed at his mind.

"God'll stop all the trains," he said, "when the time's right. In the meanwhile, we can help him when the rains arrive in November. Inspection crews will mistake rail sabotage for wash-outs and cancel runs. We won't need to flee for our lives."

Papa's words sank into me like stones dropped into a pond. He'd implied he'd never support my ancestors' timeline. Those children and ill people would die by summer. Burning brushwood crackled from the fire circle.

"But what about Magdalena's—" I said.

"I won't have people killed," Papa said, "or all of us thrown into prison."

"But my vision of Moses," I said. "The spirits want us to—"

"The matter is closed, Juanita."

Those nearby halted their conversations. Magdalena flinched. The backs of my hands and neck tingled as I read Papa's unyielding eyes. Promise, without our assigned life-saving goal, would go away.

"The matter isn't closed." Galen stood up, legs a foot apart, his expression calm. He folded his arms against his chest, his lean yet strong frame a head taller than Papa's. "We're all old enough to make decisions for ourselves."

Almost everyone else cast uneasy glances at each other, then toward Galen and Papa. The fire spewed a volley of sparks upward. Red-hot rain drifted to earth behind Papa and disappeared.

"It's not just a matter of when death happens," Papa said with a tolerant but condescending tone. "It's a matter of great suffering."

"As I see it," Galen said, "our inaction will cause far more death and suffering." He tightened one fist into a ball of knuckles. His beard, cropped into submission after each new moon, was tangled and wild, like burr clover growing on a hill. "We lack an effective purpose," he shouted. "A member of Magdalena's family faces danger. Let's do something about it."

Galen strode to the edge of the fire, repeating his storm of words. He'd never spoken this way to Papa in front of our entire community before. In nearby shadows, the arched eyebrows and parted lips of my people mirrored my own shock and alarm. Galen clasped my hand and pulled me toward him and the fire. He raised our united arms.

"I'm not afraid," he said, "to follow the directive of Moses and our ancestors. Who joins me?"

He anchored his hands upon the crests of my hips and hoisted me to his shoulder. Did fear or excitement make my head throb? Great-Grandma would have displayed bravery and determination. I extended my arm straight above my head, fist clenched.

Galen repeated his challenge. The power of his voice should have made foothills tremble. Would anyone dare to respond?

"I'll join you," a man said.

Heads turned. Wei had spoken. He planted the end of his cane against the hardpan. His stiff, gnarled fingers clutched the cane's crook. He grunted and stood, his long graying hair matted. His bent frame rocked in the firelight, as if the smoke might topple him.

"I have no fear of this new mission," Wei said. "Any who doubt should read my journal in our library."

Wei could do little to help, except to offer prayers. Whispers sped around the fire circle. A younger man with a scarred forehead touched Wei's shoulder and encouraged him to sit down. The old mystic pinched his lips tight and dismissed the suggestion with a wave of his hand.

"Let Wei speak and choose for himself," Galen said. He lowered me to the ground, then raised his arms toward the heavens. The assembled group quieted. The rhythm of crickets filled the night air. Galen motioned to Wei.

"Twenty-three years ago," Wei rasped, "an old freed-slave man—blind in one eye—decided to save a baby with coal-black skin. The two rode the relocation train in the same car. A car with a large toilet hole in the lavatory. The man hid in the lavatory with the child. When the train stopped for water, he lowered the baby down the hole, then wedged through. We found them the next day. The old man lived three months more and named the baby Galen. Then I raised the child."

Wei had told this story many times. Odd, the way he did so now. The mystic smiled in my direction, must have read my facial expression.

"I had a dream last night," Wei said. "The freed-slave pushed us all through that hole, one by one. Galen first. We crawled out from under the railcar. The train vanished. Rain clouds gathered, and the land bloomed, reborn." He coughed. "Now I understand the dream. My ancestors sent it to remind us of our new task. I will stop the train we are meant to stop, even if I must lie on the track alone."

Wei's hands trembled, and his knees bent. Still, he was strong with determination. Galen helped him return to the oak stump. Creek frogs hummed a throaty tune. The firelight dimmed, but no one rose to add another log. Magdalena twisted the end of her braid, then clasped Cole's hand.

"We'll join you," Magdalena said.

Cole nodded.

Fear's fingers molded Cole and Magdalena's faces, pushing their eyes wider, pinching Magdalena's lips between her teeth. Magdalena was rarely afraid of anything. I didn't want harm to come to her. Didn't want harm to come to any of my family or friends. One by one, two by two, villagers pledged their lives, except for Cook, Papa and Mama.

Cook removed her bandanna. She folded and unfolded the square of faded scarlet cloth several times. Papa kept looking toward Mama's thin form huddled under a blanket.

"I, too," Cook said at last. "After you're all dead, you won't need a cook."

Then Promise's leader—or was he?—raised his right hand, as if making a sacred vow.

"It must be all of us together," Papa said. "I'll plan a visit to the Cave of Light. It's my job to find the letter. Have I not agreed to the destruction of all we've built?"

"I love you, Papa," I whispered. But going to the cave would be my path to walk alone.

The others responded with eerie exuberance to Papa's declaration, some embracing each other, others weaving their mixed emotions into a cloth of chanting, into a united call to stop the train. Magdalena hooked her little finger around mine.

"After it's wrecked, where'll we go?" Magdalena said. "Your father's right. Nothing will be the same here."

Of course, everything would be different. But no member of the village had ever deserted. My people would remain together and deal with change when the time came, even as I would soon deal with the Cave of Light. Still, Billy had mentioned understanding the ancestors in order to cope or survive. Moses had stressed the importance of accomplishing our mission properly and on time. They must have issued warnings for a reason. What if Galen were killed when we sabotaged the train? Or Mama and Papa? Or Magdalena?

Coping... Wei's story about the brave old man with black skin. Why did so many people abandon their babies? Did they ever feel remorse?

"We need to find your sister's baby," I said to Magdalena. "Someday I'd like to find my natural mother and father, too. After I'm certain I've forgiven them."

"We'll stick together," Magdalena said. "Besides, you and Galen will need my man to locate drinking water."

"Yes," I whispered. The evening breeze shifted direction. The chanting subsided. Such a bleak, sandy landscape I pictured. I felt as if I'd aged a thousand years. "No one finds water like Cole."

7. Blue Light and Rattling Bones

A CURTAIN OF darkness hung behind manzanita bushes and poison oak, ten or fifteen feet above me on the hillside. This had to be the opening I'd detected the day the council met. The threshold to the Cave of Light.

I edged upward, prickly brush scraping my arms through the sleeves of my ankle-length tunic. Some types of Indian spirits stayed with their bones instead of going to the Shadow World. The spirit of the Yokut shaman's bones in the cave ought to know where that magic letter was, plus how to reach it without encountering malicious spirits or falling down a shaft. If the crumbling path didn't give way beneath my sandals, I'd soon learn the truth.

The truth... My people had accepted the Shadow World's mission to sabotage an asylum train by summer. Promise would continue to exist. But where? I glanced heavenward. Sunset dressed the western sky in muted pinks and grays, as the waning moon's pale outline slipped behind multicolored clouds. Each truth had its own time of discovery.

My empty stomach gurgled. Supper time was an unavoidable truth. Papa and the others would have noticed my absence by now. The way here from Promise was too steep and treacherous to dark-walk, particularly with quarter moon only five days away. No one could do anything before dawn about my disobedience. I had until after sunrise to find the letter.

A ledge jutted from atop a granite outcrop, rather narrow and mostly cloaked by chaparral. The ledge led to a deep indentation in the hillside. One step. Two steps. My destination was almost within reach.

Still, a lonely being of bones might desire my company for eternity. Locating the shaman's skeleton might not be the best thing. My stomach muscles tightened as I found the next foothold.

I squeezed behind scratchy bushes, then stretched my arms high. I pushed off the hillside with my feet and pulled myself onto a shelf of smooth, gray rock. An opening in the hillside waited. I snaked on my belly into a dim, rocky passage, the ceiling too low for standing. Somewhere, water dripped. So far, no spirit lights or skeletons were in sight.

Within a few feet, the passage opened into a chamber several times my height. I maneuvered into a sitting position. No blue-green light shone. Only the faint daylight from outdoors. Dusk drifted toward night. I could explore little farther until sunrise. I'd hoped for an obvious clue. Had I come to the wrong place?

My stomach rumbled, louder than before, although I'd eaten nuts, acorn bread and herbal broth for breakfast. I usually fasted longer, one full night and day, before visiting spirits. A taboo broken. My transgression could offend the shaman's spirit. Still, I'd only eaten with the community this morning to mask my intention of coming here. I had the will-power to sacrifice comfort for duty. A serving of mashed beans, however, would have tasted wonderful right then.

I scanned the shadows of the cave, my eyes adapting to darkness. If only I'd brought a lantern. Perhaps I could explore this chamber anyway. Not a good idea. Vertical shafts to lower chambers could ensnare me. The Voice of the Light—the Virgin of Guadalupe?—could only try to help. I should invoke the spirit of the shaman's bones.

"Dearest shaman," I called as I faced the cave's dim interior. "The Shadow World has bid me to come here. May I trouble you to assist me?"

I introduced myself, in case he'd forgotten the little girl who'd loved his mint and berry tea years ago. The night breeze rustled through unseen leaves outside the cavern. I repeated my request six more times, a total of seven. A strong number. An owl hooted. Not even a mysterious hoot. My chest heaved a deep sigh. All this evening's efforts had been wasted.

A wind arose outside. A chill cut through me. I crawled several feet into the cavern and curled up on the floor. Warmer now, I yawned. Should I sleep? The shaman's spirit might visit me in a dream and tell me what to do next.

From the darkness came a soft, repetitive high-pitched knocking. I tensed. Rattlesnakes preferred to slither about in daylight, but one of them might call this cave home. I'd better not move.

A shuffling sound led to another rattle. An eerie blue-green glow—a fist-size ball of light—swayed within the cave. The orb, maybe thirty feet away, divided into twin spheres and drifted closer to me. Glints of ivory triggered a tingling sensation in my fingertips and toes. Bones could rattle. Ivory was the color of bones.

Two clenched rows of teeth wobbled in the air. A death head gleamed. Blessed saints, the blue-green radiance came from eye sockets. Human eye sockets. In a skull, attached to a human skeleton. Oh, dear Lord of this world and the next. The being approached, rattling, arms by its sides, mouth frozen in a horrific grin. Strips of rags dangled from its hips. The beams turned deep blue. I couldn't move, cry out, do anything but widen my eyes. I was awake and not in the Shadow World. The dead walked the earth in more than spirit form.

A spirit capable of holding a heap of dry bones together must possess great mystical powers. Powers strong enough to hold me captive for the rest of my life. Run—I needed to stand and run. I tried to rise. Two bony hands reached out and clamped my wrists. The skeleton pushed me against the ground and dragged me deeper into darkness.

"Aiyeee," I yelled.

My cry echoed as the skeleton pulled me across the cave's bumpy floor. I twisted my body but couldn't break free. Water drops plunked against rock. Bony hands released me. The being of bones had moved me beside dripping water. Ancestors be praised. The skeleton motioned for me to drink.

"Bones will lead the way," the Voice of the Light had said.

"Thank you." I knelt and cupped my hands under the steady drip of cool liquid. What other secrets did these bones know?

A shuffling sound arose behind me. I swallowed the water and turned. Another figure stepped from the shadows and into the pool of unearthly blue light—a beardless man wearing close-fitting trousers with silver buttons down the side of each leg. Did Mexican men still wear calzoneras? And his hat, with the low crown and wide brim, was of the old vaquero style. A glint of light off metal—the man's lowered hand gripped a pistol. Or was it a pistol? It was larger than any handgun I'd ever heard of, and some sort of dial sat above the handle. The barrel, the colors of copper and brass, had a bulbous base and narrow shaft, like a vase used to hold a single long-stemmed flower. A thick thread of metal coiled around the shaft.

"Please put your gun away." My kneecaps pressed against the cave's floor.

"As you wish." He tucked the gun under his crimson waist sash.

Then I noticed his ebony hair, shoulder length and fixed in tight little braids.

"Are you alive?" I pushed back my own dangling braid.

"It matters not," the man said. His chest neither rose nor fell beneath his loose-fitting shirt. "Study my eyes."

He moved closer, his hazel eyes gleaming, as if they could burn through my soul. Compassion, strength, determination—his gaze projected the wisdom of ten thousand men. He tossed his pistol toward me. I refused to touch such a thing. The gun vanished as I recoiled.

"My eyes shine with a hero's fire. Remember them well." The man laughed and fingered a golden pendant around his neck. "You shall meet many men whose eyes contain selfish desire. Trust only those with hero's eyes."

58

Rough rock vibrated beneath my knees. I lurched, thrusting my hands against the ground. An earthquake. This was an earthquake. The hillside could collapse and bury me. Where was the way out?

I turned away from both stranger and skeleton. A hint of light shone through a distant archway. Moonbeams? I crawled on quaking ground in that direction. A force thrust me one way, then another. Smoke with a tang of sulfur stung my eyes. Liquid fire poured out of a cracked rock.

"Billy! Great-Grandma! Help me." I scrambled to my feet.

"But they are not allowed here," the red-sash stranger said.

He laughed and ushered me away from the burning rock. The quake ended, and a tiny circle of flames danced in the palm of his hand. The flames blackened, jumped onto my finger and became a ring with a dark stone.

The man shrank smaller and smaller, until only his golden earring remained where he had stood. I couldn't shake the warm ring off of my finger.

"Do not be afraid, Juanita," his fading voice said. "This ring will help you find the magic you seek to step upon the Black Mountain. And to become a true engine woman."

A true engine woman? What did that mean? And how did he know my name?

A force slammed my back and pushed me downward. My hands and knees hit the cavern floor. Bones clattered against my spine, tapping one place, then another. I lay on my stomach—one side of my face against ground—beneath a heap of enchanted, dancing bones.

Rattle...clatter...tap... If I ever got out of this cave alive I'd murder Billy, despite my mystic's obligation to respect him. And despite the fact he was already dead.

8. While the Bones Slept

THE DEEP BLUE glow of mystery met my eyes. The magical skull, no longer attached to the rest of the skeleton, floated just above the cave's floor toward my face. The shining death head settled near my nose. Such a macabre lantern, this was. The beams bathed rock, dank earth, and me. Whether the light was good or evil, I couldn't tell.

The body of the skeleton, or at least part of the thing, pressed without movement against my throbbing back. The bones slept. They didn't lead the way anywhere.

Half the night must have passed since I'd entered the Cave of Light. If only I'd located the letter, I might have slept, too. As it was, I had no idea whether the letter was a talisman or a set of sabotage instructions. Well, Papa and Galen would set out at dawn to search for me. I needed to rise and do some finding. Besides, I couldn't tolerate my sore spine much longer. I'd have to stand and stretch, even if my movement awakened the dead.

"Dear spirit of the bones," I said. The ring on my finger warmed again. "Please don't think ill of me if I continue on with my assignment from the Shadow World."

I wiggled my ankle, then my hand. Nothing bad happened, although spirits could be unpredictable. I rolled from my stomach onto my side. Bones spilled off me, soft, hollow sounds marking their landing upon the ground. I should wait a bit before proceeding, to be polite, as Wei had taught me. Seven times I counted to seven. I stood.

Long bones lay here, ribs and the breastbone over there. I'd scattered the skeleton's parts upon standing. What a jumble. Magic no longer held them together. It would be thoughtless to leave a spirit's dwelling in such disarray. I picked up one of the small bones and studied it in the blue light from the skull. Did this smither of yesteryear's life belong to a foot or a hand? I could never

60

rearrange the skeleton's pieces in proper order by sunrise and find the letter, too.

There was only one course to take. I assembled all the bones in a pile and placed the glowing skull on top. I stroked my signet ring, the former fire from Red Sash Man's hand. The carved, black ring stone resembled a hawk's head. Hawk was the great messenger and observer of the sky, or so the old shaman had told me years ago. A fitting piece of jewelry from a man with hero's eyes.

"Please accept my apology," I said to the skull, "for bringing disturbance to your resting place."

The deep blue light dimmed and might extinguish before daybreak. I knew I'd better use the remaining glow to my advantage. The faint light I'd headed for during the earthquake still beckoned from the cavern's inner reaches. The skin under my signet ring itched. A spirit could be prodding me to explore the cave further—or to return to the entrance. I rubbed my fingertip against the carved hawk. I'd walk toward the distant point of light for a few minutes and see what happened. If I suspected danger, I'd return here to the glowing skull.

Several cautious steps led me in the direction of the faint beacon. The ground sloped downward, a fact I hadn't noticed during the earthquake. An underground canyon likely separated me from my destination. The skeleton might have pushed me away from this path during the tremor to protect me. Or to prevent me from discovering secrets. Regardless, walking in the dark no longer seemed like a good idea. *Bones will lead...* I clenched my toes and inched back to the pile of bones.

"Dear *cráneo*," I said, careful to pronounce the Spanish word for skull the correct way. Some of the ancestors liked me to use Spanish words. And I didn't know Yokut. Maybe this skull would prefer Spanish over English, too. "*Por favor*—please—would you light the way for me? For the sake of my ancestors in the Shadow World."

I grasped the skull, pressing my palms against the sides. How cool the bones were. The blue light intensified yet gave off no heat. Caused no pain of any sort. Nothing whispered or buzzed in my ear. The *cráneo* must have agreed to help me. Or at least do me no harm. Yet.

Clutching the skull, I edged back down the slippery incline, my heartbeats like thunder. A mystic died when the Shadow World decreed. Yet this cave had the power to hold me as a living captive, prevent me from stopping the train, from fulfilling my obligations to my Shadow World family. The cave could even trap my spirit when I finally did die, the way it must have done to Red Sash Man. Such strong magic could separate me from Galen and everyone else I loved forever. Death alone was far from the worst fate tonight might bring.

The slant of the cave floor steepened, the small distant light now above me and no closer than before. Something was wrong. I grasped the skull tighter. Sticky; the *cráneo* felt sticky. Red shadows danced like flames on the cavern wall beside me. The lantern's eye sockets gleamed crimson. Blood! The skull bled mystical blood.

I faltered. The death head tumbled out of my grasp. I grabbed at it. Dear God, I missed. The red glow swelled and plummeted like a shooting star into the blackness below. Gone. The spirit of that skeleton would not be pleased.

No light at all, then, not even the distant one. I poised on the brink of some vast unknown. My pulse pounded in my ears. I couldn't suck in enough air. Up became like down. Down became up. Laughter echoed from every direction.

The cave's mouth—I needed to return to the cave's opening. No matter if the skull had turned to blood to warn or to trick me. It was time to escape to safety and reevaluate my plans.

I crawled, grasping damp, rough rocks. Upward, I figured, by the way I kept slipping backward. I shouldn't have come down this incline. What had I been thinking? My foot groped for the next stepping place. The primitive pathway had a fork with a wall of rock in the middle. I hadn't noticed an additional passage on the way down here. Maybe I'd turned left from a left tunnel on the way down. Would be on my right, now. I entered.

Another rise, another curve. Water dripped onto my nose. The rock walls and ceiling closed in around me, became a tunnel. I'd gone in the wrong direction. The next curve brought even less space, no room to turn around. I'd have to back out of this narrowing.

But wait, a pool of light rippled ahead, the distance from here no more than the length of Promise's sleeping place. Not like the distant glow I'd sought before. This was daylight. I was sure. Morning and the path to freedom arrived together.

Papa and Galen would be on their way to the cave to find me. When they reached the base of the hillside, I'd better be down there to greet them so they didn't become entrapped or worse. I squeezed through the tunnel, crawling on my stomach, moving bit by bit over dank soil and smooth rock, my arms bent under my chest. Another narrowing ahead. I couldn't progress much farther without getting stuck. Fresh air filled my lungs. It must have flowed from the outside. Freedom was both close and far away.

Blue-green light swelled within the tunnel and flooded my eyes. Years ago, a light had blinded those miners. My lids squeezed shut. The illumination blazed through them, as if Moses had returned.

"A child of the Houses Navarro and Jame must be born," a feminine voice said.

It was the same voice I'd heard near the Shadow World's Black Mountain, when I'd cowered in Billy's airship tin. With eyes closed and head throbbing, I wiggled forward. What was going on? Then the floor, walls, and ceiling of the cave pressed against me. I could barely breathe.

"Dear spirit of the blue-green light," I said in a ragged voice, "please consider helping me squeeze through this passageway."

"This is your path to crawl," the light said, becoming deep blue.

What an unhelpful thing to say. This spirit tested me. I inched forward and grunted. Something about Promise's library tugged at my memory—the sketch of a woman's face in Wei's journal. Blue-green at a distance, the journal claimed, and deep blue up close. Like this light. Like the skull. I had to find out if evil or good gave this cave power.

"Are you the...?" I said, still afraid to open my eyes. "I mean, I thank you for your confidence in me, and would be grateful to know if you are the Holy Virgin of Guadalupe."

"I am known by many names," the Voice of the Light said. "Never forget, though, names are less important than deeds. Open your eyes."

And be blinded? I inched forward a little more, my chest aching, the signet ring rubbing against my finger. I should respect the spirit's request, open at least one eye. Something on the ground warmed the side of my forearm. I backed into the cave a little and lifted one eyelid. Illuminated by the Virgin's light, a dusty gold pendant on a chain lay in a shallow bowl of rock. Red Sash Man had worn this jewelry.

I opened my other eye and grasped the gritty circular disk. The ring. Where was the signet ring? The carved, black hawk's head had been on my finger only moments ago. It couldn't have slipped off when I'd moved backward. Pressure against my chest increased, making each breath of air even harder to pull. More than the narrow passageway or panic affected my breathing. An unknown power far exceeded my own. I had to get out of this tunnel.

I crawled forward around a bend. The blue spirit vanished. Beams of morning sunlight shone through the mouth of the passageway. The world beyond the magic cave lay a few feet ahead. Fresh air flooded my aching lungs. I'd done it. Escaped alive. A feat neither the Yokut shaman nor Red Sash Man had managed to accomplish. Tears stung the corners of my eyes. Still, I'd failed to find the letter and would need to return.

I clutched the pendant tighter. Red Sash Man could have left it for me on purpose. For good luck. I wiggled clear of the tunnel.

"Just wait until Papa and Galen arrive," I whispered.

They'd be upset, yet wouldn't scold me for long. And surely my boldness would please Magdalena. Well, once she stopped pouting from being left behind. Maybe I would even thank Billy, instead of murdering him.

I stood, legs shakier than I'd expected. Wind whipped at my clothing. My tunic was ripped and sandal laces broken, my braid more gray than black. I slipped the chain around my neck, then worked my way to the bottom of the hill.

My pendant deserved a kiss. I raised it to my lips. Why, the metal was engraved. The marking appeared to be the letter "W." No Spanish surname I knew of started with a "W." Maybe the given name of Red Sash Man was Wilfredo. Or his family name was British, or—

Letter. "W" was a letter. Wei's journal hadn't referred to writings on paper or parchment, but to an engraved letter on a golden pendant. This was the talisman I sought. Somehow, the bones had helped.

Three people approached in the distance. Galen, Papa and Magdalena, I figured. I waved.

"Juanita," Papa shouted. There was no mistaking that stern voice.

"I found the letter of magic," I told them when they reached the base of the hillside. "Maybe now visions will come to me from the Black Mountain."

"Thank God, you're alive." Magdalena's eyes avoided mine. "You were crazy to come here alone."

"But we need to know," I said, "the best way to—"

Galen pressed his finger against my lips, then held me close. Even Papa, eyes glistening with tears, appeared more relieved than angry with me. I hadn't wanted to worry those I loved.

"You've passed a test of worthiness most would fail," Galen whispered into my ear. "Walk the path with me to the lookout tonight, my angel. What better place for a vision to visit you?"

Walk with Galen to the lookout and watch for the asylum train. What an honor. I squeezed his hand.

Yet the talisman's powers might draw my spirit from my body, take me to the Black Mountain. Whether heading for the lookout or the Shadow World, I'd better not meet that headless skeleton's spirit or any of his friends.

9. Hero's Eyes

I AWAKENED. SOMEONE snored. Galen knelt beside my mat in the darkened room, his hand against my shoulder.

"It's time," he whispered. "Today's last freight train will have passed hours ago."

Scant moonlight shone through the window of the sleeping place, yet enough to paint Galen's handsome face with a soft glow. His eyes resembled those of Red Sash Man. But, wait. I sat bolt upright. We had to get going to the lookout to keep watch for the asylum train.

I laced the deer hide tops of my sandals, wound the free ends of the ties around my ankles and secured them with double knots. I stood. My fingers brushed my loose tunic, one of the women's spares. The Cave of Light had damaged my own beyond repair. Perhaps traveling healers would bring another bolt of homespun hemp after the summer solstice. A tingle plunged across my shoulders. The feeling shot to my fingertips and toes. Promise might exist elsewhere by mid-June.

Galen led me toward the door. The hinges sighed with creaks and groans. The comforting sounds of home. California must have other safe and secluded places to live. Best to have courage and accept the future the Shadow World planned.

The cool touch of the night air in mid-spring enveloped me. How romantic to venture from the village this way with Galen. Oh, to spend the perfect life with him—healthy children, Mama well enough to read to them, bean plants topping the trellis, and water for weekly baths, even in the summer. In such a world, there would come a reunion with my lost parents. Magdalena would raise her sister's baby. Murders in asylums would cease.

I strolled with Galen past the darkened kitchen, the moon almost down to a quarter crescent in the star-studded sky. I touched the jewelry around my neck. A duet of frogs harmonized with countless crickets. So beautiful, knowing life, even if that life could never match the one in my hopes and dreams.

Still, in the Cave of Light, magical blue illumination had prophesied the birth of a child in my family. Galen and I might become the parents of the baby. Well, having any child would happen years in the future. I needed to menstruate for the first time. Marry Galen, who'd never even kissed my lips. Warmth spread across my face. Maybe he would try to kiss me on the mouth tonight.

Another thought crawled into my mind. What had that prophecy meant about me becoming a true engine woman? Plus, Billy had called me "Little Engine Woman" when I'd operated the throttle of his airship tin. Did he expect me to run a real airship? A far-fetched idea. The only mechanical thing in Promise was the rusty wind-up man that didn't work.

Ahead, the dirt path leading to the lookout curved through the bean garden then twisted away from the stream and up a rugged hillside. Not in the same direction as the Cave of Light. I'd often walked this section of the path. This time, I stepped through familiar territory with care and watched for animal eyes catching a glint of moonlight. Animals hid themselves and their families well. The people of Promise tried to do the same thing, although local Yokuts knew the location of my community, and always guided traveling healers here.

"My ancestors loved to eat rabbits and cows," I said, feeling the need for conversation. "I mean, we've no choice but to eat some meat. But my ancestors told me they even ate eggs. Can you imagine eating something that's waiting to be born? I don't think I could ever do that."

"Things can change," Galen said.

We approached a cluster of oak trees. Certain things— my love for Galen—would never change. The two of us would labor together by day, then hold each other close by night. Finally, our spirits would glow side-by-side in the Shadow World. Those of my great-grandparents did.

The rusty gate marked the edge of Promise. Time to dark-walk, so Galen and I didn't become separated. He tied a rope around my waist. I felt the steady pressure of his hand against my abdomen as he slipped his fingers under the rope sash. His hand lingered. I stiffened. Did his touch have more than one meaning?

"If it's too snug, Juanita, it'll burn you," he said.

He gave the middle of my braid a playful tug and laughed. Tension drained from me. I could trust Galen. He wrapped the free end of the rope around himself, leaving a yard of line between us.

I knew the rules for dark-walking. Galen, so familiar with the path, would lead. I'd jerk the rope two times if he walked too fast for me. Three times if I needed to stop.

"No talking until we reach the lookout," Galen said. "There are noises that aren't good to hear, yet it's wise to listen for them."

Papa had reported bear droppings on a trail. Had Galen referred to bears—or Mendozas?

Galen walked, his pace slow. I followed his shadowy form with ease, stepping where he had and maintaining slack in the connecting rope. I shifted my focus between Galen and the path. Even in the dark, this trail proved easier than the one leading to the Cave of Light.

I leaned forward as I climbed. Galen changed direction. The path disappeared, replaced by an obstacle course of stones. I stumbled. The rope pulled taut. He waited. I moved forward, my heartbeats almost as fast as a hummingbird's wings. My ankle hurt, but I could walk without limping.

It would have been better to memorize the way at dawn, as Galen must have done. South California and the Mendoza family weren't far away. The men of Promise over-protected our women and children, liked us to stay close to home. A good thing Galen understood the importance of bold actions.

The angle on the tether sharpened. I followed its slide around boulders, my ears searching for unwanted noises. Galen turned and grabbed my hand. We moved to the center of a wide rock and sat on its uneven surface. A different sort of void encircled me—even less comforting than that of the Shadow World. Something cold waited out there, something bad. I listened to Galen's breathing, as if only he could shield me. His odor—the smell of man and sweat and so much more—coated my tongue and nostrils. Oh, for that odor to cling forever.

"Where's the train station?" I scanned the darkness beyond the lookout. Nothing but a velvet sky interrupted by moon and stars, and the hint of a reflection off scattered patches of terrain.

"In a while," Galen said, "the locomotive's faint ball of light will crawl along the ground, way over there." He pointed. "If the asylum train's going to stop at Thistlewood Station, the movement of the light will slow. That's all we'll see."

"Might an airship fly above the train?" I said. "To guard it?" They had airships in South California.

"Airships never guard asylum trains," Galen said.

That was good news. Still, much distance separated Promise from the train station. Great-Grandma, and Galen's rescuer, too, had escaped the train and carried us for miles. My people and I would have to lug our belongings even farther if pursued by the authorities. Where would we hide after completing the sabotage? I didn't want friends and family to die in the process of getting there. I had much information to pry out of Billy, more than just the timing of the work. When would I meet him next?

Galen squeezed my hand, as if he knew my fears. I shifted my buttocks against the rock, turned my face toward him and smiled. He tilted my chin upward. Darkness hid his pupils. His face drew closer to mine.

He was going to kiss me. Right then. Should I close my eyes? Heartbeats sounded within my ears. My eyelids lowered. My lungs held onto their air. Galen's warm lips settled against mine. Even my ankles tingled. Oh, to make this kiss—this night—last forever.

Then Galen's arms wrapped around me, the palms of his hands firm against my back. His wooly beard tickled my cheeks and chin. Such a softness in the way his tongue entered my mouth. Dared I let his tongue caress mine? He smelled so good. Tasted so sweet. We were betrothed. Kissing this way couldn't be wrong.

Galen pulled back a few inches, as if he needed to catch his breath.

"I love you," he said.

"I love you, too." I would adore him always.

He held me near, the side of my head pressed against his chest, his fingers stroking my hair. His were strong, good hands—hardened by manual labor, yet soft enough to wipe tears away.

Dearest Galen. No matter what our mission involved, he mustn't die before I did. Life without him would be too lonely to bear.

10. God Bless Mexico

THE SWEET MEMORY of Galen's lips against mine returned over and over the next day. By the time I sat beside him after dinner, even my toes tingled. No wonder my head felt light. Papa served tea. I reached out to grasp the tea urn by its handles.

Then darkness closed in on me. Just like that. I hovered in a vast, silent place. The corridor between the worlds of the living and the dead—I had to be there. But how? And where were the Guardians of the Portals and the window back to life?

A light shimmered in the eternal night. Billy's yellow-brown glow approached me. Wait... Billy had mentioned something about a quick way to travel to the Shadow World.

"Let's get this over with," Billy said, his gruff greeting less hospitable than a cactus-covered chair. He reeked of tobacco.

"Get what over with? Why am I here?" Billy shouldn't have interrupted my special time with Galen. "I need some real answers."

"You've been getting plenty of answers from us," Billy said, "here and in the Cave of Light. You just haven't been asking the questions that go with 'em. You'll find tonight's set of answers as tasty as slurping down a mess of raw eggs."

"What do eggs have to do with answers?" I knew I flashed exasperation orange.

No use being polite to Billy, despite my status as a mystic traveler. Demand was the only thing Billy seemed to comprehend, if he understood anything I needed at all.

"Tell me," I said, "once we sabotage the train, where will we hide? And speaking of sabotage, when, where, and how should we?"

"You're asking about a different batch of eggs," Billy said. "You're on the Black Mountain now."

"Oh." I saw no mountain.

Billy had said my magic pendant would keep my earthly body alive while I traveled within the Shadow World. Found in the cave, it connected me to all this.

"Will I experience something that happened to Great-Grandma, like when the river talked to me?"

"Not this time. You'll be in British South California. Destination 1870."

Mist swirled around me, forming walls and a ceiling. A steady rain tapped on the roof. Tonight's experience would begin indoors.

I sat upon a hard wooden chair. My sturdy left hand—a man's hand—clasped a glass on a circular table. How could I be a man? Something was wedged between my teeth—a cigar. How had I known that? The tobacco tasted strong and good. I stared at a jagged crack down the length of an adobe wall, as if its presence had secret meaning. I, no, the person I was becoming, knew this place all too well.

•

Billy puffed on his cigar and surveyed the cantina. Several men in his corner of the bar nursed their drinks. Twenty feet away, a dozen off-duty railroad men in greasy overalls made sport of an unlucky thirteenth. Someone ordered a bottle of bourbon. Billy sipped his Scotch whisky—cheap and smoky—and focused on the cracked wall. He knew when to mind his own business, particularly when in South California.

Chair legs squealed against the floor two tables away. The luckless thirteenth—a medium-built man, butt naked—slumped over the seat of a piano stool. A clean-shaven bastard with his pants down and a glass of bourbon-and-soda in his left hand took aim at the pair of spread buttocks. He missed. The room resonated with coarse guffaws. This bunch was as rancid as last year's butter.

A seated man with narrow eyes and a big gut tossed a large silver coin onto the chipped tile floor. The dollar wobbled. Tails.

"I'll wager you can't get it in," Gut Man said, a pair of goggles fastened like a hatband around the base of his top hat, as if the likes of him had ever done a day's work beside a coal-burner or in swirling sand.

The bourbon-and-soda bastard missed again. The unfortunate thirteenth puked a puddle of booze and half-digested beans. His bloodshot eyes opened. He groaned. The drunken men beside him whistled, slapped their thighs, and propped his butt higher.

"Here's five more the prick don't score," a barrel-chested man said, his ruddy cheeks highlighted with blond stubble. A few feet away, a smaller silver coin was flipped through the air. The money landed with a metallic clink.

What right had those bastards? Billy puffed hard on his cigar. The stink of tobacco penetrated his mouth and nose, coated him, as if lodged in his pores. He picked up his glass. The smoky Scotch stung its way down his throat. A man could hide behind smoke. Well, sometimes.

"Two gold nuggets—and all the money on the floor," Gut Man said, "to any bloke who gets it in on the first try." His paunch jiggled under a paisley vest and cream-colored shirt. "But that's a wager. Be prepared to fork over your own money, if you lose."

A tall thin man with a waxed mustache and derby hat threw a Spanish dollar, then a gold sovereign. More coins followed. Billy could sure use some of that. He stared down at the money. One hell of a lot of dough stared back.

Disgusting. A den of Mendoza corruption, this place, although the feared Gabriel Mendoza lived at least forty miles away. One of life's darker angels, Gabriel. Hell, Gabe was the devil in cowhide boots and a top hat. A compelling reason to get himself and Juan to Mexico soon, before 1870 turned into 1871.

He sipped his Scotch. Gabriel wanted Juan. That bastard had no right to touch the love of Billy's life. Time to quit being one of Gabe's frigging locomotive engineers, as of tonight. No British Army airship hovered above this cantina with a pair of free tickets to safety. Without more money, he'd never escape over the border with Juan. Additional coins landed on the floor, just daring someone to earn them.

The cigar moved from his teeth to the ashtray in slow motion, as if directed by another's hand. Billy stroked the stubble on his jowls and scratched his crooked nose.

Black Mountain or no Black Mountain, he shouldn't have to relive this frigging night. Juanita shouldn't have to know it ever happened. But Billy wasn't the one making the rules. If he knew what was good for him, he'd better stay on script.

Billy stood and walked over to the slumped railroad man. His brain added up the money.

A sudden tightness gripped Billy's chest. The squeezing pressure came from inside. The figure of the unlucky thirteenth blurred and turned gray. Saliva welled in Billy's mouth and tasted sour.

●

My spirit tingled. The cantina was gone. A shapeless yellow-brown glow hovered in the Shadow World's night. Billy's light. I was myself again. The nightmare on the Black Mountain had ended.

Billy's cigar tin scooped up my ether, as if I were a silver coin. The tin closed. The wail of mystery winds built to a deafening pitch. What had happened? What had anything meant? And dear God, Billy was a locomotive engineer. Was this how I would become a true engine woman?

The mixed aromas of a fire and mint tea coaxed open my eyes. Galen—dearest Galen—sponged my forehead with water, his pupils intense and wide. The torch in Papa's hand burned with thin curls of black smoke. This was the world of life. The Shadow World had freed me, at least for now.

"You had no pulse." Galen's eyes and cheeks glistened in the firelight. "One minute you were reaching for the tea, and the next... We thought. Oh, my love, I thought—"

Galen cried. I blurted out a reply in broken sentences. I'd had a vision. Our mission would happen. Holding back the full truth made my stomach hurt.

"After we stop the train—" I coughed, then sucked some water from a sopping cloth and swallowed. "We're to head for Mexico. We'll probably meet some horrible people on the way."

Cole offered me a drink of tepid water. The rim of the metal cup felt cool.

How could Billy and Great-Uncle Juan, two men, have fallen in love with each other? How could Billy even have contemplated earning that money in the cantina? Far worse, Billy had run a train, could have—must have—carried thrown-away people to the prison, workhouse and asylum in South California. What had the Guardians of the Portals been doing when Billy's soul had floated from his corpse to the Shadow World? Sleeping or playing cards?

I looked into Galen's eyes, deep with amber sparkles. Those of a hero. How different he was from Billy.

"You had no heartbeat," Galen said, his voice unsteady. "No breath. Something else must have happened."

"I...I had visions of railroad men." I had no idea why I'd nearly died, but would die from embarrassment if I described the ugsome details of tonight's experience. "Most of those men were not living worthy lives."

"Was that all?" Galen said.

"I—I think so."

I touched Galen's forehead and cheeks, even as my own burned from the memory of Billy's mixed revulsion and temptation. Billy was part of me. I was part of him.

Billy's words from a different night trickled into my mind. The day would come when I would curse my ancestors. If I didn't understand and trust them, I'd neither cope, nor survive. My hand clung to Galen's, as if only he could save me, keep me from whirling toward the Black Mountain.

11. Strength of Ten

THE MORNING AIR chilled me as I knelt by the creek with the laundry. I could still see Billy—me—sipping Scotch the night before. Setting down the glass. Standing up. All right, Billy's knowledge of trains had value, despite the way he'd acquired the information. Understanding the mechanics of British airships might help, too. Knowing what men did with men, however, was a different pot of shucked acorns. The cantina experience couldn't possibly help me save lives, plan sabotage, or escape to Mexico.

"Tell me how to lead my people to safety," I demanded, as if the spirits hovered beside me. "You want me to stop the train. So, give me the information I need to do the job and keep safe those I love."

I slapped wet homespun tunics against a large flat rock in the widest section of the creek. My hands, wrinkled from moisture, reddened and tingled as I wrung out the clothes. Coins had tumbled on the floor. Thick tobacco smoke had filled the air. I scrubbed another garment. I couldn't evict flashbacks of the cantina from my mind.

Either Billy had gone ahead and earned those coins or he hadn't. Maybe I didn't want to know.

"Great-Grandma," I said. "That history lesson about Billy could have waited three hundred years."

God, I was a mystic, shouldn't vent my anger at Great-Grandma. I needed to regain self-control, rinse out my mind, talk to someone. Magdalena would likely make sarcastic remarks. The current tugged on a soggy garment and carried dirt away. Only one person in Promise could help me cope with my inner turmoil—Mama, who I trusted most.

•

I headed toward the sleeping place after the time of high sun, a Bible wedged under my arm. I read to Mama almost every afternoon while the nurse woman, Isobel, got food. An Old Testament story should prove useful today. The one about Sodom and Gomorrah might help introduce the subject of being Billy.

No, that tale wouldn't do. Evil had dwelled within Sodom and Gomorrah. Mama had said so, but without many further details. Billy's love for Juan was good. I had felt his actual feelings. I knew. Considering forcing a man or actually doing it—and for money—had brought Billy shame. I bit my thumbnail. According to the Old Testament, God had chosen a harlot to help Joshua's spies escape Jericho, the way the Shadow World had selected Billy to guide me. The tale about the harlot would be the better choice.

The wooden porch of the sleeping place creaked under my feet. The door sat ajar. Isobel waited in the entry corridor, the side of her forefinger pressed against her dry lips. Her eyes, large and perpetually crossed, perched above prominent cheekbones.

"Your mama's worse today." A scratch in a crevice of Isobel's furrowed brow twisted, like a red river snaking through a valley. "She's taken no food or water."

Mama, so fragile, would soon die without water. My chest tightened. I rushed toward the far end of the single-story building.

Mama curled in a pool of sunlight on her sleeping mat. Her emaciated frame, half covered with a stained blanket, shifted against the woven straw. Tiny purple blotches dotted her frail yellow arms. The pottery basin near her head smelled foul.

A single orange poppy lay wilted on the corner of the mat. I'd picked the flower only that morning. The poppy had been radiant with life then. I looked away. A bird chattered beyond the open window. I set the Bible on a square pine table. I had to coax Mama to drink.

I poured water into a metal cup, then sat on the floor, the vessel nearby. My hand stroked the bony angles of Mama's frame. The swelling between her rib cage and abdomen was more noticeable today, the toll from a liver malady. I clasped Mama's warm, scaly hand. Yesterdays had vanished so soon.

"Juanita?" Mama rasped, as if sand layered her throat.

"Yes, it's me."

I brushed her cheek against the blanket and inhaled. Oh, to recapture a scent from the past. Her aroma had once been sweet and pungent, like cactus flowers in late spring. She smelled of urine, now.

"I've poured water for you," I said. "Will you drink some, just for me?"

Mama's lips produced a dry, sucking sound. She closed her eyes. I touched her arm. What would convince her— only thirty-five—to fight death?

"I need your help," I said, the words choking their way from my throat to the air. I wanted to shake Mama, scream and make her drink. Instead, I clutched her baggy brown robe. My cheek, wet with tears, rested against her chest.

"Remember when I was little and got really sick?" I said. "I couldn't help you in the kitchen for weeks."

"Weeks," Mama said, her voice feeble.

"You soaked the sleeve of your robe," I said, "so I could suck water. Put wads of bean paste on my tongue so I wouldn't starve. I felt so helpless. Useless."

I wedged a rolled blanket under Mama's head and shoulders. I dipped my fingers into the water cup, then patted the dry crust of her lips. Her jaw relaxed and her teeth parted, exposing a pasty tongue. She accepted the water I sprinkled into her open mouth, so I siphoned more from the cup with the end of my sleeve. Mama sucked the wet cloth. Praise the spirits. After pouring another cupful, I eased her into a sitting position.

"You claimed you could do my work and yours until I healed." I tilted the cup against Mama's lips. "You told me my voice gave you the strength of ten women."

Mama swallowed a little water, her eyes glazed, almost as if part of her already dwelled in the next world. Her second sip of fluid trickled down her chin.

"Don't stop fighting," I said. "I love you. I need to hear your voice." And she needed to hear mine. "The ancestors have given me a job, but not enough directions. I'm scared. What if I fail, if babies or those I love die because of me?"

Mama slipped her hand atop mine and squeezed. It would be all right to talk about Billy then. Mama always knew the right words to say, always knew everything. I kissed the rope of her black hair and stroked her sweaty forehead, cheeks, and shoulders. May my needs give her new life.

"There's something else," I said. "I have visions where I'm other people. Uncomfortable things happen that I don't understand."

"A memory." Mama closed her eyes and nodded, her lips curved in a weak smile. "Find a fond memory and pray for strength."

Countless memories of Mama flooded my mind. Mama had taught me to cook and weave, to read and add numbers, to fashion wildflower crowns. We'd rolled in wet meadow grass, sung silly songs, chased butterflies, dug irrigation ditches, and slapped wet clothing against flat rocks. We'd gazed at the stars.

Mama made a guttural grunt. She grabbed at her stomach, then her throat. Her face contorted, jaundiced eyes wide. A vile red liquid spewed out of her mouth and nose, spattering her face, neck, clothing, hands, and me. Dear God.

"Isobel," I shouted. "Anyone. Help!"

Mama sagged against the mat, doubled up on her side, and gasped in spasms. I wiped the bloody vomit from her face. Isobel would know what to do. Where was she? Mama mustn't die.

Then Mama lay as still as a tiny flower sheltered from breezes. No trace of breathing remained. Gone. Mama was gone. On my knees, I cradled her lifeless body against me. I rocked Mama from side-to-side and wailed.

•

At sunrise, the women cleaned Mama's corpse with sand and brushed her hair until every strand gleamed. The men dug a grave. I fasted and spent the afternoon in

80

meditation. A mystic should perform last rites well. I had to contain my grief.

I sat cross-legged on the ground beside Mama and concentrated on the memory of the little candle, the humble light pictured in Wei's journal. I'd demanded answers from the spirits yesterday, and done so in anger. Somehow, Mama's death was part of their answer. Oh, if only I'd remained a humble light.

The people of Promise gathered by the fire after sunset. Galen beat his ceremonial drum. A river of tongues-against-palates clicks flowed. Papa's silent prayers for Mama reached my heart. Spinning around and around, I concentrated on his feelings of love and loss. Time reversed for me. When my body fell, the ground rose to meet it. My freed spirit floated.

The scent of cactus flowers greeted me. Mama, an ivory glow, waited in a passageway between the realms of life and death. "We must focus on fond memories," I said.

"No," Mama said. "We must illuminate the path of miracles. You accomplish your part. I'll take care of mine."

Mama had died. No miracle could restore her life. Things didn't happen that way. I escorted her ether to one of the Shadow World's portals. The sweet smell of warm honey greeted us. So did Great-Grandma's odor of chocolate. The river of crimson lights parted. Those guardians who judged souls permitted Mama to pass without delay. She must have never done anything wrong. I hovered until darkness swallowed the last glimpse of Mama's ivory light.

"Mama," I said. "Great-Grandma. Forgive me. Please."

I returned to the living. I stood with Galen by the embers of the fire, my brown tunic damp with perspiration and tears. I'd lost my temper, demanded the Shadow World obey my wishes. I'd violated Wei's teachings. Now I had to live with the consequences.

I sobbed against Galen's chest. I inhaled the odors of hair and skin and life, while a part of my soul dried up and blew away.

And I still didn't know when to sabotage the train.

12. Think Like an Hombre

THE SLEEPING PLACE appeared empty of light. I sat cross-legged on my mat and fingered my ragged wool blanket. Nearby, several of my people on floor mats snored. I ought to rest, too. Yet summer would arrive this month, and the murderer would put his plan into action. Little time remained to complete the Shadow World's mission. *Cease to exist.* My memory of Moses brought on a shudder. Mama was dead. Dear God, the loss continued to hurt so much. Who would die next? Were Billy and I still part of each other?

A gruff voice called to me. A shapeless apparition hovered, its shimmering, yellow-brown mist stretching from ceiling to floor between a cluster of sleepers and a clothes chest. The ghost reeked of cigars. Billy. But I was awake and not in the Shadow World.

The spirit cloud twisted and swirled into the figure of a man. Tall, slender, and clean-shaven, he was, his black hair tied at the nape of his neck. Goggles stretched around the base of his hat. He buttoned his leather vest, the backs of his hands brown as unskinned almonds, then scratched the end of his nose. Billy, in his faded blue shirt and trousers, breathed and looked flesh-and-blood real, even more real than Red Sash Man had in the Cave of Light. This wasn't right.

"How do you look so alive?" I said. "You don't even glow."

"There are times when the dead can walk the earth this way." Billy sat down cross-legged on the dirt floor and rested his elbows on his knees.

An important character in a Bible story had died and walked the earth. A tingle shot to my fingertips and toes. I clutched the blanket against my chest.

82

"Are you," I said, "like Jesus?"

"That's rich, kid." Billy chuckled and rubbed his chin. "All dead can walk the earth and appear alive to the chosen, although we usually aren't allowed."

"Is it all right to touch you?" I peered into his deep, mysterious eyes. If only Mama could join us here.

He stretched out his hand. I squeezed each finger, touched each yellowed tip and dirty nail. He felt real. Cold, but real.

"I've got to tell you about the train," he said. "Before your people wake up."

I peeked under both long shirt-sleeves. His hairy arms radiated no warmth. He pulled a stubby cigar from his vest pocket, then hunted through his other pockets, finally producing a match.

"A train comes tomorrow night," he said. "It's got one blazes of an engine." He bit off the tip of the cigar.

"Do you mean the train?" My stomach muscles clenched. "The one we're supposed to stop?"

"Yup." He struck the match on his boot. "Its driving wheels are six feet high. Got four sets, too."

"I don't know what wheels you're talking about." I smoothed the patched cloth of my night robe. *The train. It's on its way.*

"Driving wheels are the ones the steam turns, the ones that roll on the rails." Billy laughed, the cigar bouncing in the grip of his crooked, yellowed teeth, and gave my single braid a playful tug.

An engine with wheels as tall as Galen would be far larger than the one Great-Grandma had encountered. Billy breathed in and out. He ought to look more dead. I gripped my blanket tighter.

"You and your *amigos*," Billy said, "have to sabotage the track before next sunset."

"Now wait a minute," I said. Tomorrow was too soon. "At dawn, I get up and say tonight's the night? Forget about cooking, eating—maybe even about living—and try to stop the train?"

"That's the picture," Billy said.

He puffed out several rings of twinkling smoke. They drifted toward me. My lungs itched until I coughed. The acrid rings floated through the room, touching each community member. None of the sleepers reacted. Perhaps Billy's smoke couldn't affect them. Billy offered me the cigar. I pushed his hand away.

"This will help you think like an hombre," he said. "Like me." He slipped one end of the cigar between my lips. "Draw in but don't inhale."

All right, I'd take a puff, although Mama would not approve of me smoking a cigar. The smoke triggered more coughing. "That's awful." I glanced around the room. No one had awakened.

Billy produced the airship tin used to transport me in the Shadow World. He raised the cover. An eerie golden glow bathed his face.

"I'll be with you tomorrow night, the best I can." He retrieved the cigar and clamped it between his teeth. Brown saliva dribbled from the corner of his mouth. "But the only way you'll recognize me is by the smell or taste of tobacco." He spat out shimmering brown flecks. "Look into the box."

An image of a train formed within the tin. I jerked backward, a rush of fear shooting through me, as if the train might leap from the container, enlarge and become real.

"The train will run without passengers and show up earlier than usual." Billy rocked the cigar into my mouth. "But I don't know by how much." He raised the tin closer to my face. Ashes dropped into the strange glow. "See that man?"

"Yes," I mumbled. Thank God no passengers would die.

Billy reached into the box and withdrew a cloud of yellow mist. The image of a large-boned man in denim overalls staggered in his hand.

"The engineer." Billy sneered. "Frigging drunk, the bastard." He blew the mist back into the tin and replaced the cover. "Get the picture?"

On the Black Mountain, the drunken railroaders in the cantina had been in no condition to operate anything mechanical. The cantina... Afterward, had Billy remained faithful to my great uncle Juan? Lives would depend on Billy tomorrow night, yet he sometimes seemed unfeeling and neglected to tell me important things. I could put my trust in a faithful man.

"What do I need to do?" The cigar almost slipped out of my mouth.

"In the morning," Billy said, "tell your people to gather what they need to survive. They'll need your Papa's crowbars, shovels, and pickaxe, too."

He reopened the tobacco tin, just a crack. Bilious smoke oozed from under the lid. It encircled his hand, then condensed into a train track and the landscape around Promise. The night of the train was really going to happen. My teeth clamped Billy's cigar. I puffed without coughing, teetering on the brink of a canyon of consequences.

"A maintenance crew will check the rails in the morning," he said. "They'll be gone before the sun's high." He pointed at a section of straight track near a post. "Dig away some of the gravel under this side of the rail. Have the men pull the spikes. Plan's to misalign the works. You'll know the piece of rail I mean. Shorter than the rest." He shifted his finger to the adjacent rail. "Do the same thing on this side, forty feet downtrack."

Dig gravel. Pull spikes. I puffed on the cigar. The tobacco tasted better than before. I could almost hear Mama groan. Billy blew the magic mist back into the airship tin. He set the lid in place.

Smoke and words produced a queasy stomach. I returned the cigar to Billy. He stubbed it against the heel of his work boot. Golden mist seeped from inside the closed tin. The lid lifted itself. Ebony smoke billowed around the image of a blood-red track.

85

"One more thing," Billy said. "All your people must help. When the job's done, it'll be dark and unsafe to return to Promise. Sand the fire and head this way, south, toward where the train'll come from. You must sand the fire. Otherwise the railroaders will see it and brake. Dark-walk as far as you can." He guided my finger up the image of the track. "Walk past here."

He slammed the cover on the tin. The airship exploded in a burst of crimson and golden ash. I clutched my blanket.

"The steam pressure. How far will it—"

"She'll blow shrapnel a quarter mile or more. And there'll be a couple freight cars loaded with black powder. Explosive as hell."

Billy turned silver. I could see right through him. My people stirred. Night drew to a close. So much to do. Could I trust Billy not to forget a crucial detail? Time to ask him my other question.

"All those years in Mexico, did you love my great-uncle Juan more than life or being?"

"Damn right I did," he said. "Still do."

I smiled. Billy wasn't the sort of person my natural father was. Billy was loyal, as Galen, Great-Grandpa Javier, and Papa were. He would do his best and not desert me.

"I bet you never felt like less of a man," I said, "just because you loved Juan instead of a woman."

"I'd only be less of a man if I had no room for love at all." He removed his hat, then bent down and kissed my forehead. "Little Engine Woman, this is the beginning of what must be."

Billy's spirit dissipated into morning shadows, leaving a hint of cigar smoke behind. I captured the residual aroma with my nose and memory. He'd given me so many instructions. What if I forgot something important?

"Mama," I said. "Please give me strength."

No aroma of cactus flowers lingered anywhere near.

13. Night of the Train

I HIKED ALONG a flat dusty road, a crowbar in my arms and a waterskin tied against my back. The mid-afternoon sun was hot, the load heavy. In the distance, a sloped hill of gravel stretched in a straight line, like an endless burial mound. The railroad track bed. I grinned at Magdalena and Cook, who plodded under the weight of picks and waterskins. Ahead, Papa, Cole and three other men shouldered long iron rods and quickened their pace. Step by step, my group neared our destination. The people of Promise and I would complete our mission soon.

All members of my community knew the plan. At breakfast, they'd claimed to have received instructions in their dreams. Five men were to extract spikes and misalign a twenty-foot piece of steel rail, plus a longer section. Several women would undermine those rails to facilitate the process. Galen and the rest would arrive before sunset. Billy's smoke rings had touched everyone last night and must have been magic.

I unloaded my gear at the track bed and read the sky. Four to five hours of daylight remained. We had little time to rest.

Papa wielded a six-foot pry bar and wrestled with an embedded railroad spike. Rivulets of sweat trickled down his brow. The working end of the bar slipped, scraping the metal plate at the end of a wooden tie. He mopped his forehead with the floppy sleeve of his gray tunic.

"I need help," Papa called.

"Hold your horses," Cole said. He and the three other men pried spikes from a section of downline rail.

"If I had horses," Papa snapped, "I'd use their muscles, not mine."

"Tempers." Magdalena clutched a trowel. "A little water might cool them so you can *help* each other." She shot a glance at me.

Magdalena had just emphasized the word, "help." Might she still be upset about being left out of the Cave of Light adventure? If so, she'd meant her comment for more than Papa and Cole. She stood and stretched, feet straddling a wooden tie. I assisted her in pouring water for the workers. Tomorrow we should settle our differences in private. I had other things on my mind right then.

The journey to Mexico could take months. We'd need to hide from those sure to pursue. The foothills would have the good hiding places. The most direct route to the asylum—where Magdalena's niece or nephew would end up—would be where the railroad ran. I stoppered the waterskin with a wooden bung and selected a pick. That tool might work for undermining rails. If only tools could give advice.

"Can railmen detect bad track at night, or did your ancestors say?" Cook poked a crowbar into the gravel railbed. Her mouth puckered, as if sucking sour fruit.

"They didn't mention," I said. "I'm certain they would have, if it really mattered."

"What do you suppose'll happen when a speeding train hits this track? Will we really be any better than railroad men?"

"The engineer won't be sober," I said. "The accident will be his fault, too. And there shouldn't be more than four or five people aboard, all of them crew."

Such an inner chill. How many people would we save by derailing tonight's train? Fifty? Five hundred or more? Billy hadn't mentioned how long service to the asylum would be interrupted, or how long snooping newspaper reporters could deter the murder of inmates already there. I touched the pendant around my neck, the jewelry from the Cave of Light. So many questions remained unanswered.

•

The sun bled red and pink above the horizon. Galen and a dozen men, packs across their backs, trudged toward the track bed. My love! I grabbed a canteen of water, then raced to meet him.

Grit coated Galen's skin and torn tunic. Scrapes and blisters marred his hands and shoulders. Dried blood crusted a makeshift bandage on his forearm.

"What happened?" I said.

He gripped my shoulders and kissed my mouth, almost pushing me backward. He tasted of man and baked earth, his action rough, surprising and urgent. Galen had kissed me with such tenderness at the lookout. And what would Papa think? Galen pulled away.

"A couple of us," he said, "slipped on the climb up the first hill."

"I took a bad step," Galen's friend, Rodrigo, said, his palms and shins scraped. "Mistakes happen."

"Galen tried to grab him," Salvatore, said, "and missed." He took a drink of water, laughed and snorted fluid out his nose.

This was serious. They could have been killed.

"Let me clean your wound," I said to Galen.

"My friends washed it," he said, "with their own water. Clean enough for now."

They had urinated on it?

"Injuries need proper tending." I lowered my voice. "So do escape plans."

I peeled back Galen's soiled bandage, rinsing around the jagged cut on his arm with water. He didn't flinch.

"Where will we all head to in the morning?" I whispered. "I'm scared."

"We all are," Galen said, his voice low. "Your papa has some ideas, though."

Magdalena brought rolled strips of clean cloth. She folded her arms against her chest as I bound Galen's wound in silence.

"First, I wasn't important enough to go to the cave with you," Magdalena said. "Now, you won't carry on your conversation with me around."

"We were just talking about being afraid." My face warmed. "Allies forever," I mouthed.

Magdalena pursed her lips, her delicate facial features like those on a painted doll. Then she shrugged and turned away.

"Let's talk later." I let out a deep sigh.

•

A thin glow of day's end stretched across the flat western horizon. The men built a fire with sagebrush and dry scrub. Gnats gathered in little swirls, away from the smoke. Cook spooned cold bean paste from a blackened pot into waiting hands.

I moved closer to Galen. He would need more food to help heal his wound.

"You must eat some of my beans," I said.

"I can't do that."

"Please." I extended my open palm. "I love you."

Galen nodded. His tongue gleaned food from my hand, curled between outstretched fingers, and pushed against each indentation. A small, candle-lit chapel, pungent with the aroma of burning wax, filled my imagination. What a perfect place to marry Galen after my people had reached Mexico and were safe. I would wear a white shawl embroidered with red roses, a type of flower I'd seen in a picture. Magdalena would fix my hair. Cole would give Galen advice.

"Juanita," Papa called across the fire circle. "When should we pack up?"

"Before the train arrives," I teased. Papa had interrupted my thoughts. I winked at Galen, who stood and offered his outstretched hand.

"The train usually rolls through two, maybe three hours before dawn," Galen said. "Plenty of time till then."

"It'll be sooner tonight," I said.

Galen and I glanced beyond the fire, into the darkness concealing the railbed. He scratched his chest. Clouds drifted past the pale moon, fat but no longer full. A good omen? Or bad?

"We'd better ready ourselves now," Galen said. "Did you hear that?" he shouted to the others. "Let's clean up and break camp. Sand the fire last, after we're grouped and ready to head out."

"How far do we dark-walk?" Papa tightened the lacing on his sandals.

"As far as we can," I said, "in the direction the train comes from."

"How long'll it take us to die if you're wrong, child?"

If I was wrong, so was Billy. He couldn't be mistaken, could he? I turned and squeezed Galen's hand, listening for a reassuring whisper. Night responded with a distant, haunting wail. A whistle.

A whistle? I couldn't move. Galen's lips parted, his face daubed with moonlight and disbelief. The train. The train was coming. Right then.

A woman screamed. Gravel crunched. Shadowy figures shot off in all directions, jolting me from my state of shock. Everyone needed to run toward the train. Hadn't they remembered Billy's instructions? Galen swept me into his arms and raced through the darkness.

"Follow my voice," he yelled. "All of you. This way."

He gulped for air between each order. His feet pounded the earth, a single ankle-twist away from disaster. I clung to his neck. I bounced against his chest. My lower legs dangled. I prayed the others followed Galen.

He approached the fire. No one had put it out. Railroaders would notice the flames.

"Put me down," I said.

He kept running. Billy had insisted the fire must be sanded. I wiggled and pounded my fist against Galen's scraped shoulder.

"Drummer, put me down."

He set me on my feet. How close was the train? At least a minute had passed since I'd first heard the whistle.

"You must be the leader," I said, "for all. And I must hide the fire." I turned and stumbled toward the glow. "Keep calling and I won't be afraid." It was a necessary lie.

Galen's call waned. The whistle didn't. Wei, the old mystic, sat hunched by the fire, motionless. I dove to my knees and tossed sandy soil into the flames.

"Help me," I called. Wei didn't respond. I scooped more sand, frantic. "Old mystic man, I need a strong magic."

Wei lurched forward and toppled into the fire, smothering the flames. The smell of his seared flesh ripped at my senses and soul. The whistle screeched. Dead—Wei was dead. A surge of vomit rose to my throat. I clutched my sickened stomach and fled toward the approaching ball of light. A mystic dies when the Shadow World decrees.

My sandals thumped hardpan with an uneven rhythm. I reached gravel and skidded. I dared not fall. The one-eyed steel serpent tore along the raised embankment of the railbed with a fury that should have rent the ground. The whistle screeched. The monstrous black engine roared. If only I could hear Galen.

"Get down," a voice called.

Who'd said that? I saw only the locomotive's headlamp, sparks from the stack, the hellish outline of raging iron and steel. Then I tasted tobacco and rolled against the embankment. The serpent passed, shuddered and groaned, barreling into the night. The train should have veered.

The left—the train pitched toward the left. No, the serpent glided, as if on ghost rails. The long silhouette arched, rode the air and aimed downward. A mountain of metal collided with ground.

A burst of flames leaped heavenward. Fire fanned out to scorch earth. An explosion flattened my body. A fireball swallowed the moon.

Steam, shrapnel and screams—how could this horror happen to me and my friends? We all should have dark-walked to safety hours before the train arrived. What had gone wrong? Then came silence, the most frightening thing of all. The air refused to yield a single groan of life.

I lay motionless, the right side of my face pressed against rough gravel and sand. I smelled a pungent, organic odor. Fuel and grease.

"Galen," I called. "Galen."

No answer came. Perhaps my voice was too weak. Still, I kept calling Galen's name. Time crawled by, its length kept secret. My throat grew hoarse. A soft wind brought the stench of blood and burnt things. Excrement, too. My stomach twisted. Wei toppled into the fire again and again in my imagination. Perhaps I should try to stand. Galen might hear me if I stood.

My brain instructed my legs to move. They wouldn't. It begged my arms to help. They couldn't. Where were my legs, my arms? Surely I'd know if the explosion had ripped them away.

I concentrated on my limbs, searched for the sensation of them pressing against the ground. Part of me seemed heavy in that same way. I breathed in with short gasps, trying to purge the taste and smell of death from my mouth and nostrils. Faceless images of broken, charred bodies flashed through my mind. My people! Who lived and who didn't?

"What have I done?"

Hours passed, perhaps a thousand years. Morning's first light arrived. My arm curved in front of me, healthy and brown, but unresponsive. Beyond my arm lay a chilling object, round yet not round—with hair. Dearest God.

I snapped shut my eyes and whispered apologies to the dead. The buzzing of a fly replied. I retched. Fluid trickled from the side of my mouth. How could I look at the body part? How could I not? A fluttering sound took that choice away.

I opened my eyes. A raven sat on the severed head, picking at flayed flesh. One side of the face was gone, the other bloodied and gray. Yet even in dawn's light, I recognized the features. Only yesterday they'd appeared so delicate, like those on a painted doll.

Magdalena!

I closed my tear-filled eyes. The flutter of wings announced the arrival of a second scavenger. *Cease to exist.* The spirits had known this would happen. They'd never meant for my people to survive. Bad enough they'd taken Mama before her time, let Wei die so his body would hide the fire. I'd devoted myself to my ancestors. And they'd used me to murder those I loved.

"I hate my ancestors," I cried. "I have no ancestors."

"You can't get rid of us that easy," a gruff voice whispered. Billy! "Hate us all you want, but stop the trains."

Mucous clogged my nose and slimed down the back of my throat. My head throbbed. Galen was dead. So were Papa and Nurse, Cook and Cole. The rest of my friends. Nothing remained but an impossible assignment.

"Take me." I wept. "Take me, too."

The sun edged higher in the sky. Vultures and more ravens gathered to feast. Neither searing rays nor hungry birds touched me, as if my helpless body lay beneath an invisible shield. A wildflower withered. Still, I felt no thirst. The pendant from the Cave of Light chilled my chest. A mystic doesn't die until the Shadow World decrees.

Journal of Passage, Year 1894

14. Pilgrimage to the River of Tears

SOMEWHERE, THE SUN crept high in the sky. Dead walked the earth. My mortal form slept in their care, my body shielded. My spirit drifted, aware and alone, through a dark and silent place.

Beyond California's great valley, snow-capped mountains spawned icy winds. Their howls summoned men who understood the languages of wilderness. All these things happened. I was sure. Otherwise, my soul would have hovered at the Shadow World's portals while birds picked my bones clean.

The Shadow World wanted me to stop more trains. How dare they ask? Let Billy walk the earth and do the job himself. I should have died with Galen, Papa, and Magdalena.

Yet the light—deep blue up close and blue-green from afar—had appeared to me in the cave. A child must be born. The chosen parents could be me and Galen. If so, Galen must still live, may even lay injured and unconscious near the railroad track. I had to find him. And I had to find, or at least protect, the child of Magdalena's sister.

•

A song of a single bass note aroused me from stupor. Pain blocked my return. Agony's knives twisted within my body. Even breathing hurt. My encrusted lips released groans. A heap of crushed, dry leaves. That's what I felt like.

The song repeated, as did three words—River of Tears. Green linen rippled like an enchanted river. Muscular arms protruded from its depths. I floated along, pain's captive.

This wasn't the Shadow World or Promise. I lay on my back, tied to a hard flat surface slung between two rows of men. Several chanted the story of a healers' shrine in California's Inyo Valley. Their smocks, the color of spring grass, bloomed in my peripheral vision. They were pilgrims to the River of Tears.

My head, the only body part that seemed to acknowledge my will, was somehow immobilized. Above, the edge of a crude canopy of frayed fabric flapped. Rays of sunlight highlighted the material's coarse weave.

I groaned louder. I should ask if the men carried Galen, too. The pilgrims lowered my litter to the ground and sponged my lips with water. Tepid drops dribbled onto my parched tongue, which rolled, thick and useless. The drops vanished, unable to reach my pasty throat that begged for relief.

The men asked me questions—my name, age, and village. I managed to utter Galen's name. Something stroked the palm of my hand. A finger? A pilgrim told me to grasp it. My hands wouldn't work.

"Water," I said, so thirsty.

The pilgrims tipped my litter. I took one spoonful of liquid at a time. Nothing had ever tasted better. I smiled, recalling the canteen I'd brought my man. The river of green linen flowed again.

Pain, water, and brays from pungent mules punctuated the moments of my ensuing days. Thin gruel and baths in sand happened, too. This was my new life. Again, the men asked questions about my name, age, and village. I needed to know about my betrothed—my only purpose for living, then.

"Galen," I said.

The men gave me odd glances. Galen's injuries could be worse than mine. Some of the healers might have taken him to a secret place to help him regain strength. These kind pilgrims didn't want me to worry.

•

I awakened screaming. Angry muscles in my back and legs twisted and stretched like caged snakes protesting confinement. My cries pierced the night air. The moon should have shattered.

Strong arms braced my neck and pressed on my shoulders. Hands kneaded my thighs and calves, massaged the curve of my spine. I screamed over and over. The torture finally ended. I panted. A back muscle twinged. What if the cramps returned?

A pilgrim crouched beside me and rearranged my blanket, his deep voice reassuring. He said his name was Victor, then coaxed me to accept a spoonful of medicine. The fluid smelled minty and tasted bitter.

The glow of the torch waned. A younger man with a flat nose and pimpled forehead knelt by my litter. He stroked my fingers and made soft sobbing sounds. Locks of curly brown hair framed his beardless face and extended to his shoulders, hidden beneath his green smock. He stuttered a prayer.

The youth looked older than me but younger than Galen, and so sad. Oh, to clasp his hand and offer what little solace I could. Was he a novice studying the profession of healing? I concentrated, picturing Galen's hands, callused and strong. The novice gasped, then turned toward the others and shouted.

"She's m-moving her fingers," he said. "It's a m-miracle."

The men gathered. One relit the torch. They pointed and hugged each other. The novice whistled and danced in circles. I curled my fingers, clenched my fists and released. My hands worked. It was true. The torchlight sputtered, as if astonished, too. Then men and flame blended together, drifting from focus. The bitter water began its work.

I whispered for Galen, over and over. His face had been so kind, and his eyes, those of a hero. If dead, Galen would have comforted me in dreams. He must be alive.

•

A gravelly voice spoke. I opened my eyes to a man and the afternoon. The trim, large-boned stranger wore a pale blue shirt, buckskin vest, and long denim trousers, all victims of hasty mending. A patchwork of shadows and fading sun adorned the afternoon.

"Just one more day to flat land," the stranger said, tipping his hat and sounding as if he knew secrets of heaven and earth. "The most difficult grades are behind us now."

A curved nose dominated his wide chestnut-colored face, jutting from between sculpted cheekbones like the beak on a hawk. Narrow white braids protruded from under the borders of the striped bandanna he wore beneath his hat—a top hat of sorts, only not as high, with goggles fastened around the band. Like Billy's hat had been. A ball-shaped gold earring festooned the lobe of his left ear. He stood straight as a pine.

I blinked. Who was this beak man? His hazel eyes sparkled, dusted, perhaps, with embers of a hero's fire.

"You mustn't move your neck yet," he said. "The healers want it braced until the ceremony at the river bed. We should arrive in three days, with luck." He tightened my chest strap but loosened the restraints on my legs, hips, and arms.

I wiggled my fingers. My toes took more effort. How marvelous to actually move below the chin. My fingers found the golden pendant, still safe around my neck.

Should I attempt to raise an arm, shift my rear end, or just scratch? Bending a leg would be wonderful. Sore, wasted muscle responded with reluctance. An angry nerve proved more assertive. Tears formed, and my vision clouded.

"What's wrong now?" I groaned.

"You're still bruised inside," the man said. "You can't expect...I mean, the way I found you, it's a miracle you're even alive."

I regressed to exercising my fingers and toes. A line of healers in green smocks and baggy tan trousers lifted the board and carried me to the fire circle. The beak man sat

98

on the ground, legs crossed, a tawny skin bag across his chest.

"They're starting the fire in the trench," he said to me. He picked up a stick, the length of my arm. "It'll be a couple of hours before dinner. Are you hungry?"

"I must be."

I'd spoken little to the pilgrims, although they'd tried to initiate conversation. The pain of my loss overshadowed my desire to make new friends. The beak man was different, though—his gait, eyes, voice, even his odor. One couldn't retreat from such a man.

"You eat meat?" He withdrew a knife from a tooled sheath then whittled the tip of the stick.

"When I must."

"I'll roast you a dough cake." He tapped the end of the stick and sharpened it more. Thin curls of wood flicked onto my blanket.

My upper teeth pressed against my lower lip. This man had found me. Had he heard the howl of winds or interpreted the languages of the wilderness?

"Tell me what happened to Galen," I said. "The tallest of my people with the darkest skin."

The man scratched the abundant white stubble on his chin and cheeks. His forefinger and thumb twisted his earring. He then stood and strapped the sheathed knife to his thigh. Why didn't he answer my question? He uncorked the skin bag and offered me a drink.

I opened my mouth, expecting a squirt of water. The liquid tasted strange, like spoiled fruit. I winced. He laughed.

"It's wine. Good for the soul."

The beak man raised the bag to his mouth and tilted his head back. A thin stream of berry-colored liquid arced through the air in my peripheral vision. He recorked the bag, licked his lips and then fiddled with his earring.

"We wondered if your name was Galen." His voice sounded odd.

"I'm Juan...Juanita."

"That's pretty." He drank more wine. Vertical creases lined his brow and the leathery skin between his eyes. "You were the only one."

"What do you mean?"

The beak man knelt, his face revealing no emotion. Smelling of sweat and wine, he cupped his large hands around my shoulders.

"The only one found alive," he said.

Galen couldn't be dead. The beak man's firm grasp thwarted my upward lurch. Galen's ghost had not visited me. This man's words couldn't be true. I screamed and thrashed. The green linen river of men encircled and restrained me, until only my eyes, nostrils and mouth could move.

"Believe me," the beak man said. "We searched a full day." His expression softened. He shook his head. "I'm sorry. We did all we could."

My temples pounded. My guts ached as if wrenched away. The price was too great. I wailed long and loud, like the whistle of the train. The men relaxed their grip, clasping only my hands. I wept until drained of everything but misery.

After a while, the pilgrims cooked dough cakes. A balding man roasted a small animal he'd caught and skinned. The stink of cooking flesh tainted even the aroma of fresh bread.

"At least drink water," the beak man said.

"Why do you care?"

"I found you by the wreck," he said. "The desert entrusted you to me."

The man sponged my face and hummed a pretty but melancholy tune. He uncorked a skin bag and dribbled water across my lips. I'd brought a canteen to Galen the night of the train. I drank. The beak man tore cold bread into bits and danced them down my cheeks. Hadn't I wanted Mama to regain strength? I accepted the food the man offered. Later, he slipped a basin under my hips, the way Nurse used to do for Mama when she needed to urinate.

"Who are you?" I said.

"No one important. Just an old guide man who leads pilgrims through the wilderness."

I studied his face, the taut skin creased slightly at the outer corner of each eye. He didn't look old, despite his white hair and whiskers.

"Why haven't I seen you with the pilgrims?" I said. "I mean, before today."

"You didn't have to see me. I watched you."

He took the basin and disappeared from sight. I shut my eyes. Galen was dead. All hope and most reasons for living gone. The banter and fire sounds triggered my memory of Wei, framed by firelight before a drumming.

"When you are worthy," Wei had said to me, "your ancestors will place in you two pains that are sources of great power. The day you learn to control those pains— those spirits—to tear them from your bosom and put them back at will, you'll be a true healer. Only a mystic can live with spirit pains. An ordinary person would soon die."

I clutched the pendant around my neck. Perhaps I could learn to live with spirit pains, if required to remain alive at all. The pain from lost love would sear me until the day I died.

•

The hot dry air exploded with whoops and guffaws. One pilgrim kissed the ground. Another removed his sandals and rubbed his toes. Still tied to the litter, I glanced from side-to-side, capturing displays of excitement and relief. We must have reached the River of Tears.

Guide Man dismounted his dun gelding. He tipped my litter, allowing me to glimpse red and brown mountains towering in the distance. He rotated me in the opposite direction. A second range appeared—snow-dusted mountaintops enveloped in blue haze.

Desiccated terrain stretched between mountain ranges, flat, as if God had wielded a huge heated stone to smooth the land. Honey mesquite trees, their bark reddish brown, reached out with scrawny limbs and spiny twigs. Scrub grew low, more gray than green. How different from Promise's blue oaks, buckeye trees and tumbling stream. Not even tears from a river ran through here.

"Hard to believe," Guide said, "that this land has known water and meadows." He still wore the hat with the leather-and-glass goggles attached, as if it had eyes of its own.

"Why do the pilgrims travel here for ceremonies?" Direct sunlight assaulted my face. I squinted, shading my eyes with my hand. "Looks like a place to end life, rather than renew. And why did they walk? You rode."

"They walk for atonement," he said, "and for the challenge." He returned my litter to horizontal and replaced the canopy. "It's claimed spirits reside here, where Yankees once murdered many Mexicans and Indians. Communication with those spirits improves the ability to heal others, or so the men say. Today, they hope such interaction will mend you. Of course, only one in my group is a mystic traveler. Most are ordinary herbalists or physicians who wish to learn more about spiritual healing and augment their skills."

"Why did no women come along? Both men and women healers used to visit Promise together. And where's the water? We'll shrivel to dust."

"There are times when men feel the need to be without women, to reflect on life and search their souls. As for water, we're counting on God's help. Or the spirits." He twisted his earring and stared down at me. "You've told us nothing about the train wreck, and you don't have to. But the pilgrims and I need to know if you fear the judgment of your ancestors."

"I hate my ancestors." The image of Magdalena's severed head and the stench of my people's broken bodies would blaze forever in my memory. "I have none."

The guide frowned, a small frown, the edges of his mouth turned down with a gentle slant. The sparkle in his eyes dulled, and the adjacent skin crinkled. His brows seemed to thicken, like two bushy albino porcupines raising their quills.

He led the dun horse away. The shuffle of sandals replaced clomps of hooves. Pilgrims lifted my litter. They moved past tethered mules and beyond the camp kitchen. The raised hoods of the men's capes masked their facial profiles. They set the board on the ground, in the shade of a honey mesquite tree, and left. This had to be the place of ceremony.

•

Afternoon merged with dusk. The twenty pilgrims returned and formed a semi-circle around me. None spoke. Victor, their mystic, followed, stripped to a loincloth, a knife sheath strapped against his leg. How indecent to wear so little in front of a woman. Wei, Papa and Galen would have agreed.

Victor carried a long wooden staff, its tip whittled sharp. His brown, hairy skin glistened with sweat. I'd cursed my ancestors, not without good cause. This mystic's primitive and shocking appearance had to be a bad omen of what awaited me once spirits gathered.

Two of the pilgrims laid more kindling in the fire trench. Another placed a silver chalice on the ground. Several others approached me, their faces solemn. My heartbeats quickened. The pilgrims untied the ropes that bound me to the board. I didn't dare move, not yet, for I might break an unknown taboo in error. These men deserved respect, even if my ancestors didn't.

The throb of my temples rose and receded, as if living tides set the rhythm of my pulse. Victor squeezed fluid from a skin bag into the silver chalice. He walked around me with his staff, drawing a large circle in the dust to separate the two of us from the rest. When finished, he cast the staff outside of the circle. The chalice remained.

"You've not been truthful," Victor said, his voice deep and hard. "We offered compassion. You repaid with lies."

"What do you mean?" I said.

"We found you by the tracks." He drew closer, his shoulder-length hair wild and free, his chest and upper arms engraved with small scars. "Twin spirits, the mark of pending death, hovered above your head. We vowed to carry you here. If we couldn't save you, at least you could join your ancestors with dignity, in a sacred place."

I fingered the dusty fabric of my robe. Victor scowled, flaring the nostrils of his broad, sunburned nose. He looked and sounded disappointed I still lived.

"The twin spirits no longer hover," he said. "They disappeared early this afternoon, yet you've neither died nor recovered. There's but one explanation. You've inhaled them." He stepped backward, but not outside the closed circle of magic. "Only a great mystic can inhale or exhale spirits at will. You could walk if you wanted. Instead, you feign injury and shame our profession."

"The pain is real," I said. How dare he accuse me of lying? "And I have no powers, not anymore. I've cursed my ancestors, not inhaled them."

"We shall see." Victor spat on the ground. "They sit in judgment."

He lit the ceremonial fire. Dry brush caught quickly, crackling as if fueled by vengeance. He tossed powder into the fire, producing a momentary green blaze, the color of patina on copper. He must have signaled spirits.

Those outside the circle sat and chanted, clinking spoons with an abrasive rhythm. Victor stretched out his arms, first toward the heavens, then the earth. He unsheathed his knife. Why?

"Mystic traveler girl, I am ready to face the Guardians of the Portals," Victor said. "Are you?"

My galloping heartbeats slowed, calmed by the familiar words of ritual. Had he learned them from the ghost of Moses, as Wei had? No matter. If the spirits judged me unworthy to live, they would take my soul. Although the dead might keep my spirit separated from Galen's as a punishment. These men, despite their current appearance, weren't evil and would never intentionally hurt me.

"I'm prepared," I said, "but no longer have the power to release my spirit."

Victor nodded and raised his chin. The pink and lilac hues of the lowering sun accentuated his stocky brown frame. He knelt beside the chalice, dipped his knife blade into the cup, and rose, vessel in hand.

"Fly to us," he said, "all you who are no more."

I took a deep breath and smiled. Galen would want me to smile. I searched for a comforting thought and remembered one from Wei's journal. *Life is a dream, and death, the mystical awakener.*

"We have walked here to atone for the evil in all mankind, past, present and future." Victor's voice resonated in an eerie way.

He nicked his chest without flinching and collected drops of blood in the chalice. Oh, dear God. What did he have in mind?

"Those who drink this potion," he said, "are yours to judge and claim. Or heal."

The chants of the pilgrims grew louder. Victor laid the knife upon my chest. Perhaps my blood had to join his in the potion so I could travel with him.

"It's time for a journey," he said.

He offered me the cup, his free arm lifting my head and shoulders. Bitter liquid trickled into my mouth. Galen might hover near the Shadow World's portals, waiting to see me. I needed to be brave and swallow. Victor raised the goblet to his own lips.

"Do no harm," he said, and recited several sentences in a strange language. He crossed his arms against his chest and performed the slow spirals of a mystic's dance.

My head ached even worse. My vision blurred. The world spun and pulsed chants. Lights flashed with each pulse—purple, crimson, yellow and orange. The potion worked fast. Victor's knife pivoted above me on its own power. A skull, alive with beetles, pressed against my chest. The bony jaw laughed Magdalena's laugh and merged into the mystic's blade of steel. Mist gathered from nowhere, folding my hands around the knife's hilt. Would Galen want me to make the thrust, to try to join him now?

"A mystic must earn the peace of death," the voice of Wei cried. "Your work has just begun."

Just begun? Had Wei been chatting with Billy? Clouds of sand swirled up from the ground and glowed plaid. From within them, a bagpipe wailed. How had I known what that sound was? Sand tore the knife away, and a man called my name. I couldn't see him.

"Say yer bonnie words, yer prayers," he said, "and walk seide-by-seide wui me, yer great-great uncle. Ethan's mah nam."

His speech was so strange. I reached toward the sound of his kind voice and stood. Pain jolted me like bolts of lightning. No doubt about it. My spirit remained inside my body. A spiral of cactus flowers and plaid sand supported my wavering frame. Wind and mist howled through a curtain of long black hair and brought me the mystic's chalice.

"Look at your reflection," Magdalena said. She let out a high-pitched laugh.

"No!" I'd caused Magdalena's death—everybody's. I couldn't face my reflection or my friend.

"You can't escape your destiny," Magdalena said. "You don't have our permission." The mist shimmered with the delicate features of a painted doll. "Look at your eyes."

I clutched the chalice. The reflection of my emerald eyes gleamed from polished silver.

"Hero's eyes!" Magdalena's laugh swelled and echoed. Her spirit blew through me, as if flesh were gauze. "Your papa says to finish what you and Billy started."

I screamed and dropped the chalice. I could never wreck another train. An explosion of colors erupted through sand and air.

"Listen, and listen well," Magdalena said. "You've made California's newspapers focus on that asylum and the trains, but in a year or two, people will forget the whole damn thing. My sister just had her baby girl, so get busy.

And your great-grandma says not to curse the family who loves you."

The wind shifted and calmed. A blue-green glow sparkled. A gentle breeze reeked of cigars. I inhaled the twin spirits the Shadow World must have chosen to guide and watch over me: Magdalena, who'd once saved me from drowning, and Billy, who knew about life and trains.

The breeze bore a floral scent then, so lovely and comforting, the air should have glowed lavender. Lilacs, perhaps, not a spirit odor I recalled. I closed my eyes.

"Bring Galen to me in a dream," I said to Billy.

I dreamed not of Galen, but of Ethan. He played his favorite song on the bagpipes: "Amazing Grace."

"Ah learned the pipes frae mah deid fowk," he claimed. "How to speak Scots, too."

I guessed he referred to his ancestors. In my dream, I think he glowed tartan and held my hand.

•

I awakened. The guide man kept vigil. The evening fire glowed with new beauty. The pilgrims' guide helped me sit. Movement hurt less than expected. Cloth rustled. Victor approached, again dressed in a baggy linen smock and trousers, his hair tied at the nape of his neck. Our hands joined, his skin rough and warm.

"Thank you for summoning spirits for me," I said. "Even with the potion, I couldn't release my soul."

His finger brushed the golden pendant around my neck, the jewelry from the Cave of Light.

"This pendant holds magic enough to guide you to the Shadow World's portals," Victor said. "I can tell. You just need to discover the key."

I smiled. If true, someday I'd go see Galen, apologize in person to all my friends and family. Promise's people would tell me how best to stop the asylum trains without taking more lives. The firelight beyond Victor shimmered. I pressed the engraved disk against my chest, the power of magic more comforting than that of any knife.

"The memory of that night," I said. My ears echoed with the whistle of a train, thunder of driving wheels and screams of dying friends. "Will the night of the train always burn like fire?"

"Healing doesn't mean forgetting," Victor said, resting his hand upon my shoulder. "I can only guess what happened that night, but its horror will burn as long as you live."

I lowered my eyelids. Oh, to hear a ghostly drum.

15. A Nameless Man

THE PILGRIMS BROKE camp. I sat on my litter in the patchy shade of a honey mesquite—a scraggly tree, close to twenty feet high. Not as towering as my assigned purpose.

Three days had passed since the ceremony at the dry riverbed. Yesterday, men from the north had brought fresh water and other supplies. Too bad they hadn't traveled from the south. Then they might have known the location of the orphanage I sought, the one with Magdalena's niece.

I stretched my legs straight, kneaded my thighs, and watched the white-haired guide direct placement of packs, waterskins and a rifle on mules. My scrawny calves reminded me of twigs on sprouting pines. The Shadow World wanted me to stop all the asylum trains. I may have regained a purpose but couldn't even hike.

The guide hollered at the pilgrims. He wiggled one pack rope, then another. When he wasn't shouting or spitting up phlegm, he whistled a song. A bony yellow dog darted through the maze of mules and men, yapping. Mule tails flicked at flies.

Drummer put me down...keep calling...the last words I'd spoken to Galen repeated in my brain. But that chapter of my life had closed. I needed to talk to someone alive.

"What's your name?" I called to the guide.

"Guide Man," he said with a rough voice, as if he'd gargled with gravel. "I've already told you."

This man had found me by the railroad tracks, saved my life. Already, strands of our destinies must have intertwined. I ought to learn the correct way to address him.

"What about your real name, the one your mother chose?" I leaned back, braced by my hands and arms.

He secured a lead rope and patted a grazing mule's neck. Morning wind rippled the rolled-up sleeves of his loose-fitting denim shirt. The silk bandanna tied around his neck looked damp.

"The desert ate my name," Guide said. "I have no other."

"What?"

Maybe a few extra inches of airspace had muddled Guide's words. I leaned out from the shade of the tree and burlap canopy. Sunlight warmed my head and neck. The short-haired yellow dog ambled toward Guide, panting. The mongrel wagged its tail and dripped saliva. Guide scratched the dog behind the half-pricked ears of its cocked head.

"There's no place on earth sealed with my name," Guide said.

"What sort of nonsense is that?" I brushed away an annoying fly.

Guide Man was so strange. I picked at a bit of biscuit stuck between my front teeth and waited for his reply to my question. Twenty feet away, the milk goat chewed at its tether. The dog barked and dashed off after a scampering lizard. Guide turned toward me.

"Discover why no place is sealed with my name, and you'll know who I am."

Such a puzzling remark. Better to listen to the shouts of men, clanks of shovels and the incessant yaps of the excited dog.

The twenty pilgrims shuffled to and fro, green, long-sleeved smocks and baggy trousers flapping. They tightened ropes and buried the fire. One rolled and tied his pant legs above his knees. Made his pants look like breeches. Strips of rawhide laced his elaborate sandals from toes to calves. Guide Man wore dusty leather boots with thick, medium-high heels. There was so much for me to observe.

I twisted. My back pinched and my rear end ached. I folded my thin blanket to improvise a cushion. The nanny goat broke loose before I finished folding, and it nibbled on the blanket's free end. The animal twitched its head, claiming the wool prize. Should I make a sudden move? I studied the scraggly, pungent creature. The milk goat in Promise had died when I was only five years old. I had little memory of being this close to a goat.

I reached out my hand with caution. The animal explored my fingers, then chewed on my sleeve. Guide approached and grasped the stub of the goat's tether rope. He separated its mouth from my tunic, his thick-fingered hands broad and agile. His unwrinkled, sun-bronzed skin appeared so youthful. Maybe he was only in his thirties and a curse had turned his hair white.

"Goats," he said, "always invite themselves to the wrong dinner table."

"You put your fingers in her mouth," I said. "Aren't you afraid she might bite?"

"Goat and I understand each other." Guide shook the dust from my blanket. "I don't ask about her given name, and she doesn't bite."

Guide was sensitive about his name. I wouldn't prod him again. He grinned, exposing the tips of straight white teeth. He tossed me the blanket and led the goat away—two white-haired companions. The nanny's teeth found the corner of a handkerchief poking from his rear pocket.

I tucked the blanket under my buttocks. The warm earth and thirsty desert scrub triggered memories of the night of the train. I shouldn't have stopped to sand the fire that night. Galen might not have died if he'd had more time to escape the explosion.

•

The procession of healers navigated the cracks and ruts of the dirt road. Horses and mules plodded along the road's crusty border. The sun climbed in the morning sky. The pilgrims took turns carrying my litter, an obvious burden.

"Let me walk awhile," I said.

"Your muscles have grown too weak," a short man said, his skin the shade of burnt sugar. His free hand mopped perspiration off his brow and adjusted the green bandanna and straw sombrero protecting his balding head from sun. "Exercise when we stop."

Guide Man dismounted the dun gelding and tipped the short top hat he wore over his head bandanna. Maybe he'd fastened the goggles around the hat's base in case of a dust blow. Guide walked beside my litter, leading the horse.

"Would you like to learn how to ride?" Guide said.

The horse snorted and seemed so huge. Should I try? I nodded. Guide motioned for the nearby pilgrims to stop. He pulled something small from his pocket. I stood.

"Introduce yourself to King Solomon with this." Guide handed me a lump of sugar. "Use an open palm, not fingers."

The gelding's soft, wet muzzle tickled my hand. A light odor emanated from the animal's body, something like the smell of urine. After the horse consumed the sugar, I inched toward the saddle.

"Boost me up," I said.

Guide hoisted me to stirrup level. Unsteady, I swung astride, a long distance from the ground. Guide led. Solomon followed, slow and steady. God, my feet dangled above the stirrups. I clutched the pommel. This was almost as scary as sitting on a high branch of an oak on a windy day.

A breeze played with the unbraided white hair protruding from underneath Guide's hat and bandanna. What might his name be? I stroked his horse's ebony mane, which was gritty with trail dust. Maybe Guide had an odd name, such as Xerxes.

"You don't have to tell me your real name," I said. "In Promise, our cook hated hers."

Solomon stopped and nibbled a patch of scrub grass. Guide pulled a wedge of biscuit from his shirt pocket. He always saved a piece of breakfast biscuit to eat mid-morning. His marvelous white teeth bit into the bread and he chewed.

"And how do you feel about your name?" he said.

"It's a good one, given to me by my great-grandmother." I patted King Solomon's sun-warmed neck. "Juanita Elise Jame-Navarro. I'd never want a different name."

Guide Man wiped the crumbs from his face and clasped the leather bridle. His tongue made sharp clicks. The gelding followed him. Shifting against the hard saddle hurt my bottom.

"What about when you marry?" Guide said. His boots crunched smithers of rocks as he walked. "You'll take your husband's last name."

"But I'll never marry, not now."

Even as I spoke, grief brought the familiar sting of tears. I'd talked and ridden enough, for then. Guide helped me dismount and return to the litter. Afterwards, he grasped King Solomon's saddle horn, his left foot greeting a stirrup.

"You're a pretty girl. In a few years, you'll be even prettier." Guide straightened himself in the saddle and prompted Solomon with his knees. "Some young man will try to change your stubborn mind."

I pouted as Guide rode toward the string of mules. A child must be born. Ancestors probably expected me to carry on the family line. An unlikely happening. Life had some rivers I could no longer cross.

I stretched out on the litter and stared up at the canvas canopy. Healers carried me. Sleep would bring escape from a guide's puzzling words and a drummer's song. My eyes closed.

Magdalena's voice echoed from within. I must finish what Billy and I had started. Yes, that superintendent who planned to poison inmates would again grow bold. Wisdom, cleverness, courage and determination. I'd find a nonviolent way to end the use of the terrible asylum or prevent murderers from working there. Next time I'd not turn my allies into bits and pieces.

•

The smell of smoke—the campfire—awakened me. The moon waxed full. In Promise, drummings had often occurred at full moon. What a magnificent drummer Galen had been. I fingered my special pendant. Someday I'd visit him in one of the Shadow World's approach passages. The necklace would reveal the way.

Several healers congregated around a large blackened pot. They chatted and took turns stirring, sipping from a communal cup of brandy. For a while they discussed medical things—the best way to set a broken bone or avoid wound corruption, the most effective herbal remedies for pain. They chatted about their many friends and colleagues who didn't believe in spiritualism. How could so many not believe the truth? After more brandy, the tone of conversation changed. The men's voices lowered to snickers, a sign they told vulgar jokes.

I stared at the moon's mysterious face, stroked the sides of the litter. Oh, for a bowl of mashed beans blended with sweetpod-and-acorn meal. Time to hobble to the fire circle. The evening gruel smelled unappetizing. At least the snickers had stopped. Guide Man sat down next to me, holding a bowl of the usual thin porridge. He offered me some. I declined.

"A lamp is extinguished without fuel." He filled the spoon and danced it through the air, his eyes expressing concern. "Such a lovely young lamp should eat and flare brightly."

"The pilgrims don't cook the food of my people."

"You'll have to teach your husband how to cook." He laughed. "These men won't change their ways."

"But I won't take a husband." Had he forgotten our earlier conversation?

"Then take a wife, but eat." He wiggled the spoon.

A wife? My mouth opened in surprise. Guide thrust the spoon inside. Dinner had the consistency of watered sand. I made a face, swallowed the porridge, then covered my lips with both hands. Guide swirled the spoon in the bowl and winked. I endured three more tepid spoonfuls, each grittier than the one before. Guide finished eating the gruel and poured water into the bowl.

After the water, we shared a little wine. The deep red liquid tasted like the milk goat smelled, but imparted pleasant warmth. Guide and I sat huddled under a blanket together. A canopy of stars twinkled between broken clouds. Shooting stars appeared when loved ones died, didn't they? *Dearest Galen.* I watched for a blaze of light. None appeared.

"Galen's upset," I said. "That's why he doesn't visit. I made him leave me at the fire on the night of the train."

"At the fire?" Guide's voice sounded odd.

"He was supposed to lead the others to a safer place," I said, "while I sanded the fire. I didn't want the railroaders to see our fire and brake."

"You were involved with what happened?" Guide glanced around, as if nervous.

"Of course." Why had he lowered his voice?

"I would've thought that—"

"Thought that a woman can't do the job of an hombre?"

"No, but I'm surprised." He rubbed the back of his neck. "Surprised your people put a girl—pardon me—a young woman, in jeopardy."

"I was the mystic for the people of Promise." I glanced at the edge of the clouded moon, then toward the glowing fire. "The Shadow World sabotaged the train through me."

"Your words," Guide whispered, "they're dangerous." He drew closer, scant moonlight bathing his short whiskers and solemn expression. "You must not repeat those words to anyone."

He stood and spat toward the fire. Was he angry or just concerned for my safety? Perhaps I shouldn't have admitted responsibility for the disaster. He'd been a stranger—not a friend—when he'd saved my life. Our destinies might not have intertwined after all.

•

Thunder awakened me. Sheets of rain descended. The sky boomed like the Shadow World pounded giant drums. Half-naked men scurried around in dawn's light, unfolding tarps and sheltering dry clothes and supplies from the storm.

I rose and slid my bedding under a sheet of canvas. Storms and rituals could change acceptable manners of dress with such ease.

Guide Man, garbed only in his drawers, gold chain, earring and bandanna, called to me. I hadn't seen him this way before. How embarrassing. Water rolled off swirls of his white chest hair. I avoided glancing lower. The back of his left shoulder bore a tattoo—a number.

"If you want to bathe, you'd better do it before the sky turns off the spigot." He laughed.

I itched from the dust of travel. The healers had bathed my injured body and already seen me unclothed. Guide had, too. I pulled my wet tunic over my head, then removed my filthy camisole and drawers. Water pelted my skin. With my eyes closed and lips parted, I savored the pleasant chill of the rain.

The deluge subsided. Raindrops tapped my face and shoulders, as if playing tag, then stopped. I shivered, my bare arms crossed against my undeveloped bosom. I studied Guide's dark blue tattoo.

Guide draped a thin wool blanket around me, slipping itchy gray fabric under one of my arms and knotting two corners on the opposite shoulder. How thin my arms were compared to his. He improvised a belt for me from a piece of narrow rope, scraped mud from his feet and then dressed.

"What's that number on your shoulder?" I said.

"My identification." He put on his short top hat. "So I don't forget who I am." He twisted his earring. "It's nothing, just a number. The others have numbers too, but on passports, so the Brits and Yankees can tell which side of the border they belong on."

Cole, who had traveled with healers, had possessed some sort of passport. Why would someone rather have a tattoo?

I unbraided my waist-length hair and asked Guide to comb out the tangles. His touch was so gentle. Twenty feet away, two pilgrims coaxed wet sticks to burn. Several other men rattled metal pots and wooden cookspoons. Their pant legs, sandals and boots were muddy. None had yet combed his hair.

"Do you think they would let me help cook?" I said. "I ought to help."

"Willing hands are always welcome," Guide said. "But this morning, tell me about Galen while I braid your hair."

My throat pinched tight. Sorrow stung my eyes, and tears flowed. How heavy my legs grew. Guide handed me a handkerchief, wadded and stiff from previous use. I mopped my cheeks and the corners of my eyes. I would love Galen forever, ache until I reunited with him in the world beyond.

"He was very tall," I said.

"A mountain's tall," Guide said.

"He could almost touch the stars."

Guide hummed and parted my hair to fix two braids. Galen had liked my hair that way. His own had been a wiry charcoal-black frizz. How I'd loved to touch the bush of his hair.

"Tell me about his eyes," Guide said.

"His eyes were those of a hero." Did I hear the snip of scissors? I glanced over my shoulder. Guide stuffed a strip of scarlet cloth into his shirt pocket. "You've cut one of your own red bandannas to tie my braids."

"Just an old one," he said. "Now hold still."

Guide had sacrificed one of his beautiful silk bandannas for me. Telling him about the night of the train may not have been a mistake, after all. He made the ragged, guttural sound of clearing phlegm from his throat.

"You told us Galen had dark skin," he said.

Inner emptiness again, as if I were a hollow log. I crossed my arms against my chest and rubbed my shoulders.

"His skin was a lovely black," I said. "As dark as skin could ever grow."

"His skin was that dark?" Guide Man, still standing behind me, relaxed his grip on my hair, must have stopped braiding. "Are you sure?"

"As black as the stone in your finger ring," I said. "Well, almost."

Guide slipped his right hand in front of my face. "Black as this onyx?"

"From head to toe," I said. "Is there something wrong? You searched for other survivors. Surely you remember."

"Of course I remember." He shook his head. "Nothing's wrong. This old man's been in the wilderness too long, that's all. Death turns black skin a bit gray."

Death and grayness... I sat down on a knee-high rock, the upper surface smooth. When the Shadow World became my home, I'd project a vivid emerald light, the color of my earthly eyes. What color might Galen's light be? Perhaps regal purple. I looked away, toward the healers cooking breakfast. My gaze met the novice's stare. He glanced down, then stirred a thin stream of dry meal into a pot of boiling water. Guide stooped in front of me, his breath warm. He inspected the end of my tight braid, then secured it with red cloth. Guide and the pilgrims were so full of life, as my people once had been.

"You're not old," I said. Cook, at thirty-nine, had looked older than Guide. "Now finish my hair."

He nodded and stepped behind me. I'd guess his secret, which couldn't be anything really bad. He was too kind. Guide tied the end of my second braid. Dark clouds gathered, obscuring the sun.

"It's time to choose where tonight's camp will be," Guide said, "although that sky may make its own selection."

He retrieved the chart cylinder from a pack. The tube shed bits of weather-worn metal when opened. He wiped his hands on his trousers, then extracted a long roll of parchment.

"This shows both topography and roads," he said. He unrolled the chart, handed me one side to hold, then pointed to a collage of colors, curls, and bold lines. "Right now we're here, on the eastern side of the Sierras, straddling the North-South California divide." Guide slipped his finger across the map's surface and rested it on the junction between patches of beige and faded green. "Promise would have been approximately here," he whispered. "Once we cross the Sierras, we'll either end up north or south of it."

I focused on the chart, as if the people of Promise were faces in hidden pictures, the imagination game I used to play with puffy clouds and murky streams. Galen, Magdalena, Cook, Nurse, Papa—I could imagine them all.

"Which route is better?" I needed to fight the urge to cry.

"Neither, Juanita, but for different reasons." The skin near the outer corners of Guide's eyes crinkled. "The southern road runs this way, through British territory." He pointed while his other hand steadied the map. "It's in poor condition. This initial section is steep, treacherous. The rest's long and dry."

"And the northern?"

"More gradual climbs, more water, but—"

"But what?" I said.

Wind rattled the parchment. Guide rerolled half of the map. I tightened my grip on the open edge.

"There's a Yankee checkpoint on the northern route," Guide said. "The presence of a young woman on a men's pilgrimage is apt to raise more than one eyebrow, particularly with the news of a train wreck still in mind. They'd check identification closely. And you don't have identification."

"Tell me about this road." I slipped my hand over his and pointed below the southern route. "Is it better?"

"It goes to different mountains—the Tehachapis. Only one thing goes there."

He returned the chart to its case, then wiped rust-streaked fingers on his denim shirt. Something about the way Guide had emphasized the word "Tehachapis" bothered me, as if his tattoo or secret were the reason.

"What thing?" I said.

He rubbed the back of his neck, then twisted his gold earring. "Fold your braids atop your head." He rested his right thumb under his chin and stroked his lips with his bent forefinger. "If you crop your hair and dress like a novice—"

"My hair? Must I?" I clutched my braids so brightly bound with ribbons of bandanna. My hair was part of who I was.

"You can wait a night or two," Guide said. "Hair grows back. On the living."

The memory of Galen's drum returned. The weight and freedom of my tresses as I'd spun.

"Oh, did I forget to tell you?" Guide lifted my chin and smiled. "About the thing that crosses the Tehachapis. If you cut your hair, someday, I'll show you."

"Show me what?" Once more his breath was warm.

"A train." Guide lifted off his hat and winked. "Just like the one you sabotaged."

I pulled away. Guide would show me an asylum train. What had he implied? That he might help me complete the mission my people had started? Or take me to the asylum to find Magdalena's niece?

But he didn't know my future plans, or even about Magdalena.

16. A Chunk of Sky

I COULDN'T CUT my hair, even a full two days after Guide's recommendation. A pilgrim cut it for me, a stocky man named Bernardo with an oily pony tail and a deep, resonating voice. While snipping, he sang a silly song about a barber. Perhaps he sensed my inner turmoil and wanted me to laugh.

The other nineteen healers gathered in a circle, their whisker-framed smiles projecting encouragement and support. Each bite of the scissors—each metallic snap— spewed acid from my stomach to my throat. My locks fell to the ground like murdered children. The gentle wind scattered a few tufts.

Guide Man dug a shallow hole between a twenty-foot-tall Joshua tree and a struggling pine. The upraised arms of the Joshua, matted with dead leaves and tipped with fists of long spines, seemed to protest my disfigurement. Guide and the novice placed the tresses into the grave.

"We'll bury your robe and tunic, as well," Guide said. "The desert has too many eyes."

I patted what was left of my butchered hair, which extended no more than an inch below my earlobes. An unseen bird trilled from the pine. I donned borrowed clothing—a green smock and tan trousers. The sleeves extended to my knuckles. The pant cuffs flopped over the tips of my sandals, forming two little heaps of cloth on the beige earth. The donor of my new clothes smiled and told me to roll the waistband, probably pleased anyone was shorter than he.

The novice gleaned a lock of my hair from a clump of scrub and slipped it into his pocket. He didn't realize I watched. Did he like me? How sweet, but my heart had no place for a new love. I joined the hikers—the line of knapsacks, bedrolls and walking-staffs. The novice worked his way to me. Exchanging few words, we traveled uphill side-by-side, through a pass where pines thrived, to the brink of a precarious spiral chiseled into a desert mountainside. In the distance, the snow-capped Sierras stretched skyward.

Leading the group, Guide Man jogged King Solomon's reins. His gelding whinnied and snorted. Guide leaned over the horse's neck and whispered. Solomon steadied.

"And this is the good road?" I said, my dusty toes clinging to dustier sandals. I practically balanced on the edge of the earth.

The yellow dog nipped the mules' heels and ducked their hooves. The line of pack animals plodded forward. The goat ambled behind, picking its way around chunks of fallen rock with playful ease. The Black Mountain should have taught me to be a goat.

"We'll rest at the first plateau," Guide called.

My sandals slipped against loose gravel. A deep canyon waited for unwary steps. Endless heartbeats later, the broad expanse of the plateau greeted me with a blaze of blue lupine and wildflower golds. I prodded verdant brushes and grasses with my hiking stick. Nothing scurried or rattled warning. It was safe to let the shaded earth soothe my blistered toes. Flowing water babbled nearby. I swatted a mosquito.

"The creek's over here," I called.

We'd have to ladle from the center of the creek where the water would be deeper and moving. The animals should drink farther downstream. I tugged at the goat's lead rope. Goat buried its nose in a thorny tangle, ignoring orders, pleas, tug-of-war and enticements of clothing. Then I noticed what occupied its fancy: blackberries.

•

We travelers made camp with purple tongues and fingers. I collapsed on a hollow log, exhausted. Let the men build the fire. How useless I'd become.

"The road was difficult," Guide said to me.

"The others are tired, too." I rubbed my fist against the curve of my aching lower spine. Sometimes, Guide could almost read my mind the way Billy did. "I should be helping."

Guide massaged the back of my neck and shoulders, then lower. I stretched my legs straight. His hands kneaded my sore calves. He unlaced and removed my sandals, the soles worn thin, then gently rubbed my scraped and blistered feet. How well he treated me, as if I were his daughter or younger sister. He would make a good ally.

"Would you like to learn how to clean the animals' hooves?" Guide said.

"Oh, yes."

He stood and offered his hand, the way Galen had done. A strong grip, so full of life. I shivered as I rose. Guilt about my survival chilled me from the inside.

"Will we find deeper water tomorrow?" I slipped my feet back into my sandals. "I'd love to take a nice, cool bath."

"Not tomorrow, but the day after," he said. "There's a lake, then the river drops fast. Very fast."

"Does that mean another good road?" How easy it was to joke about earlier terror.

"The road will be very good," Guide said, "if no one slips off."

He picked up a buckskin satchel and headed toward the animals. I followed. The two horses and string of mules stood tethered in knee-high grass. While their mouths grazed, their tails shooed flies. A mockingbird perched in a fragrant pine sang, its stolen tunes interspersed with imitation squawks and chatter. A facade of tranquility in treacherous country.

"The mountain today was scary," I said. "Trips to the Shadow World are less frightening than that third bend."

"We'll take care of King Solomon first," Guide said. "He tolerates a pedicure better than the mules."

"Weren't you even a little afraid?" He'd ignored my confession. "Tell the truth."

"I fear not the mountains. Old friends who respect each other rarely have serious quarrels. It's the Yankee federalmen beyond these mountains who worry me."

I nodded. Roads were impartial. Malicious men weren't.

Guide made a clicking sound with his tongue. King Solomon pricked his ears and followed his master to an area where stubby grasses grew. I limped over to them. Guide lifted one of Solomon's dusty forelegs, exposing the bottom of the hoof.

"Do you see the way he lets me do this?" Guide said. "We understand each other. Trust each other."

Guide's gaze met mine, his eyes so deep, as if the light that entered them sped directly to eternity. Before the train wreck, Billy had talked about trust, coping, and survival. He hadn't revealed his last name or the dangers I would face. Who was Guide, and what did he really mean? Were our destinies entwined or not?

Afternoon turned to evening. A pilgrim and I hoisted a water pot onto the fire. My foot faltered against a stone. Water slopped out of the blackened pot and sizzled. It wouldn't be hard to slip on the next steep trail.

I rubbed my ankle. Solomon might rear and pitch Guide. Checkpoint guards might demand identification and arrest me. In Promise, most women had kept close to the village for a good reason.

Anxieties about the road and federalmen festered within me. By the following night, the river roared in my nightmares. A wall of water gushed down a black canyon, sucking Guide beneath its churning foam.

Something touched my shoulder. I opened my eyes. Guide had roused me from my torture. He moved our bedrolls closer. For a while, I gazed at the star-studded heavens, pretending Papa offered me a dipper of mint tea. Then I focused on the irregular rhythm of Guide's snores. Papa had snored. Guide wasn't Papa, though. Building true trust would take time.

•

Morning came, and I soon faced the brink of a river canyon. Twists of an eroded trail clung to walls of crumbling rock. The sloping path was twelve to fifteen feet wide in one spot, and in another, barely enough to accommodate a horse—like a giant beast had bitten into the road and torn a chunk away. The warning call of rushing water echoed from the unseen canyon floor. The hairs on the backs of my hands stiffened.

I laced my sandals tighter, then rerolled the waistband of my trousers. The novice entered the line of hikers and stuttered instructions. I'd step where he did, as I'd done with Galen on the way to the lookout. My gaze drifted between the road ahead and the ragged sky. What if rain hit before I was down?

Guide selected several pilgrims to lead the mules. I agreed to herd the goat. All needed to walk single file, maintaining a slow pace. Time for more wisdom, cleverness, courage and determination. Good practice for the future, when I'd free Magdalena's niece and destroy another train.

"If an animal balks, everybody behind stops," Guide said. "And stay to the left. The outer edge of this trail could cave." He tucked an unbraided lock of his white hair under his bandanna. "Anything or anyone that falls off is gone. Do you understand? I won't risk lives in a futile rescue attempt. I've learned that lesson."

The group proceeded. Granite boulders slept in cradles of sedimentary sheer wall, waiting to awaken and crush life. There was no place to hide if a landslide occurred. If anything bad happened, Guide and the others would be unable to help me. Such an uneven path, each step a new challenge. I clenched my stomach and toes.

The trail widened at one bend, its center overgrown with thorny brush and weeds. The goat nibbled a clump of straw-colored ryegrass, while the men passed on the left with room to spare and disappeared around the next turn. I pulled the nanny's lead. The goat shook its scraggly head, as if laughing.

"We're already the rear of the line," I said, tugging the rope.

The animal didn't budge. How annoying, it was. I turned and left it behind. The edge was way too close. I walked on the outer side of the trail. The center line of brush stretched uphill for fifteen feet and down for twenty-five. No sounds from the pilgrims reached me. Backtracking would waste too much time.

I took short, careful steps down the grade. Ten feet. Twenty. Something yanked my pant leg. I tripped and lunged. My body crashed against hot crumbs of rock and skidded.

Grab something—I had to grab something. I thrust one arm toward bushy scrub. I missed. Momentum propelled me into a chunk of sky. My hands clung to rock and soil. My feet didn't.

Wind whipped through my hair and clothing. Dear Lord, what had happened? My hands and forearms hugged the edge of the trail. The rest of me dangled over the canyon.

I opened my mouth to scream to God, my ancestors and the mountain. Nothing came out, as if a hand restrained my cry. Earth crumbled in my grasp. My feet slipped against a sheer rock wall. There were no sounds of rocks landing, just slipping away.

I had to overcome gravity and panic, pull myself back on the trail. The goat stared with a puzzled expression, its mouth clutching a scrap of my tan trousers. That awful creature! Yet its lead rope extended from its neck to the ground, less than a foot from my right hand. Before, I'd been unable to tug this beast down the path. I'd failed at pulling the goat away from the berries, too. *What if...* I inched my scraped fingers across loose rock. The goat's head lowered. Time and hooves stood still.

More rock crumbled, and the distant river called. My arms ached. The full force of the wind tossed dirt into my eyes. Then I couldn't see at all. If only I'd had goggles. My fingertips found the rope. I wound its slack around my wrist and breathed out.

"Goat," I whispered, "play tug-of-war. Like before. Please."

I wiggled the rope, blinking to clear my eyes, to see the animal's outline. The wind's hot breath hit my face. The goat clomped backward. Would it have sufficient strength to rescue me? I'd no other hope. I tugged harder, my arms afire with pain. The goat pawed the ground and clomped again. My chest scraped level rock. My left hand lunged for the rope and connected.

The goat dug in with each step, pulling. The tops of my thighs cleared the precipice. I snaked forward, still clutching the lead with both hands, the raw skin on my forearms burning. I trembled and stroked the ground. The animal nudged my shoulder with its nose. It acted disappointed the game had ended. Game? The stakes had been my life. Its sloppy tongue licked my cheek. Just for a moment, the goat's breath reeked of cigars. Billy. His spirit had saved me.

"Thank you," I said, as my daze receded.

The beast trotted down the narrow trail. I fingered my pendant, still safe against my chest, then followed. This talisman from the Cave of Light possessed powers I'd yet to discover or confirm. Somehow, the jewelry connected me with the spirits.

When I reached the meadow, the novice raced in my direction with red and tearful eyes. I shrugged and tried to make a joke about what had happened, although I wasn't sure I really knew. That stupid goat! At least my head no longer felt light as hot air and feathers.

I brushed red-brown dust from my disheveled smock and ripped trousers. The novice poured water from his canteen onto a wadded rag. He sponged my bloodied arms, knees, and shins. Guide strolled over, grinning and arms folded.

"I see you stopped to chat with my friend, the mountain."

"Oh, yes," I said, my tone drier than stale hardtack. "Your friend, the mountain. We had an interesting debate."

I studied Guide's expression. Not one I'd learned. He seemed to be waiting. I asked for his handkerchief, wiped my face, then fed the material to the goat.

"Your goat," I said, "your handkerchief."

I rerolled the waistband on my borrowed trousers and brushed more dust off the sleeves of my smock.

"What happened up there?" Guide said, his voice lowered. "We've been sick with worry."

"What happened up there? Just look at me, at the hole torn in the back of my trousers. Can't you guess?"

"We couldn't go back." His gaze locked on mine as if his pupils were extensions of my own. "There are paths through life and mountains that each must walk alone."

"Oh, there are?"

Didn't he think I knew that? What sort of verbal game did he play? I inspected my grimy, broken fingernails, the way Magdalena might have done.

"Well, there are riddles and secrets each must guess alone," I said. "And I have one for you." I folded my arms and stood tall. "When is a nanny goat a Billy?"

17. Lampglow, Spiders and the Dog

RAINDROPS SPRINKLED MY face. Dark clouds blanketed the sky. A few hours ago, I'd nearly fallen off a mountain. God, I didn't need a storm. A faded red barn lay ahead, potential shelter for me and the men.

The warped, splintery sides of the barn sagged under a half-collapsed roof. A nearby L-shaped adobe house, nestled under pines and topped with a patchwork of tiles and beaten metal, fared better. Both structures appeared long-abandoned, at least by residents with two legs.

Inside the single-story house, rust and mold streaked the cracked walls. Musty open beams in the large main room sloughed vermin. Spider's lace hung silken in the shadows, undulating in the cross draft between broken windows. A pilgrim—Bernardo—tossed a manzanita branch to me. I brandished the makeshift broom while the gray skies offered light, whisking insects and rodent droppings from a damp floor. No time to prepare a meal before dusk, and we were down to our last few candles. Not good.

I batted a fat black spider crawling on a wall. It plummeted and displayed its red-hourglass belly. I leaped backward, flinging my branch against the concrete.

"I'm not sleeping with black widows," I said.

Bernardo laughed and eliminated the arachnid in one unceremonious splat. In the Shadow World, hourglass-red had been my color of fear. Dead or alive, this spider represented a bad omen.

After sunset, the men sat cross-legged on blankets in a circle. I joined them and watched three squat candles flicker. Wicks in pools of hot candle wax burned, yielding thin curls of black smoke and the aroma of jasmine.

"Light conquers dark," Victor, the mystic man, said. "Choose for our feet safe paths home." He recited a different prayer line by line, for all to repeat, then upended his small wooden keg and poured the last of his brandy into a communal cup.

Safe paths. I glanced toward the corner where Guide's rifle rested against the wall. Not even a river touched by angels could subtract danger from my future. I ought to get used to the idea of treacherous journeys. Words came easier than actions.

I swallowed my paltry share of the liquor. Guide contributed his last bota of wine. The pilgrims passed around a pouch of nuts and raisins. Rain drummed above on the makeshift metal shingles and echoed, as if this gathering happened under a giant, inverted galvanized tub. The tempo of the watery dance accelerated. The three candles sizzled—death by drowning. Aching, cold, and hungry, I prepared for sleep and listened to the sky drip.

"Guide Man," I said. "Will there be anything left of the road but mud?" Water dripped on my head. I shifted my bedroll.

"Oh, yes," Guide said.

"Will the road be slippery?"

He grunted and turned.

I curled closer, almost unable to discern his outline in the dark. I sought comfort in the smell of unwashed man and denim, a sweaty, musky odor reminiscent of Galen and Papa. A pungent smell of precious life.

"The road will be wider," Guide said. He cleared phlegm from his chest. "Not as steep."

Wind throttled boughs and rattled wooden slats. The storm continued to build. A branch cracked and thudded against the ground. Metal roofing shuddered, but held. I smelled tobacco. My skin tingled, as if brushed by spidery feet. First had come the hourglass color of fear, the bad omen. Now this. Billy's presence was a warning.

"Easier to walk on, that road," Guide said. "Until the federal checkpoint."

"Something's wrong," I said. "The spirits—"

130

Another branch cracked and clamored against metal. A lone plate of window glass shattered in reply. King Solomon whinnied, softly at first, then louder. The dog joined in with a barking frenzy. I bolted to a sitting position and attempted to rise. Guide grasped my wrist, jerking me back to the floor.

Metal clicked, a small but ominous sound. Guide held a hand gun. He pushed me flat. I caught the blanket in my hands. Outside, the dog snarled. It yelped.

"We're being watched," Guide said, his tone cold as frost.

Lampglow hovered beyond the newly broken window, illuminating the edge of the brick hearth. Light oscillated and swelled, then retreated. Inside the house, slow and regular breaths returned. The intruders had left.

"Best to stay inside until daybreak," Guide said.

"The dog," I said.

"We can't help her now, Juanita."

Guide stroked my head, over and over. The elements finally quieted. I cried, muffling my sobs as best I could. Had thieves or federalmen killed the dog? Guide gripped my hand.

●

I found the dog after sunrise. The back of its skull had been bludgeoned, its eyes now fixed in that last eternal stare. Rain had erased all other evidence of intruders. At least no possessions were missing. Victor set the body under a pine. The novice transferred a flat leather folder— the size of a billfold—into my hand. What was this? I looked inside.

"But this is yours—your paper of passage," I said. "I can't."

"Keep it," he said. "I won't n-need it as much as you when we reach the checkpoint tomorrow." He smiled.

I inhaled long and slow. He was so sweet. I pressed the folder into his palm and closed his fingers around it, searching for appropriate words. I didn't want to hurt his feelings.

"What makes you think you're immune?" I said. "Some men like to harm boys."

I looked away, toward the distant snow-tipped mountains, remembering the night I'd been Billy in the cantina. What really would happen when Yankee checkpoint guards learned I had no identification?

"Each of us must face what is ours to face," I said. I laid my scraped hand on his shoulder, his green linen smock dusty but soft. "If we're lucky, we'll bluff our way through the checkpoint. If not..."

The novice fidgeted with the folder, then ambled back to the shelter, his body swaying, both a child and a man. I nibbled on the tip of my forefinger. Oh, no, I was doing the same thing Magdalena used to do when we discussed romantic matters. I jerked my finger from my mouth. Magdalena's ghost laughed inside my mind.

"I'm sorry," she said. "Just wanted to see if I could talk to you inside your head. I don't know how I did what I just did. I'll try not to let it happen again."

18. Checkpoint and Beyond

I APPROACHED THE Yankee checkpoint on heavy, ineffectual legs, as if dream-walking. The stationhouse, a single-story adobe with a red brick patio, lurked at the edge of a clearing beneath an ominous sky. God, I could still picture the dog's body, left under a pine the day before.

A thick-waisted man with brown hair lumbered out of the station. Wind whipped at his long-sleeved, gray flannel shirt. He brandished a gun with more length and width than five weapons needed. Each thud of his heavy boots flattened helpless blades of wet grass. He was about as congenial as a giant trapdoor spider selecting its next meal.

"Halt!" the spider said. "Line up with your papers. Over there." He motioned toward Guide. "Old man—off your horse."

Guide dismounted and held King Solomon's reins. Two other guards appeared, shirtsleeves rolled up past their elbows, their guns longer than Guide's pistol but shorter than his rifle or Spider's. The first guard had a small, tanned head and big belly, like a bloated tick. The second, broad-shouldered yet lean, wore tattoos of dragons stretched over his muscular white arms. I hid in the middle of the pilgrims' line next to the novice, watching the guards watch them.

The federalmen checked passports. Bernardo placed his folded paperwork into the tick man's heavy-boned hand. The tick read out a number. The tattoo man thumbed through dog-eared sheets of paper in a leather folder.

"Clean." Tattoo Man pushed back a lock of his oily blond hair.

"That's the l-list of registered travelers," the novice whispered. He glanced around with a nervous expression. "And passports reported stolen."

The tick called out another number. The guards moved down the line of pilgrims, ever closer to me. What should I do or say? Would a low-pitched voice help deceive the federalmen, or just sound phony? The spider stared in my direction, his tongue rimming his fat lips. A metal clasp pinged against a flagpole. The backs of my hands tingled.

"453111," a gruff voice said.

I looked up, startled. The tick man stood six or seven feet away. How could it be my turn already?

"Listen, kid," the voice said, "453111."

I smelled tobacco—wretched, wonderful, stinky, precious tobacco. Billy. I let the aroma fill my mouth and nostrils, coat my lungs and cling to my skin. He repeated the number several times. Then the tick faced me, fingering the strap on the gun slung over his shoulder, making a clicking sound with his tongue and palate.

"Dig out your papers," he said. "I don't have all day."

I froze, listening to the flagpole's metallic pings, unable to remember the number. The tick scratched his chest.

"You deaf or something?"

A fly landed on my ear. The insect buzzed and whispered. My grip on the hiking staff tightened.

"The river ate my passport," I said.

"I didn't ask for sass."

"I...I don't mean no disrespect." I offered my scraped hands for inspection, then met his gaze. "I nearly fell off the mountain, that's all. My papers—my whole pack—the river has 'em."

He scratched his chest and smirked. The odor of tobacco grew stronger. I needed to fight panic. Things would be all right if Billy were nearby. Or would they? I'd smelled Billy's tobacco on the night of the train wreck.

"Listen," I said, "I know the number. It's 453—"

"The blazes with the number, kid."

The tick bellowed toward the building. Another guard emerged, a length of chain dangling from his left palm. The chain clinked as he approached. He uncoiled his right hand without warning and grabbed my shoulder.

"No!" the novice said. All turned in his direction. "It's m-me who lost the passport. He gave me his."

"Lock 'em both up." The tick cursed and motioned with his gun.

The guard with the chain tightened his grip on my shoulder. Blessed saints and ancestors. How would I escape? Guide stepped forward, his arms clear of his sides.

"These are boys," Guide said, his gravelly voice turned smooth as lamp oil. "Mere children. Let them pass without trouble." He glanced at me and the novice, shaking his head. "They'd lose their own butts down a latrine, this pair. Let them by."

"We're just doing our job," the spider said. "Anyone without papers gets detained."

"We all must do our jobs." Guide twisted his gold earring. "Mine is to bring these two safely back to their families. This one with the thick black hair—and thicker skull—it won't go well for me if he's harmed, even delayed." Guide rubbed the back of his neck. "His family is of high station."

"We've heard that before," the tick said. He fingered the leather gunstrap pressed against his shoulder.

"He's my godson." Guide removed his hat and tapped the goggles. "You've heard of the Mendoza family, I'm sure."

The Mendozas? Guide pretended I was a Mendoza? The spider pulled a tobacco pouch from his pocket and rolled a cigarette, sometimes looking at Guide, other times at me. Breathe. I needed to take slow, quiet breaths. The buzz of a horsefly resonated. The guard's grip on my shoulder remained steady.

"Mendoza, eh?" the spider said. He lit the cigarette.

"I run a reputable business." Guide half-turned toward his horse. "My permits are in this saddlebag if—"

"I'll open that," the tick shouted, lunging forward.

"Be my guest." Guide stepped farther away from King Solomon, producing a sweeping gesture. "And my pistol's on the other side, not with the papers."

The tick withdrew a stubby cylinder from the leather saddlebag and tossed it to the spider. The cigarette balanced between the spider's lips jiggled, shedding the plug of ash. He examined the discolored metal case. As he wrenched the lid free, a gold coin tumbled into his palm. A bribe? He transferred the money to his shirt pocket, then shook loose a roll of documents. For several minutes he studied them, inhaling deeply and purging smoke through his nose. If only I could read his mind.

"Your godson," the spider said. "He knows his passport number?"

"Yes," Guide said.

"Tell me the number." The spider's cold gaze locked to mine.

I recited the first three digits. What came next? My tongue felt curled in knots. The odor of tobacco swelled and I completed my response.

The spider flicked the cigarette butt into a shallow puddle of mud. Another guard submerged the butt with the tip of his boot.

"Please accept my apologies for the delay, sir," the spider said to Guide. "You may all continue on your way." He dug in his pocket and retrieved the gold coin. "This belongs to you, I believe."

"Just something I found on the trail," Guide said. "It would've been bad luck not to pick it up. Keep it for luck."

Guide adjusted his hat and bandanna, then mounted King Solomon. The novice slapped my back and draped his arm around my shoulders, as a comrade might do. I owed Guide a gold coin and a golden deed.

I walked with the youth for several minutes, each moment like hours, my heart racing as if I ran up a mountainside. The guards might change their minds and pursue. And why had Guide mentioned the Mendozas? That family had a terrible reputation.

The road curved, revealing a down slope. The crack of gunfire came from behind. The novice lurched, clutched his shoulder and stumbled. A crimson pool welled through his green linen smock. He'd been hit. Victor's hand muffled my cry.

"Keep him walking." Victor's palm cupped my mouth harder. "If you scream," he whispered, "and sound like a girl, he's dead. We all are."

Two pilgrims held the novice upright, their hands and smocks spotted with blood. The novice groaned, his breathing labored. At least he still lived. But for how long?

The men lowered the young man to the ground. The novice grunted, the right side of his pimpled face pressed against a carpet of withered grasses. Bernardo sliced away strips of bloodied shirt. Victor knelt nearby.

"There's no time for potions or a litter," Victor said. "Those bastards might choose to follow." He touched the novice's arm, then dipped the thin blade of a small knife into a jar of clear liquid. "You're a man now."

The youth nodded his head. Several healers pinned his torso and legs against the earth. I clasped his cool, sweaty palm. The knife tunneled through his flesh. The novice jerked. Nausea swept through me as if the blade had cut me, too. The novice's short ragged nails dug into the back of my hand and drew blood. I winced.

"F-filthy men," the novice said between sobs. "Filthy Mendozas."

Mendozas. Guide had concealed his name. Was he one? Victor rinsed the bullet wound with salted water. Why had a guard tried to kill this innocent young man?

Pilgrims propped the novice on the spare mount, a docile chestnut mare with a white blaze. Bernardo grasped the horse's hemp lead. Several others walked alongside chatting and watching—always watching.

•

The pilgrims and I hiked past a cultivated field. No more fresh aromas of deserts and mountains. Just the stink of dung. Men and boys in one field—their clothes similar to the pilgrims' garments—drove teams of mules or oxen. Others, wearing overalls, toiled as human mules and oxen, the way the people of Promise had done. Bent women wearing ankle-length dresses hand-pumped water from wells. Women and girls with soiled bonnets carried buckets to stooped field hands and lean-to shelters. Some waved toward the pilgrims. One woman asked a healer for medical advice.

I passed the line of pack mules and walked beside Guide. Bits of rocks pressed through the worn soles of my sandals. How nice to have callused feet.

"Why did the guards try to kill the novice?" I said.

"They didn't try to kill him," Guide said. "Just send a warning."

"He was bleeding like—"

"Just a warning," Guide said, reining Solomon to a halt. "That's all." His voice sounded different, so unfeeling. "They only miss the heart or head on purpose."

I searched for a reassuring odor—the sweaty, musky smell that had comforted me on previous occasions. Had he ever shot someone? The stink of manure from the fields intensified.

"What were those papers?" I said. "The ones you let the guards see?"

"A collection of permits to travel this area with Americans or Brits."

Guide dismounted and slipped the reins over Solomon's pricked ears to lead. He had both a kind and a disturbing side. I wanted to ride with and run from him at the same time. Instead, we walked past a fenced feed lot. A half-dozen pigs picked through refuse or wallowed in mud. I batted away a swarm of gnats.

"Where did you learn that number," Guide said, "the one you recited back there?"

"Spirits, I think. They whisper things in my head."

"Passport numbers that end with three ones are special." He brushed several fat flies away from Solomon's nose and eyes, his expression somber. "They're only issued to the Mendoza family, but most don't know that."

I hiked beside Guide, my mind jumbled amidst orderly clomps of hooves. A dry stretch of road puffed red-brown dust. I had to ask my next question.

"Was Mendoza the name on your permits?"

"Yes," he said, his voice calm. "Not my real name."

"Oh."

Well that was good news. Still, I leaned hard on my hiking staff. My knees, back and hip joints burned. Guide walked so tall and strong. Even with the riding, he should have looked more tired.

"The pilgrimage is almost over," I said. "What will happen to me?"

"Without identification, you'd better stay with me. At least for a while."

"And be a Mendoza?" I said.

"No, Juanita. Be named Mendoza."

Papa had spat on the ground at the mere mention of that family. If Papa's ghost were here, it would blaze the color of fury. I didn't even want to be a pretend Mendoza.

"Why are those people so hated and feared?" I said.

"There are reasons." Guide shrugged. "They live mostly in South California but have done U.S. federal business in North California for over fifty years."

"What sort of business?" The sun beat against the back of my neck.

Guide unscrewed the lid of his aluminum canteen. He took a long drink, then passed the vessel to me. I gripped the coarse surface of the canteen's homespun covering and drank.

"These days, Mendozas issue papers," Guide said. He took the canteen from me and secured the lid. Skin crinkled near the outer corners of his eyes. His mouth curled in a frown. "Tickets to ride the train."

I parted my lips, unable to speak. Mendozas controlled who went to the bad asylum. And which prisoners were housed hundreds of miles away from their families. I could never live with Guide. Yet what other choice did I have?

The line of healers and mules passed me and Guide, raising yellow-brown dust. Billy's voice called my name. Ethereal tobacco smoke wafted to my nose.

"Smile sweetly," Billy's voice said. "You're going to go with Guide to British South California and bide your time. A year or two. Maybe a little more. If you learn to outsmart the Mendozas, you can stop all the trains to hell-on-earth. With the proper motivation, that family could shut down or clean up the South California asylum. Even build a new center in the north."

And help me get custody of Magdalena's niece?

"That, too, once the train thing's done." He chuckled. "If you let those Mendoza bastards outsmart you, you'll wish I'd let you fall into that chunk of sky atop the river canyon."

The buzz of a fly droned near my ear. In the mountain pass, I'd clung to the canyon wall, unable to scream. The Shadow World must have silenced my cry so only Billy could save me. Now, I owed him my life.

If a living person saved the life of a friend, their destinies intertwined. A ghost, however, could extract payment for the same type of favor. Billy's order to go with Guide made clear the price he planned to extract from me.

Less clear was the new feeling gnawing at my gut. Billy had to know I already intended to stop the asylum trains. Why would he feel the need to coerce me?

Journal of Awakening

19. Coming of Age, Year 1896

A VOICE FLITTED through my mind as I lay in bed. Magdalena's ghost. What was the problem? I needed to sleep, not listen to jabbering. Magdalena ought to stay out of my head for a while. I rolled onto my back and grumbled at my dead friend by thoughts, as usual. Guide snored next to me. Magdalena persisted.

Something had excited Magdalena—maybe my estimated eighteenth birthday, only two days away. Two years had passed since the night of the train. By now that murderous asylum superintendent, the one Billy had told me about, prepared to carry out his wretched plans. The spirits of Promise's people might have devised a new idea for stopping him—a plan that wouldn't harm anyone innocent. This very moment, the Shadow World could be plotting to outwit the Mendozas and keep Magdalena's two-year-old niece—Carla—safe.

Except plotting and action were two separate pots of beans.

I fluffed my feather pillow and sighed. Few people came to visit Guide. Without a passport, I dared not leave his property for any reason. I'd never meet Mendozas to outwit, not even the owner of the estate adjoining his.

The Shadow World didn't even want me to tell Guide about Carla yet. It made no sense. Guide could write a letter to the asylum. Make arrangements to bring Carla into our home.

A quill poked through the mattress ticking and found my thigh. I shifted, straightening the long skirt of my white muslin nightgown. My ankle brushed against Guide's left leg, his skin hairy and warm. Even my toes tingled. Life in Promise seemed a thousand years away.

Well, almost.

A glint of metal shone from the corner of Guide's bedroom, then disappeared. Clouded moonlight played hide-and-seek with Clockman, the mechanical wind-up person he'd repaired. Its broken form had just shown up at our front gate a year ago. A gift from a neighbor, Guide had claimed. But I knew every speck in those amber irises. A miracle I couldn't understand reconnected me with the machine from Promise's library.

Parts of my past and future were one.

Promise. Galen. The train wreck. Checkpoint guards. I shivered, then let the irregular rhythm of Guide's snoring soothe me. The main reason I'd shared his high four-poster bed for much of the past two years. In fact, sleeping apart always brought me horrific dreams. Too many times I'd awakened screaming.

The red tile floor faded in and out of view. I inhaled the spicy aroma of Guide's new hair oil. Forget Promise, for then. In my imagination, Guide's fingertips explored the contours of my womanly bosom. He'd never touched me that way. The moon would shine purple stripes first.

"Your ancestors have a saying," Magdalena said. "You can't get hot chocolate without boiling the water."

"You can't boil water without water," I said by thought.

I fingered the polished oak headboard. The outline of Guide's broad chest rose and fell. The spacious room smelled of woman and man.

"You want to catch Guide for a husband?" Magdalena laughed. "Catch him off guard."

"Go be a dream."

I snuggled against the curve of Guide's left arm and shoulder. That arm could muscle a bale of hay with ease. I stroked the soft mat of hair on his chest, exposed by the v-shaped neckline of his flannel nightshirt. My palm touched the fabric against his flat stomach. His body had the firmness of a man Galen's age.

A breeze stirred the shadowy curtains, as if Galen's spirit hovered near the open window. I retracted my hand. The thin cotton curtains billowed, then stilled. Moonlight settled on Clockman's leather face. His amber eyes sparkled, then turned dark as Papa's had been. Knots in the ceiling timbers peered down at me. I inhaled but detected no odors that might belong to Papa or my first love.

Galen never visited. He didn't even want me to travel to the Shadow World, according to Magdalena. If Galen still loved me, he'd send a sign. Whisper to me from pattering raindrops. Comfort me when I cried. But he did nothing at all. I twisted my ropy black braid around my fingers. In my fantasy, moonlight painted the bed and floor with purple stripes.

•

A hint of dawn shone through the bedroom window. I yawned. Guide had risen already and taken Clockman with him. The daily routine awaited me. His three-hundred-acre estate demanded attention.

No sense in enslaving my waistline in a corset this early in the morning. I donned my petticoats, camisole, and high-necked yellow tea-gown, then headed downstairs where I'd left my shoes.

Elena, the hired woman, waddled from one kitchen chore to the next, her matronly fat jiggling like mounds of flan under her loose ecru dress. I lit the rest of the fuel lamps on the lower floor of Guide's two-story home, except for the one in his locked den. Only he ventured there.

Elena set off to gather eggs and milk the goats. I cajoled the stubborn water pump in the brick courtyard. The apparatus squealed and sucked air. A burst of cold water splashed my high-top button shoes.

"Give me a nice, dependable creek," I muttered, then recalled how undependable creeks were in summer and fall.

I lugged water to the kitchen. The damper on the stove took some fiddling to adjust. Yesterday, the new crateful of thumb-sized charcoal fuel blocks had arrived. Wet mud would burn easier than those blocks did. It would take an hour to heat the cast-iron grill to a suitable temperature. Angel—Elena's husband—and Guide would have to enlist Clockman to replenish the troughs and scatter chicken feed. A little lamp oil and sawdust encouraged the reluctant fire. Elena joined me, bearing a wicker basket of eggs and a wooden pail half-filled with milk.

"It's time you learned to scramble eggs." Elena cracked one and removed a bloody spot. "If I ever take sick, the men will starve."

"I could do the scrambling, if I had to."

Preparing food I wouldn't eat held little appeal. I turned away from the broken yolk and slimy white. Soon Elena sloshed her wooden spoon through a dozen raw eggs. The spoon tapped the sides of the ceramic bowl. Those eggs could have grown into cute baby chickens.

I twisted my slender arms back and forth, transforming a pasty ball of masa into a smooth tortilla. I hummed the melancholy tune Guide often strummed on his guitar. As I slapped more dough into thin disks, bits of masa lodged in the embroidered daisy on my apron and the pleated yoke of my tea gown, the most loose-fitting dress I owned.

Elena wet the tip of her middle finger with her tongue. She flicked moisture onto the iron grill. The metal replied with a halfhearted sizzle. Not ready yet.

The uncooked kidney beans for tonight's dinner still soaked in a pot of water. I might as well drain them. I tipped the vessel until a thin stream of cloudy pink liquid flowed into a catch bucket, then added fresh water to the pot and hoisted it onto the rear of the stove. My hands flattened more balls of masa. If only I had the fixings to prepare mashed beans the way the women of Promise had done.

"Someday," I said, "I'm going to get a passport and gallop out our gate with Guide. We'll go back to the mountains when the mesquite's in bloom. I'll collect a sack full of sweet pods and acorns. Then you'll taste real beans."

"I pray to God this house never has to resort to leaching acorns." The nostrils of Elena's flat nose flared.

Elena had no comprehension of how sweet the acorns near Promise tasted. She minced a dried green chili pepper and tossed half into the beaten eggs.

"Put in the whole thing," I said. Elena worried too much about Angel's digestion. The pepper was a jalapeño, not a fiery habañero. "The men like the tang."

I plopped the first tortilla onto the hot grill. The dough sizzled, yielding the pleasant aroma of sweet corn. A horse whinnied. I peered over the top of the faded scarlet café curtain and out the window.

Guide, astride King Solomon, approached the house. The top of his denim work smock hung open, exposing the soft white hair I'd stroked the night before. Magdalena had married Cole at age seventeen. Great-Grandma had married young, too. I knew how to run a household, was old enough to wed. And I wasn't too young for Guide, who couldn't even be forty. In Promise, Cook had married a man twice her age when she was twenty.

How sweet Guide's lips would feel against my own. I turned the tortilla, glad my honey-colored skin could conceal a blush.

•

At breakfast, I served Angel first. He wore his coarse black hair, tinged with silver, loose this morning instead of tied back. His luxuriant mustache framed his narrow lips. He was muscular, nearly as tall as Guide, and had the appetite of a horde of locusts. When he ate, bits of food lodged in the ends of his mustache, like flies trapped in a spider's web. The first time I'd watched him eat scrambled eggs, thank God I hadn't puked. Angel was hard working and cared for the estate as if it were his own. He was respectful of women. A good man, overall.

Guide ate less then Angel did. Elena often claimed he ran on air. This particular morning he inspected the stack of tortillas and chose two—one cooked to perfection and the other with little burnt spots. He decorated the good one with goat cheese and red salsa, then placed it on my plate, reserving the burnt one for himself.

"Golden brown." Guide laughed and disguised his tortilla's blackened flaws with eggs and cheese. "Just like my mother used to make."

He chewed as if each morsel of food must be savored, then pulled two small boxes, tied with long crimson ribbons, from the side pockets of his denim trousers. He set the boxes near his plate. Were they for me?

"Happy Birthday, one day early," he said.

"Such beautiful ribbons." I nearly spilled the coffee.

"Better than strips from an old bandanna?"

Guide wiggled one of my thick shoulder-length braids and chided me to finish eating breakfast. The skin at the edges of his eyes crinkled. Bet he wanted to appear stern.

Silk ribbons—how pretty they would look in my hair. The black lacquer boxes, one square and the other rectangular, appeared expensive and mysterious, each cover painted with a golden rose. I took a dainty bite of tortilla and chewed well before swallowing. The next mouthful I gulped down with haste. Excitement was difficult to contain.

At last Elena cleared the plates, and Guide slid the gifts within reach. His hazel eyes gleamed with pleasure. I untied the first ribbon and fixed a bow around my left braid. What would fit in a flat box? I raised the lid. A single gold earring stud sat atop a folded piece of paper. This was the sort of paper shown at checkpoints along the North to South California border. I'd be free to ride beyond Guide's property.

"Today, I'll pierce your left ear," Guide said. "Like mine." He pointed to the number on my passport, the same number Billy had buzzed in my ear two years ago. "Just remember, though. Pretty young girls shouldn't ride alone."

146

I twirled around the kitchen, laughing. I had a real passport. Now I could meet a real Mendoza. I swished the ankle-length skirt of my buttercup-yellow gown, then snapped my fingers above my head.

"There's one more box," Guide said. "If you can float down from the clouds."

I danced back to the table and claimed the other ribbon for my right braid. The flowered box contained two items. One was a single mesquite pod. My hands tensed. The familiar sting of tears kissed my eyes. I clasped the pod to my bosom and stroked the tiny homespun pouch within the box. Then I withdrew a leached acorn. It had to have come from a blue oak near Promise. Guide must have met someone who'd traveled to that area in recent weeks.

"Sorry I couldn't get more." Guide smiled a narrow, closed-mouth smile. "Your memory will detect the flavor in the beans tonight, even if your tongue can't."

"Your gift is beautiful," I said. "Perfect."

•

Clothed only in my earring and magic pendant, I sucked my stomach flat. I posed before the rectangular mirror in the bedroom. The rooster crowed from the barnyard. Guide's distant voice called to Angel. I placed my hands on my hips, legs parted a few inches, and examined my image in profile.

Food was so plentiful in Guide's home. Was I too plump? I daubed my tender earlobe with alcohol, then rotated the smooth golden ball of my earring. Being eighteen felt different, although my exact date of birth remained unknown to me. I always celebrated it on June seventeenth. Regardless, the three-foot-high plate of silver-backed glass cast the same reflection it had the night before. How disappointing.

The fan-shaped flame in the fuel lamp flared. Shapeless shadows danced on the wall. A soft whistling sound, like the early call of a rising storm, arose within my mind. Magdalena had roused.

"You're five-feet-two and can't weigh more than a dozen ten-pound sacks of beans," Magdalena said, thought to thought, as usual. "Elena's overly plump. You're not."

"Maybe Guide doesn't like his women so wiggly."

"Maybe he doesn't like his evening wine either."

I turned the ends of my mouth upward, my emerald eyes wide. "Does this expression look suggestive?"

"If you want to be suggestive," Magdalena said, "ask Guide if you can take a bath tonight."

Baths were for Saturday afternoons. How could I ask to take one at night in the middle of the week? I balanced on the balls of my feet and stretched, admiring the way my thick ebony tresses brushed against my sloped shoulders. The fine black hairs on my legs looked soft and feminine.

Magdalena laughed. "All you have to say to him is..."

She jabbered on, offering advice about attracting Guide's attention. My cheeks grew warmer than melting butter on a stove. A sharp rap on the door interrupted the conspiracy.

"Tortillas don't cook themselves," Elena called, "even on birthdays."

I fumbled with my underwear, then put on tan trousers and a cotton, shirtwaist blouse. I stepped into the long skirt I'd split for riding astride.

"Why can't riding clothes look flattering without a corset?" Tight cinching was for sausages. Or getting admiring glances from Guide. "Guide should've left Clockman to lace me up."

"Just be glad he invited you to accompany him this morning," Magdalena said. "One nice ride leads to another."

I hurried toward the kitchen, the glass chimney of my fuel lamp rattling in its brass frame. Just for a moment, a ghostly shadow glided on the adobe wall beside my own, nibbling at the tip of its forefinger.

•

After drying breakfast dishes, I put on my top hat and veil and met Guide by the stable. The horses waited, saddled and bridled. I mounted without assistance. No side saddle for me today. Angel swung open the steel gate to Guide's estate. The rusty hinges creaked. Within a few exhilarating seconds, I passed from the confinement of Guide's barbed wire fences to the freedom of an open road.

With freedom came new vulnerability. I gripped the reins tighter. Why had that old thought popped into my mind? I carried a passport. Guide escorted me. Today of all days should bring little trouble.

I hugged the mare and saddle with my legs and braced for action. New vulnerability, indeed. In my imagination, I raced with the winds. Even thoughts about outwitting Mendozas, marrying Guide, and adopting Carla could wait until later.

"Where are we going?" I said. "May we gallop?"

"Hold both your horses." Guide laughed, and rested his hand on the pommel of King Solomon's saddle. "We'll gallop on the way home."

"Must we wait that long?" I let out a musical sigh, doing my best to project disappointment.

"I've business with our neighbor." His hands practically squeezed the leather reins. "I need a few slow miles for contemplation."

I nodded, knowing he referred to Antonio Mendoza. Guide rarely talked about that man. When he did, his face always looked clenched and tight, as if he held a chunk of rancid meat in his mouth yet feared to spit it out. Maybe today I'd get a better idea of what I was up against.

We rode through a small but fragrant grove of eucalyptus, live oak and pine. Cones and acorns dotted the path, amidst leaves and dry needles. I breathed in, slow and deep.

"Why doesn't Antonio pay us calls?" I said.

"He doesn't visit friends anymore," Guide said, touching the brim on his top hat. "Only enemies."

What became of those enemies? The backs of my hands tingled. Antonio might be one of the Mendozas I would need to outsmart.

The path forked at the clearing. The horses veered to the left and trotted across an open, flat stretch of land bordered by distant mountains. My bosom jiggled under the pleats of my blouse. My silk camisole and undervest failed to restrain my breasts. Guide didn't appear to notice. Antonio might, though, and would think I wasn't a lady. I should have worn my corset.

Ahead, a barbed wire fence enclosed an orchard of apple and plum trees, their boughs heavy with fruit. What sort of man grew bountiful trees but never visited friends?

•

Antonio's property abutted ours, yet Guide and I must have ridden for an hour to reach the main gate. A guard with a blackened front tooth unlocked the ten-foot-long steel barricade. His collarless blue shirt and the gun across his back made him look like a checkpoint guard. Over fifty miles separated this ranch from the border between North and South California. Regardless, it was good I carried my passport in my saddlebag. I touched my pendant through the fabric of my blouse.

I dismounted near a brightly-painted green barn and stood close to Guide under a date palm. The stable boy led our horses away. Other guards approached, odd-looking guns slung over their shoulders, ochre dust covering their silk shirts and buttoned vests. My heart thudded, like a fist pounding a huge ceremonial drum. I was a guest, needed to calm down. Antonio knew nothing about my mission. Things would be all right.

A trim, large-framed man, even taller than Galen had been, appeared from behind the barn. The ugly snout of a gun poked over the crest of his broad shoulder. The weapon was harnessed diagonally across his back. A slender band of sculpted beard curved around the man's jowls and connected his sideburns with the tips of his goatee. His tight little ebony braids, like clusters of oiled worms, extended several inches below his earlobes. He tipped the brim of his short, top hat—identical to Guide's—but didn't smile.

The man gestured toward a circular courtyard of red bricks and slate-gray flagstones. Behind the yard lay a two-story structure—a mansion of adobe and wrought iron. He walked with long, quick strides in my direction. The legs of his leather pants brushed against each other and produced soft swishing sounds. He blocked my path, his dark eyes intense and unblinking, as if he could steal my very soul. I skirted to the right to avoid a collision and forced a polite smile. This had to be Antonio.

The walkway was uneven. The toe of my boot grazed the protruding edge of something. I stumbled and pitched forward, releasing a cry of surprise. Antonio's warm arms broke my fall. He steadied me against him, the forcefulness of his grip unexpected. This man had the strength to crush bones.

I tried to speak, but the combined odors of Antonio's sweat and perfumed hair oil—more pungent than Guide's—assaulted my senses. Nausea swept through me, flushing my face and chilling my shoulders. Antonio...the gun...the house...all seemed to drift and fade. What business had Guide with this man? Why couldn't I control my emotions? Whatever happened, I mustn't faint and demonstrate my greatest weakness—fear. I reached out, as if determination could clutch consciousness. My legs buckled like two slashed bags of sand. I slumped downward, as helpless as a rag doll.

•

Someone lifted me. Male voices spoke. The scents of leather and perfumed Macassar oil grew strong. Warmth encased me. A sensation of movement, uneven and jerky, followed. Antonio was carrying me in his arms.

I'd never fainted before, except when Billy had grabbed my spirit and taken it to the Black Mountain. A bad omen. Best to remain unresponsive, keep my eyelids closed and my ears open.

"What does one do," Guide said, "with a stubborn girl who refuses to eat meat and eggs? No wonder she faints. Her blood's thinner than a beggar's gruel."

"Frig'em sweet and often, and they all do what they're told." Antonio's deep, guttural laugh was even more offensive than his words had been.

"What do I owe you for catching her?" Guide chuckled, like he tried to change the topic of conversation. "God," he added with a sober tone, "just include all of today on my running tab. It's beyond repayment. What's the difference?"

"Our friendship isn't about repayment," Antonio said.

This crude man couldn't possibly be Guide's friend. I heard the metallic creak of door hinges. The ride turned smoother then. Repeated rhythmic clicks meant several men in boots crossed a tile floor. The air cooled.

Antonio lowered me onto a plush, cushioned surface. Clinks of glassware and a sloshing sound suggested the pouring of water. I stirred, pretending I'd been unconscious the entire while. He'd placed me atop a tawny leather sofa with a sheepskin throw.

His thick-fingered hand, as dark as Guide's brandy, felt my pulse, then tilted a crystal goblet against my lips. The water tasted of lemon. The gray gun, shaped like two side-by-side rifles but not as long, still lurked across his back. His overall appearance, though, was less evil than before.

Perhaps Antonio actually believed Guide was his friend. He might have blocked my path to test my mettle in some perverse way. How childish my overreaction had been.

"Can she ride home when you do?" Antonio said to Guide. "Or will you need a carriage?"

Guide put his hands on his hips, his heels planted a foot apart from each other on a braided green rug. Ochre dust coated his leather riding boots and clung to the legs of his loose-fitting denim trousers.

"I think she can ride," Guide said, "on the mare."

Antonio smirked a sort of half-smile. The left corner of his mouth curved upwards and the right, slightly down. The movement accentuated a thin diagonal scar on his left cheek.

"I'll lead the stallion," Guide added.

Guide owned three mules, two mares and a gelding. What was he talking about? Perhaps Antonio had asked him to train a horse to saddle. I grasped the rounded top of the leather sofa and sat upright.

"Did you say stallion?"

"You're feeling stronger already," Guide said. "Amazing what a little word can do."

I pressed my fingertips against my lips. I'd begged him for a spirited horse last spring. Now the striations in Guide's eyes gleamed like polished agate in bright sunlight, the way they had when he'd given me the two lacquer boxes. He must have purchased a horse. My joyful squeal danced through the air.

"The stallion," Guide said, "is from Tony."

I faced Antonio. Why would he present me with such an expensive gift? A hunger burned from the depths of his dark brown eyes. I didn't need Magdalena's assistance to interpret that expression. Antonio wanted me. I did not want him.

"The horse," Antonio said, "is for a good girl who does as she's told. His name is Ibn Sina."

The chunky links of a gold chain showed through the open necklines of Antonio's silk shirt and paisley vest. Focusing on the jewelry let me avoid his gaze. Two years ago, Billy had issued an icy warning. If I let the Mendozas outsmart me, I would wish I'd fallen into a river canyon. Antonio was powerful and dangerous. Frightening in a way I hadn't anticipated. Freedom. New vulnerability. I'd better speak with care.

I crafted a gracious smile, then thanked Antonio with a soft, meek voice. He shifted one shoulder loop of his gun harness and tilted his head, as if amused. A two-legged rattlesnake.

"Ibn Sina is nine years old," he said. "Half Arabian and half ghost. Your man says you'll make a good combination."

Antonio offered his hand and pulled me to my feet, his broad palm sweaty. He looked me over, like a cougar sizing up supper. I should have worn that corset. He had better believe Guide was my man. Guide and he clasped each other's arms, then embraced.

Between Guide and Antonio, I stepped from the shelter of the cool adobe into the hot sunlight. Several of Antonio's men followed. In the brick courtyard, King Solomon drank water from a circular concrete pool. A stable boy, shorter than me, clung to the taut lead rope of an unsaddled foam-white horse. The animal—a stallion—jerked to the side, its head and silvery tail arched high. The horse whinnied and fought the lead, as if poised to sprout wings. Only Ibn Sina would have such spirit.

Ibn Sina flared his nostrils and reared. Shod hooves pounded the air, the animal's trumpeting call like a battle cry from some ancient land. The stable boy's wide-open eyes projected raw fear as he fought to steady the stallion. The horse reared again, missing the young man's head by mere inches. Ibn Sina was unmanageable.

I shot a glance in Antonio's direction. He grinned and stroked the slender band of beard from the tips of his sideburns to his goatee. The stable boy shouted. I turned. Twelve hundred pounds of unrestrained horseflesh lunged in my direction. Oh, dear God.

Guide darted for the lead rope. He missed. The guards dodged sideways to safety. I dropped to the brick patio and flattened myself. My forearms shielded the back of my hat and head. I scrunched my eyes tight. May my pendant and ancestors provide deliverance. Antonio's deep laugh resounded through the warm air. The man was insane. A soft nicker replaced the angry sound of hoofbeats. I opened one eye. Ibn Sina stood a foot away from me, shaking his head, neck and arched tail, as if fending off flies. I smelled beer, the odor of my great-grandfather's spirit. The stallion nuzzled my shoulder. The aroma deepened.

Antonio had claimed my new horse was half ghost. The animal might actually be possessed. I sat up and stroked the velvety nose that had nudged me. Ibn Sina nodded, as docile as trampled grass.

I squealed out girlish laughter. Great-Grandpa Javier controlled Ibn Sina. The horse would never kick, bite, or throw me. I stood, not even bothering to brush the dust off my blouse and skirt. My fingers grasped the stallion's coarse, silvery mane.

"Boost me up," I called to Guide. He cast a wary look at both me and the horse. "Please."

Antonio stepped forward, his front teeth exposed by his grin. He'd known Ibn Sina wouldn't harm me, but how? He cupped his hands to meet my foot. As I swung my right leg over the back of the ghost horse, one of Antonio's hands moved upward and supported my left thigh. Ibn Sina snorted and pawed the brick patio, his hoof producing a sharp clicking sound. Antonio released me.

"I hope to see you again," Antonio said, "now that you have a passport." He scratched the side of his neck. "Soon."

"But, of course." I'd rather spend an afternoon vomiting. Two years ago, no wonder Billy had tried to blackmail me into dealing with the Mendoza family. He hadn't believed I'd cooperate of my own free will.

Guide mounted King Solomon and rode through the gate at a walking pace, leading the chestnut mare. I followed. Antonio waved to us from the shade of a live oak. I filled my lungs and breathed out hard. If only I could expel the memories of my benefactor's grip and stare with such ease.

A vertical tree snag, rough bark ridged in the shape of leg bones, stood near the path. Antonio was a Mendoza and somehow connected with the operation of the asylum trains. Resuming the Shadow World's mission would trigger an inevitable confrontation between us.

"I don't trust that man," I said.

"You've no need to fear Tony unless you cross him," Guide replied. "He knows about Promise, about almost everything."

Antonio knew I'd helped sabotage a train? No wonder he'd blocked my path and intimidated me. He'd wanted to determine if I posed a threat. The spirits might have induced my fainting spell to ease his concerns.

"Tony's obnoxious," Guide said, "but I've known him for years. He arranged for your passport. I told him you're my woman."

Sudden warmth flushed my cheeks. What should I say?

"The word about availability gets around," Guide added. "I had to lie." He patted King Solomon's neck. "Unsavory suitors would have littered our front doorstep like night crawlers after a hard rain."

"Do you want me to, you know...to be...." I glanced down, then toward the apple and plum orchard, my heart rate quickening.

"You belong to Galen. I respect that." Guide twisted his gold earring. "Just as Tony respects the claim you belong to me."

Images of Galen hoisting me to his shoulder beside a flickering fire flooded my mind. He didn't visit me, even in dreams. Did I still belong to him? Magdalena's excited talking broke into my thoughts with the force of a driving rain. Guide cared for me and would be a loyal husband. Magdalena wanted me to entice him. Should I?

Ibn Sina snorted, a reminder that Great-Grandpa's spirit was near. I couldn't seduce a man in front of my family. Besides, Galen might be furious if I experienced that physical part of love we could never share.

A warm breeze hit my face. The air over the open stretch of road tasted dusty. Guide looked away without smiling. Did uncertainty plague him, too?

"Do what I suggested," Magdalena said. "This is the chance you've waited for."

My stomach ached, like I tried to digest a handful of stones. My calling as a mystic traveler required me to heed the advice of my two guardian spirits. And I wanted so much to catch Guide.

"Since you respect I belong to Galen," I said to Guide, "may I ask for something special?"

"What now, Juanita? The sun, moon or stars?"

"I want to soak in a bath tonight. After Angel and Elena go from the main house."

Ibn Sina stopped and pawed the ground. Guide shifted in King Solomon's saddle. The well-weathered leather creaked.

"I want to feel clean," I said. "To smell nice."

"That's a lot of water to pump in the dark for a womanish whim."

"I'll use the water to scrub clothes tomorrow." I tensed my legs against Ibn Sina's warm sides. "Please."

"Extra fuel blocks to heat water, lamp oil to light the kitchen." Guide reached behind his head and tightened the knot in his bandanna. "Do you realize what that costs?"

"If it costs so much…" I nibbled on my thumbnail and prayed Great-Grandpa wouldn't make Ibn Sina do something unsociable. "All we have to do is heat the water. Only an inexpensive little candle will give enough light."

Ibn Sina walked, hooves thudding against the dirt road and ears twitching. The grove of pine, oak, and eucalyptus lay a quarter-mile ahead. As the horses clomped, flies buzzed louder. My forwardness had embarrassed Guide. I should have ignored my inner longing and Magdalena's crazy prodding.

"I suppose I could manage one bite of beef with the beans tonight," I said. That should please him.

"A tub of hot water," Guide said, "will cost you more than that."

Ibn Sina halted and nibbled a clump of tall dry grass. Flies crawled near its eyes. Great-Grandpa didn't let the stallion flinch.

"All right," I said. "Two bites."

Guide faced straight ahead and prompted Solomon to trot. Ibn Sina matched the pace. I bounced with the uneven ride, yet felt as if I floated in a dream. Magdalena whispered ghostly advice.

"Will you strum your guitar tonight?" I said. "You know, do a serenade?"

Guide reined Solomon to a standstill and peeled off his top hat, pushing his sweaty bandanna toward the back of his head. He squinted in my direction. The skin around the outer edges of his eyes crinkled.

"What scheme's churning through that brain of yours?"

Guide had bushed his eyebrows, a sure sign of disapproval, but might have done so to appear proper. I gathered the courage to speak.

"You want Tony to be convinced I'm your woman, don't you? I mean, even if we don't, well, you know."

Guide slung his hat over Solomon's saddle horn. He fiddled with his gold earring, his mouth clamped tight.

"Elena's got keen hearing," I said. "And I bet she loves to gossip in town." I shrugged and did my best to form a coy little smile. "After tonight, even fish'll think we're lovers."

Guide sat motionless. Ibn Sina pawed the ground, then peed.

20. The Bath

THE PUMP IN the moonlit courtyard squeaked as I worked the metal handle up and down. Guide helped me haul bucketfuls of water into the house. Some went to the kitchen, most to the metal bathtub on the adjacent laundry portico. We took turns holding the fuel oil lantern, gripping its brass handle while shadows danced on the wall. Each bubbling call of the kettle, each journey across the threshold of the enclosed porch, etched a path of no return. So awkward, this was. Guide probably felt the same way.

"Ibn Sina's a fine horse, no?" Guide said. "Spirited, yet tame for you." He upended a bucket of unheated water into the bulky five-foot-long tub.

"Where did Antonio find him?" I said. At last, he'd spoken. My kettle chortled as its steaming contents spilled into the bath.

"Who's sure where Tony gets anything?" Guide swished his hand in the water. "Two more kettles and we're done."

"Excuse me?" Magdalena said inside my mind. "Two more and things get started." She laughed. "Don't worry, I'll leave you two alone as soon as you head for the bedroom."

Guide fumbled in the top drawer of a pine utility cabinet and withdrew a thick candle, six or seven inches tall. He wiggled the base into a brass sconce.

"Tony insists that one of your ancestors possesses your horse, although he didn't explain how he knows. Is it the ghost who controlled the goat on the mountain?"

"Do you mean Billy?" What a ridiculous idea. I must have neglected to mention Billy's former occupation. "An engineer wouldn't understand about being a horse."

"Engineer?" Guide faced away from me and struck a match against a small brick.

"On a train," I said with a little shrug. "Ibn Sina's possessed by Great-Grandpa Javier, a wise farmer who understands horses."

Guide carried the candle to a low pine chest near the tub, cupping the flame with his left hand, his gaze directed down.

"Billy was an engineer on a train?"

"Yes, but don't think ill of him." I removed the spare kettle from the burner, my hand protected by a quilted potholder. "Billy wasn't an evil man. He ran away from doing that sort of thing—to Mexico."

Guide extinguished the fuel lantern. He stared at the floor. Candle-glow flickered through the sooty glass chimney of the lamp. This might not have been an appropriate occasion to mention Billy.

"Are you all right?" I said.

He took a slow deep breath and exhaled with a faint whistling sound. Lines formed around the corners of his lips. He nodded and opened his guitar case, then sat on the red tile floor, his back hunched against the wall. His callused fingers strummed the strings on his guitar. The instrument emitted pensive music, as if it cried.

Antonio's family was involved with the asylum trains. Guide's reaction to Billy's engineering days seemed strange. The last kettle of steaming water went into the tub. I stepped out of my long skirt, then removed my puffy-sleeved blouse. During the past year Guide had laced and unlaced my corset many times, although lately, he'd encouraged me to use the help of Clockman when Elena wasn't available. Still, taking off my clothing in front of him tonight felt uncomfortable. The strings on my drawers jammed in a granny knot. I glanced at Guide. He wasn't even looking at me. Just as well.

"He sees more than you think," Magdalena said. "Let water simmer at its own pace."

I unbraided my hair and combed each section with quick strokes of my fingers. My shadow grew tall on the wall, temporarily engulfing Guide's. I removed my underwear, then immediately climbed into the tub and sat in the hot water to hide. Maybe I shouldn't have let Magdalena talk me into doing this, no matter how much my heart longed for Guide. Galen might watch from the Black Mountain, angry and hurt. Where was the Juanita who'd sworn she would remain true?

I leaned back against smooth, sloped metal, squeezed the washrag against my shoulders, and listened to Guide's fingers pick the steel strings. He hummed, his deep voice uneven but soft. A child must be born, or so the Virgin of Guadalupe had told me inside the Cave of Light. If I were to bear the child, Galen's time to father the baby had passed. My destiny now entwined with Guide's. Within my mind, Magdalena rattled off more suggestions.

"Is your throat sore?" I said to Guide. I shifted lower in the water. "Your humming is rough. You need brandy."

"Some brandy," he said in a monotone.

"Yes." I swallowed on impulse, although my mouth felt dry. "A nice glass of...cognac."

"Would you like a glass as well?" He rubbed the back of his neck with one hand, then put down the guitar.

"That's all right." I twisted the wet ends of my hair around my fingers. "Why dirty two glasses? I'll sip from yours."

He brought me a crystal brandy snifter, walking with slow, short strides, like a man condemned. Magdalena had sworn lovemaking always excited men. Guide acted more frightened than I was. This didn't seem normal. I listened for Magdalena's cue.

"You look forlorn," I said to Guide as I accepted the drink. His eyes tried to avoid my body—I could tell. I swished my tongue in the liquor. Maybe too suggestive. "That's very nice, like this water," I whispered. Our glances met. I hummed a short, wistful sigh. "It's not right to use so much precious water for only one."

"Water," Guide whispered.

He undressed, vest and shirt first, in silence. Then he unbuttoned his trousers. I stared at his naked chest, the swirls of white hair on his sun-browned skin. I knew I ought to glance lower. My hands tensed. His stomach was flat and his hips, narrow. I focused on his muscular thighs.

"Concentrate on the important part," Magdalena said.

I didn't have to stare there yet. Warm water splashed around me, the level rising as Guide climbed into the bath. We sat facing each other with knees drawn close to our chests, sharing the snifter of brandy and a cotton washrag. Guide was so dear to me. To win him for a husband, I must initiate the next advance.

"Do you remember when it rained on the pilgrimage?" I said. "We bathed together in the downpour."

"You were beautiful in your innocence."

"Am I less beautiful now?" I cupped my hands around my bosom.

I drew his palms to where mine had rested. He held both breasts, as if my flesh were blown glass and might shatter. I studied his hazel eyes in the candlelight. They expressed either the wisdom of deserts or the resignation of a lost traveler. Galen's eyes had been darker, yet less mysterious. He would have been a fine husband, too. But Galen never visited, nor had he ever touched me this way.

"It's tempting for an old cat to seek a tender mouse," Guide said. His thumbs rubbed my nipples. "Does this please you?"

I nodded, warm and dizzy, the lower half of my body weak. I'd never even imagined such a feeling. If only the sensation could last forever. I closed my eyes and let the pleasure from stimulation, bath, and brandy blend.

"What does this make you want?" he said.

"I think—more."

"I once tended a garden for a man," he said. "There was a rose bush, such a splendid and precious thing." He massaged my breasts a little harder now. "It's right for a caretaker to admire a budding rose, even to stroke its petals, if the rose is pleased."

"This rose is very pleased."

162

Dared I touch him? I wouldn't have to look, not yet. The wet warmth of his tongue explored my breasts. I pressed his head closer. Surely Guide felt the vibrations from my pounding heart. He suckled, then pulled away.

"This caretaker is not too old to claim a young flower," he said, his voice gentle and kind. He kissed the backs of my hands, his eyelids lowered. "It would be so easy, but so very wrong."

I stiffened. Why had he said such a thing? Maybe he wanted to marry me first. Yes, that had to be the reason. Galen had felt the same way. Then I saw Guide's tight, pained smile and the squint of his soulful eyes. Something else bothered him.

"When a man turns his back on honor, he has nothing." Guide reached for the snifter of cognac on the floor. "I won't touch you that way, Juanita. Not now. Not ever."

"Not now? Ever?" What sort of words were those?

Guide downed his brandy. He clutched the empty glass, his face devoid of any readable expression. Dear God. Guide didn't love me and never would. A barrage of tears flooded my eyes.

"Galen didn't die the night of the train wreck," Guide said.

"Alive? Galen alive?"

My hands shot from the rim of the tub to my lips, as if they flew on their own. Galen, living? Breathing? How? I'd called his name for hours after the derailment. That just couldn't be.

"We found no bodies with dark black skin." Guide set the snifter on the tile. "Once you complete the tasks the spirits have assigned, I think they'll let you find him."

I blurted out a pained cry. Guide had to be mistaken. I'd never forgotten the way Galen had run past the fire, carrying me in his arms. Even now, the memory of his footsteps echoed like peals of thunder in a storm. Galen had loved me, had risked his own life for my sake. He never would have left me alone to die.

"You're lying," I said.

Guide grasped my shoulders, his touch firm. His fingertips nudged a lock of my damp hair away from my eyes. The ruts of skin on his forehead projected distress.

"Galen couldn't see you by the rail embankment," he said. "The healers couldn't, either." He turned away. "You were in plain sight for me to find."

I retreated a few inches with a slosh of warm water. Galen couldn't have overlooked me. Guide's claim made no sense. Then I glanced at his ring, the one with the onyx stone. On the pilgrimage to the River of Tears, my description of Galen's dark skin had surprised Guide.

"If this is the truth," I said, "why didn't you tell me before?"

He rubbed the back of his neck. A rivulet of water trickled down his forearm. He took a slow, deep breath and exhaled through his beak nose.

"I had to be the one to find you," he said. "The one to bring you to my home. I had to fall in love with you. Your ancestors planned it that way."

"My ancestors aren't like that. You have no right to say such a thing." Billy should have hinted about Galen, yet he sometimes neglected to mention details I considered important. "They're not Mendozas."

Guide climbed out of the bath with an ungraceful splash. He wrapped a towel around his waist, then poured more brandy. The candle flickered within the glass chimney lamp. He swirled the cognac in the crystal snifter and faced the shadows on the wall.

"To the south of here's the Tehachapi Mountains," he said. "There's rails through the pass. They climb 3,600 feet in 50 miles—a 2.5 percent grade. Do you know how steep a 2.5 percent grade can be, I mean, for a train? It takes skill to run an engine over that terrain."

I clutched the washrag. The Tehachapis had nothing to do with Galen or my ancestors, except for Billy. Why did Guide expound about mountain grades and passes when I needed to hear about Galen's fate and my own?

164

"There are seventeen tunnels," Guide said. "A gateway through the mountains. South California's main prison and its miserable, rat-infested asylum and workhouse are on the other side, seventy miles south of Tehachapi Station." He faced me and raised his glass in a toast. "Take down those tunnels and they'll not get put back for years."

He sipped brandy. His smooth brow made him appear so calm. How good, he cared about stopping the trains, yet some terrible fact weighed upon his mind. Had the U.S. or British government imprisoned Galen? Antonio might have passed on such information. I parted my lips, my words racing through my muddled mind yet trapped within my body.

"An engineer running the Tehachapis needs a good hand at the firebox." Guide twisted his gold earring. "Your ancestors haven't visited me, but they want me to fire for you and Billy."

"What are you talking about?" I said. "You know nothing of—"

"I can fire a locomotive." Guide drained his glass with a single swallow. "I'm damn handy with explosives, too."

I sat motionless in the tepid water, like I'd turned into a pillar of salt and watched my own body dissolve. Guide had worked for the railroad? This was—had to be—some sort of bad dream. The real Guide would awaken me soon and kiss this nightmare away.

"I know every foot of rail through the Tehachapis." Guide picked up the brandy decanter, then set it down hard. "I was a member of an engine crew on an asylum train."

No! I wailed long and hard. My throat tightened. I gasped for air. Lord of all, might Guide have run the train carrying me and Great-Grandma? This couldn't—mustn't—be true. Maybe, if I didn't listen. I pressed my palms against my ears but found no escape.

"I thought I'd never have to tell you who I am," Guide said. "Or what I've done."

Guide reached for his clothing. Strange, the way his nakedness evoked only a dull, empty feeling, as if my stunned spirit occupied a dead shell. He pulled on his leather boots and tucked the ends of his trousers inside. He buttoned his shirt then put on his wool vest.

Streams of tears warmed my cheeks. My mind groped for any possibility that Guide could someday earn forgiveness as Billy had done.

"Swear that working the firebox was the worst," I said.

Guide faced me. He tossed me a towel. The thick cloth slipped from my grasp, soaked up bath water and sank. His cold glare pierced my very soul.

"Mendozas purchased my mother two months after my conception." Guide placed his guitar into a black case. The vibrating strings produced an eerie metallic twang. "Mendozas fed her an elixir they'd concocted, something that changed the very fabric of my fetal form. I was their experiment. They owned me. There's little I haven't done."

Then I pictured it all like I stood on the Black Mountain. Guide running the train. Beating a chained prisoner. Devouring his own ample dinners while deformed children in his care starved. Letting dying lepers rot in their own wastes. A demented man screamed obscenities, hour after hour. I could see Guide force a pillow against the man's mouth and nose. The victim's breathing stopped.

"Murderer," I hollered. "You're a murderer!"

I hurled the sopping towel in his direction. The soaked cotton squished against the tile floor. Out of the tub, I scrambled, then raced dripping and naked from the enclosed porch. My wet feet slipped in the darkened corridor. I collided with a wall. My head throbbed with pain.

"I hate you," I shouted, over and over. The hallway and stairwell echoed my anguished cries. "I wish you were dead!"

I slammed the door to our bedroom. Volleys of spiteful words spewed from my mouth and reverberated to my ears. Guide had found me, had brought me to his home. He could destroy the tunnels. Billy, Magdalena, Great-Grandma—their spirits had known about Galen and Guide. The Shadow World had betrayed me, the way it had on the night of the train wreck.

I collapsed on the bed and sobbed, my insides wringing themselves out. Was there no one left to trust in this world or the next? Another rush of tears wet my pillowcase. No, there was still someone. Galen. If only I knew where to find him.

•

A ghostly candle lamp illuminated the bedroom with a lavender hue and floated to rest on the chest of drawers. Guide's empty rocking chair tipped forward and backward on the floor, creaking. I smelled tobacco. Billy had come here to launch another scheme.

"Go away," I said.

I buried my face in a pillow and sniffled. The room's chill cut through my muslin nightgown. The creaking sound stopped. I raised my head.

Billy's translucent figure hovered in a standing position, his image gaining substance as he materialized. He wedged his thumbs into the front pockets of his denim trousers. Stains dotted his tawny suede vest.

"You wouldn't have believed us," Billy said. "The truth had to come from Guide."

"You could have tried to tell me," I snapped. "I nearly let him—"

"Nearly let him?" Billy belted out a round of coarse laughter. "I think you're confusing the horse with the saddle. You engraved the invitation. Guide just fondled the envelope."

"The bath was Magdalena's idea."

I jumped to my feet and launched my pillow in Billy's direction. He leaped aside. Couldn't I hit anything? I reached for another pillow. The muslin case smelled of Guide. I collapsed on the bed and wept, clutching the pillow and the smooth fabric of our silken quilt.

Billy moved to the bed and sat on the edge, an unlit cigar in his hand. He patted his vest pockets. One tobacco-stained finger scratched the dark stubble on his cheeks.

"What's your problem with Guide?" he said. "If your ancestors expected you to keep company with saints, you'd be sipping tea with Paul or Joan of Arc."

"I could have handled anything but murder," I said between sobs.

Billy unbuttoned his vest and dug out his match tin. He lit his cigar. Rings of gray smoke drifted across the room.

"You and I aren't so frigging clean. We didn't exactly ship those brake and enginemen to Acapulco." Billy's raised eyebrows were lopsided now, and his lips stretched into a grin, exposing his yellowed teeth. "Guide just did it one helluva lot more than the two of us, that's all."

I sat up straight. The night of the train wreck, I'd followed Billy's orders. He deserved most of the blame. I pulled the silken quilt around my shoulders and drew my knees close to my chest.

"That was different," I said.

"How so? Because only crew members were aboard and they were a bunch of bastards?" Billy puffed on his cigar. "Even bastards can change." He chuckled. "Well, sometimes."

Billy, without a hint of sympathy, tugged on a lock of my hair. The tip of his cigar glowed in the shadowy room, as crimson as fresh blood.

"Get used to the concept that you, me, and some lucky third party are going to demolish at least ten of the tunnels through the Tehachapis."

"Not him!"

I twisted around and flailed Billy with my fists. He vanished, cigar and all. Ten feet away, he reappeared and brushed off his shirt-sleeves. He straightened his vest.

"Mystic traveler girl, I think we need to review some basics. Your continued status as one of the living is tied to certain professional duties and obligations." He tightened the rawhide strand that bound his shoulder-length hair.

168

"We're going to heist an unmanned freight train and blast shut the tunnels. It's the best way to start correcting a lousy situation. And we need his help. Do I make myself clear?"

I draped Guide's pillow over the nightgown-covered caps of my bent knees and sobbed into its softness. I was miserable and Billy didn't understand. Again he sat on the edge of the bed. His form indented the mattress, as if he were alive. He offered me his ghostly handkerchief, the stained fabric like a gentle wisp of smoke.

"The Shadow World gives me grief, too," he said. "I'd like to take you to Galen, but can't until the train job's done."

He pulled his magic tobacco tin from his vest pocket and opened it in the palm of his hand. Spirals of fluorescent green mist curled upward, encircling his face.

"If you want to know the truth about Guide, dare to ask the mist."

Guide might have murdered a member of my own family. I couldn't bear that, couldn't ask the mist, at least, not right away. The fabric of Guide's quilt felt soft and expensive. The covering could have been a gift from Antonio, another disquieting possibility. However Guide might have sinned, Antonio was worse.

"Truth will show itself," Billy said, "even if you don't ask."

Billy thrust the magic airship tin toward me. Fiery pain tore through me and hit again. My skin burned all over, as if scraped raw and rubbed with cut lemons. I let the pain take me, carry and overwhelm me. So much better to hurt from magic than from the truth of life.

Guide's image appeared in miniature beside a tiny bathtub in the tin. He pointed a handgun into his own mouth. I screamed and bolted toward the bedroom door.

I never should have uttered those terrible words. The door catch jammed. I couldn't claw it open.

"Guide, stop," I shouted. "Put away the gun."

My fists hammered against the oak planks and iron hinges. The barricade stood fast. I hollered Guide's name over and over, then dropped to the cold tiles and wept. Billy knelt beside me, setting his magic tin on the floor. He wrapped the silken quilt around me and stroked my head.

"His expression. His eyes." Guide really loved me, was probably sorry for all the evil things he'd done. "Stop him, please."

"He has to stop himself."

Billy dispersed the green mist with a sharp puff. The next cloud billowed with purple hues. I hid my face in my aching hands. Wisdom and courage be damned. I couldn't look again. Billy clutched my hair, his grasp powerful enough to rip out the roots.

Purple smoke erupted to ruby red within the box. The image of a bloodied figure screamed, over and over. Assailants thudded rods against his bludgeoned flesh. I recoiled. Billy held me fast and yanked my hair hard.

"Find your Guide," he commanded.

I scanned the demonic faces, my heart thundering. I'd rather die than witness Guide's willing participation in this horror. Then I beheld a tattoo on the victim's shoulder. Guide's number. I slumped against the floor. The tin slammed shut.

On the pilgrimage two years ago, Guide had told me some odd things. The desert had eaten his name, he'd claimed. No place on earth was sealed with his name.

Billy rested one shoulder against the wall and extracted a railroader's watch from his vest. He checked the hour. As he pressed a small silver button, the timepiece chimed.

"They left him for dead," Billy said. "After all, that assault would have killed any normal man." The tune repeated. "He healed eventually, physically, at least." He dangled the watch from its chain and grinned. "Bunch of jackasses had no clue he'd been both built and born."

So that's what Guide had meant about the elixir and the fabric of his fetal form. Some sort of medicine or magic potion had made him physically different from other people. I let Billy cradle me against the soft mist of his chest. The aromas of chocolate and cactus flowers blended with that of burning tobacco. Inner strength returned, like feeling to numbed limbs.

"He refused to fire a prison train," Billy said. "Some of the condemned convicts were as young as you are. All innocent. A British warden threatened to shoot him. A fight happened. Guide got his hands on a crowbar and bashed in his opponent's skull. Then he ran like hell."

The aroma and taste of sweetened chocolate permeated my nose and tongue. Great-Grandma. Whoever Guide really was, whatever wretched deeds he had done, the ghastly beating had changed his character forever.

"Couldn't he have escaped both North and South California?" My own whisper seemed so distant. "You did."

"I wasn't property." Billy again wrapped the quilt around my shoulders. "Mendozas have a way of finding who they own."

I touched his rough, unshaven face, then his soft suede vest. How could a ghost hold me close and seem so real? I clasped his wrists.

"Am I property of the Shadow World's?"

"No. You're like a ray of mystic light from the Black Mountain, on loan to the world of life for a while."

"Will he pull the trigger?"

"I don't think so." Billy turned translucent. His illusion blended with the woven brown rug hanging on the wall. "Although you hurt him as much as his assailants did, in a way."

"What do I say to him?" More tears stung my sore eyes. "What do I say or do ever again?"

"If you care for him, both actions and words will come."

Billy left in a flamboyant manner—all blues and oranges, like an instant sunset. I edged into the corridor with the quilt and an unlit lamp. Once downstairs, I lay on the hard floor outside Guide's locked den. Each time I awakened, I pressed my ear to the carved door, listening for a snore, a cough, anything at all.

●

The grandfather clock in the hallway chimed four times. I arose then lit my hurricane lamp. My ears buzzed. No, they rang and buzzed. Icy tiles cramped my feet as I returned to the bedroom. I brushed then braided my hair, soon festooned its short black ropes with crimson birthday ribbons. I poured water from a blue ceramic pitcher into a matching washbowl. How soothing, the cool liquid I splashed upon my face.

An odd feeling brought a shudder, as if someone watched. I turned. Clockman stood facing me. Its leather hands clutched my corset. It must have taken the undergarment out of my clothes chest.

"Of all days," I said, "I'm not wearing that."

Of course, it neither heard nor understood my words. No machine had those abilities. Its innards were probably set in the corset lacing mode. Still, it pointed at the garment, then at me, as if it actually had a mind. Its fingertips tapped the corset's stiff front closure, stroked the drab linen concealing the thin steel bones. Maybe the strange things Clockman sometimes seemed to do weren't my imagination. If it had stepped toward me, I would have fled the room.

My toes caught in the strings of my drawers as I struggled to dress. I wobbled into my embroidered tea gown, tied the sash, then left the room. I could have sworn I heard a metallic groan. Could a spirit—good or evil—possess an automaton? Well, Guide's state of well-being concerned me far more.

Only the tick of the grandfather clock greeted me as I tiptoed by Guide's closed den. My stomach churned. Then came a familiar snore. Guide was alive. I pinched my lips together and continued toward the kitchen.

The tub sat empty on the portico. Guide must have bucketed it dry while I'd sobbed on our bed. So much water wasted. I scraped ashes from the cast-iron stove, then used fuel blocks and dry twigs to lay a fresh fire. The stove was warming and the tortillas ready to bake when Elena waddled into the kitchen.

"Gather the eggs first," I said, half-facing the stove to conceal my puffy eyes. "I'm doing the scrambling this morning, and I'll need extra time."

Elena pressed her warm palm to my forehead. She mumbled something about red eyes without fever and diseases of devils, then left with the wicker basket. Had she overheard the argument last night? When Elena returned, I accepted the eggs and smiled. Elena felt my cheeks with the back of one hand.

"I'll be with the goats," she said. Her long skirt rustled as she moved from the kitchen to the wash portico. "If you get dizzy, stay clear of the stove."

The porch door banged behind Elena. The tread of boots clicked on the entryway tiles. The front door creaked. Voices of two sleepy men converged and trailed into the courtyard. I whispered a prayer of thanks. The next move was mine.

The eggs, nine white and four brown, glared up from Elena's basket as if they were eyes. Thirteen was an ominous number. I smelled tobacco—Billy.

"Help me. I've never cracked eggs open before."

"You've watched Elena," Billy said, his shapeless glow yellow-brown.

"I've tried not to watch Elena." Billy knew how I felt about eggs. "If I find a developing embryo—"

"You won't," Billy said. "Just tap the middle of one against the edge of that bowl."

I did as instructed. Nothing happened. I tapped a little harder.

"You could break it faster by coughing," he quipped.

"Don't laugh at me." I whacked the egg against the pottery bowl. The shell imploded.

"Jesus, not that hard," Billy said.

I stamped my foot and sniffled, my fingers coated with egg white. I didn't want to serve the men scrambled eggs and shells. And Elena would return soon.

"Be my hands," I said. "Do what you did with the goat on the mountain."

"You mean, possess you?" Billy's spirit light flickered. "That's tricky business with people. It's one thing to tick and tock in your brain and another to be the frigging mainspring. This ain't the Black Mountain."

"I think Magdalena possessed me for a minute on the pilgrimage," I said, remembering the novice. "I was thinking about something she liked."

Billy's spirit light congealed into a ball. "All right, close your eyes. Concentrate on...well, I don't know. How about Scotch whisky?"

Scotch whisky. I drew in a deep breath. My mouth tasted of tobacco. I was becoming Billy.

Billy patted his pockets for matches. Not finding any, he splashed a jigger of brandy into a ceramic mug and downed the shot.

He tapped each egg against a pottery bowl and used his thumbs to pry open the cracked shell. Soon a dozen fat yolks glistened in a lake of albumin. He plopped in the broken one, strained of shell, then wiped his sticky fingers on his dress. As he reached for the wire whip, my hand stretched without his help. I breathed out his spirit.

"I love you," I whispered to Billy as the aroma of tobacco vanished.

The porch door squeaked. Elena carried a wooden bucket into the kitchen and set it by the sink. She eyed me in a strange way, then picked several goat hairs out of the milk. Elena peered into the egg bowl, arched her eyebrows, and nodded with approval. I minced a dried green chili. With luck, Elena wouldn't detect the smell of brandy on my breath.

"Please get me a jar of salsa from the pantry," I said. "A small one from last year. Habañero."

"Are you plotting murder?" Elena's upper lip twitched. "That batch was so hot it cooked itself."

Guide had done the murdering. I plotted reconciliation.

"The salsa, please."

•

Guide and Angel came to breakfast forty-five minutes later, without the usual morning banter. Guide sat at the oak table, folding and refolding his napkin until an old coffee stain no longer showed. He rubbed the back of one hand.

"Stains don't all wash out," I said, pouring coffee. "Your eyes look horrid. Didn't you sleep well?"

"Not really," he said, his voice soft and low.

"What a coincidence. I didn't either."

I plunked a small bowl of golden salsa by his plate, clamped my teeth together and smiled. His eyes widened, as if prepared to roll down the slope of his beak nose. He opened his mouth without speaking. Good. I served the warm tortillas on a flowered pottery platter.

"Take the three on top," I said to Guide, "the ones with no ugly spots. Don't be shy. I made plenty, a stack of seventeen."

He just sat there, his fingertips touching the edge of the breakfast table.

"Seventeen is a good number, no?" I plopped three tortillas onto his plate and carried the egg platter to the table. "Lots of things can come in seventeens—seventeen tortillas, seventeen chickens, seventeen ears of corn." I dumped a serving of eggs onto his tortillas. "Seventeen tunnels."

Guide cast his gaze low, breaths shallow. He obviously understood what I meant. Angel and Elena probably didn't. I served the others. Angel plunged his fork into a tuft of eggs.

"My, there's a little left," I said, still holding the platter. I scraped the eggs onto my own plate, hoped I wouldn't gag, then sat down at the table.

Guide coughed, as if food had gone down his windpipe. Angel froze, his fork poised in mid-air. He delivered his eggs to his whiskers rather than to his mouth. Elena slopped coffee and made no move to mop up the spill. I sprinkled goat's milk cheese onto my eggs then wrapped the mixture in a limp tortilla. After taking a generous bite, I chewed slowly and swallowed with an exaggerated gulp.

"An eighteen-year-old woman is different from one of seventeen," I said. "She sees the world in a different light." I turned toward Guide and flashed a quick smile. "An eighteen-year-old woman knows how to digest repulsive things."

The others sat still, like surprised moles stunned by bright sunshine. They must have thought I'd rather die than consume eggs.

"But you're not eating," I said to Guide. "Is my cooking too bland?"

I dribbled a few drops of the habañero salsa onto my own food. I bathed the eggs on Guide's plate with two generous tablespoonfuls. His facial coloration seemed odd. I pushed his plate closer. May Great-Grandma Zetta provide me the strength to continue. I licked the residual salsa from the teaspoon. My mouth burned, practically afire.

"Eat hearty," I said. "Pain purges many ills."

21. A Special Gift

ANGEL RUSHED INTO the morning room, his open mouth drawn into a small circle beneath his drooping mustache. Anxiety flickered within his dark pupils, and he clutched a folded piece of paper in his hand. Dirt caked his field boots. Angel rarely forgot to wipe his feet at the doorstep. Someone must have sent disturbing news. I clipped a thread and returned a torn pair of overalls to my sewing basket. I accepted the note. Eternal saints. Antonio requested the honor of my presence.

Freedom and new vulnerability. A cold, sick feeling hit me. Antonio found me appealing. I wasn't prepared to cope with him so soon after yesterday, despite my mission. I hurried into the kitchen and peered out the window, eyes still sore from too much crying the night before and not enough sleep. Men on horseback waited in the courtyard, guns strapped across their backs. The screen door to the portico squeaked. Guide entered the kitchen, holding my leather riding boots and felt top hat. His eyebrows scrunched, a sure sign of alarm.

"Must I go there today?" I brushed bits of sewing thread off of my five-gore skirt, then straightened the front of my jacket bodice. "I'm not dressed for riding."

"When a man of such power summons friends on good terms," Guide said, "they go immediately and without question." He twisted his earring.

I changed into my riding boots, tied on my hat with a veil. Guide ushered me through the courtyard toward the barn. Five or six of Antonio's men, dressed in work denims, lurked in my peripheral vision. Wide-brim sombreros shaded their heads. I would not ride astride and show my ruffled drawers to these brutes.

The crunch of dry grasses accompanied each footstep as I walked beside Guide. The gray barn and wire chicken coops drifted out of focus. Now those structures appeared doubled. This was not a good day to match wits with Antonio. An inappropriate comment might slip out and provoke his wrath. I unlatched Ibn Sina's stall and entered, finding comfort in the odors of horse and hay.

"What if one's not on good terms when Tony summons them?" I hoisted the blanket and side-saddle onto Ibn Sina's back, not sure I wanted a reply.

"Little difference," Guide said. "Except to carry a rosary." He touched my hand with his fingertips, as if he thought I'd rebuke any gesture of affection. "I'd accompany you, but I've not been invited."

"If something happens," I said, "I'm sorry about last night, the wretched things I yelled."

"Are you?" He lowered his gaze and fingered the hem of his blue flannel shirt.

I patted the stallion's withers, then fastened the leather girth strap, hunting for the words to convey my true feelings.

"I slept by the den and awakened over and over, listening for sounds." I brushed back loose strands of my hair. "I was so afraid."

"I meant it." Guide handed me a bridle. "The part about falling in love."

"If not for Galen." My words wilted before I could form them. "I'd still offer all."

Guide seemed to study my expression. His hazel eyes had no sparkle. They looked like they belonged to something dead. He kissed my forehead.

"It's not wise to keep Tony waiting. Or do anything to incur his displeasure."

I mounted my horse, praying in silence for Great-Grandpa's protection. Ibn Sina snorted as we approached the waiting escort. The stallion broke gait, whinnied and bared teeth.

•

Antonio greeted me in his library, his mustache and goatee trimmed and his narrow braids oiled. The neck of his white silk shirt hung open. His unbuttoned coat

178

revealed a patterned vest. Leather pants, the color of wet earth, hugged his flat stomach and conformed to the contours of his sturdy thighs. He bore no gun. Little relief that brought. His overall appearance made me uncomfortable, as if grave worms crawled down my spine.

The guards left the room. Antonio offered me a glass of wine. The diamond of whiskers between his lower lip and chin barely shifted position as he spoke. He didn't smile. I countered with a polite refusal, attempting to appear calm. He moved closer, smelling of leather.

"I do not care to drink a fine claret alone," he said.

Such an unpleasant edge to his voice. I tightened my stomach muscles. Guide owed substantial debts to this man, might even be in danger of losing his land. I mustn't create trouble.

"A small glass, then," I said. "For a small person."

He clapped his hands three times. A guard entered with an amber bottle and two crystal goblets. I feigned interest in one of the many shelves of thick and dusty books that lined an entire wall. Antonio was trying to intimidate me, the way he had the previous day. Guide had taught me how to handle wine or brandy. Things might turn out fine, if I controlled my fear. The guard poured red wine and left.

Antonio raised one glass in a toast then presented it to me. The onyx ring on his forefinger appeared identical to Guide's. Why? I sipped the claret. He tensed one hand into a fist when I wasn't drinking. Each time I swallowed, his hand relaxed. Yesterday, he'd mentioned being a good girl and doing as told.

"You may wonder why I invited you today." He refilled my empty goblet. "I have a gift, a special gift."

"Oh?"

I searched his icy expression for any hint of warmth. He raised his glass, prompting me to do the same. As I drank, the corners of his mouth curved down. Whatever he had to offer would not be welcome.

"Remove your bodice," he said.

"You mean..."

I tightened my hand around the goblet. I couldn't do such a thing. Not here. Not for him. There had to be a way to say no without sounding insulting. I thought to Magdalena and pleaded for advice.

"But you are shy, of course, a modest woman." Antonio took my wineglass and gestured toward the door. "My guards, they will assist you."

"I...I don't need help."

I fumbled with the top buttons on my jacket bodice, fastened below my throat. Yesterday, he'd believed I was Guide's woman. What had happened? Then I remembered the red, puffy eyes I'd faced in the mirror this morning. Tony suspected I'd fought with Guide. I didn't know why he'd sent for me, but he considered me available.

Antonio positioned his hands, ready to clap for the guards. I pictured their thick lips and burly bodies. Even Antonio would be better than that. I slipped off my long-sleeved bodice, exposing my silk camisole and undervest. God, another day I'd not worn a corset. Antonio's eyes surveyed me like those of a hungry vulture circling a fallen doe.

"Such a perfect body," he said, "even with those red, swollen eyes. A vision to stir any normal man." He stood beside a straight-backed oak chair, sipping wine. "Your Guide's quite fortunate." His glass clicked to rest on a polished rosewood table. He fondled the crystal stem. "Sit down."

I edged away from him, over red tiles toward the leather sofa. He frowned and tapped the top of the oak chair. I nodded and sat on the wooden seat. Antonio stroked my cheek. His large hand progressed across my throat to my shoulder.

"It would be a shame to mar such exquisite beauty," he said.

I clutched the smooth, curved side of the chair's seat and prayed to Magdalena for guidance. There had to be a way to escape and still remain in his good graces. Did Magdalena keep silent because she felt powerless, too?

"Things are right between you and Guide, are they not?" Antonio said.

"They're fine."

"Are you sure you give him no grief?" He touched one of my eyelids.

"Well, perhaps some, just a little." That had sounded wrong. "An occasional misunderstanding."

"Perhaps one last night?" He fingered the magic pendant between my breasts, his tongue rimming his upper lip.

"Perhaps, yes."

Antonio slid his hand along the outside of my camisole and massaged the top of my bosom. How dared he! The wrist on his free hand twisted twice with a quick, wide motion. The gleam of sharpened steel appeared from nowhere—a knife. He was going to cut me.

"No," I whispered. "Please."

"I love this man, Guide." He scowled, pressing his knife against my breast. "This little misunderstanding, it's settled, no?"

"It's settled," I said. "I swear."

"That's good." He released me and twisted his wrist again. The knife handle split open and closed around the blade, becoming a protective sheath. "Mendozas shouldn't quarrel with their own."

Too close. I expelled my breath, the meaning of his comment elusive. Guide and I had fought, but he wasn't a Mendoza any more than I was. He used that name on his papers because Mendozas had owned him.

Antonio returned the knife to his coat pocket. As his hands massaged my shoulders, I studied his onyx ring. A plain stone, this was, not like the carved hawk in the Cave of Light. Perhaps many Mendozas wore this simple type of stone. Guide had lied to me about other things. He might be a Mendoza, after all.

"Turn around and straddle the chair," Antonio said.

I obeyed and faced a massive brass-framed mirror. He curved my arms around the wooden back of the chair. His powerful hands kneaded my neck and progressed down my spine. At least he touched me in a civilized manner. Then his hand slid up my back and stroked my throat. Bile spewed from my stomach toward my mouth.

"I had unusual dreams this week," Antonio said. "In one, I stood on a dark mountain. There were two handsome young women—one with ivory skin and a long red mane flowing in the wind. The second was shorter, chestnut-skinned with ropy black braids. Not as pretty as you." He blew against the nape of my neck. His leather pants swished as he shifted. "My touch doesn't offend you, I trust."

"It's fine," I lied. The women in his dream might have been my ancestors. I needed to hear more.

"The redhead was willow thin," Antonio said. "She held a staff and reached outward to the sky and river. But the river and sky disobeyed. So she gave the rod to me. 'Only you can part the waters,' she said. 'Only you can make skies rain plagues.' They showed me visions, these women. I awakened quite cold."

The dream reminded me of the story of Moses. Moses had once committed murder, but God had chosen him to do great things. Then I recalled the strange message written by my once redheaded great-grandmother. *He who would piss on the babe in the bulrushes shall be made to part the Red Sea.* So that was the Shadow World's plan. They wanted to recruit Antonio, as well as Guide, to their cause.

"When I was young, I was not so superstitious," Antonio added. "I might have shrugged and said, how can the dead talk to the living in dreams? But I don't grow younger, and the dead have enough disdain for me already." His nails pressed against the soft flesh of my upper arms. "I've sent so many before their time."

The wet warmth of Antonio's tongue pressed behind my ear. His perfumed Macassar hair oil smelled of eucalyptus and mint. If only I could put on my bodice jacket and leave. Yet to gain his support, I needed to play his game. For then.

"When spirits visit for a chest-to-chest talk—a little persuasive chat—it's wise to pay heed," Antonio said. "They want me to help you, these women."

Antonio exhaled a gentle puff of breath into my ear. I tensed my arms around the chair. My ancestors should have enlisted the assistance of a decent Mendoza.

"Now, for that little gift." Antonio clapped his hands three times.

The sound of heavy footsteps led to the creak of the library door. The large mirror before me revealed the image of a guard in denims. He mustn't see the outline of my bosom. I pressed my chest against the carved chair back. The guard delivered a tray to a nearby table, then left. The pewter tray held small glass jars, towels, and a flat leather case.

"I'm going to give you a sort of picture." Antonio opened the case and transferred several needles to a bottle of clear fluid. "A nice little drawing under the skin, on the back of your left shoulder. Guide's number."

"Not a tattoo!"

"I could brand you, as we do horses." In the mirror, Antonio's thick lips formed a half-smile.

My throat tightened. Magdalena's voice cautioned me. It was a dangerous time to challenge this man. God, even a ghost feared him. My mouth went dry.

How could he behave this way and claim to love Guide?

Antonio exposed my shoulder and cleaned a patch of my skin with wet gauze smelling of alcohol. He dipped a needle into a jar, the dye as blue as a jaybird's feathers. I clutched the chair back and braced myself.

The first jab hit. I winced. I concentrated on the mirror, trying to become only an image that couldn't feel. The needle bit over and over, permitting little time for recovery. Tears trickled like salty rain down my cheeks.

"It's good when a couple wears the same number," Antonio said. "Obligations to each other are less easily cast aside. And it's good for identification. Sometimes a body is brought to me and the face is gone. The shoulder is always left if there's a tattoo. A courtesy."

He unscrewed the lid of a different jar, one containing a dye as crimson as fresh blood. I closed my eyes. How much more pain could I endure? My thoughts focused on Guide and Galen—both strong and stoic men. The needle grazed a nerve. I jerked and groaned. Fresh streams of tears wet my cheeks. He rubbed another patch of my skin with alcohol-soaked gauze.

"This train business," he said. "Dreams tell me Guide and you plan to embark on a dangerous journey. If returned to me, perhaps I may recognize only your tattoos." His image in the mirror frowned. "If Guide is brought to me that way, you had better be, too."

The backs of my hands tingled. So that was his meaning. He believed I could betray Guide. Antonio's needle pierced my skin. Then he stepped back, teeth clamped around the knuckle of his forefinger. He grabbed my left braid and twisted the rope of hair around his fist. I wanted to cry out but didn't dare.

"If you cross me," Antonio said, his every word precise and cold, "if he dies and you don't, I'll find you. My blade will cut you, piece by piece. Your breasts first. Then your face. If you're still alive after that, I'll keep slicing. All of your ancestors put together won't be able to save you. Do I make myself clear?"

Antonio's words twisted into me like knives rotated in raw wounds. His fingers, even his smooth silk shirt, seemed to burn into my skin. And the mirror. The man's reflection loomed dark and tall, so terrifying that his image almost had its own breath. My image receded and blurred, as if he'd extracted my soul from my body.

He steadied me against the chair, no longer tugging my braid. I must have wobbled to the side. He kissed the top of my head, then positioned a hand mirror behind my shoulder and a second before my face. The tattoo—the ugsome string of little red and blue numbers—could have filled the room.

"My art," he said. "Does it please Guide's rose?"

184

"Guide's rose?"

The previous night, Guide had compared me to a rose. Antonio really did know about the bath with Guide, the story of the garden caretaker, and the argument. There was only one way he could have gained such knowledge. The heat of anger flushed through me. My family had taken this monster to the threshold of the Black Mountain in his dreams and given him lurid visions of me. They were as ruthless as the Mendozas.

Then a dark thought stirred from the depths of my mind. I tried to push away that distant memory of Billy's self-introduction, but his words swelled like rice in a pot of boiling water.

"Just call me Billy," he'd said to me that night in the Shadow World.

He'd never told me his last name, only that it wasn't worth skimmed piss. In fact, the only ancestors who had provided their last names were on my father's side of the family. The name of my mother's house had never been divulged. Except, possibly, for a monogram, the "W" on the pendant from the Cave of Light. That magic pendant had protected me on the night of the train. Someday it would help me release my spirit from my body again.

An upside-down "W" was an "M."

I turned toward Antonio and gasped. A tingling sensation spread across the backs of my hands. Guide wasn't the Mendoza Antonio had referred to after he'd threatened me with his blade. I was.

Why hadn't my dead family told me?

Antonio retrieved my jacket bodice from the table. I extended one leaden arm to accept. He dropped the garment onto the floor, beyond my reach, then knelt by the front of the chair. He turned me to face him, his eyes glowering, dark and hungry pools. This man, a relative, had the connections to demolish the tunnels through the Tehachapi Mountains, maybe even to build a new asylum or prevent murderers from working in the old one. The Shadow World had dangled images of me, like bait, within his dreams. Spirits had offered me as a reward for his cooperation. Maybe even an easier time when the Guardians of the Portals judged his soul.

"Did I tell you Guide's real name?" Antonio said, his breath heavy. "He mentioned you once asked."

His lips brushed the silk camisole covering my bosom. I clutched the chair seat, unwanted stimulation blending with a rush of realizations. The deceased Mendozas must have been seeking some sort of absolution for prior family atrocities. Only living Mendozas could be their hands. If I rebelled now and Antonio killed me, my mission wouldn't happen. I inhaled, then purged a steady stream of air through my nose. An implied reward had been offered to me, too—Galen. If I refused to humor Antonio, my Mendoza ancestors would keep me and Galen apart until death. Or longer.

"Tell me Guide's name."

"Then press my head close, as you did with him." He guided my hands to the back of his head. His oiled braids slithered beneath my fingers.

Oh, to scream, to claw out his eyes and run. Instead, I sat, hardly breathing, as if I were made of living sandstone, and allowed his thick lips and heavy hands to use my breasts for pleasure. I retrieved memories of pain. The repetitive stabs of his tattoo needle. My muscle cramps on the pilgrimage to the River of Tears. My great-grandma's broken foot. Pain was my refuge.

"Guide's name," Antonio said, "is one you know well, I think." He stood and motioned for me to dress. "Graham Locke."

The name, another verbal kick in the gut, hit me hard. Eighteen years ago, Great-Grandma had fled an asylum train and carried me in a wicker basket through a rain-starved valley. Great-Grandma had used a drunken sot—Graham Locke—as a diversion to stop the train. He'd been fat and bald with ruddy cheeks.

"Guide doesn't resemble that man at all."

"Guide related your story to me." Antonio laughed and fingered the gold chain around his neck. "The drunk on the train with your great-grandmother wasn't Guide, just someone in my disfavor. That man wanted his family shielded from my wrath. We cut a deal. I arranged a switch of identities to protect Guide. That's why Guide's passport states he's a Mendoza." Antonio poured wine and prompted a toast. "Guide will arrive soon. Smile to put him at ease. We have many things to discuss—ammunition and papers of passage. My guards will escort you home after dinner."

A long-legged spider spun a web on the bookcase. I sipped my wine. Half of my ancestors were Mendozas. How repulsive, the childhood fantasy to meet my natural parents.

"You see this scar?" Antonio pointed to his wrist. "We're brothers in blood, your Guide and I. Of course, Juanita, he wouldn't have a scar. He self-heals in many ways. He was an experiment to overcome the aging process. The Mendozas searched for their own version of the fountain of youth. He was their only success, or, should I say, partial success. His hair's white, and the rest of him ages, too, yet quite slowly."

Antonio replenished the claret in my glass. I'd had way too much wine already and set the goblet on a small table.

"Guide was born one hundred years ago," he said. "How fortunate to be that age and appear so young, to still gain such sweet pleasure from sleeping next to you while guarding your virginity."

My tattooed shoulder throbbed. When would Guide arrive? I could almost see him facing me at Antonio's dinner table, forcing a smile and searching my eyes. Antonio was wretched. Guide had committed murder. I was a Mendoza. Too much had hit me. I needed solitude. Fresh air.

"Bring Ibn Sina to the courtyard," I said. "Now."

•

I clutched Guide's silken quilt and peered out of our bedroom window. Stars filled the sky, like jewels sewn on black velvet. On the pilgrimage to the River of Tears, I'd curled next to Guide and gazed at stars. I'd shared the beauty of night skies with Galen, too. Such innocent times.

My stomach gurgled. I should eat some dried fruit. Maybe Guide would bring me a fresh plum or two from Antonio's. My fingertips brushed my shoulder, still sore. Future encounters with that man would occur. Who would I be by the time I stopped the asylum trains, found Galen and rescued Carla?

I sat on the edge of Guide's bed and folded my hands in my lap. Galen might not be the same man I'd once known, and he might refuse to marry a Mendoza.

A horse whinnied, the sound too shrill to have come from the barn. Guide was home. I carried an oil lamp to the top of the staircase and waited. The front door creaked open.

"You shouldn't have left Tony's early," Guide said, his footsteps heavy on the wooden planking. His entire body sagged, as if age had conquered him in a single evening. "I needed to see you." He climbed the stairs to the second floor. "To know you were all right."

"I had to get out." I hadn't meant to worry him.

He led me into the bedroom. I undressed, wincing as fabric rubbed my sore shoulder, tears spilling down my cheeks. Guide helped me slip into a nightgown. He kissed my neck and the back of my hands—not in an aroused manner—as if to cleanse away the horrid happenings of that day. Yet he avoided the patch of red and blue numbers on the back of my left shoulder. The tattoo was Mendoza property.

I stretched out on the bed, bosom pressed against the mattress. He lay beside me. I closed my eyes. Caretaker and rose. A matched pair of numbers. Did Antonio watch us from the portal of the Black Mountain in his dreams? And what visions might the dead bring to Galen?

22. Of Plans and Eighty-Niners

THE GRANDFATHER CLOCK in the hallway chimed nine times. I unlocked Guide's den. The room was musty, and laced with odors of tools and oil. Guide had promised to return home from Antonio's by dusk. The two men plotted the sabotage of the Tehachapi tunnels. What kept him this time? I set my oil lantern on his littered workbench next to a box of Clockman's spare gears and a half-assembled miniature phosphor lamp. Then I sat in a high-backed wooden chair, facing bookshelves and padlocked gun cases—keys to knowledge and cold finality.

Three months had elapsed since Antonio had tattooed me. Thank God I'd not had to see him since that day. Mental images of his ugsome half-smile still plagued me. But Guide could take care of himself. Or could he? Something bad might have happened on his way home. I could ride to look for him, or wait an hour longer. I lit the candle lamp in the corridor and watched the minute hand advance.

A familiar creak joined the steady ticks of the clock. Guide must be home. I hurried toward the opening front door. His gait was unsteady.

"Bring dinner to my workbench," he said, breath strong with liquor. He fumbled his way out of his baggy, wool sack coat.

I'd never seen him this intoxicated. He was old enough to have better sense. And he should have known I'd worry. I brought food, long cold, to the den.

"You'll have to be on time for dinner tomorrow," I chided. "It's special—a chicken."

"Tony makes his own schedule." Seated, Guide wrapped a cold tortilla around a mound of rice, salsa and pasty beans. "You know that."

I let the comment pass and unbraided my hair. Something unpleasant must have happened today. I'd prod him for details in the morning. The tortilla broke as Guide ate, dumping salsa-soaked rice onto his plate. He shoveled the mess into his mouth using his fingers, then wiped his hands on his new hemp shirt.

"Antonio teaches you bad manners," I said. "Your napkin is over there."

"Shirts can be washed," he said, shrugging. "Bring some wine."

"You've had enough, I think." I dropped the linen napkin beside his plate. "I'll bring water."

"I didn't ask for water." He wiped his fingers on his shirt with a slow, methodical motion. "I said wine."

I knew I should keep my mouth shut. Guide didn't relish the many hours spent with Antonio. Maybe liquor helped him cope. Yet his authoritarian tone of voice irked me. I wasn't his servant. I grasped the ruffled skirt of my yellow dress and curtsied.

"I'll bring wine, Guide. Anything you say, Guide. Or perhaps I should call you Antonio."

Guide shoved back from his workbench and stood, toppling his wooden chair. He lunged in my direction. My cheek stung as his palm met my face. My long hair shifted across my eyes, like a curtain hit by wind. I teetered backward. How could he have slapped me? Then he raised his tensed arm and closed in on me, poised to strike with his full strength. His glare blazed with raw anger.

I shielded my face with my arms. I cried out, like a dying animal in pain. My companion and caretaker had turned into a stranger. I dropped to my knees and wept.

"Oh, God," Guide whispered. He sank to the tile beside me. "Juanita...I'm sorry."

His arms, then gentle, drew me against his chest and ushered me to a reclining position. He wrapped himself around me on the cool floor, begging for forgiveness, his body heavy and warm. I clung to him and sobbed. I shouldn't have provoked him. When I had, he should have vented his fury with words.

Guide kissed my eyelids and damp cheeks. He shifted to a sitting position, as if embarrassed he'd pressed his body against mine. His own eyes appeared clear and dry. Why hadn't he cried, too? Maybe the medicine or magical potion his mother had ingested influenced his actions—or maybe just the way he'd lived. We stood, separated by silence. I needed words.

"You should be proud of me," I said. I combed my hair with my fingers and straightened my ruffled dress. "I promised to help Elena pluck the chicken after breakfast. I'll stuff and cook it, too."

"You're quite the woman of eighteen."

He smiled and tugged a lock of my hair. Galen had done likewise with my long tresses. I touched my cheek, although the skin no longer burned from Guide's slap. Galen never would have struck a woman.

Guide walked over to the tallest gun case. The glass panels rattled as he unlocked and creaked open the doors. He extracted an ugly gray weapon, nearly the length of my arm, with a narrow, curved appendage protruding vertically from the middle of the barrel like the dorsal fin on a fish.

I closed my eyes. In my memory, a crimson stain spread on a green shirt. Checkpoint guards had shot the novice on the pilgrimage. His nails had dug into my palm as the healers had removed the bullet. The novice, sweet and kind, never would have hit me.

"This is called an eighty-niner," Guide said, "named for the year it was first manufactured in South California. Kick's softer than most, and it withstands a fair amount of abuse. I think you could manage it. If Billy helps, of course."

Guide offered me the eighty-niner. I didn't know much about guns nor wish to learn to use them. My arms remained pressed against my sides.

"We're going to steal a train," Guide said. "Railroaders won't just let us do that."

Guide placed the eighty-niner on the workbench. He set two pistols beside the weapon and demonstrated how to load them. Then he pointed his first and middle fingers into his mouth. His tongue made a soft clicking sound.

"If they catch us," he said.

I nodded. Our mission of sabotage was really going to happen and not two or three years in the future. Very soon. I was only eighteen years old. Responsibilities pounded my mind. Guide removed guns from the case, one by one, and inspected them.

"Your rifle has the simplest operation." He pointed to a lever behind the trigger. "Position one is the safety. Number two lets you fire once. Use number three when all hell pays a visit. One press of the trigger will fire a round from the magazine." His finger tapped the vertical appendage atop the barrel.

Guide pressed the butt of the rifle against his shoulder, pointing the business end toward a corner of the room. My memory of Antonio's knife against my bosom produced a deep internal shudder. Did use of any weapon facilitate abuse? Guide set down the rifle and returned to the tallest gun case.

"This is right for me, I think." Guide removed what appeared to be a heftier eighty-niner with two barrels and magazines, side-by-side and a couple of inches apart, but only one wooden stock and trigger. He took a deep breath. "I'll do everything I can to keep from taking lives."

I watched our shadows on the wall, shadows dwarfed in my imagination by those of guns. His best intentions would not buy our escape from the inevitable, and he knew it. The time would come when he—when I—would look into the eyes of another human being and fire. Even if Billy's ghost possessed me, pulled the trigger for me, I would have to shoulder the responsibility for murder, bear the eternal guilt.

No wonder Billy had told me I mustn't find Carla until the train job ended. I might emerge unfit to raise any child.

Guide offered me the eighty-niner a second time. He and Billy had run an asylum train. Billy's side of the family

192

wanted their honor restored. The honor of all people mattered to me and the Jame-Navarro ghosts. Both sets of ancestors had chosen me, a Mendoza, to put an end to the asylum trains and the murder of children and sick people. If I remained faithful to the Shadow World, spirits would help me complete our mission in the most compassionate way possible. Maybe I would only have to fire in self-defense.

Surely Carla's life depended upon my action. It was the least I could do.

I accepted the eighty-niner from Guide, careful to point it away from us both. I checked the safety setting.

"How do I sight a target?"

Guide explained. "You might not see your targets," he added, "only surmise their locations."

I nodded. What if I couldn't evaluate dangerous situations and respond fast enough? My inability might cause Guide's injury or death. Antonio would hunt me down. The gun in my arms grew heavy and cold.

He took the eighty-niner from me and put it away. The weight of the gun lingered, or perhaps, the weight of my obligations. The light from the oil lamp blazed with enhanced brightness. I could and would do my part. Juanita Elise Jame-Navarro-Mendoza had a mission and must come of age.

"Tony told me tonight where the explosives are waiting," Guide said. "In canisters down a dry well, maybe sixty to eighty feet, where the bore narrows. It'll be hell to get them up, but at least they're well hidden from the wrong eyes."

"How far from here?"

"Five days." He snapped shut the padlock on the gun case. "Maybe six, if it's up to us to commandeer a decent wagon."

Elena kept blue-and-white canisters in the kitchen. I'd never heard of using canisters for explosives. They had to be larger than ones for sugar, flour, or corn masa.

"The stuff's pretty powerful. Or, so Tony claims." Guide untied his bandanna and folded the cloth, then picked up the oil lamp. "Let's get some sleep, Juanita."

We walked to the outhouse together. Even on his own property, Guide worried about my safety after dark. I entered first. Strange, the way his presence on the other side of the weather-warped door no longer embarrassed me.

Tonight, shadows and hues of gold blended in an unusually complex way in the flickering light. The pungent odor of latrine clung to my nose and mouth. A far better smell, though, than that of death. Once outside, I filled my lungs with fresh air.

"Tony's men'll ride with us the first three days," Guide said when he rejoined me. "We'll be weaving through the mountains on our way to a safe house."

Soon, my boots and his crunched against fallen leaves and dry grasses on the path. I'd no desire to spend three days and nights with Antonio's thugs. My foot stubbed something hard. I half-stumbled and recovered. Guide's free arm, warm and strong, threaded around mine. I flinched. Couldn't help doing so after tonight's confrontation.

Still, I loved Guide. If only I could have both him and Galen with me forever, stop the asylum trains without taking more human lives. I glanced toward the heavens to seal my wish. No stars twinkled in the overcast sky.

23. Cookies and a Chest-to-Chest Talk

FOUR ARMED RIDERS approached Guide's estate. They led an unsaddled mule. I watched from the courtyard, my eighty-niner strapped across my back. This day had arrived so soon. Angel swung open the gate to receive Antonio's men. One rider, clean shaven, pulled a red bandanna from his shirt pocket. He mopped perspiration from his tanned neck and brow, his boots and denims soiled with ochre dust.

"Our horses need water," he called.

"Over here." I pointed toward a concrete watering trough.

The animals drank. Warm September sunshine baked the morning air. I passed a blue ceramic pitcher of lemonade to the men. The guards bore hard, but respectful, expressions on their faces. Perhaps they could be trusted to keep their hands to themselves. I had to be sure, though. The first leg of our journey, after we picked up supplies at Antonio's, would last three days. I retrieved a kitchen canister from behind a decorative shrub.

"I baked something special for all of you." I opened the pottery canister of heart-shaped cookies and inhaled the aroma of cinnamon in an exaggerated manner. "These are from an old family recipe."

The men gave me odd looks. Bodyguards and hired killers probably didn't expect cordial greetings. I took the cookie on top, then offered the rest to the riders.

"Some Mendoza women claim that these cookies bring good luck," I said. "Those who share them will never cross each other."

I bit into my cookie. The men grinned, exposing yellowed teeth as I chewed. One by one, they dipped their hands into the canister. A man with a black-and-silver ponytail dismounted, half of a cookie wedged between his teeth. Crumbs flecked his whiskered chin. He swallowed the rest of his cookie, then tipped his wide-brimmed hat.

"Some Mendoza men," he said, "claim that ill-fitting gunstraps bring bad luck."

He adjusted my straps, buckles, and quick release. Two of the riders gave him nods of approval. I thought I'd done a good enough job by myself. My cheeks warmed.

"I have a daughter your age," the man whispered. "She doesn't know what the blazes she's doing, either." He kissed my forehead. "Choose with great care who you will trust."

I studied his brown eyes, kind now, as Guide's usually were. Antonio had been angry the day he'd tattooed me. The sullen expressions of my escort that day had reflected his mood. These men behaved like ordinary people did. Today's visit with Antonio might turn out far better than I'd feared. I patted my skirt pocket. The small, flat tin inside contained a single heart-shaped cookie.

The clomp of hooves prompted me to turn. Guide approached, leading King Solomon and Ibn Sina. Elena waddled behind, two extra saddlebags draped over her wide shoulders. Guide slung the bags onto the pack mule. I looked back at the two-story adobe home I loved so well. I might never see this house again.

Elena pressed something into my palm—a rosary. Tears dampened the poor woman's eyes. Dear, sweet Elena. Angel and Elena didn't know the reason for this hasty departure. They worried Guide and I might be in Antonio's disfavor. I hung the rosary around my neck and bid goodbye.

I mounted Ibn Sina and sat straight in the saddle. A breeze called my name. Pungent aromas wafted to my nose—hot chocolate, cactus flowers and tobacco. The scent of lilacs trailed behind the others, the mysterious odor I'd noticed at the River of Tears. The Shadow World would ride with me today. My knees prompted the stallion to walk. I would not disappoint my family or myself.

The group passed through the gate and trotted for a while, then slowed at the familiar grove of eucalyptus, oak

196

and pine. Words swept through my mind like grains of sand carried by wind. Last night, I'd decided how I'd greet Antonio. Now those words seemed inappropriate and stale. He could be so wretched, yet I needed his continued support. What should I say to him or do? Magdalena slipped into my mind with a facetious laugh.

"The answer to your question, Juanita, should be obvious by now," the spirit said. "You're either going to outsmart Tony, or do anything he wants."

Ibn Sina's ears twitched. Great-Grandpa must have overheard. The horse stopped and pawed the ground. I leaned closer to its silver-gray mane. Magdalena knew a lot about getting her way with men. I whispered words of reassurance. Ibn Sina snorted hard. I jiggled the reins and coaxed the stallion to continue.

•

The entrance to Antonio's ranch came into view. The main house, with its spears of wrought iron guarding the doors and windows, appeared designed from bad dreams. Which window belonged to the library? To the bedroom? I could deal with removing my bodice for Antonio, but not more.

Antonio, wearing a fitted buckskin coat, waited for me and Guide in the courtyard. A new red bandanna, tied vaquero fashion, restrained his braided hair. No hat with goggles today. Grit dirtied the toes of his leather boots, but his denim pants were clean. He folded his arms against the front of his suede vest. He didn't look like a ruthless Mendoza.

Guide dismounted. Antonio embraced him, as if the two hadn't seen each other for years. I tightened my hands around Ibn Sina's reins. Antonio motioned to me with a broad sweep of his arm. I climbed down and strode with firm steps in his direction.

"You wear a gun and a rosary?" Antonio shook his head from side-to-side a few times, his smile warm and wide. "What sort of host do you think I am?" He gestured for a guard to take my eighty-niner, then turned toward Guide. "Go with my men. Choose spare mounts from my best unbranded stock. You'll spend the morning here and enjoy my hospitality. This afternoon—even tomorrow—will be soon enough to begin your long and dangerous journey."

Guide led King Solomon toward the stable. Antonio faced me and clasped his hands around mine. His lips parted in a narrow smile.

"We deal with each other again," he said.

I nodded. Would the words I'd rehearsed prompt him to disclose his intentions? My left hand fumbled in the pocket of my riding skirt and extracted the small flat tin.

"I have a gift for you," I said. "A special gift."

I opened the tin and revealed a single heart-shaped cookie, like the ones I'd offered to the men.

"This is from an old family recipe," I said. I stared directly into his deep brown eyes, which bore a puzzled expression. "Many Jame-Navarro women claim this type of cookie brings good luck. When two members of the same family have bad feelings between them, they share one of these to renew their mutual trust."

Antonio closed the tin. He slipped it into his vest pocket. His gaze shifted toward the ground.

"Then we will share this," he said. "Later."

I understood his meaning. I'd not enjoy his company today, but could win his support. I'd needed to know that.

He stretched his arm around my waist. We walked side-by-side toward the adobe mansion. Billy had likely traded his honor for money many years ago, in order to smuggle my great-uncle Juan to safety. I'd experienced his distress on the Black Mountain. A lesson given to me for good reason? May the Shadow World spare me from a similar fate.

We entered the cool house. A single man—unarmed—followed. Men with guns always followed Antonio. Something was wrong. I walked down a corridor, listening to the click of boots against the red tile floor. The guard opened the door to the library. I clenched my stomach muscles and entered the room.

A wooden chair sat in front of the brass-framed mirror, the seat directed away from the glass. The same as three months ago. I faced the mirror, straddled the chair, sat, then leaned forward against the straight back. The women of the house of Jame-Navarro were strong. Magdalena would make me even stronger. A glass pitcher of water and a small plate of sliced lemons rested on a nearby table. Antonio poured water into two large crystal goblets and added a garnish. The lemon wheels floated like dead fish in a poisoned pond.

"At least it's not wine," Magdalena said inside my mind. "God, look at that insect's eyes. He tastes you already."

I sipped water while Magdalena jabbered. Having my best friend here helped. Antonio stood behind me. His strong hands kneaded my neck and shoulders. He bent over and blew into my ear. I smelled the perfumed oil in his braids. If I concentrated on the bookshelves—on anything else—perhaps I wouldn't feel his touch.

"I've had strange dreams this week," Antonio said. "In them, you rode Ibn Sina through *bandido* country alone. A rider pursued you. You cried out for my help."

"It was only a dream," I said. "You've chosen good men to escort me and Guide. I'll be safe."

"Little rose." Antonio bent over and kissed the nape of my neck. "You understand nothing about this part of South California. British law reigns from Los Angeles to San Diego but not here. Only my finest men will escort you. Those who accompanied you this morning place too much value on the lives of strangers they meet on the road."

Antonio pressed his mouth against the side of my neck, his breath warm. What was he doing? He sucked my skin. The mirror revealed the bruise he'd left. I felt ashamed but didn't know why.

"This will be my special gift to you," he said, "to mark your body in this way." He dragged his thumb across my throat, as if feeling every contour. "Your escorts won't dare touch what they see is mine."

I wasn't his and never could be. He knew that. I'd keep a civil tongue, though, at least for then.

"Your thoughtfulness pleases me," I said, "but Guide and I will stand watch for each other at night. I'll be safe. Your marks aren't needed."

Antonio massaged my shoulders, this time from the front. He fingered one of the pleats on my cotton bodice. I refused to yield to him further without first attempting to reason. Provoking his anger, however, would be unwise. He unfastened one of my buttons. My hand tightened around the stem on my water goblet. Magdalena whispered encouragement and advice.

"This day is warm, Juanita," Antonio said. "Surely your many layers of outer clothing will induce another fainting spell."

"I think not," I replied.

Antonio played with the gold chain around his neck, his head tilted to one side.

"I have sealed two letters," he said. "My messenger will carry one of them soon. The first letter instructs a particular stationmaster to rearrange freight schedules, keep himself and his crews at home on a designated day. I request use of their roundhouse to relieve an untrustworthy man of his miserable life." His lips formed a lopsided half-smile. "The second letter warns that same stationmaster about pending sabotage."

Antonio took my water glass and set it on the nearby table. How could he send that second letter, after all the arrangements he and Guide had made? This had to be a bluff.

"Tony's threat's for real," Magdalena said inside my mind. "Let that cockroach decorate you or you might as well head back home." Her ghost made a strange sound, like she needed to breathe. "I'll give you strength, as best I can."

I stood, my lips pinched shut. I'd not let Antonio gloat over my defeat. Not today. Somehow, my hands removed my riding boots and outer garments. The ticks of the grandfather clock grew loud. I faced the mirror, my arms by my sides and eyes closed. If only my spirit could crawl inside that clock and hide.

Antonio sucked a mark on my neck, then unlaced my corset. He moved to my shoulders. His tongue licked me, like that of a deer seeking salt. He unbuttoned my camisole and moved down to my bosom, his lips and breath warm. That bastard! Magdalena's strength surged, and I didn't flinch.

Babies, poor men and women. Carla. They'd be safe once the tunnels came down. There was only one decent asylum and almshouse in North California, but Mendozas could change things for the better. Antonio knelt, untied the waist on my calf-length drawers, then gripped my hips. He pressed his mouth against my abdomen. Soon his tongue brushed a secret and sensitive place. God, I wanted to strangle him. Instead, I let the sound of the clock fill my mind, every tick bringing me closer to escape. Antonio moved behind me and worked his way upward. He spared my buttocks and legs, perhaps because I'd have to ride.

He finished, turned me around in front of the mirror. So many ugsome blotches marred my skin. How would I face Guide today? He would see—know—where Antonio had touched me. My toes rubbed against a crack in a floor tile. Guide's expression of helplessness would be far worse than anything Antonio could ever do.

"Little rose, I know you don't appreciate what I've done." He poured two fresh goblets of water, as if nothing of any consequence had occurred. "There are occasions when I must deal with certain unpleasantries. To take care of unpleasant tasks, one hires unpleasant men."

Antonio handed me a glass of water. He withdrew a folded knife from his pocket and turned it over in his hands—the butterfly knife he'd opened during my last visit. My body tensed.

"Such men use offensive language," Antonio said. "Occasionally they touch forbidden things. My rules, they're very clear, but men are men."

Antonio twisted his wrist. The knife case clinked and split lengthwise, exposing the gleaming blade. Another twist and the case pieces reunited to form the grip on the formidable weapon. I'd done as told. Why this? I inched backward, tying the waist string of my drawers. Was there a paperweight I could throw at him? If I could reach the door, Guide might hear me scream.

"Do you see what I mean?" Antonio laughed and withdrew the blade. "The clearest path from the world to the brain is through the eyes. Instruct with a graphic image, and the lesson stays. Ears are less reliable. Messages can go astray."

Two twists of Antonio's wrist returned the blade to its hiding spot inside the knife handle. He took a sip of water and prompted me to drink, too. The tang of lemon offered no refreshment. My legs felt as if they'd dissolve.

You know," he said, "once I ordered a man to give a special woman safe passage through South California. The message never made it from his ears to his brain. So I decided to instruct his companions in a more effective way. When a man's ears hear screams, the message is not so clear. Screams are made for many different reasons. When a man's eyes witness an offender's private parts amputated and shoved up the ass, the message is never misinterpreted."

The crack of glass against tile resonated. Why, I'd dropped the goblet. Stem and bowl had severed without shattering. In the mirror, the image of Antonio's leather boot nudged the broken goblet away from my stocking-feet. This man was worse than insane.

"Marking you with my kiss is for the graphic image," Antonio said. "Your escorts have witnessed what my wrath can do. You are under my protection now, as is your Guide. I once marked him, too."

"I don't believe this," I whispered. "No man—no devil—could be as evil as you."

Poor Guide. Dearest Guide. Only horrible circumstances would have forced him to yield in such a shameful way. Antonio had no right to mistreat him. The heat of anger pulsed through me. I faced Antonio with clenched fists and fury.

"It's bad enough that I can't find Galen," I yelled, "that I sleep with a murderer who's too honorable to make love to me. But you... Your heart pumps more cruelty than blood. My God. I'd choose Billy before you. And he prefers men and is dead."

I spat in Antonio's face. He grasped my wrists. I kicked and twisted, but couldn't wrench free. A bright glint arose in his eyes, an expression of pleasure. He enjoyed my struggle. My anger awakened his excitement.

Antonio used his full strength then. He pushed me downward. His hand clamped my mouth. Magdalena shouted escape instructions, but the heft of his body pinned me against the cold floor. His knee jammed into the crevice between my legs and forced them—and the crotch opening in my drawers—apart. His hardness pressed against me, first from beneath his clothes, then as flesh. I tried to twist, to flatten my hips against the floor. His first thrust missed. I knew the second one wouldn't.

I purchased all the leverage I could and wrenched to one side. Antonio wedged my arms against the tile. He forced his mouth on mine and quelled my scream. The strength of his hips immobilized my own. Was there any way to slam my knee into his crotch?

A faint, ghostly droning sound crept into the library. Surely I imagined the noise. No, a distant bagpipe wailed. A tartan light shimmered against the ceiling and wall. The glow had to be my ancestor, Ethan. High-pitched notes from a chanter joined the approaching background drone. Dear Ethan was here to help me. And he played his favorite tune, *Amazing Grace*.

Antonio's grip relaxed. He rolled off me, his face contorted and strange. He must have heard the bagpipes, too.

Ethan materialized all at once—eight feet tall, three feet wide, dressed in a kilt and little else. He hunched, arms spread in battle-ready position, his red hair and whiskers gleaming. His eyes blazed. Ethereal blood dripped from the dagger in his grasp. His body stank like putrid meat baking in summer sunshine. Ethan's ghost was the most wonderful thing I'd ever beheld.

Ethan lunged toward Antonio and cornered him against the wall. Antonio stuffed his man thing back into his jeans and fumbled to button the closure. Magdalena jabbered something unintelligible, but I already knew what must be done. Antonio had abused and humiliated me. Although I still needed his cooperation and support, the time for revenge had arrived. I retrieved Elena's rosary. I stepped in front of Antonio, stood on my toes, then sucked a little mark on his disgusting neck. He didn't budge.

"Did you know," I said, "Scotsmen were some of the fiercest soldiers ever? They piped as they marched into battle, and the smell of their sheepskin bags could be foul."

I unbuttoned the top of Antonio's shirt. My tongue curled against his exposed skin. I sucked again, then turned. Ethan's lips moved, yet I heard nothing. Perhaps he delivered a chest-to-chest talk, a little lesson about proper behavior, inappropriate for my ears to hear.

"Ear to brain, eye to brain," I said to Antonio. "Maybe even stink to brain. The Scots were formidable, and their message got through." I gazed upward at Antonio's horrified face and produced my sweetest smile. "They scared the shit out of their opponents."

That bulge in Antonio's vest pocket. I'd almost forgotten the tin I'd given him. I had power, if only for a limited time, and an opportunity to grate at his self-pride a little more. I extracted the box and replaced it with Elena's rosary. The heart-shaped cookie, baked to renew our mutual trust, had broken during our struggle. I nibbled on a piece and stuffed a different one into his mouth. He grimaced. The two of us chewed together, bathed in Ethan's tartan glow. The cookie tasted of sugar and cinnamon. It crumbled in my mouth, just the way I preferred.

"You're under my protection now," I said, and blew toward Antonio's ear. "If you send the correct letter to that stationmaster—"

"Put the rest of your clothes on," Antonio said. "Shut up and get the hell off my land." He sank to a sitting position on the floor, his back pressed into the corner. He covered his face with his palms. "Christ, I'll help you—to get dressed, to leave, to blow up a goddamned mountain. To do any frigging thing you please."

Anything? I delivered a salute of approval to Ethan and grinned.

"Let me tell you," I said, "about a toddler named Carla in an asylum."

24. Bruises

AS I STOOD by Ibn Sina in the courtyard, Antonio fastened a buckle on my gunstrap. He rested his palms on my shoulders. His mouth curved in a smile. A glint of satisfaction lay within his deep-set eyes, and no visible trace of his earlier terror remained. This man acted victorious, not vanquished. I peered around him at my eight escorts, armed and unshaven men, heavy-boned with meaty hands. Antonio could ill afford to reveal his fears or defeats to these men.

Oh, to escape his touch and the musky smell of his oiled braids forever. Dear Ethan, so protective and flamboyant in the library, had blazed to my rescue just in time. Spirits weren't permitted to walk the earth as they pleased. They needed special permission to materialize in their once-living form as if alive. Ethan probably faced some sort of reprimand, maybe even from God. What if he couldn't show himself that way again? Several bodyguards offered me polite nods. Any sign of Antonio's weakness could erode their sense of obligation, endanger me and Guide on our three-day journey. Plus Antonio had promised to write a letter on Carla's behalf. A chance existed he'd abide by his vow. I needed to act with care.

I let Antonio boost me into the saddle. He tilted his head and winked at me. His hand lingered upon my knee. If only I could spit in that disgusting face, jab his flat gut with my boot. I clasped my palm over his knuckles and forced a shy smile.

Surely my eyes would convey innocence, if I glanced toward Guide. Astride King Solomon, he turned away, his expression as blank as an unused sheet of paper. I knew the word filling his mind, the one burning inside Antonio's guards—harlot. Oh, how I wanted to scream, to let them all know my body remained pure. Instead, I slid Antonio's hand up to my lower thigh. The sun warmed my shoulders but not the chill in my soul.

"Perhaps we will meet again," Antonio said, his lopsided smile a warning sign, like the rattle of a coiled snake. "Go with God and our ancestors, Juanita Mendoza."

"That I will, my dear cousin." What scheme churned inside his brain?

I didn't know our true family relationship, nor, I suspected, did he. Odd, the way he'd referred to our joint ancestors a minute ago, not mine alone. He had enunciated each syllable of my name. Why?

"Protect this woman with your lives," Antonio called to his men, his fist clenched.

A guard mopped sweat from his scarred forehead. Another strapped a knife sheath above the top of his leather boot. Grime covered the denims, bandannas and sombreros of all eight bodyguards. They looked like vicious dogs waiting to be tossed raw meat.

My fingers touched the side of my neck. Antonio had branded me with his mouth for good reason. He should not have tried to force his way into me, though. That could not be forgiven.

Ibn Sina pawed the ground, as if impatient. I prompted the stallion with my knees. The group of riders moved forward. I'd explain the truth to Guide later. We would hold each other close, as always. The story of Ethan's ghost might even make him laugh.

How inappropriate to joke about near rape. I should be in a state of shock. Still, Antonio's desire had terrified me less than his knife had during our previous encounter. Perhaps shock would hit later.

The horses broke into a trot, the warm breeze refreshing against my face. Such bright sunlight. I adjusted my top hat and veil to protect my eyes.

Ethan and protecting—a thought surfaced, one that should have in Antonio's courtyard. Antonio had some knowledge of spiritualism and mystic traveling. He may have deduced what constraints bound Ethan. Thus the remark about meeting me again. Antonio planned to stalk me as he had others, strike when I was vulnerable and alone.

Had my natural mother ever been vulnerable and alone? The idea slid into my mind before I could shut it out. My own conception could have resulted from rape. Had my natural mother placed me on the train out of hate for my father?

•

The day's shadows lengthened. Hovels clustered in the distance, like an abandoned clutch of eggs. I rode with the men toward a town at the foot of a mountain.

A guard removed a brass spyglass from his saddlebag, then scanned what lay ahead. Our horses' hooves clomped against eroded land. Soon, the unmistakable stink of latrines hit my nose. This place didn't smell abandoned. A gray rat appeared from behind a heap of adobe rubble and scampered away.

People lived here. Where were they? Maybe they always hid from strangers.

The riders in front veered to the left. I followed. A woman in tatters scurried across the road ahead, a naked toddler clutched against one hip. Open sores dotted the woman's brown forearms. The people of Promise had been wealthy in comparison. I offered a silent prayer of healing. If only I could do more.

I halted with the others, looked and listened. A breeze rustled through the vegetation. Guide pointed toward an uneven street lined by the peeling wooden frames of dilapidated wagons and homes.

"I doubt the people here welcome uninvited guests," Guide said.

The people might outnumber us and have guns, too. And dusk neared. I pressed my knees against Ibn Sina's sides, anxious to find a safe place to camp for the night.

•

I helped the men set up camp by a cluster of oaks. It was my job to gather dry wood and build a small fire. Antonio's men drew lots for guard duty and agreed upon shifts. Guide took off for the bushes, a short-handled shovel in his grasp. I sat on the ground by Ibn Sina's saddle, waiting for his return. After draping a saddle blanket around my shoulders, I drew my knees toward my chest.

A guard with a skull-shaped tattoo on his forearm offered me a piece of hardtack. I accepted the dry biscuit and thanked him with a polite smile. The man stirred the adjacent fire with a long stick. His eyes seemed to track my every move. Not the eyes of a hero. I patted my neck, where Antonio had left a mark. The guard turned and walked away from me, as if my skin oozed poison.

Guide returned. We shared a strip of deer jerky and chose a place to sleep. I snuggled into the curve of his arm, hoping to inform him about Antonio's defeat. Ten feet away, two guards spoke in low voices. I stroked my neck in the darkness, over and over. Thank God, saints and ancestors for the protection of Guide and the guards' fear of Antonio Mendoza. I'd tell Guide about Antonio after the men left us at the safe house and could no longer eavesdrop.

•

Barbed wire fences lined the road as far as I could see. The safe house must be near. After three days of travel, much of it on mountain roads, a real bed would feel nice.

The estate, hundreds of acres, sprawled in a broad valley. Autumn clothed the distant hillsides in amber hues, and the sun hung low in a cloudless sky. Inside of the compound, date palms lined a gravel road. A grove of lemon trees smelled sweet.

As I rode toward the main house, I counted two dozen or so cottages beyond the stable and fields, plus three barn-like structures of sun-grayed wood. Red geraniums bordered a tidy green lawn in front of the predominant dwelling. The red tile roof had no obvious cracks and appeared new. This estate might be the place where Guide had once tended roses. So much beauty and luxury for so few to enjoy.

A whirlwind of stewards greeted our group in the circular brick courtyard. Ten clean-shaven guards flanked the stewards, eighty-niners slung across their backs. Guide glanced at me and pressed his finger against his lips. I nodded. He could do the talking. He dismounted and assisted me down from the saddle. The stewards ferried away our horses and other possessions. Two guards in work denims and black leather boots escorted me and Guide to an isolated adobe cottage, about a half-mile from the courtyard. The guards left.

I stepped into the cottage, which appeared to consist of one spacious room. A clear glass jug of red wine, a crystal brandy decanter, and a covered platter waited on a polished table near our bed. A steaming bath beckoned from the adjoining alcove, most of the porcelain tub tucked behind a hand-painted screen. The partition was gold with a border of poppies.

"Who owns this place?" I noticed two fresh oranges behind the decanter. "And what sort of host doesn't personally welcome his guests?"

"One who doesn't wish us to see him, or he us," Guide said.

I touched the side of the dome cover on the food platter. Warm. My empty stomach gurgled. I removed my dusty riding coat and sat on the firm bed. Best not to think about the identity of our host. I pulled off my boots and knit socks, then burrowed my sore feet into the luxurious pile of a tawny sheepskin rug. The tiles on the floor contained so many colors—green, orange, ochre and azure. I stretched, tempted to take a bite of dinner before washing.

"Where did these people get so much money?" I said.

"Two Mendoza brothers discovered gold in the Sacramento area," Guide said, "in 1826. They kept the strike secret for years, hoarding what they found. When others discovered gold as well, the Mendozas sold supplies to prospectors. They used their profits to acquire water rights, open land, and South California oil seeps."

Guide placed his visor and bandanna on a chest of drawers. He sat in a straight-backed chair and pulled off his dusty leather boots.

"The Yankees plotted to take California from Mexico. The British did, too. The Mendozas sold guns and purchased loyalties. Once California was stolen from Mexico and divided, the Americans encouraged Mexicans to leave the northern half of the state. The British welcomed the exiled labor force and honored their agreements with the Mendozas, although some looked for ways to eliminate the Mendoza family, one key member at a time."

No wonder Antonio and our current hosts employed so many bodyguards. And Billy had been right. The Mendozas did have enough influence and money to build a new asylum and improve the old one. All my living family lacked were compassion and motivation.

Guide set his boots by the bed, then disappeared into the alcove. I peered into a shallow closet and the drawers of a cedar-lined chest, all permeated with the aroma of dried spices and flowers.

"We should bathe." Guide stepped back into the main room, his shirt unbuttoned. "You can use the tub first."

I slipped out of my riding clothes, the fabric coated with road dust and ripe with sweat. Guide unlaced my corset. He stripped to his undershorts, then unbraided his white hair. I liked the look of his body—strong and firm. A mirror, three feet high in a brass frame, hung on the wall. I inspected my bruised skin and frowned. Some of the marks were in embarrassing locations. I'd not had the opportunity to talk to Guide in private since the episode in Antonio's library. Guide had stroked my bruised neck and flashed a hurt glance, but had asked no questions.

He peeled an orange. I untied the ribbons from my braids and used my fingers to comb my hair. I climbed into

the hot bath. Guide brought me the sectioned orange. He touched my hand.

"The bruises will be gone in a few more days," Guide said. "On the outside, at least."

I bit into the sweet fruit, again angered by Antonio's arrogance and cruelty. Juice spurted onto Guide's lower arm, producing a muddy streak. He needed to wash, too. I dislodged a bit of orange pulp from my eyetooth.

"Join me," I said. "This tub's big enough to float Noah's ark."

"Is it safe?" He smiled, just a little, a hint of uncertainty in his hazel eyes.

"Tony didn't do any real damage. I'm still your rose to guard." I lathered my arms with soap, then motioned to reassure him.

Guide removed his undershorts. He swished his foot in the water. The level crept high, almost cresting over the porcelain rim, as he lowered himself into the tub. I faced his back. A dozen moles studded his chestnut-colored skin. I soaped his shoulders, drawing little swirls with the suds. I needed to talk to Guide about a lot of things. Trains might be a good place to begin.

"When do we steal an engine?" I said. "Friday night after next?"

"That weekend's too soon. We'll need more time to get at the explosives. I'm not sure what we'll have to work with and how it's packaged." He splashed his face with water. "If it was stabilized enough to lower it down a well, I guess it's safe to raise."

We both turned around. I slipped the bar of soap over my shoulder. Guide's hands felt good against my bare back, although his touch didn't arouse my passion. I closed my eyes. Someday I'd lather Galen from his head to his toes.

"Tony did get you everywhere but the legs and rear padding." Guide touched my shoulders and lower back, as if counting. "And he left no bruise inside?"

I splashed water in his direction. I couldn't blame Guide for doubting me. I'd tell him about Ethan's ghost later. Conversation about such matters would feel less awkward after a glass of wine or brandy.

"We had a little chest-to-chest talk," I said. "Now tell me more about the explosives."

"A wagon's supposed to be arranged." Guide rinsed the soap off my back. "A team's another matter."

"We already have three horses besides Ibn Sina. My family will make them behave." I splashed more water in Guide's direction. "Just like they made Antonio behave."

"That's a feat no one else has ever managed."

"My great-great uncle isn't like anybody else." I cleared my throat. "You didn't finish what you were saying about the explosives."

"The stuff to rig the detonators are buried in a cemetery." Guide squeezed the washrag on my shoulders, dribbling warm water down the curves of my bosom. "Tony wanted to make you feel at home."

"What an insect," I said. "You saw my backside. He put a mark right above the...well, you know." I glanced down at the gray soapy scum in the water. I ought to say what was on my mind. "That time with you, did he put one there?"

Guide's silence answered my question. My prying probably embarrassed him. Best to drop the subject and get dressed. I climbed out of the tub. He followed. We wrapped ourselves in white towels. Guide poured claret into two stemmed glasses, then searched my eyes with a pained stare.

"Of which time do you inquire?" he said.

I opened my mouth but couldn't even gasp. A tingling sensation shot across the backs of my hands. How many times had Antonio shamed him, and in what other ways? Guide took a timid step toward me. I turned away and put on a white nightgown.

"Will we take the engine on a Friday night," I said, "or a Saturday?"

"Saturday night. When the crews have gone home or are drunk."

He gestured toward our dinner. I sat on a cane chair at the table and fingered the stem on my wineglass. Disquieting imagery welled inside my head. I took a sip of the claret. Did Guide prefer men? My betrothal to Galen might not be the real reason he'd never made love to me. I poked my fork at the meat and rice dish, finally taking a bite.

"Is this chicken?" I said. "It's stringy."

"Pork, I think."

"First it's eggs, then chicken." My fork clattered against the china plate. "Now a pig?"

"Wash it down if you have to." He poured more wine. "Food's going to get scarce soon enough." Guide raised his glass in a toast, an uncomfortable reminder of Antonio. "You can sleep it off tomorrow. Besides, this will be the last liquor either one of us'll touch before Mexico, assuming we get there alive. Rule number one of the sabotage game—keep a clear head or have it blown away."

Inside my mind, Magdalena groaned. Guide didn't have to remind us about her severed head. I nudged a clump of shredded pork to the side of my plate. The rice smelled of nutmeg, like one of Elena's desserts. I scooped some into my mouth.

I didn't have the faintest idea how to blow up a tunnel or drive a train. Billy would have to possess me, the way he had when I'd broken eggs into a bowl. Eggs. Guide was right about not wasting food. I nibbled on the pork, then downed the meat with a hefty swallow of wine. He should have trusted me, though, told me about him and Antonio.

Guide chewed a lump of pork and scraped the last grains of rice from his plate. The legs of his chair squeaked against the tile as he stood. He stepped behind me. The mirror beyond the table reflected our images. He massaged my shoulders, the way Antonio had done, his mouth curled in a lopsided smile. I gripped the edge of the table. Was I frightened or just overwhelmed?

"Everything is changing too fast," I said.

"You have to cope by faith," he said. "Without honor, we have nothing. Without faith, even less."

He bent over and blew into my ear. I jerked away from him. How dare he mock me with Antonio's sort of amorous innuendo? I stumbled from the chair and wheeled around to face Guide. He grasped my wrists, his jaw set firm. I tried to twist free. Locks of my damp hair tumbled across my face, then tossed in the opposite direction. I wrenched my arms downward, unable to break his hold. My wrists burned.

"Let me go," I said.

"Reassure me you didn't sell the treasure that could have been mine," Guide said, his voice cold and hard. "The one I didn't claim because of Galen."

Guide's face—the wrinkled brow, squinted eyes and beak nose framed by expressions of mixed anger and pain. I'd fought Antonio, not enticed him. I was innocent. Guide had no right to treat me like a slut.

"If you doubt me," I shouted, "finish the job Antonio started before a giant ghost changed his mind."

Guide released my wrists. I collapsed on the bed, tears stinging my eyes. My head pounded. My chest heaved with deep, heavy sobs. I'd not meant to hurt Guide by being alone with Antonio. If only I could have told him what had happened right away. I shivered, as if iced inside and out. Guide draped a dry towel across my back.

"Why does all this even matter?" I said. "If Tony had done it to me, would I be worth less than before?"

"No," Guide said. "But I would."

He walked around the screen to the alcove, probably to use the chamber pot. He was such a strange companion, this man who could strike me or consider me the worthy one. That painted border of orange poppies, vivid and neatly arranged—life ought to be as perfect as painted flowers on a screen.

"We really could use extra help to get the train," Guide said. "Tell Billy to bring a brakeman's ghost to signal when we couple the engine and tender to the rest of the train."

I tensed my stomach muscles. Courage—Guide had pulled his emotions together. Time for me to be strong and do the same. Sniffling, I sat on the edge of the mattress. A lace-trimmed handkerchief sat folded on the nightstand. I blew my nose.

"What's a tender?" I said.

"The car that supplies water and fuel to the locomotive. I won't need to see the signals, as long as you and Billy can." Guide, wearing a nightshirt, emerged from the alcove. "Three miles an hour is coupling speed. More than four's a collision. Not a good thing with a load of nitro, even if it's stabilized."

He cleared the dishes, then unrolled one of his charts on the table, talking about trains all the while. Boilers, air brakes, valves—I couldn't picture most of the things he described. He wasn't talking to me anyway, just at me.

"This is where we are now." Guide pointed to an insignificant spot in South California, near the irregular north-south border. "This is where we pick up the explosives. The detonators will be here." He tapped the chart. "And here's the trainyard."

"How long does it take to steal a train?"

"Depends," he said, shrugging his broad shoulders. "Billy and I will have to see what's available."

Guide delivered another monologue, this time about tunnels and explosives. Explosions had shattered my life on the night of the train wreck. Would I ever find Galen?

I traced my finger down the chart. The tunnels were marked, numbers one through seventeen. Guide had circled the ten most important ones to destroy.

He poured some brandy and swirled it in his glass. I fidgeted with the ribbon on my nightgown. Guide knew so much about trains, as did Billy. I kept thinking about the two of them and about Antonio. Then I remembered the night Guide had slapped my face.

"When you came home drunk and hit me," I said, "you'd let Tony use you like a woman." I focused on the floor tiles and counted colors. I raised my head. "Tell me you had no choice."

He ran his hand down the side of my neck. "Tell me you had no choice."

216

I cried, my tears as soft as the first hint of dew. Guide stretched his arms around me. Oh, to find comfort in his warmth. His callused fingers wiped the tears from my cheeks.

"I need to tell you some things," he said.

Guide gestured toward the bed. I sat on the mattress, bracing myself for what he might say. He unbuckled one of our saddlebags and withdrew a loop of wire cable and a bulky steel clasp, about four inches long. He opened and shut the catch, then set the equipment beside me.

"Down the well," he said, "where the explosives are. You're going to have to fasten these to the cable quickly, by feel alone." He smiled a thin smile. "So much of life must be addressed by feel alone."

I understood his meaning. I picked up the clasp but couldn't manipulate the stiff catch. He placed his hand over mine and guided my thumb. The catch opened.

"As you know," Guide said, "thugs left me in a pool of my own blood twenty-six years ago. A man I knew found me unconscious. He carried me by wagon to what is now Tony's ranch, then owned by his father, Gabriel Mendoza. Gabriel owed his life to me and sent for the physician in the nearest town. It took three years and all of the doctor's skill for me to heal."

Guide slipped a loop of cable through the catch. The metal snapped shut. His action seemed connected to his story.

"Gabriel could have a hard heart," Guide said, "colder than fish packed in snow. Tony, who I had mentored for years, reached out to me to survive."

Guide turned the clasp over and over in his hands. The steel cable rubbed against the inner edge of the catch with a metallic sound.

"Gabriel was assassinated," Guide said. "Tony and I continued to eat together. Often slept in the same room. When we traveled, we watched out for each other's safety. We were as close as two men who are not lovers could be.

Then something changed. Slowly, like steady drips of water erode a sandstone slab."

Guide offered the clasp to me. He prompted me to release the cable. I worked the stiff catch halfway open. The cable lodged in the steel jaw.

"Tony kept a mistress," Guide said, "a two-day ride away in North California. Another man got to her by force. Tony finally learned his identity and rode out on a manhunt alone. The night he returned, I saw both Gabriel and Satan in his eyes. He demanded I submit to him. I valued my life and obeyed. Then he cried."

I fingered the clasp and cable. In Antonio's grip, Guide and I were like that metal loop. Yet Guide sounded so calm. I could never possess that much self-control.

"I couldn't live at his ranch after that," Guide said. "He deeded me land. I hired out as a guide. When my money ran short, Tony paid the bills. Most of the rest you know."

Guide stood. He rolled up the chart. I hung the towels. Then he sat on a cane chair. His eyes glistened, wet with tears.

"That night, he wanted you. I was the next best thing. I had to talk about you, while he..." Guide closed his eyes and clenched both fists. "That was the first time I ever wanted to kill him. He knew it."

Guide rasped out half-sobs. I pressed close to him. Where was the hero who had rescued me from the desert? Fed me with a spoon and soothed away nightmares? Where was the foolish mystic traveler girl who'd believed that men, living or dead, could be perfect?

I stroked his white hair, damp from bathing. His chest heaved deep breaths. He fingered the gold chain around his neck. His breathing evened.

"Where did Billy and your great-uncle cross the border?" he said, like that had been our main topic of conversation.

"California to Baja."

"We may have to cross farther east."

Guide fluffed my pillow and dimmed the lamp. He climbed into bed. I wasn't ready for sleep. Would I ever lie

218

beside Galen at night? Even if I did, Galen might have changed in the last two years. Strife might fill our marriage as a result.

"If methane's seeping from the bore of that dry well," Guide said, "this could be the last real bed we share. If you're not asphyxiated first, we'll both be blown to kingdom come."

I sat on the edge of the mattress, my image in the mirror like that of a stranger. So much had happened in a single hour. I stretched out on my back beside Guide. He clasped my hand. During the weeks to come, what if I had to put the gun to both Guide's head and my own to avoid capture? There were fates far worse than methane in a well.

25. Baptism by Dry Well

BIRDS CHIRPED FROM a charred brick chimney. Insects buzzed among wild grasses and chaparral. I noticed no evidence of a well near the fire-ravaged house. I reined my horse to a stop behind Guide's still mount and again surveyed the flat landscape. Such a peaceful desolation. Disaster must have befallen years ago.

Guide checked a small map of upper South California. He dismounted near an oak snag and navigated an uneven dirt path. I did likewise, trailing fifteen feet behind him. The distant foothills appeared so harmless. Did British soldiers live there, or desperadoes? Maybe thieves already had found the well and explosives. Antonio's guards should have stuck around longer.

Guide turned and motioned for me to hurry, a grin plastered on his unshaven face. Near his feet, a glint of metal shone through sandy soil. The tap of his boot produced a hollow sound.

"The well's closing plate," Guide said.

"You're a human divining rod." I laughed. Maps and charts practically talked to Guide, the way water in the ground had spoken to Magdalena's husband Cole.

Guide scraped sandy soil off the plate with his boot. His brow furrowed now, like a field prepared for planting. Something worried him. I helped wiggle the weighty metal rectangle, even as rattlesnakes and black widow spiders crawled through my imagination. He lifted the plate with a grunt. A bevy of insects scurried from the underside of the metal. No widows, though.

I peered into the opening of the well, which was approximately four feet wide. Bricks formed the first section of the inner casing. Beyond that, shadowy hints of stone faded to blackness. My descent wouldn't be fun.

"How deep did you say this is?" I said. "Sixty to eighty feet?"

"The top section, yes. After it narrows, who knows? Someone tried to drill their failed water-well to find oil." Guide extracted a match tin from his pocket. "There's supposed to be a metal plate covering the lower drill hole, so you don't end up wedged in a pipe half-way to China." He slid open the tin and winked with a somber expression. "Mystic traveler girl, are you ready to face the Guardians of the Portals?"

A year ago, I'd described the rituals of mystic traveling to Guide. At the current moment, I didn't appreciate his flippant remark. Galen and Wei wouldn't have, either.

Guide suspended a lighted match over the well. What concentration of methane gas would trigger an explosion? I held my breath. The flame flickered for fifteen or twenty seconds.

"The match burns, but not the air," he said, as if he'd never been concerned. He tossed a pebble into the void. The stone produced a faint metallic clunk. Guide grinned and patted me on the rump. "Time to see how well the rest of Tony's instructions were followed. If the game's been played in our favor, the rig that lowered the canisters down this pit shouldn't be too far away."

•

Gravel along the inner wall of a cracked foundation veiled an eight-foot long cylindrical bundle. The package, rolled in a tarp, had to contain the rig. I hugged Guide. We clinked our canteens in a toast then kicked the ends and middle of the bulky package. No rattles of snakes. I helped maneuver the bundle into the wagon, tipping one end against the bed and inching the other high enough to slide into position. The process was reversed at the well site. Sweat trickled down my sides as I helped unwrap the rig. The work hadn't been easy.

"Er, this is very nice." I'd no idea how to assemble the jumble of equipment on the tarp. "Three metal poles, sort of stuck together at one end. Straps, ropes, dangling things, a lifetime supply of impossible-to-open clasps, a key to wind a giant clockman and two fishing reels big enough to catch Jonah's whale."

"It sets up as a tripod," Guide chided. "Like you might use to hang a pot over a fire."

He tossed me a jumble of straps and buckles. I rotated the harness in several directions, including inside out. The leather contraption wiggled its tentacles as I held it by a metal ring.

"How do I put this on?" I said.

"Over your clothes." Guide chuckled, the way Billy sometimes did. "I'm not Tony."

I hurled the harness toward him. Guide stepped aside, bellowing a hearty laugh. He removed his low top hat and made a sweeping gesture of apology. The warm breeze fluttered the rolled sleeves on his hemp shirt and locks of his white hair. I heaved a deep sigh and let him tug one of my braids. Guide had to cope with Antonio's unsavory personality in his own way.

We set up the tripod, unshaded from the late morning sun. My cotton blouse clung to the contours of my bosom. Sweat glistened on Guide's forehead and arms. The tripod teetered on rocky, uneven ground and required multiple adjustments. Guide threaded cables through pulleys and attached clasps to the free ends. He let out and retracted the cable twice. Finally, he stepped back, twisting his earring. I took several swallows of tepid water from my canteen. Would the rig hold together?

"Use these." Guide offered me a pair of leather gloves with the fingers cut away.

He secured the harness straps around my thighs, hips, shoulders and chest. Leather strips encased my torso, as if I'd been stuffed into a fishnet sack, and my head, arms and legs poked through the holes. Guide clamped the lifeline to the metal ring of my harness. The connection rubbed, just below the nape of my neck.

My heartbeats quickened. What if the pit swarmed with rats? If intruders attacked Guide and left me buried alive? And the connection to the lifeline might fail. If only I could double-check the hookup myself.

"I want to hear your lovely voice, Juanita," Guide said, "when you're working down there. Tell me you love me, loud and often. Once every minute or so, unless you're giving me information or directions." He kissed my forehead. "Tell me when your hands can touch the top canisters. I'll stop paying out your line and send down the tow. We'll raise them one at a time."

"All right." My throat tightened.

"The canisters have been secured shut with thin cable," Guide said. "Call 'up,' after you make each connection and 'down,' if you need more slack."

Guide reinspected the buckles and clasps. He tightened my chest strap, then again checked the lifeline.

"Try to stay calm," he said. "Unnecessary shouts and panic waste oxygen."

I sat on the edge of the well and gathered courage. Gravity had evoked terror the day I'd dangled from the cliff on the pilgrimage. Now the threat was entombment alive. *Mission and purpose.* I glanced up at Guide and fingered my magic pendant.

"A mystic dies," I whispered, "when the Shadow World decrees."

I slid into the well's maw, swaying. As I descended, the surrounding air grew damp and cool. Visibility diminished, as did the cranking sound of the hand winch. My flesh tingled, as if covered with spidery feet.

"Love you," I shouted toward the pool of daylight.

I drifted deeper and prayed for Billy's help. My lungs filled with air, yet felt empty and starved. Darkness encased me. My chest tightened. Then came the smell of tobacco. Saints and ancestors be praised.

"Quit with the jitters," Billy's voice said. "Shout to Guide or he'll haul you up."

I called to Guide. An eerie echo replied. I brushed against the rough well casing and pulled away. At least this wasn't the Cave of Light. No skeleton waited to dance on my back.

"Get ready to land," Billy said. "And always clip the clasp to the ends of the canisters. Those things are too long to raise sideways without a helluva lot of grief."

I gripped the straps on my harness. My boots contacted a hard, uneven surface. I knelt and shouted for the hoist cable. Billy rattled off more instructions.

I groped for the end of the nearest canister. The container lay on its side, its cold, metal surface gritty. The flat, circular end had a diameter twice the spread of my hand. I clutched the wrap cable and waited for Guide to lower the hoist cable. When the line arrived, my left hand grabbed the hoist clasp. My thumb pushed against a jammed release. I couldn't see to fix it. This wasn't going to work.

"Concentrate on Scotch whisky," Billy said.

I did as told, and Billy's spirit surged from my brain to my fingertips. I opened the clasp and snapped it around the wrap cable. When I let go, my hands moved by my own power.

"Up," I shouted. An echo answered.

I guided the bulky container's path until it ascended beyond my reach. The canister was approximately the length of my arm. I searched for the end of the next canister and waited for the hoist cable's return.

More connections followed. I didn't count the number. Guide would. I shouted to him again, hoping the canister tally neared thirty. The cable didn't move. An unmistakable retort penetrated the blackness and my being. Gunfire.

"Freeze," Billy said.

Good God! I clung to the cable. Guide shouted, but I couldn't decipher his words. Had he been shot?

"He's calling to you," Billy said. "Answer."

I looked upward. "You all right?"

Guide didn't answer, although the canister swayed and ascended toward the light. Something awful must have happened. My lungs struggled for air. Oxygen. The limited supply of oxygen. I had to calm down or risk losing consciousness. Several canisters later, I knelt on a flat surface, my hands feeling for additional containers. There weren't any.

The metal surface beneath me rocked. The closing plate Guide had mentioned. A narrow well bore lay hidden below. If the plate tipped, my body could become trapped.

"My turn to go up," I shouted.

I clutched the umbilical cable and listened to the faint crank of the winch. My fingertips pressed the coarse lifeline against my gloved palm. Darkness yielded to shadows as I ascended, the shadows to light, the touch of the well casing no less ominous than on descent.

Guide might be bleeding from a bullet wound. Maybe he'd killed someone's hired thug. I dangled and swayed, lungs fighting for fresh air. The sunlight's warmth reached my face and chest. Guide gripped my shoulders. My feet touched firm ground. My legs buckled. He was safe. So was I.

Guide freed me from the harness, his voice steady and calm, his fingers working fast. I sat on the hardpan, coughing, not even sure what he'd said. He offered me some water. Warm liquid trickled into my mouth, so cool and refreshing. Normal breaths returned.

"What happened?" I said. "I heard shots."

He wiggled aside on his knees and pointed toward a carcass, twenty feet away. "Rabid, I think."

The remains of a tawny cougar lay slumped near ragged clumps of grasses. Guide screwed the lid on the canteen, then dismantled the entry rig. Sweat dampened his brown arms.

"Gunfire has a habit of being heard, and men are curious by nature." He rolled the equipment in the tarp, taking no time to brush off loose dirt. "Let's get this back where we found it and clear out."

I scanned the hillside ruins and pictured Antonio's scowl. Unpleasant men would be the most curious of all.

26. The Cemetery

I DROVE THE open wagon. No sounds of a load shift. I glanced behind to confirm the lashing on the canvas tarp held fast. Dangerous, those canisters of explosives. At least they couldn't be seen. I gripped the reins of my two-horse team with both hands. Best to keep the pace slow.

Ibn Sina swished his silvery tail and nickered, likely talking to the other member of the wagon team, a bay mare possessed by somebody's distant cousin. The spare mount, a shirt-tail relative, trailed behind. Guide rode shotgun with his eighty-niner on Solomon, the gelding inhabited by the spirit of Great-Uncle Raúl. The few riders we passed skirted around us and made no move to initiate conversation. Just as well. How fortunate, the way my family—at least on my father's side—liked to stick together.

The cemetery, invaded by thick-bladed grasses and thorny chaparral, lay on a level stretch of ground, east of a sleepy village. A few oaks and pines bordered one side of the graveyard. On the opposite side, a modest adobe building rose from a patio of haphazard bricks. A creek ran forty to fifty feet behind the structure. What a blessing it still had water this time of year.

Ibn Sina gave no warning whinny. Guide and I explored the one unlocked room of the adobe. A collection of old candle-stubs littered an altar. Remnants of candle wax coated parts of the earthen floor. This was a chapel.

"They've got food in Sweet Springs," Guide said. "We'll need more tomorrow. And much of that creek's probably stagnant. We'll be low on iodine, too."

"I know, I know." I'd purchased a dozen tortillas from a home in the nearby village and gleaned local information.

I unharnessed the team so the horses could forage. Guide blocked the steel-rimmed wagon wheels with short lengths of chain. Dusk would come soon. Would darkness bring intruders? Regardless, I'd have to stay and guard the wagon tomorrow when he traveled to Sweet Springs. That town was inhabited by more than thugs or desperation, according to him, but not much more. An inner tingle shot across my shoulders. Better to focus on our project in the graveyard—finding the buried detonator caps.

"Let me take the lantern when it's good and dark," I said. "As soon as I find the right spot to dig, I'll signal and we'll switch."

Guide's eyebrows appeared as bushy as tree squirrels' tails. He disapproved, hardly a surprise. I slung a saddlebag over my shoulder and walked toward the chapel.

"A place of the dead," I added, "is a safe haven for a mystic."

We shared most of the remaining hardtack and some potable water, waiting for evening. The horses stayed nearby, their nickers soft and calm. All was well. The sun lingered in a ragged sky. Night's shroud finally arrived. Clouds hid the moon and most of the stars.

I set out on foot with an oil lamp, listened to the barks of a fox and followed Magdalena's lavender glow. Through the maze of headstones, I wove, many cracked and broken. A loose layer of weedless soil covered one plot. It appeared recently disturbed. When I found nothing more promising, I returned to the plot. Limp, pink trumpet flowers lay scattered on freshly turned earth. Magdalena materialized, translucent. She inspected her fingernails and picked burrs off her long tunic.

"These flowers haven't been here all that long." I nibbled on the tip of my thumbnail. "What if detonators aren't all that's buried?"

"So what?" Magdalena shrugged.

"A mystic can't desecrate a grave." I raised the lantern and glanced around. "Somebody's apt to get offended."

"A grave's a corpse, box, and earth." Magdalena played with a lock of her unbraided black hair, twisting it around her fingers. "Nobody on our side's going to get all that angry. Listen, not even someone who enjoys pain would lounge around inside a dead body. When I died, I was out before the first fly landed."

"Don't some Indian spirits stay with their bones?" The shaman's spirit in the Cave of Light had. I peered over the top of an adjacent headstone. "What if an Indian spirit of the bones is floating about to check on who comes to pay respects?"

"If anybody was here, I'd know," Magdalena said. "Now, go tell Guide where to dig, and we'll watch the wagon."

The lantern flame flickered. I adjusted the fuel pin. Magdalena could be mistaken. We should seek permission from the dead to dig. I knelt and straightened one of the wilted flowers. I shot a pleading look at Magdalena, who shimmered orange.

"Do you realize how many people die every day?" Magdalena said. "What am I supposed to say? Attention all spirits—any of you folks just get planted next to a stash of detonator caps and alarm clocks?"

The lantern flickered again. Magdalena headed in the direction of the old chapel. I tried to catch up without tripping. Spirits could drift in and out of all kinds of places. Maybe Magdalena could go see if the grave were real. She flashed deep purple at the suggestion.

"You're asking me to go curl around a bloated corpse? That's revolting. Don't you remember what it stunk like after the night of the train?"

"Please." I knelt in a patch of soft earth and raised my clasped hands. "I'd do the same for you."

Magdalena's image hovered, her arms folded and lips pursed. I could hear my own breathing.

"All right," she said. "But don't get the idea your judgement is always the best. For example, it was dangerous to tell Antonio about Carla."

"I'm sorry. I thought—" Oh, God. He might hurt the poor child to get even. How stupid I'd been.

"Wait here."

I lowered my eyelids. Inner darkness revealed a curly-haired little girl screaming for help. I opened my eyes fast. Magdalena was gone. May Carla stay safe. I returned to the gravesite. Clouds drifted apart. Moonlight peeked through. An olive green froth encased me.

"It's a grave of sorts." Magdalena materialized from the foam, looking like she'd bubbled her spirit through pond scum.

"Oh." I glanced at shadowy ground.

"Tell Guide to open the casket," Magdalena said. "Under no condition may he even consider looking in any of the ammo cases." She winced, pinched her nose shut, and flashed a disingenuous smile. "Some man in another's disfavor, I think. Lovingly shredded—well, most of him."

"Antonio's doing?" I clutched the lantern tighter. I didn't want the gruesome details.

"Even that pig has limits," Magdalena said. "But who knows?" She gestured for me to fetch Guide. "There's little down there left to desecrate. The damage has already been done."

Billy had said something disturbing to me over two years ago. If the Mendozas outsmarted me, I'd wish I'd fallen into a river canyon. Antonio had a score to settle with me. Soon others would, too. The explosives in the wagon were far more manageable than some members of my Mother's family.

27. Treacherous Trek

THE RISING SUN spread soft light inside the chapel. I remained curled up under my blanket, my cotton nightgown damp with sweat. Unknown dangers waited in Sweet Springs, the nearest town for replenishing our dwindling supplies of food and iodine. Billy had warned me during the night.

I rubbed my shoulders. Guide had already risen. Clad in knee-length underwear, he splashed water from a shallow metal bowl onto his face. New days brought new problems, ones water couldn't wash away.

I stood and stretched. A wagon full of explosives, if seen, could set off a flurry of rumors in town and attract British authorities. Leaving it unguarded here or elsewhere might cause trouble, too. Either Guide or I would have to travel alone by horseback to Sweet Springs.

Guide, a former bodyguard for the Mendoza family, would insist on trekking for the supplies. Still, I feared for his safety as much as for my own. Enough deaths—those from the night of the train wreck—weighed upon my conscience already. And I might have put Carla in even more danger. Such an inner shudder. Staying with the wagon wouldn't ensure my safety. Antonio, or someone worse, might show up and take advantage of the situation.

I needed clothing proper for the day ahead—my divided skirt and ankle-length pantaloons. A corset would squeeze, pinch and bring misery. Instead, I'd wear my heaviest undervest. I dressed, then pulled on my leather boots.

"I'm riding to Sweet Springs this morning." I splashed my face with water. "Alone."

"You'll do no such thing," Guide said, buttoning his vest.

He gripped my left wrist. The edges of his eyes crinkled.

"Let go of me," I said.

Guide freed me and stepped aside, his mouth open. He didn't know what to say. He plunged one arm, then the other, down the sleeves of his denim jacket. I braided my hair, searching for my own convincing words.

"Listen, a mystic doesn't die until the Shadow World decrees." I rolled my bedding. "If I go to town, I probably won't die. On the other hand, if you go...well, who knows? All our work will be for nothing."

Guide twisted his earring, his frown framed by unruly gray-and-white stubble, chaparral at the base of a beak-nose foothill. I brushed by him, determined, and whistled for Ibn Sina. I was perfectly capable of selecting our supplies. Guide could rig the explosive charges while I was gone. My main problem would be getting to the store and back.

I shuffled with the bulky saddle toward my horse. It was hot out here. In a couple of hours, perspiration would glue my undergarments to my skin. How soon would the weather turn cool?

Guide rigged King Solomon to be my packhorse. He shook loose dirt from my canvas riding jacket, a size too small for months and stiff from sweat and soil. I hated that thing.

"Eighty to ninety degrees by noon," I said. "The jacket stays here."

"You jiggle." He handed me the garment, his expression firm.

Warmth spread across my face. I couldn't help being a woman or disliking corsets. Guide buttoned the jacket. He slung my eighty-niner across my back, then adjusted the gunstrap and kissed the tip of my nose.

"Smile at no one," he said. "Ride angry."

I nodded. Too bad I hadn't practiced ruthless expressions in front of a mirror. Yet no scowl would discourage Antonio, if he waited along the way.

•

The trail to Sweet Springs wound through a chaparral-filled valley between amber hills. My legs hugged Ibn Sina's sides as I rode. My horse maintained a conservative but steady stride, ears pricked. He trotted as we passed a cluster of oak trees, turning his head, a wild look in his eyes. King Solomon matched the pace, moving abreast of the Arabian stallion. Hooves clomped against the packed earth. Despite the presence of my great-uncle and great-grandpa, I wasn't safe from harm.

The sun beat on my back. A pitcher of cold water, flavored with lemon slices, would taste so refreshing. Heat stroke would finish me unless I opened my jacket. My fingers fumbled with the buttons. Finally, I exhaled down the top of my exposed bodice. Anything to evaporate sweat and get cool.

With freedom, comes new vulnerability. There was that unwelcome thought again.

A cluster of hovels dotted the dusty landscape to my left. The structures weren't near the road. I scowled, nonetheless. Further down the trail, I took a swig of water from my canteen.

Water—a tender car on a train could hold as much as twenty-five thousand gallons, according to Guide. How long would it take for a person or windmill to pump that much water from a well? I adjusted my sombrero, its wide brim curled upward on the sides. No fancy top hat and veil today. I needed to look like a desperado.

Then Billy's denim-clad illusion, oily black hair tied back with a rawhide lace, materialized astride King Solomon. One of Billy's translucent hands grasped the reins. The other scratched his scalp. No doubt, the vision was only for my eyes.

"Tell me what you're going to do when we hit town," Billy said.

"Everything you told me in my dream."

"Remember," Billy said, "concentrate on Scotch whisky if things turn sour. I'll want a surefire way to zip into your engine room. Those words worked well before."

I nodded. With luck, he wouldn't have to possess me and use my body to kill. Billy bit off the tip of a fresh cigar. He struck a match on his airship tobacco tin and cupped his left hand to shield the flame.

"Before we reach town," he said, "take a few of those gold and silver coins out of your inside pockets." A rivulet of brown saliva trickled from the side of his mouth. "Keep that frigging jacket buttoned in public."

I turned away, muttering. Wretched jacket. I should've had a tiny bosom.

•

The general store in Sweet Springs, like many of the structures along the brick-cobbled main street, stood adjacent to a bar. Several men clad in faded shirts, vests and canvas trousers lounged on the portico of the tavern, their heads unruly jungles of hair. They leaned against a cracked adobe wall, passing a mug of beer and polluting the morning air with coarse laughter. I glared as if the lives of others meant nothing.

"Stay clear of that cantina," Billy's voice whispered from inside my mind.

I'd figured that out by myself. I dismounted between my horses and left them unhitched. Great-Grandpa and Great-Uncle would keep the animals from wandering. I tucked several empty canvas sacks under one arm and walked with determined strides toward the store. Whistles and catcalls burned into my ears. I clasped my gunstrap and maintained a belligerent facade.

The screen door to the grocer's creaked as I opened it, revealing a dim interior. Boxes, bottles and cans jammed floor-to-ceiling shelves. The aromas of spices, must, and stale cigarette smoke hung in the air. I stepped inside.

A man with a drooping mustache sat on a stool behind a long wooden counter. The countertop held a brass cash register, a platform balance scale, and several glass bread cases swarming inside with fat flies. I wouldn't be buying fresh bread or rolls in this store. Two small boys and a girl, the color of gingersnaps, sat playing cards on the floor in a corner. The boys' features resembled the man's. The girl had overlapping teeth and narrow eyes that made her appear sleepy. Carla would be even younger.

I had a gun. Why did there have to be children here? I snapped my fingers at the proprietor.

"I need seven pounds of hardtack, and I don't pay for maggots or weevils," I said. "One pound of jerky, deer or beef—no horse. Two pounds of dried fruit—whatever you have is fine, as long as it's not crawling. And iodine for treating wounds and bad water."

"Pick out what food pleases you." He motioned toward a row of wooden barrels. "I don't want no trouble."

I clenched my stomach muscles and opened the first barrel. Small insects peppered desiccated bread. Everything moved. Fewer bugs had congregated under the closing plate of the well. I evicted the unwelcome diners from several wheels of hardtack, then moved on to the dried meat. How would I tell one type of jerky from the next? I pried the lid off a thirty-gallon barrel.

"That's horse," Billy whispered.

Ugh! I advanced to the adjacent barrel. The dried meat inside looked odd, almost gray. At least it wasn't horse. I plunged my hand under the surface layer and took eight pieces. Then I scooped some dried dates out of a galvanized bucket.

I returned to the counter. The proprietor waited with a brown bottle of iodine. He placed each of my bags on one of the scale's platforms, adding brass weights to the other platform until the sides balanced.

"Ten shillings," he said. "I don't take no Yankee money."

"Tell him ten's too much," Billy said. "This crap's barely worth five. Plus he's charging you for the weight of your own bags."

I scowled and scratched my shoulder, my heart beating hard. How would the storekeeper react to confrontation? Whatever happened, I mustn't appear vulnerable or hurt the children.

"Five shillings or ten bullets. Deal?" I gestured toward the boy and girl. My stomach twisted.

The proprietor glanced around. He twitched one eye. The children in the corner stopped talking. The young girl's cards fluttered to the floor. The man's right hand edged toward the inner rim of the counter. Was his gun nearby? I stretched out my arm and clamped his wrist. My stare met his. He placed both of his hands on the counter, palms up.

"Five shillings are fine, woman," he said. "I made an honest mistake."

Thank God.

I slapped five silver coins onto the counter, then marched out as aggressively as I'd entered. I headed for the horses, feeling Billy's invisible presence. Lord of all, I hadn't backed out of the store. The man could have shot me from behind.

I scanned the street. Three thugs in overalls stepped out of the adjacent cantina. One staggered. Another's face bore a jagged scar. All carried two-barreled versions of eighty-niners across their backs. The men didn't look the sort to be intimidated by one woman or one gun. I stuffed supplies into King Solomon's saddlebags as fast as possible.

"Think Scotch whisky," Billy said. "We're shipping those bastards south in a pine box."

I understood his meaning but buckled shut the last saddlebag. All I wanted to do was mount Ibn Sina and flee. I glanced up, saw the approaching men, and reached for my horse's reins.

The thug with the scar shifted his rifle to his arms. Ibn Sina trumpeted and reared high. The man ducked, hit the ground, and rolled in the dust. The stallion reared again, legs boxing the air. Billy shouted. I jerked backward and my brain screamed *Scotch whisky*. Someone strong grabbed me from behind.

28. The Grandfather Clock

DARKNESS SURROUNDED ME. My spirit floated free. I was sure. A loud clicking sound—a steady tick—filled the air. Faint amber light glimmered from an unknown distant place. The aroma of tobacco grew strong.

"Billy? What's going on?"

The ticking sound grew louder. Two male voices jabbered a few sentences in Spanish. Ethan muttered an unintelligible reply. Where was I? Not outside the cantina.

My spirit drifted toward a dangling piece of metal. A counterweight. A long pendulum swung to and fro. I was in a grandfather clock. Something was terribly amiss.

Great-grandpa had once spent hours inside an alarm clock. When dead. That cantina—those thugs must have killed me. No, that didn't make sense. Or did it? The clock ticked.

Perhaps the Shadow World had found a more competent person to help Guide, one with more mechanical abilities. Oh, I'd never be reunited with Guide or Galen when alive, never raise a family—not even Carla. No more sunrises. No more raindrops dancing against my cheeks. I shimmered a color, caught flashes of washed-out blue. Ethan's plaid glow edged next to me and hovered.

"There ur worse places than a clock," he said, making an unconvincing attempt to sound cheerful. "Ye coods be in a bagpipe."

"Shut up, Eth," Billy muttered. The reek of cigars intensified. "I suppose this frigging thing chimes the hour."

I perched next to Billy's yellow-brown cloud of mist on the clock's escapement, half-expecting the toothed metal wheel to be uncomfortable, or at least to tickle. The lack of such sensations wasn't good.

"Am I dead?" I said. "I want the truth."

Billy retreated to the cabinet's baseboard. The clock ticked—not a tick-tock sound, just a tick.

"Juanita," Billy said, "you're being raped."

"Raped?" I whispered. "Oh, dear God!"

I hovered, my spirit shaking. The air around me chilled. Those wretched men, they were worse than Antonio. How would I tell Galen? Guide? My spirit congealed, like a wad of cold bean paste clinging to a spoon. I might get pregnant. Guide would blame himself. Galen wouldn't want me for his bride. And the baby... I uttered a long and mournful cry.

Ethan wafted beside me, stuttering a jumble of sympathetic words. Billy floated back up to the escapement and gathered his amorphous essence into a sitting position.

"If it makes you feel any better," Billy said, "Magdalena slammed one of the shits in the balls and nearly scratched his eyes out."

"What are you talking about?" I said.

"She's in yer body." Ethan sank downward as the pendulum sliced through his spirit. "So the rogues won't think ye're dead and dump ye down a dry well."

"That woman's one hot pepper," the ghost of a Navarro patriarch said. "It took three hombres to drag her into the cantina."

I bellowed a wail of mixed hurt and disbelief. How could the men in my family be so callous, leave Magdalena at the mercy of those brutes? Magdalena liked men to notice her, not rape her. I blazed a color, even several, as if I exploded in all directions. Thugs shredded my honor, and Magdalena was miserable. Didn't Billy and the others care?

"What sort of men are you?" I said. "Magdalena's my best friend. She once saved my life. Help her. Help both of us."

The patriarch dropped to the bottom corner of the clock case and hid behind a cobweb. Ethan transformed into a plaid see-through turnip. The clock ticked louder. The minute hand advanced several times.

"Rape—*violar*," the patriarch said in a timid voice. "Pardon me, but I can't believe I've forgotten. Is that an irregular verb?"

"No," another male voice said. "I think it's pretty common."

"This is no time for bad jokes," I snapped. That clod of a spirit had to be a Mendoza. "Do something to stop those men."

I again vented my fury, then sulked in an upper corner of the case. Ethan neared me, extending a few fingers of ectoplasm, as if tiptoeing up creaky stairs at midnight.

"For Pete's sake," Billy muttered, "we're doing what we can, all right? We've already been stretching rules like they were elastic. Ethan's on God's list of shit-duty for the next thousand years." Billy made a guttural noise. "Javier got Ibn Sina to trample the bartender before the son-of-a-bitch could unbutton his trousers. They smashed the house stash of booze in the process."

The steady tick of the clock triggered the memory of Antonio's touch. I'd wanted to hide in a clock that day he'd bruised my skin. I'd not wanted to feel what was being done to me. This grandfather clock protected me from horrors far worse than Antonio's sucking kisses. Maybe I'd been unfairly harsh to Billy and the other family spirits.

I shrank into an innocuous sphere. A disturbing compulsion spread throughout my being. I wouldn't be in this predicament if I'd let Billy possess me. Nor would Magdalena.

I knew I blazed an ugsome color. My world had turned all upside down and inside out. Ethan encircled me, the contours of his spirit shaped like two arms.

"Ye know, we ought t' play a round of cards," he said. "A pinochle game gives minds something more constructive to do than bauchling or revenge." He patted me and motioned to Billy.

"You've got to materialize in human form to play cards," Billy said. "There's not enough room."

"We coods be the size of wee faeries," Ethan said and assumed the tiny shape of a scruffy-haired gnome with dragonfly wings. "The lassie can keep score."

Billy materialized in miniature, balanced on the escapement, and fished out a deck of cards.

"I'm being raped—ruined—and this is all the great Billy Mendoza can think of to do?"

Billy shrugged and searched the pockets of his denim jacket. The Mendoza clod slicked back his thinning hair with ethereal spit. The patriarch pulled up an imaginary chair and sat down by the illusion of a small square table. Ethan, now dressed in a kilt and a fringed buckskin shirt, stroked his bushy red beard and sat cross-legged in the air. He flapped his wings and looked ridiculous.

The men of my family were crazy. They meant well, but were nuts. My soul wafted under the translucent table. The shuffle of cards blended with the ticks of the clock.

"You're not even going to answer me, are you?" I said. "This really is all you can think of to do."

My poor body. Did the men hit me as well as rape me?

"Don't worry about the marriage and purity thing." Billy dealt the cards and turned one up. "If Galen gives you any trouble, I'll arrange a chest-to-chest talk."

"You'll do no such thing," I said.

God, I'd die of embarrassment if Billy ever materialized between me and Galen in bed or elsewhere. My spirit shot upward and flashed colors above the table.

"Carumba," the patriarch said to Billy, "just give'm a wet dream." He studied the cards in his hand. "Threaten to make Galen prefer men if he doesn't marry Juanita."

"Don't you dare," I said.

"Ye canna expect Galen to fall for such a rabble o' nonsense," Ethan said. He fingered four cards, then melded only two on the table. "Men who want men gie born that way. Weren't ye born that way, Billy?"

I floated above the others. What sort of stupid plan was this? Besides, Galen should marry me because he wanted to, not because ghosts coerced him.

"All this is a quare gunk, but ye're bonnie still." Ethan stuck his head down through the middle of the table, like he'd forgotten I'd moved. "And Galen loves ye. The night o' the train—when that poor man nae coods find ye..."

The talk about Galen's feelings struck me in an odd way. The train wreck had happened so long ago. Since then, Guide had entered my life and affection. His rebuke would be as painful to bear as Galen's.

A muffled rumbling came. Something was happening. Billy slapped an ace from each suit on the imaginary table. It and the chairs vanished, cards and all, leaving all four ghosts sitting on air.

"The cavalry's arrived," Billy said.

"Javier and Raúl went to recruit a team," Ethan said as he turned toward me, "huge as Clydesdales and hitched to a beer wain." His scruffy face beamed. "This place is about to turn more blooding than the Battle of Culloden. Ye can escape awa in the bedlam."

Ethan fluttered his dragonfly wings and sputtered out a string of instructions, his dialect thicker than smoke in a burning room. I deciphered his intent. He wanted Billy to possess me until I cleared town. The ticks of the clock echoed around me. My words of agreement slipped out with ease.

"The bastards that got to you won't give us much grief," Billy said. "The beer wagon just busted through the doors and kegs are flying. On the off chance they interfere, we'd be doing them a favor, planting nice clean bullets between the eyes. By tomorrow morning, Tony'll order them filleted."

Antonio had no knowledge of all this. What did Billy mean? *Oh, no!*

"Don't you dare give Antonio a dream," I said to Billy. He mustn't humiliate me in that way.

We drifted through a dark corridor toward daylight. The hallway echoed with hoof beats, swearing and sounds of shattering glass. I floated faster. My body, wherever it was, needed to draw me back inside. The stench of vomit, booze and blood permeated the surrounding air.

"After you blow up the tunnels," Billy said, "your life and Guide's won't be worth fried shit. Not on this side of the Mexican border." His voice grew distant. "A dream will remind Tony of his promises and obligations."

Instruct with the graphic image. Antonio had said that. I'd been defiled today. Tomorrow he'd seal a death contract with drops of his own blood. So be it. My attackers deserved to be sliced into pieces until they died.

No, wait. Papa had claimed even railroad men had value to their families. Mama had always taught me to forgive. Who or what had I become?

The clock ticked. I shuddered. I'd crossed the bridge away from innocence. In the world of life, time moved in one direction.

29. The Cleansing

I HAD NO NEED to explain my tardy arrival or my ripped riding skirt and trousers, held together with a clasp pin and knots. Guide knew why I reeked of booze, urine, and things more unsavory. I could tell. He stood by the chapel with a lantern, a pained expression contorting his stubbled face. His hazel eyes, clear and dry in the amber lamplight, stared directly into my own, as if he wanted to cry but had used up his tears long ago.

I shifted to dismount Ibn Sina and winced, my inner thighs—and higher—sore. How had I managed to ride for five miles? My rear end hurt from the inside, a burning sensation. Someone must have done it to me as if I were Billy.

Guide set his lantern on the ground, then peeled the rifle off my back. He eased me from the horse and carried me in his arms. His sweat-soiled denims and bandanna smelled so good. I let the odors perfuse me. I drank them in, the way a person rescued from the desert might gulp water. Thank God I was here, safe. For then.

The aroma of burning wood mingled with the cool night breeze inside the shabby chapel. Near a paneless window, a bed of coals glowed red under a blackened pot. Guide lowered me onto the earthen floor, away from the path of potential smoke. He brought the lantern, a wash basin and some rags.

"I'm going to have to look at you to do this," he said. He scratched the side of his beak nose, then twisted his gold earring. "Do you understand?"

The foul smell of my body left no doubt what had to be done. But I didn't want Guide to see the evidence of my shame. His company was precious, though. I nodded and unbuttoned my floppy denim overshirt, the garment King

242

Solomon had snatched from a clothesline this afternoon. Guide helped pull off my riding boots. He stripped away the remainder of my tattered clothing. He spread a canvas tarp on the floor. I felt both close to him and distant, childlike yet old.

Guide sponged my arms and breasts with warm, soapy water. Valuable boiled water—it should have been used for drinking. He'd cleansed me with his kisses after Antonio had tattooed my shoulder, had rinsed me with his tears after Antonio had bruised my skin. I listened to the dribbling sound of water being squeezed from a washrag. The damp cloth stroked my stomach, then daubed tender flesh. Another splash. More dribbles. I closed my eyes. A coyote howled from some distant place, as if nothing in the world had changed.

"Turn over," Guide said, "while I get fresh water."

I rolled onto a dry section of the tarp. I wished Guide would say more, yet was glad he hadn't. Words could wait until another time. He sponged my backside, then changed the water and repeated the process. He dripped iodine and alcohol onto a square of gauze.

"This will sting," he said.

I winced when he pressed the gauze between my buttocks. Another wave of shame spread through me, like flames in a box of tinder. A rush of tears overflowed my eyes and kept traveling. Guide upended the blackened cook pot and splashed the last of the hot water into the basin. He mixed in some cold water and swished a sprig of greenery in the liquid. A faint aroma of mint wafted to my nose.

"For your hair." Guide smiled and cast his glance toward the corner of the room where the chipped pitcher sat.

I sniffled, helped him untwine my shoulder-length braids. I knelt and bent over, letting my loose locks tumble into the water. Then, draped with a wool blanket, I lay on my back. The comb in Guide's grasp teased snarls from my wet tresses. He'd untangled my matted hair before, on the pilgrimage to the River of Tears. So long ago.

I gazed up at an open beam in the ceiling. The wood appeared charred in the diffuse lampglow, spoiled. A memory drifted through my mind. After Mama had died, I'd helped the other women of Promise clean her corpse with sand. Isobel, the nurse, had brushed Mama's crowning glory until it had gleamed like polished onyx in sunlight. The ritual had been one of communal grieving.

I felt the itch of wool against my bare skin, the gentle tug of Guide's hands on my hair. He hummed a melancholy tune and was so careful not to hurt me. How could I ever leave him, give him up for Galen? The lantern cast our shadows on the adobe wall. I whispered a chant.

Journal of the Train, Year 1896

30. Reunion in the Roundhouse

AN EERIE QUIETNESS blanketed this edge of Brigand's Bend. A bit northwest of Bakersfield. British territory, it was. I leaned back against the wagon seat, my team of horses already reined to a halt. Ten feet away, Guide shifted astride King Solomon, his jaws set tight. No doubt he surveyed the surrounding brick courtyards and the low, adobe buildings they adjoined. I fidgeted with the buttons on my embroidered blouse. Guide had said little since my rape six days ago. He probably blamed himself.

I turned toward the nearby road wrinkled with dry ruts. A trainyard and terminal sat on the road's far side, an eighth of a mile to the west. Rangy manzanita flanked the one-story terminal, a wooden structure with faded green trim. Guide would scout the station and yard while I watched the wagon. Then we would steal a train and destroy ten Tehachapi tunnels.

I crossed my arms, wrists marred with yellow-blue blotches, against my chest. My attackers must have gripped me hard. If only the late-afternoon sunlight could cleanse my skin and soul. A muscle twinged below my waistline. I ought to change my pad soon, although this period was very light. I bowed my head. At least I wasn't pregnant.

Guide dismounted, the long sleeves of his denim shirt rippling in the late afternoon wind. Air currents played with the bottom cuffs of his striped bib-overalls, slate blue-and-white and layered with the dust of travel. He kept looking at the terminal. Had Antonio cleared out the building as promised? A kept promise might also mean he'd written that letter to protect Carla.

"If you hear gunfire when I'm in the terminal," Guide said, "don't investigate unless you're Billy."

"I won't make that mistake again."

Ibn Sina nickered, projecting Great-Grandpa's sympathy. I climbed down from the wagon and patted the stallion's warm neck. Guide put on his railroader's cap and tucked his goggles into one of his pockets.

"You were lucky," Guide said. He looked away, facing the distant amber hills. "Those men could have smashed in your face or slit you to ribbons."

What had happened was bad enough. I didn't need details about anything worse. I offered Guide a drink of water. His sun-bronzed hand accepted the metal canteen. My arm remained extended, holding only air as he drank. He brushed my fingers with his lips—so politely—and returned the canteen.

Guide ought to rub my shoulders or kiss my nose, make me feel like nothing between us had changed. Until six days ago, I'd been an unbruised rose. Now I felt like a shunned and trampled weed. He unstrapped his twin-barreled eighty-niner and wedged the butt end under his right arm.

"How does it happen," he said, "the transition to Billy?"

"When he says it's the right time and I smell tobacco, I concentrate on the words *Scotch whisky*. It's a little tricky for him to take over, because my own spirit stays inside me."

I smiled, rocking a loose brick on the patio with the toe of my boot. Perhaps Guide would respond to my smile. His left hand rummaged through a leather saddlebag. He stuffed a small wrench and a pair of pliers into the pockets of his overalls, his facial expression as cold as snowmelt. I counted slivers of broken brown glass on the ground. Was I considered damaged goods?

"Will your thoughts be only Billy's," Guide said, "or a blend?"

"Mostly his," I said, "as if almost all the real me got pushed into a drawer of my brain." I played with the tufted end of one braid, trying to maintain composure. "I'll be Billy and answer to his name. My thoughts will call me Billy, as well. Yet deep inside, I'll know who I really am."

Guide didn't have to know possession might kill me. Besides, that story would sound contrived, like a scheme to regain his affection.

"Will you have access to all Billy's thoughts?" Guide said, his voice lowered.

"Just those he selects." I studied his stern eyes. "Why do you ask?"

"Did Billy ever tell you that he and I were friends?"

"How good of friends?" Had he been like a woman to Billy, too?

"We weren't lovers, if that's of concern." Guide scratched his cheek, clean-shaven the day before. "I fired for Billy when he was an engineer." He tilted his head. "Seems odd he didn't mention it."

Mouth open, I twitched my upper lip. Why hadn't the family let me know? I traced little circles in the air with my forefinger, then flashed an accusing glance at Ibn Sina. The stallion snorted and flicked his silvery tail.

"After you're Juanita again," Guide said, "will you remember everything you did and said as Billy?"

I'd recall most things, even if not right away, but why would that matter? He twisted his earring. Then he didn't look at me.

"What dark secrets are left to purge?" I touched his arm.

"The secrets are Billy's to tell this time." Guide faced me, tightening his grip on his eighty-niner. "I'm just going to prod him to clear the air."

"Does Billy suspect you'll do that?"

"I'm sure he does."

Guide flipped a small lever on his weapon. The safety device disengaged. He turned and crossed the open ground toward the terminal. If only he'd glance back and offer a demonstration of affection, a reassurance of my worth. The distance separating us increased by more than footsteps. What sort of confrontation awaited me as Billy in the trainyard?

Guide disappeared from sight behind manzanita bushes. A yellow-brown vortex of light approached me and hovered, like a spoiled lemon dangling on a string. Had to be Billy. That ghost needed to do some explaining.

"I've never worn the rag," Billy's spirit said. "This is going to feel unnatural."

"It's my last day," I said. His comment about my monthly bleeding had been inane.

A small drab bird landed fifteen feet away and pecked cracks between the bricks for dinner. Billy just kept hovering. Maybe he watched the bird. More likely he stalled, didn't intend to tell me about him and Guide. There was no use harping at him. I'd have to discover the truth myself.

"Let's get this switch over with," I snapped. "It's time to steal a train."

Billy responded with a grunt. I scrunched shut my eyes and pictured a glass of Scotch whisky, browner than over-steeped tea. A shot of liquid smoke. I could feel his spirit curl around me, try to crawl inside my brain.

A slow, deep breath of air filled my lungs. The smells of tobacco and liquor intensified, permeated my being, even oozed from my pores like sweat. The backs of my hands tingled. My chest and throat stung, as if spattered with white-hot ashes. I'd become Billy before, but this possession differed.

A faint recollection of some railroaders welled within my mind, the memory of a lot of booze. I'd drunk way too much. No, Billy had done the drinking—twenty-six years ago. Was I him? I glanced down at my girlish blouse, riding skirt and embroidered trousers. These duds would never do. Billy had better find some overalls fast.

•

Billy fiddled with his silk undervest as he walked toward Guide's wagon. Juanita's damn breasts flopped around worse than beached fish. At least he didn't have to put up with a frigging corset. He expectorated onto the gravel, still not ready to stare in the direction of the trainyard. There'd be hell to pay when Old Man Locke cornered him in yonder roundhouse and vented his pent-up wrath.

A blue denim shirt, trainman's cap, goggles and striped overalls waited for Billy in the wagon. At least Guide didn't expect him to dress like a woman. Guide...Billy had referred to him by that name around Juanita for the past two years. It still felt odd. He stripped down to his underwear and noticed a pistol under the tarp. Fully loaded. He slipped into the clothes of an engineer.

Smoking something besides an illusion would help matters. He patted his pockets in a habitual manner. The search yielded little more than a hairbrush and spare sanitary rag. Crap. Probably time to watch the stationhouse, anyway. He strapped on his eighty-niner. When he squinted into the lowering October sun, he saw double. He'd have to get used to peering through real eyes. The Union Jack fluttered up the pole—an all-clear signal from Guide. Rule Britannia, no duplicate image.

Billy scrambled into the wagon seat, the damn thing way too high. He sure could have used an extra seven inches of height. His hands grasped and jiggled the reins. The wagon rolled forward with a rattle, the load in the bed as snug as two diamondbacks coiled in a spittoon. His gut muscles tensed. Billy couldn't hide from his past any longer.

•

Dusk's light bathed the roundhouse, and the place was far too quiet. What the hell had happened to the shop's boilers? No shop boilers meant no shop steam. Shit on a sausage. Billy had counted on in-house steam to wake up a cold locomotive.

He moved closer to the engine house, a semicircle of linked concrete stalls with support posts for walls. A metal-roofed stable for locomotives. Each stall contained an engine, section of track, service bay and smoke vent. All sections of service track led to the usual outdoor steel turntable, about thirty feet in diameter and flush with the ground, used to aim rolling stock in the desired direction. The combined structure—the roundhouse—was large as a city-sized block. The trainyard doubled the real estate.

Tools hung inside the stalls on every section of post a man could reach. Spare parts littered the concrete floor. Billy glanced up at the high ceiling, far taller than any locomotive.

Guide waited near the opening of the first stall, the one closest to the terminal. He and the roundhouse blended together. What the blazes should Billy say? Maybe he should state the obvious.

"How's a body supposed to heist a train around here without piped steam?" Billy wedged his hands into his overall pockets. "Burn rotted ties in the firebox?"

Guide didn't look directly at him. His eyes scanned a silent engine, as if searching for something, perhaps appropriate words.

"Well, it won't be the first time, Billy, now will it, starting cold?" The skin crinkled around the outer edges of Guide's eyes, projecting the disapproval Billy knew all too well. "Who'd've thought I'd fire for you again on this side of hell?"

Billy's mouth turned dry. His chuckle gained a nervous edge. This damn meeting felt even more uncomfortable than he'd anticipated.

"Ever see such junk?" Billy gestured with his thumb toward the nearby engine streaked with rust. "Not like it used to be."

"What is?" Guide turned away. "Something here'll hold steam." He took a slow, deep breath. Sucking air was a great way to hold back words. "After all, they pull trains out of here to Los Angeles. Even to Yuma."

Billy coughed. An ache in his gut gnawed with rat teeth. Their last run together had originated in Yuma, Arizona—U.S. property. Guide had overseen Gabriel Mendoza's railroad project investments and often helped operate locomotives. Once back inside South California,

250

the Brits had conscripted Guide to fire a prison train across the Mojave Desert. Guide had wielded that frigging crowbar in response.

"Why don't you break into the office?" Billy pointed toward the far end of the barn. "Find out what they've cleared to run. I'll check out the engines."

"As you wish," Guide said. "Your call, now as always." The outer edges of his eyes slanted down under his bushy brows. "That's what they paid you for, wasn't it? To make the tough decisions? As engineer, I mean."

Guide turned and strode away, his every breath and footstep determined and controlled, the master of bridled emotion, undeniably in command. He could have waited a few hours to start the insinuations.

Yuma and the Mojave—hot as blazes in summer and blazing worse inside Billy for twenty-six years. Guide had known about Billy's screw up, how railroad constables had sniffed him out. Billy hadn't intentionally turned him over, though, despite what Guide believed. He'd been stupid, not disloyal.

Forget the nearby multi-ton rust bucket. Billy moved to the next stall, reached up and grasped a vertical iron bar beside the ladder of another locomotive. He balanced on one foot and lifted the other to meet a horizontal steel rung. Using both the grab iron and rungs for support, he climbed. A misjudgment of distance produced a barked shin. Annoying, Juanita's petite stature. This bouncy bosom just made things worse. The men in the cantina had shredded the only decent underwear she'd owned.

Once in the engine cab, Billy searched for the posted results of the most recent engine inspection. Everything was current. His tongue rimmed his lips. Success so soon? His hand glided across the valve handles on the fireman's manifold and up to the boiler water glass, edging its way toward the throttle and Johnson bar like a cautious suitor. He fondled the four-foot Johnson—the manual reverse. A small cylindrical object at the base of the bar caught his eye. A red glow shimmered, followed by a flash of plaid. Ethan's warning signal.

He released the bar, then took a closer look. Thin wires protruded from a metal tube. An explosive trap. Mendozas or their family's enemies must have put two and two together. So much for secret sabotage plans. Guide would need to know right away. Billy edged down from the engine cab. He wiped his greasy palms on his overalls.

The night of the train flared into memory. Tragic, that loss of good lives and a majestic machine. Promise wasn't the sort of assignment Billy would have chosen if eternal atonement got purchased with cheap apologies. Yet that sabotage had focused press attention on the South California asylum, the place all of California dumped their lepers, unwanted orphans and madmen—which included Mexican and Indian troublemakers conveniently declared insane. So the thwarted superintendent and would-be murderer had waited. Now the lives of four hundred adult inmates and one hundred children were again at risk. Too bad public interest was so frigging fickle.

"Watch out for explosive traps." Guide approached, a clipboard clutched in one hand and an unlit brass lantern swinging from the other.

"So I've noticed." Billy claimed the clipboard.

Guide tossed him a ring of keys and turned in the direction he'd come from. Billy pocketed the keys, then flipped through some report sheets. One locomotive, Number 9029, had been oiled and cleared to pull fuel and water tankers. A notation on wheel arrangement might help pinpoint the equipment's location. He checked another page. Number 9029 had four sets of eighty-inch drivers—the wheels turned by the piston rods—and two sets each of lead and trailing wheels. He scanned the open entryways of the engine service areas. That 4-8-4 would be a thunder of a big engine. Where was it?

Staying beneath the front edge of the roof, Billy headed toward the opposite end of the building and the entrance to the trainyard. A voice, not Guide's, called from the shadows of a service bay. A watchman? Billy dropped and hit pavement. A lantern crashed. He rolled toward a locomotive, then recovered, his belly pressed against the floor and eighty-niner ready to fire. Guide, stomach side down and horizontal, backed him up, fifteen to twenty feet away.

"Put those things down before you do something stupid," the familiar voice admonished. "Unless, of course, you prefer to kill me."

Antonio emerged from behind a locomotive, eighty-niner across his back, his hands stretched away from his body, palms up, holding only air. Well, wasn't that sweet? Antonio advanced with slow steps, the edges of his mouth curved down. Dust coated his leather pants. His silk shirt hung loose under his unbuttoned vest, one sleeve torn and soiled with grease. An unkempt garden of stubble sprouted around the remnants of his once-manicured beard.

"I suspect you won't kill me," Antonio said, "regardless of what I've done before." He stopped and half smiled. "You need all the help you can find right now, no?"

"You're out of character, Tony," Guide said. "You don't leave your sanctuary for altruistic motives, remember?"

"Why so suspicious?" Antonio peered down the bridge of his long straight nose. "Do you forget my lessons so soon?" He smirked, offering the old man a hand and ignoring the rejection. "Rule number two of the sabotage game is very simple. Have an unpleasant task? Hire an unpleasant man." He glanced toward Billy. "I bring a gift, a special gift. You won't panic if I reach into my pocket?"

"Just keep it slow." Billy motioned with his eighty-niner. Having no help would trump hiring the wrong help.

Antonio extracted a leather pouch from his vest, the bag big enough to hold a derringer or small grenade. If only Billy could read this sidewinder's thoughts.

"Toss it on the deck," Billy said. "I think not." Antonio's upper lip curled. "You'll have to trust me, Billy. You trusted my father, after all. Well, sometimes."

He drew closer, his arm extended and the pouch cradled in his broad palm. Billy's heartbeats quickened.

Did this bastard have an explosive device? Had he planted the two traps? Billy aimed his rifle at Antonio's head.

"Freeze, Tony," Guide said. "If Billy misses, I won't."

"You too?" Antonio called over his shoulder with a hurt tone. "If I had it in for either of you, would I have been foolish enough to select this time and place?" He smirked again. "Open the pouch, Billy. Don't feel it first. You'll spoil the surprise."

Billy stood and stretched out his arm as if shaking hands with the devil. A ticking sound. Did Antonio hand him a frigging bomb? But if so, he'd join the collateral damage. Not his style. Billy fumbled with the knotted drawstring. The pouch contained a railroader's watch and a half-dozen cigars wrapped in a clean shop rag.

Something was wedged around a narrow cigar—an onyx ring, its polished black stone shaped like a hawk's head. Gabriel Mendoza had worn such a ring. Billy once had, too. Billy pointed the barrel of his rifle toward the ground, staring at the piece of jewelry, a likeness of the one belonging to the mysterious ghost in the Cave of Light near Promise. That had been a Juanita thought. Antonio slipped the ring onto Billy's left forefinger. The fit was perfect.

"Wear this in good health or ill," Antonio said. "Like it or not, the three of us are wedded to each other until Juanita's job is done."

Billy just stood there. What the Sam Hill could he add? Antonio had won this particular round, and there'd be more.

"Your engine is on a west siding in the yard," Antonio said. "The rest of your train's parked near the east gate. Five tankers—two with oil, three with water—and five boxcars. Do refrain from lighting up when inspecting the rear boxes. They're loaded with dynamite and drums of black powder." Antonio rubbed the plain onyx stone in his own ring and grinned. His coffee-brown leather pants made a sensuous swish as he shifted position. "Everything's set, except to unload your wagon and fire up. Destination—Tehachapi, even Yuma, who knows? Life's full of little twists."

So was death.

254

31. How Long Does It Take to Steal a Train?

THE SILENT LOCOMOTIVE, unlit and fifteen feet tall, waited under the night's blanket, its massive driving wheels blocked with lengths of steel chain. Streamlined. Modern. Jesus, this engine was a beauty. Billy did a preliminary check of the exterior, then climbed into the engine cab. His eighty-niner clunked against iron.

Guide and Antonio joined him. Billy reviewed the posted inspection sheet in the light from Antonio's oil lamp. Pressure test. Brakes. Most items looked all right. One way or another, he'd reach those tunnels and blast them to kingdom come.

He stepped back and bumped into Guide. The cab, a two seater, wasn't much wider than a pair of privies. The black, enameled cast-iron firebox and steam boiler took up the majority of the space in front. Insulated pipes and most valves sat overhead. Two glass and metal tubes, each twice the size of a beer mug, projected from the boiler. Guide manipulated the gauge cocks.

"The water glasses are reading true," Guide said.

"Good," Billy said. The level stood at half-a-glass, the amount of water in the boiler ideal.

He eyed the engraved metal plate below the dual glasses and above the firebox door, the delineation of the crown sheet's location. The crown was the roof of the firebox, and its boiler side had not been recently inspected. Any trouble would come from there.

Antonio sat down in the fireman's seat to the left of the boiler, clunking the lantern against the firebox. He rested the tip of one elbow on the lower frame of the side window, which was paneless and open to the elements.

"I know how to repair a clockman," Antonio said, "but little about the mechanics of engine cabs."

"A boiler's mostly a helluva big teakettle," Billy replied. "It gets hot enough to generate steam, yet keeps the firebox below it from melting."

"Now there's a mistress," Antonio said.

"A poorly tended boiler's a one-way ticket to disaster," Billy added, determined not to react to his remark. "Let the water in the glass creep too high and you can blow a piston. Drop the level too low, and you'll blow the whole train."

Guide offered an affirmative grunt and dug in one of his pockets. He pulled out a small phosphor lantern with a beam focuser, attached to a lanyard necklace. Probably something he'd assembled in his workshop. A long step edged him around Billy. Use of a foot pedal opened the firebox door. Then he knelt and looked into the box.

"Brickwork and flues look clean." Guide stood.

Billy peeled off his eighty-niner, claimed the focused-beam lantern, then wedged the top half of his body into the firebox. He twisted onto his back and looked up at the crown sheet. Metal plugs embedded the thing. Did boiler scale encrust their reverse sides? Scale could raise the melting point of the solder in the plugs. If the firebox overheated, the plug cores wouldn't melt in time for boiler water to flow downward and quench the flames. An explosion—far more severe than one triggered by a small explosive trap—might result. He extricated himself from the box and found Guide scanning the inspection sheet. His face betrayed no hint of the concern Billy knew he felt.

"Hand me the light," Guide said. "I'll make sure the tender's full."

"You've other things to do." Billy hung the phosphor lantern around his neck. "I'll walk the top of this thing."

"Want some help?" Antonio said. "So you don't fall off?"

"Cut the sarcastic crap," Billy said.

The engine cab had no rear wall of its own. The front end of the tender car, with its exterior grab irons and ladder, provided one. A broad, hinged metal floor plate covered the coupling bar between the cab and car. The arrangement made the tender appear an integral part of the locomotive.

Billy grasped a ladder rung on the tender. His muscles tensed as he tilted outward and scaled. Once on top, he raised the nearest hatch cover. Water tank full. He pulled the stick gauge from its slot in the adjacent fuel tank. Plenty of oil. He replaced the stick, then climbed over to the top of the engine.

The steel cowl atop the locomotive concealed the exhaust stack, except for the rim, even hid the dome storing sand for traction. A fuel-efficient design. The brass bell showed. The main steam valve did, too. But the rounded, bare topside left plenty of places to take a tumble and few to recover. Twenty-six years had passed since Billy had last run a locomotive, but some things about the top of an engine hadn't changed. They were all dirty, and if a worker wasn't careful, deadly, too.

Billy wrestled the main valve open. Juanita's body lacked the muscular strength of his previous one. Damn inconvenient.

"All set up there?" Guide called to him. "Can I open the manifold?"

"All set," he replied.

Billy leaped from the engine toward the tender. Shit, he'd miscalculated. He might fall. He landed with a thud on the edge of the tender and teetered off-balance. His arms flailed. Sweet Jesus! Stability returned. Operating by reflex was apt to get him into trouble. He wiped his greasy hands on his shop rag, then climbed down into the engine cab. He'd have hell to pay if he harmed Juanita's body.

Burning sagebrush crackled in the open firebox. Billy assumed his place on the right-hand side of the cab, checking the positions of the steam throttle and reverse. Exciting, to smell the fire. Guide maintained a sober expression. No doubt, vitriol sloshed behind those calm eyeballs. Billy glanced at the steam gauge.

"How long to get to 230 pounds pressure?" Billy said. How long would it take the old man to spew out what had poisoned his mind for twenty-six years?

"Four to six hours," Guide said. "After the train's loaded, you and I should spell each other to grab an hour's sleep. Could be our last chance until Monday."

"Only if we're ready to couple up the train before two-thirty." Billy would handle the forty-hour run without rest if he had to. "We need to highball it out of here by four." He fiddled with one strap on his damn camisole while the bastard in leather maneuvered a sack of fuel pellets into the cab. "Will you give me a hand with the ammo cases?" he said to Antonio.

"My pleasure," Antonio said. "Your place or mine?"

Billy extended his right middle finger in reply. He put on his eighty-niner, backed down the boarding ladder, then stretched his left leg off the lower rung. The toe of his boot brushed against the ground. He hopped off the ladder with the grace of a drunk. Billy needed to occupy a man's body.

"Watch the tracks." He motioned Antonio toward the stationhouse. "One car rolling free'll ruin your day." A messy way to die.

"We should walk together," Antonio said. He lifted his oil lantern, a bulky thing that burned with a soft hum.

They crossed tracks. Billy grunted. Their train had ten cars, according to Antonio's earlier comments. A real shorty. The cars would be hitched in a logical order for the sabotage—water and oil tankers alternated up-front and a stock car for the horses next. The boxcars containing explosives would comprise the rear. No caboose needed. Ethan's ghost could signal without a comfy place to ride. What sort of an arsenal had Antonio arranged? Doing explosives hadn't been Billy's strong suit.

Once past the tracks, Antonio motioned for Billy to halt. A soft click. He'd released the safety on his eighty-niner. Billy listened for other sounds. An owl hooted.

"Wait here," Antonio whispered.

"I'll cover your back." Billy readied his weapon.

Antonio moved on, his shadow suspended between flickers of lamplight and the glint of his rifle. No warning shimmer came from Ethan. Still, Billy wouldn't relax yet. The rear door of the darkened stationhouse creaked open. Antonio swung his lantern back and forth—the signal to join him. They edged across a tile floor toward the front door and window, then peered outside.

"Are those horses your relatives?" Antonio said.

"Yeah." Billy chuckled and slung his eighty-niner back over his shoulder. "Got a wire cutter?"

"Not on me."

"There's one in the wagon," Billy said. "Snip open that fence over there, enough to squeeze the wagon through. And, by the way, I want you to switch the tracks later, to get our engine across the yard to our train. You think you can do that by lamplight?"

"How will I know what gets switched?" He frowned and rubbed his overgrown goatee.

"A recent acquaintance of yours'll be around." Billy grinned, recalling Juanita's memories of the bagpipes in Antonio's library. "One who's figured out how to, shall we say, communicate essentials."

Antonio's face contorted to a pained scowl. His upper lip curled, exposing the gleam of white incisors. His shoulders slumped.

"Bloody thunder," he said, "not the Scot."

Billy gave Antonio's upper arm a playful punch. He opened the front door, producing an unnerving creak. Outlines of his horses were visible beyond the portico. Their hooves pawed the ground, over and over. A warning. His relationship with Antonio was one of tenuous tolerance, at best. He yanked his camisole strap back onto his sloped shoulder and headed toward the wagon.

•

Antonio stood beside a line of railcars, his oil lantern lifted high. Billy jumped down from the wagon to roll open the boxcar doors. The end door, painted the color of rust, budged a mere inch. He leaned back and grunted. The blasted thing wouldn't slide.

Antonio thrust the lamp into Billy's hand, then opened each boxcar with ease. Damn showoff. He readied the stock car. Billy unhitched the horses. The animals nickered and clumped up the ramp into the car, not pausing to snort at Antonio or bare their teeth. Once inside, they buried their muzzles in a trough of oats. Four-legged traitors.

Time to move on to the adjacent boxcar. He helped Antonio maneuver the loading ramp into place. Antonio's hand, callused and warm, curved atop his. Billy pulled away from him.

Antonio shrugged, then rattled off a list of the boxcar's contents—everything from food and water to bullets and bags of sand. He'd even brought a wind-up mechanical person. Looked like Guide's, except someone had dressed it in overalls.

Billy stepped closer. The automaton was nearly as tall as he was and damn imposing. Deep within his mind, he felt Juanita's shudder.

"What do you plan to do with a clockman?" Billy said. "Have it serve tea?"

"They come in handy," Antonio said. "When I do a job, it's done right." He smiled, that disgusting blend of smirk and deadpan best described as a half-smile. His tongue wet his lips.

"Focus on unloading the wagon," Billy said.

Antonio extracted the nitro canisters from the wagon, one at a time. He transferred each into the butt end of the third boxcar as if cradling newborn babies. Billy moved the other cargo—mostly medicine, food and clothes—to the front of the same car, except for Guide's spare bowie knife. Best to strap that sheathed weapon to his thigh. Finished first, Billy grabbed the lantern and watched Antonio from the top of the ramp.

"Put that down," Antonio exclaimed. "Outside the car, for God's sake. There's some powder in here, too."

Billy couldn't see a drum or keg. What was that bastard up to? Antonio knelt by the nitro and motioned for assistance. Billy hung the light just outside the door and set his eighty-niner beside a bag of medicines. His fingertips patted the hilt of Guide's knife. He took several assertive steps, his boots thumping against the wooden floor of the dim railcar.

"Drag those sand bags closer," Antonio snapped. "Then snug up the ropes around the kegs."

"You plan to tell me how to run this train as well as load it, like one of those bleeding three-day-wonders the Feds used to send around to do inspections in North California?"

"Don't push me," Antonio said. "It doesn't suit my mood." He stood like a straight pine towering over a puny shrub. "My word's law in the ammo cars."

Billy's rifle sat several seconds away. He blinked and noticed the outline of three kegs against the far wall. Antonio hadn't lied. Billy dragged a sandbag over to a canister. Antonio lifted two bags with ease.

Billy tightened the rope restraints around the three kegs of black powder. He fastened the metal grounding clamps. Antonio stepped behind him and blew into his ear.

"Back off," Billy exclaimed.

Billy wheeled around, unsheathing his bowie knife. Antonio spread his arms and leaped clear of the blade. With a couple of motions of his wrist, his butterfly knife clinked open.

"You've lost your touch, Billy," Antonio said. "Care to try again?"

Tension flowed through Billy's muscles. He stood with his legs apart, poised for a fight. His family's mission hung in jeopardy, but Antonio needed to learn where limits lay.

"Sheathe that thing." Antonio spat into the air. "Listen, I could carve you for dinner. You know that."

Billy could slice him, too. How much clearance was behind him? Could Antonio pin him against the kegs? If Billy edged to the left, there might be more room to maneuver.

"I didn't blow into your ear because I wanted to cut you." Antonio's tone softened from a growl to a treacherous purr.

Sweat dribbled down Billy's face. More beaded between his breasts. Antonio's arms were long, and his reach, deadly. Billy would have to strike at precisely the right moment. Antonio inched closer, the stink of unwashed man and leather strong. Billy tightened his hand around the hilt of Guide's knife.

"So dismiss my proposition." Antonio stood motionless, just out of range. "But at least extend the courtesy of consideration."

Billy was within Antonio's reach. That meant Juanita was, too. Damn! He sheathed Guide's knife. Quick rhythmic motions of Antonio's wrist and lower arm closed the butterfly blade.

"Think about it." Antonio pocketed his knife and turned.

Antonio snugged up the canisters with the last two sandbags, his taut muscles obvious, even in the dim light. A familiar but unexpected hunger welled within Billy. His skin tingled. He clenched both fists. How the blazes had Billy's physical desire catapulted over his wall of disdain?

A distant bagpipe wailed. Ethan was ready. Antonio turned toward the railcar door. Billy dug in his pocket and tossed him the ring of keys to the switch locks, the collection Guide had commandeered from the roundhouse office. Antonio headed in the direction of the track-switching route.

Billy's loins ached. He could feel Juanita's possessed mind spin.

•

The steam pressure gauge crested the fifty mark when Billy returned to the locomotive. God, but the duet of the blower and fire igniting against the flash wall invigorated him.

Guide fired the engine on oil. The color of the flames through the firebox peephole left no doubt the old man could still set a clear stack. Graham—it just sounded right to think that name once in a while—was part train.

"Sand the soot out of the flues already?" Billy said.

The firebox flues didn't need scouring yet—a chore performed when a running engine chugged hard. Billy had loved to tease Guide about his knack for burning a clean, efficient fire.

"Not flues I've been sanding," Guide said, "but the past." His voice was as calm as a sheltered cove on a windless day. "Surprising how much carbon accumulates in the brain over twenty-six years. More than enough to coat life black."

Crap, this was it—what Billy had dreaded. He patted his overalls for matches and a cigar. Even a condemned man deserved a smoke.

"Care to sand out a bit of your own carbon?" Guide said.

"Can't this wait until another time?" Billy fumbled for his match tin. "What do you expect me to do, yell all that shit over the blower's din?"

"What better way to finally spit it out, Billy?" Guide directed the beam of the flashlight toward the water glass, then clamped his palm over the injector handle and added water to the boiler. "I screamed the night the Brits busted through the front door of that secluded cabin." He twisted a valve and produced a sharp hiss of steam. "Wonder how they knew where to look?"

Billy lit his cigar, a good brand. Tasted rotten. He crouched and stubbed the dratted thing in the sandbox.

"I didn't mean that to happen, all right? The wrong word slipped out in the wrong place, that's all." Billy pulled himself as tall as he could. Not tall enough. "You think I'd have risked my neck and Juan's safety to bundle you off to Old Man Mendoza's if I'd already sold you down the river?"

"I'd like to believe that." Guide's lamp beam illuminated the steam gauge, which registered eighty-five pounds. He clicked off the light. "Odd, the way Tony showed up here. Hardly his way. Conscience is an amazing motivational force."

Pressure mounted within Billy, a sort of cold steam. Guide sounded so detached. Why the frig couldn't he blow fire out his ears like a normal human being?

"Imagine what it feels like," Guide said, "to get bashed with rifle butts. They had a crowbar, too. There's something quite terrifying about the crunch of one's own bones."

The needle on the boiler gauge climbed to eighty-seven pounds. Billy didn't need earthly light to read the mark. The heat from the firebox sucked sweat from both his skin and soul. The gauge read eighty-nine pounds.

"Hit a man's head hard enough," Guide said, "and the brain gets pushed through the ears."

Billy clutched the edge of the adjacent seat-back, Guide's words burning inside him. His fingernails dug into the firm leather upholstery. The steam gauge registered ninety pounds.

"They must have paid well, Billy," Guide said. "Getting to Mexico couldn't have come cheap."

The needle on the pressure gauge shimmied upward. Ninety-five pounds. Ninety-nine. Shit, the pressure of torment in Billy rose ten times faster. His wail burst free as the long thin blast of a train whistle-warning its way into a station.

"You really think I screwed you," Billy yelled, "fled the goddamned country to hide? You were like my father. A man can't hide from part of himself." He could picture Guide, crumpled on the floor of that cabin like a mound of raw meat—a bleeding, swollen mound of raw meat. "I couldn't let Juan end up in Gabriel Mendoza's bed. That's why I ran." Billy's guts wrenched and his eyes burned, vision blurred by tears, just like when he'd found what was left of Guide. "Juan was sweet. Vulnerable. You know what Gabriel would've done to him? I fucking sold myself—not you—to get the fucking money to smuggle him out."

Billy removed his cap and buried his face in his hands. His fury deteriorated to sobs.

"Sixteen years. I spent sixteen blasted years in Mexico before I died there. Your image haunted me every night and day." Billy's sobs softened to hoarse whispers. "What do you want? You can't kill someone who's already dead. There's nothing left to do but say I'm sorry."

Guide extended his hand, palm up, the way a father might do when his son's tripped and skinned a knee. His expression revealed little hint of emotion. He ought to scream and belt Billy hard.

"We would both have been better off," Guide said, "if you'd sent me a note back then." His warm fingers touched Billy's.

Billy sobbed, gasping for air. He let Guide draw him close, then buried his head against the bib of his friend's overalls, the fabric ripe with sweat and engine grease.

"We've quite another concern," Guide said. "Why don't you go see how Tony's faring?" He stroked the back of Billy's head. "Pull yourself together."

Billy nodded, sniffling. Yes, he had to control his emotions. Guide kissed his forehead, had forgiven him.

"You've never looked better, Billy." Guide winked and straightened his visor. "I do believe I prefer you with breasts."

Billy chuckled. Guide hadn't lost his sense of humor. Billy put on his cap, reached out of the cab for the grab iron then turned to descend the ladder. His gaze locked to Guide's. This man had it bad for Juanita.

32. One Hell of an Engine

BILLY ENGAGED THE reverse and reached up to ease open the steam throttle. The locomotive crawled backward, finally coupling to its train with a heavy thud and shudder. The horses in the stock car whinnied. The relatives were jumpy tonight, probably worried about the nitro. He couldn't blame them. Hauling explosives never made him cozy. Plus he could tell, Juanita was as tense as an over-stretched banjo string.

Antonio stood trackside. Billy figured he'd need the bastard's strength to connect the brake hoses between cars. He climbed down from the engine cab and signaled for assistance. An engineer does what's needed.

"Hold the lantern high, will ya?" Billy said. "And pay attention."

He balanced one foot on a coupling, then demonstrated the safest technique for snugging hoses. Most people didn't appreciate the high damage potential of a train at rest. Billy traded places with Antonio and corrected the position of his body. He didn't want him squashed. Not yet.

Billy led the way to the next set of railcars. A shifting breeze brought the odor of leather. He cast a discreet glance toward Antonio's crotch. The memory of Juan, Billy's lover and helpmate, reared to revile the action. Damn, but he could see Juan's hurt expression. Juan had never been unfaithful to him. Billy's subsequent breaths came deep and quiet. Each one reinforced his resolve. He lifted the lantern while Antonio connected brake hoses, as much to provide a physical barrier as a light.

"Now we walk the train," Billy said, "look for loose bolts or machinery pissing oil where it shouldn't." He signaled to the cab for Guide to pump up the brakes. "And

Ethan might have missed a hidden time bomb. Eth's good, but we'd better check."

"How can I tell where oil belongs?"

"This stuff's normal." Billy pointed out a small well of oily muck. "But a puddle over there might not be."

Antonio faced him and rested one hand on his shoulder. Billy shifted the bastard's hand, squeezing his palm. With a quick motion, Billy dipped Antonio's fingertips into the pool of sludge.

"If you want to feel something up," Billy said, "learn to do it to the driving wheels on the locomotive. If they get too hot, she'll need more grease."

Antonio glanced at his mucky fingers. He wiped them on the front of Billy's bib-overalls, pausing at his bosom.

"Have some grease."

He fondled Billy through the double layers of denim. The sensation caught Billy by surprise. He should knee Antonio, tell him to frig off. Yet he just stood there.

"Didn't your old lady ever teach you how to take no for an answer?" Billy said, angry with himself.

"Planning to pull your knife?"

"Not right now." Billy stepped away. "But once the tunnels are down, watch out."

Antonio did an "after you" gesture toward the engine cab, a grin plastered on his lousy face. Billy climbed the ladder. If Antonio followed too closely, Billy would kick him in the chops.

Inside the engine cab, the phosphor lights were on but dim. Guide hummed a tune in a minor key and marked the fuel valve positions with pieces of wire—a feel-in-the-dark method of control.

Billy checked his watch—nearly two-thirty. They would get rolling on time. He tossed a floppy pillow and a worn leather cushion onto the engineer's boxy seat to provide elevation.

"The powder could use a nanny," Billy said to Antonio. "Go read it a bedtime story."

Antonio glowered and retreated down the ladder. Billy had held his own ground. Darned fine! He sat on the pillow and leaned out the window until the bastard boarded to the rear, then noticed Ethan's ethereal lamp. The green glow drifted high, a signal. Tracks in the yard were clear.

The building intensity of a heavy spot fire meant the locomotive was ready to get moving. Billy reached up to grasp the whistle rope. No telling who might hear a whistle blast. Better to run without warning for now.

Billy tested the feel of the steam throttle. Guide curved his fingers around the cylindrical firing valve. Sweat dripped off the end of his beak nose. He grinned in Billy's direction. Together, they coaxed the locomotive from its reverie—inching the throttle forward while upping the fire, as if two people, a ghost and an engine could make love. The exhaust blasts from the machine's arousal drowned out the roar from the firebox and the murmur of Billy's breathing.

Number 9029 dug in her wheels and crawled down the rails, swallowing the ties as the frequency of stack exhausts increased. So exciting, the combined odors of steam and burning oil. Too bad he couldn't open the throttle until the din of exhaust pierced his ear drums and made him scream.

"This is the way it should be," Billy said to Guide. "The way it never was for us before. The heat off the box, the cool night air. And there's no bloody guilt about hauling human cargo—about you and me or anything at all."

The locomotive danced in steel slippers to the rhythm of the exhaust. The only sound missing was the steady hammer of the boiler feed pump. Guide would activate that equipment soon. Billy wedged a cigar into his mouth, lit the end and puffed. No offense meant to the Shadow World, but this was paradise, as good as any existence got.

"Number 9029 is one hell of an engine," Billy shouted, as if the passing wind had ears.

33. Wet Puma on the Prowl

THE SPEEDOMETER NEEDLE shimmied at the ten mark, stuck. The blasted thing wasn't worth a squashed ha'penny. Billy pounded the instrument with his fist, then gave up and pulled out his watch. No way to evaluate track conditions or terrain at night, except through Ethan. He'd have to keep the speed low. If he clocked the time between mileposts, he could calculate the rate of travel. Ethan's pale green glow broke through the darkness and lit up each mile marker. Around twenty miles per hour, right on target. No doubt about it, Billy's skill forged full speed ahead.

By an hour before dawn, they would need to take on water. Billy scouted the night for the Caliente Station. Ethan's red light flashed, followed by a shot of plaid. Trouble ahead! He slammed shut the throttle, shouted to Guide and applied the brakes.

The train slowed, but momentum kept it rolling, the headlamp illuminating the tracks. Something lay across them. Would the locomotive stop in time? Metal wheels screeched against rails. Collision was inevitable. The frigging engine could derail.

The nitro in the rear car. Billy braced against his seat. Guide clutched the side of his window. The locomotive drifted toward the unknown object.

Then Billy blinked, no longer felt a sense of motion. The train had come to rest. A bundle of metal bars lay on the tracks, less than ten feet ahead. He expelled spent air and whistled. Someone had planted traps in the roundhouse. He would bet these metal bars concealed an impact bomb.

"Ethan wants me to check it out," Antonio called.

The engine's headlamp illuminated Antonio's form. He knelt on the far side of the metal bars. Billy couldn't see what he was doing. Probably deactivating an explosive device. An unpleasant job and an unpleasant man.

Antonio waved an all-clear signal. Billy climbed down from the engine cab to inspect the tracks. Antonio had better keep his paws off him. Still, railroads didn't sabotage their own rolling stock. Some disgruntled Brit or Mendoza must have offered a bounty for their little band. Antonio was useful to have around.

•

Billy spotted the mile marker for Caliente and shut the engine's throttle. The train drifted toward the unlit station. Guide clutched his eighty-niner with his left hand, his right one against the fuel valve. He looked like he didn't know which piece of equipment he'd have to fire first.

"All quiet out there," Guide said. "A good sign or an ambush?"

No warning signal from Ethan. Whoever had rigged the impact bomb to that stack of metal rods might not have stuck around.

"I'll lay odds the coast's clear." Billy manipulated a lever, depositing sand on the tracks as the engine came to rest near the water tower. Billy hung the focused-beam lantern around his neck. He leaned out the cab window. Antonio emerged from a boxcar and lit his oil lamp. Billy chuckled. Although Antonio had deactivated that bomb, he'd been way too obnoxious. Mission and purpose were important, but so was evening the score.

"Gimme a hand." Billy motioned Antonio toward the water tower, a wooden tank on stilts and crossbars.

The base of the reservoir sat fifteen feet off the ground. A piece of metal pipe, maybe twelve to fifteen feet long, one end more curved than Guide's nose, served as a spout. The pipe was snugged against the tower, like a hard-on restrained by a tight pair of trousers. He chuckled again.

Billy turned to scale the ladder on the tender several feet away. He whistled as he climbed the rungs. There was no mischief like good mischief. Once on top, he lifted the cistern's square cover. The metal hinges creaked. He hoisted an aluminum rod tall as Juanita and stood on the edge of the tender, his legs parted and muscles braced. He glanced down, a long way to tumble, then teased the guide rope on the waterspout within reach.

"If this spout gets hung up, climb up and free it," Billy called to Antonio, who now stood by the base of the tower.

Billy signaled for him to move to the left. Antonio stepped to the side, still holding the lantern, his head ten feet below the end of the stubby drainpipe on the tank. Just where Billy wanted him. A hard tug on the guide rope awakened the waterspout with a metallic groan. Billy maneuvered the long and bulky spout until its base slipped loosely over the drainpipe, like a mouth around the tip of a thumb. Water gushed, invigorating and cool, into the tender's tank as the spout was lowered. Antonio bellowed a string of obscenities. The inevitable deluge of cold water escaping the pipe and drain connection had hit the mark.

Antonio lunged like a wild bull headed for a matador. He charged up the tender's ladder. His fury could have lit the way. He tore toward Billy. *Hell, let him.* Juanita, deep within his mind, prepared to die.

Sopping wet and seething, Antonio halted a few feet away from Billy. It was like an invisible wall separated them. Billy grinned, still controlling the position of the spout. The cistern brimmed and water splashed onto the deck. Billy raised the pipe.

Antonio shoved the spout clear of the tender, then gripped Billy's shoulders. Billy's boot slipped against the edge of the car. Antonio's grip relaxed, an unexpected action. He even stepped backward, releasing Billy from a precarious perch. No doubt he feared Guide would shoot him if Juanita were harmed.

"How long to Tunnel Three?" Antonio snapped. "Isn't that where you want the first charges laid?"

"Tunnel Three's the place," Billy said, his smug tone as light as balsa wood. He'd bested Antonio.

"How much lead time do you want on the clocks?"

Billy scratched his shoulder. Tunnel Three was only five hundred feet long, but Number Five was over a thousand. Then there was the loop of track between Tunnels Nine and Ten. He'd need extra time to run the loop and get clear.

"You're the expert," Billy said.

Antonio slicked back a wet lock of his hair.

"I want to use Tunnel Three for practice," he said, "and to block potential traffic from the north. Tunnels Five through Ten have to blow together. The noise'll wake the devil, but the most critical part of the job will be done before Brits interrupt us."

Billy nodded. There wouldn't be too many people around early on a Sunday morning, other than those who'd planted explosives on the tracks, unless someone had tipped off the railroad constables. If Brits or Mendoza gunmen had already planned an ambush, they would likely protect the mountain and strike before Tunnel Three. Otherwise, they'd wait downtrack of the tunnels, too far away to confirm the location of the Tunnel Three explosion. Enemies might even assume, if they heard anything at all, their own impact bomb had worked. Antonio's plan sounded all right.

Billy inhaled Antonio's odor. He smelled like a wet puma on the prowl, so different from Juan. Once again, Billy slammed the door on temptation without throwing the deadbolt.

"Why don't you and Guide spell each other for a bit of rest?" Antonio said, his voice softer than before. "As soon as there's daylight, I'll set the clocks and we'll get rolling."

Antonio squinted, as if he'd noticed something odd. Billy nodded without smiling. What the hell had he just seen?

34. Tunnels at Dawn

BILLY YAWNED AND rubbed his eyes, his mouth dry as mummified mice in the desert. Beside him, Guide minded the firebox. Now they'd both rested. Hell, Juanita had rested, too. Beyond the engine cab, red-and-gold banners of Sunday sunrise unfurled along the horizon.

"Nitro's ready," Antonio called. "Let's go."

Guide stretched and stood. He pulled the lever to blow accumulated crud from the boiler. Outside the engine cab, horizontal billows of steam roared from the locomotive's valves and shot twenty feet across the ground. The vapor dissipated, as if by magic. In the Shadow World, Billy had missed such things. Life came to an end way too soon.

They got the train going, then passed through Tunnels One and Two. Tunnel Three would be the first they'd destroy. The train curled and squealed up the grade in its direction. The rear cars swayed. No sign of an ambush yet.

The Tehachapi Mountains wore their fall coat, slung over the remnants of spring and summer grasses. Isolated oaks kept green on a pallet of amber and variegated straw. The steel drivers slipped against the rails. Billy held the running speed to fifteen miles per hour. Antonio clung to a grip on a boxcar, motioning with his free arm, silken shirtsleeve billowing like a ship's sail in the wind. Another signal.

"Tony just switched on the first timer," Billy said to Guide. "We've got one hour to set up Tunnel Three and get clear."

"Stop her close as you can to the tunnel," Guide shouted.

Billy nodded and braked the train to a full stop just short of the bore. The light from the headlamp revealed an earthen interior plastered with soot. He plucked the cotton plugs from his sore ears. How crazy, his earlier longing to endure the din of such a massive engine.

The boiler water glasses contained foam. Alkali must have contaminated the water in the last tower. This was a lousy way to operate a vessel pressurized with steam. The contamination could have been deliberate.

"I've seen fewer suds on wash days," Billy said.

"She's stable enough for now," Guide replied.

Antonio waited by the side of the track bed, a coil of rope and a harpoon gun in his grasp. A bucket-sized spool of narrow-gauge cable sat on gravel. A leather tool bag rested on the spool's top. Guide climbed down and helped haul the equipment toward the tunnel. They looked ready to scale a wall.

The men put on their goggles and miner's phosphor-lamp helmets. They entered the tunnel, beyond earshot but within Billy's view. Both men pointed upward. The wooden support beams would be twenty-five feet or so above the tracks. Antonio lifted the harpoon gun. Its attached rope dangled. Guide signaled for more light. Billy ran the engine closer, until the stack sat within the bore.

Antonio rounded his shoulders and appeared to cough hard. Guide unscrewed the lid on a canteen and wet down a spare bandanna. He pressed the cloth against his mouth and nose.

Billy's chest tightened. He hacked. His eyes stung and teared. Exhaust fouled up the air in the cab and the tunnel. Talk about an egg being smoked and boiled at the same time. He put on his goggles and prepared to back up the engine.

Guide coughed, motioning for the harpoon gun. He stood, head and weapon tilted upward, his legs apart. The harpoon lunged through the air. The line dangled from the beam above. He'd snagged the target. Antonio tugged the rope. It held fast.

A damned good shot.

Billy backed up the train, holding his breath until the stack met open air. Guide and Antonio, hacking like they had consumption, emerged from the tunnel. The two offloaded several drums of black powder, then maneuvered the barrels downtrack and against the tunnel's wall. They sure as hell deserved the salute of approval he gave them.

Planting the harpoon had taken longer than expected. The ticks of detonator clocks pounded inside Billy's brain. He checked his pocket watch. His supply of wiggle room shrank faster than a cheap cotton shirt in hot suds. And the water glasses foamed worse than ever. Shit.

Inside the tunnel, Antonio shinnied up a rope, like one agile snake climbing another. He dangled in mid-air. No easy task, fastening a pulley to a support beam. Guide hoisted the canisters.

"Come on," Billy muttered.

Antonio slid down to the track. Guide and he headed back, bundled with looped rope and cable. Billy tugged a warning on the whistle rope. Guide scrambled up to the fireman's station. Antonio flung the equipment and himself into the nearest boxcar. His boots hung out the opening.

"Say a prayer," Billy said to Guide.

Billy gave the engine more steam. The driving wheels slipped against the sanded rails with less traction than banana peels on ice. Seconds dragged like hours. The locomotive finally broke inertia and crawled. Five hundred feet through the tunnel was going to be a helluva long ride.

The train rattled under the canisters and past the powder kegs. Hallelujah. Nothing ignited. The locomotive met daylight and a corridor walled with rock.

"We've got three minutes to get ahead of the shock wave," Guide shouted above the engine noise. "Your turn for prayers."

Only three frigging minutes? Billy's whole body tensed. He could feel Juanita's mind do the same. The engine needed more steam. No, the locomotive would jump the track for sure. Either way, they'd never get clear in time.

"More throttle, Billy Boy," a voice called.

Billy looked up in surprise, greeted by Ethan's green glow. He opened the throttle. Then the train ran too fast for the blasted track. He reached for the brake valve. Ethan hollered and shimmered plaid. Billy gave the engine more throttle.

The explosion roared like peals of thunder in a storm. Billy lurched. The train shuddered. Booms echoed off the hills. Christ on a calliope. Were they clear? Something clamped his throttle arm—Guide's hand. Billy reduced the train's speed, leaned out the window and let the wind pound his face.

"We've won," Guide said, "for now."

The tunnel had lost, though. As with the locomotive Billy had wrecked near Promise, the tunnel had done nothing wrong. He needed to smoke and patted his pockets for a match. Echoes of exhaust chugs ricocheted off the ravine like supernatural cannon fire. Tunnel Five would be next to rig.

"I'll get ulcers doing this another nine times," Billy said.

"You're a ghost, Billy," Guide said. "You can't get ulcers. You and Tony can get Juanita pregnant, though." He glanced at the water glass.

"I've some sense of honor," Billy exclaimed.

Billy took a swallow of water from his canteen. Guide's concern for Juanita had prompted his comment. There was no reason to take offense.

"Real men don't cheat," Billy said to Guide and winked.

•

The train vibrated through Tunnel Five and rolled to a stop, its stack exhaust venting toward blue sky. This left the rear parked five hundred feet or so down the hole. Billy leaned out the engine cab. Antonio headed off to uncouple the end boxcar, which contained enough black powder, dynamite and detonators to destroy the tunnel. Ethan would help him out.

Billy's stomach spewed acid up his chest. The thought of a haunt trying to turn a bastard into a brakeman wasn't the reason. He'd forgotten how well sound carried in this terrain. Soon, five tunnels would explode simultaneously. The racket could bring a swarm of railmen, like hornets defending their busted hive. Even on Sunday. Even if the impact-bomb sidewinders had gone. A ghostly sphere of green light at the train's rear drifted up and down.

"They've pulled the coupling pin," Billy said to Guide. "Get ready to roll."

Antonio strutted out of the tunnel a minute later, waving his miner's hat. He climbed into the engine cab. Soon their train, minus one car of explosives, puffed blue-gray smoke up the next grade. They passed through Tunnel Six, then deposited a boxcar of black powder and dynamite in Tunnel Seven and a second one in Tunnel Eight. Two more tunnels until boom time.

Antonio joked as they traversed the canyon. For now, he was in a good mood. Ragged clouds coalesced in a patch of blue sky. Antonio's expression soured.

"Tehachapi Creek," he said, "how many crossings does it have?"

"Don't recall offhand." Billy, ears sore, inserted fresh wads of cotton. "Two crossings so far. I think there's still three more before the next tunnel and two after."

"Seven crossings over water," Antonio said. He rolled the wads of coarse cotton between his large fingers and stuffed them into his ears. "A good omen, no?"

"A good omen, maybe," Billy chided. That had been an odd thing for him to say. "It's October and the rains have been lousy. Creek's mostly dry."

"Speaking of crossings," Guide said, "the next one'll come up fast. Want to water at its towers?"

Billy checked his watch. They didn't have fifteen minutes to spare, but topping off the tank would help dilute the muck from the previous fill. No warning light from Ethan. He reached for the brake.

•

Flames darted from under the firebox door. Engine Number 9029 puffed hard up a grade toward Tunnel Nine.

Here came the next tight curve. A sharp pain hit Billy's eardrums as the locomotive chugged louder. Frigging lot of good new cotton plugs had done. Antonio stood on the metal floor plate in the rear of the cab, swaying with the motion of the train, his palms pressed against his ears.

Guide glanced toward Billy's throttle and brake arm, his own gloved hand on the cylindrical firing valve. Rivulets of sweat channeled through the white stubble on his face and dripped off his chin. His beak nose glistened. The work in Tunnel Nine would require use of the harpoon. Guide had better replenish his supply of sweat. Billy tossed him a canteen.

"We can save five minutes and a lot of hacking," Antonio said, "if you keep the stack outside the next tunnel."

"Won't be enough light," Billy said.

Antonio turned toward Guide. "How's your aim in the dark?"

"Good enough," Guide said.

"Got a rabbit's foot in your overalls?" Billy said. May nine be a lucky number.

The next curve started after the fourth crossing of the Tehachapi Creek. A second curve brought Tunnel Nine into view. Billy scanned the rails, tunnel and mountain. The track looped back around itself and over the top, constructed to gain the most elevation using the least amount of land. He chuckled. String enough cars on the loop, and a train could practically nip its own ass. He brought the train to rest between two parallel walls of dry earth, a corridor to the threshold of another earthen bore.

Guide twisted his earring. He had to be nervous. Billy ached to smoke. No time left. Flanked by Guide and Antonio, he walked along a section of ties to the mouth of Tunnel Nine. Daylight gleamed from the opposite end of the bore, over four hundred feet away. At least this tunnel was a short, straight shot. So why the blazes did butterflies barrage his stomach?

"Rig three canisters onto that support beam." Guide pointed toward a blackened overhead timber, fifty feet from the entrance southbound. "We'll unload the powder after we run the locomotive through the tunnel."

Billy yanked his unruly camisole strap back onto his shoulder. The train had barely squeezed by those kegs in Tunnel Three. Guide's plan sounded good.

The men anchored the harpoon while Billy minded the engine. He puffed on the butt of a cigar and watched the onward march of a minute hand. Guide emerged from the tunnel. His wrinkled brow and bushy eyebrows told the story. He was less than pleased.

"Help us unload the canisters," Guide called to him.

"Sure."

Billy slipped the cigar stub through the firebox peephole, then backed down the ladder. Warm wind rippled his shirt, a refreshing change from the heat of the cab. He strode toward the rear car, his pace brisk. Guide passed in the opposite direction, cradling two canisters.

"Take the one on the ground," he said.

Billy lifted the bulky tube, the length of a yardstick, and hauled it on his shoulder. The tunnel smelled damp, the way large holes in the earth often do. Laced with residual smoke from the stack, as well. Antonio dangled inside the tunnel, a human spider on rope silk. He rigged a pulley.

"Get me another charge," Antonio said.

"Can you do it, Billy?" Guide clasped the payload end of a hoist cable.

Billy checked his pocket watch. The boiler water glasses had been foaming less since the last tower. Leaving the engine for five or ten minutes more ought to be all right.

"Which tube do I take?" Billy said.

"The one on the left end of the row," Antonio said.

"That should be easy enough."

He reached the boxcar. Sandbags snugged the line of canisters beyond his grasp. A combination of vaulting and wiggling brought him aboard. He stood in the darkened car. So cold. And he could swear that Clockman, seated in a corner, stared right at him.

Things smelled of sulfur. A pressure squeezed his chest. His mouth tasted like he chewed an oily rag. The line of canisters on the floor undulated, blurred. Billy leaned against the ribbed metal wall for support. His temples throbbed. Something was seriously wrong.

A stroke? A heart attack? Juanita's body was too young for either. Maybe he needed more water or food. His shoulders twitched with a sudden shudder. A tingling sensation shot to his fingertips and toes.

Then I realized the problem. I wasn't Billy anymore.

35. An Explosive Situation

I LEANED AGAINST something, blinked until my eyes came into focus. Dim light. Walls made of wood. Where was I? Billy shouldn't have left my body so soon. But wait, that line of metal cylinders on the floor. Those were the nitro canisters I'd retrieved from the dry well. This had to be the munitions car on the stolen train.

Why had I entered the boxcar? The men's voices echoed within my mind, their words unclear. Had Guide and Antonio sent Billy for more explosives? My glance darted from one metal cylinder to the next. I had no idea which tube to take.

Antonio. He had said something to Billy. But what? Left. End. Row. That was it. Antonio had requested the canister on the left end of the row.

My head didn't feel right. My legs wobbled. I dropped to my hands and knees to push the canister toward the open door, but wound up on my belly like a drunken worm. If only I could close my eyes, curl up in a ball and sleep. My eyelids lowered. A flash of light jolted them open. Forest green, red and dark blue blazed in front of me—a plaid.

"Ye canna nap now," Ethan said. "The men need yer help."

My help. I snapped from my stupor. Guide and Antonio, they were working with live charges in a tunnel. They planned to escape the pending blast by train. A train that no longer had an engineer. And gunmen might be waiting to ambush them. Dear God!

I edged one hand and knee forward, then the other. Guide would need to learn the truth about Billy right away. I slid the canister along the floor, my coordination improved.

Guide could probably run the train for a short distance by himself. We could dump the rest of the explosives in the next tunnel. The three of us could escape on horseback and hide from the authorities. Things would be all right.

I climbed down from the boxcar, then aimed for the tunnel. My arms cradled the canister with care. If I dropped the stupid thing, it would blast me to Mexico. I wobbled along the chunky, uneven gravel of the railbed.

Billy must have deserted me to avoid the temptation of Antonio. No, Billy was more responsible than that. I stumbled into the bore. My arms ached. At least the locomotive's headlamp provided light.

Billy had possessed me for over a day. Maybe a ghost could only possess a person for a limited time without doing permanent damage. Whatever the reason, Billy had stayed as long as he could.

Antonio motioned to me, his torn silk shirt half unbuttoned. Wretched man. He'd tried to rape me in his library, might even think I was an easier target now. The tentative truce established with Billy was unlikely to extend to me. I'd pretend I was Billy. I'd confide in Guide when we were alone in the engine cab.

"Notch up the fire to a heavy spot as soon as you see we're done," Guide said to me. He unscrewed the lid on the tube I handed him and then activated the timer on the charge. "We'll pull the train clear of the tunnel, except for the end car."

I mopped sweat off my forehead. What was a heavy spot on a fire? I mumbled something in agreement, the way Billy might have done, then headed toward the locomotive, careful to step only on the wooden ties. This was no time to twist an ankle.

Such a massive engine—its largest wheels a foot taller than me. The locomotive's size hadn't intimidated Billy. If only I could smell tobacco and be him. *Scotch whisky. Scotch whisky. Scotch whisky.* No matter how hard I thought, Billy didn't come back. At the boarding ladder, I balanced on my toes and raised one foot to the height of the lowest rung. I stretched my arms upward and climbed.

The cab stank of hot oil. Moisture dripped and sizzled on a vertical structure of black iron, above where a fire burned. The thing reminded me of an oven. Something mechanical produced a noise, like a rising wind before a storm.

I looked up at the handle of one control, then down at a circular gauge. The modest maze of pipes and handles seemed familiar, although I couldn't recall the specific names for parts. I touched some sort of control with a handle and a little pointer, sort of like an odd-shaped sundial.

The pointer sat in a groove. A notch. Guide had said to notch up the fire. Moving the pointer one or two settings might do the job. More notches sat on the right side of the present setting than on the left. The train was stopped. The fire had to be low. I'd move the control toward the right when the time came.

My head itched. I fiddled with one braid. I might be able to assist Guide in running the train for a short distance, if he told me exactly what to do. We could take care of two more tunnels instead of just one. Enough to halt the asylum trains for at least two years. I'd have rescued Carla by then. Had Antonio written that letter? I leaned out the side window to look for him. What scheme would keep him out of the cab?

A soft hiss—a valve with a slow leak spat onto the hot rim of the firebox door. The spittle flashed to vapor. I eyed the boiler water glasses and manipulated a small adjacent valve, then jerked backwards, emitting a short gasp. Lord of this world and the next. I'd just done Billy things. Some of his train knowledge remained inside my head.

Maybe I could help run the train beyond the tunnels to safety. Guide would coach me, so I didn't do anything foolish. Billy's absence would be our secret.

Antonio's coarse laughter announced the men's return. Both climbed the ladder into the engine cab.

I stiffened all over. Antonio should be riding in a boxcar with the canisters. What was I going to do?

Guide entered first and pulled a lever on his side of the cab. A swishing sound followed. He turned toward me, watching for my next move. Antonio crowded behind him, then leaned back against the connecting car, his arms folded. I glanced at one control, then at the next. Billy's advice from another time spilled into my memory—think like an hombre.

My right hand jiggled a handle. My left hand reached up and moved something else. Several labored chugs resonated through the air, and the train crawled forward. I leaned out the window, as Billy would have done. What should I look for? The train rumbled into the tunnel and beneath the charges. Could the hot exhaust set off the explosives?

A green glow rimmed a handle near my left knee. The men didn't appear to notice. At least Ethan hadn't deserted me. I adjusted the control with my gloved hand. The train slowed to a standstill at the opposite end of the tunnel. The rear boxcar sat within the bore.

"Can you help Antonio haul powder?" Guide manipulated the valves on the foam-filled water glasses, his bushy eyebrows revealing his inner concern.

"Yeah...sure," I said.

I'd no idea how to move a powder keg. And what if Antonio made another advance? My fingers brushed against the hilt of my knife as I slipped behind Guide. I'd never dare challenge Antonio with a blade the way Billy had.

Antonio offered me a miner's helmet. The fit was loose. Billy would have known how to adjust the hat, but I didn't. I fumbled with the headgear and prayed Antonio wouldn't notice.

•

Near the end boxcar, Antonio tied a bandanna around his sweaty head and replaced his miner's hat. The helmet's phosphor headlamp emitted a modest glow. He muscled a drum down a short makeshift ramp. I studied his every motion, emulating his actions within my mind. Moving a powder keg was a little like moving a barrel containing rainwater. He shot an amused glance in my direction. A warm flush spread across my face. He must have mistaken my attentiveness for desire.

"Roll two kegs over there," Antonio said, pointing to a spot several feet up the track. He winked and grinned. "I'll move the rest to the center of the bore."

I set to work, avoiding eye contact with him. I tugged at the first keg and grunted. After several yanks, the keg tipped toward me, balanced on its lower rim. Hand-over-hand, I rolled it into position.

"This lid's stuck," Antonio shouted, a canister wedged between his thighs. His hands fumbled to twist off the top. "Get me a wrench."

"From where?"

"The open boxcar," he said. "To the right of the door."

I hiked trackside, walked up the ramp into the ammo car, then faced the sliding door. Just a broken hammer and a pile of oily rags on the right. But to the left, the tip of a large wrench protruded from beneath a clump of grease wipes.

"Nearly didn't find it," I said several minutes later. I slapped the business end of the grimy wrench into Antonio's palm. "This must have shifted, slid under the junk to the left of the door."

"To the left?" Antonio said. "Couldn't have."

I laughed, certain Billy would have done likewise. "Sure wasn't on the right. Not when I climbed in."

Antonio's mouth hung open. His unblinking eyes blazed in my direction.

"You climbed inside," he said. "Did you climb inside to get the canister, too?"

"Well, yeah," What was wrong with that?

"Bloody thunder!"

Antonio yanked off his helmet and waved the yellow metal dome in the direction of the locomotive. He wheeled back around, locks of his unbraided hair dangling in his horror-struck eyes.

"That canister on the left end," he said. "I meant as you face the train. You grabbed one on a short fuse. It's rigged up top. We've got seven to ten minutes. Bloody shit!" He bolted downtrack toward the engine cab, flailing his arms over his head. "Highball. Start the train. Haul ass!"

What had I done? I froze in place, my body unable to obey my frantic mind. The chugs of the locomotive reverberated in my ears. Guide was moving the train.

"Don't just stand there," Antonio shouted, hunched over with one foot on the canister, his wrench grinding on the metal rim. He forced off the top and dialed back the timer. "Run for your life."

My mind screamed for my legs to move. Nothing happened. Antonio placed the live charge on top of a powder keg. He shook my shoulders, slapped my face. Why couldn't I run? Then his arm shot between my legs. He tossed me across his shoulder, as if I weighed nothing, and ran.

A distant rumble brought me to my senses—the train must have looped and crossed above. Would Guide escape the coming blast? Daylight stabbed my eyes. Walls of dry earth bordered our path on both sides. We were out of the tunnel.

Antonio slung me against his chest without losing stride. He lunged from the track, skidded on gravel, and pinned me upright against the cut in the mountain. His body encased mine from behind, the side of my helmet and face pressed to rough rock. A roar belted my eardrums. Irregular clatter followed, a rain of shrapnel and rocks.

The shower of debris slowed, leaving a swirl of odors—smoke, powder, dust, leather and sweat. Antonio clutched me tighter. A warm sticky liquid streamed between my face and the rock—blood.

His grip relaxed, but my attempts to move proved futile. He still pinned my frame. His chest heaved in uneven spasms against my back.

"You or me," I said, "bleeding. Think it's you."

"Little rose," Antonio whispered.

Little rose? He must have guessed I wasn't Billy. My heartbeats quickened. Antonio mumbled something undecipherable, then groaned. His voice sounded so different, kind and concerned. He might actually care for me or Billy in some strange way. No! Antonio had tattooed me, threatened me, pinned me to the floor and jammed his knee between my legs. Men such as Antonio couldn't love. Desert dunes would sprout icicles first. Still, he'd just saved my life.

"Sweet Jesus, move along," I said, trying my best to project the character of Billy. "Time to get you patched and do the next tunnel." My arms and hands stung, scraped by the mountain.

"Are you all right?" Guide's voice called, sounding far away.

Guide was safe. Thank God and ancestors.

"Bring a canteen and some bandages," I shouted.

The crimson flow down the rock subsided. Antonio's breathing evened. He rolled to the side and braced against a vertical slab of mountain. Blood caked his hair and torn bandanna. More spotted his tattered shirt and dusty skin. His helmet was missing.

"You're lousy at—at demolition, Billy." He sat on a heap of gravel.

"Next time," I said, "don't lose your hat."

A sick feeling washed through me. My mistake could have killed Guide. And Antonio. Tony was an insect, but I didn't want him dead. Besides, his influence might help build a future asylum. Unite me with Carla. I should've admitted I was no longer Billy. Should I confess?

I sat beside him. Both he and Guide had left the comfort of their homes—everything—to help me and Billy. They would view Billy's unexplained absence as a betrayal. I couldn't admit the truth, not yet.

"Let me check you out," I said.

The cuts on Antonio's head appeared superficial. Scalps always bled a lot when sliced. No great problem so far. I checked his pulse. Strong and regular. He was probably all right but could use a bandage.

Down the tracks, Guide approached with a satchel.

Guide and Antonio—they both needed Billy, not me. Why had Billy gone away? He must have had a good reason. I motioned for Guide to hurry. I'd continue my pretense and have faith.

36. Trouble at Tehachapi

I WALKED WITH Antonio arm-in-arm through Tunnel Ten. An hour had passed since the mistimed explosion, yet his steps remained unsteady. The air hung heavy with dust. Could the structural beams crumble? I could have used Guide's help. But railroaders might come from the South. He had to keep watch.

Iodine, blood, dirt and engine grease stained Antonio's silk shirt, or what was left of it. The rain of rocks had scraped skin on his back. I clutched Guide's medicine satchel in my right hand. At least I'd cleaned and bandaged the worst of Antonio's wounds. His warmth radiated against my left arm and shoulder. Maybe he faked his uneven gait. Enjoyed being close to me.

We emerged into daylight. Guide waited at the train, a canteen slung around his neck and a burlap shirt rolled under one arm. Ten feet from the end boxcar, Antonio collapsed with a grunt.

"You don't look fit for another climb," Guide said. He offered the shirt and water.

"I'll shinny up the next cable for him," I said.

I nudged a camisole strap back onto my shoulder. Magdalena and I had climbed ropes on many occasions when children. Doing this one couldn't be much worse. Antonio made a weak attempt to rise but appeared to reconsider. I unrolled the burlap shirt and draped it across his lap. He winced as he maneuvered his way into the coarse garment.

"I want two canisters with the mechanical equivalent of a long slow fuse." Guide took a swig from the canteen. "Which ones, Tony?"

"Use the two..." Antonio rubbed his temples. "Nearest the door." He closed his eyes, hunched his shoulders. His arms encircled his bent knees.

Good instructions. There'd be no mix-up of canisters this time. An odd light gleamed from a clump of scrub oaks on the adjacent hillside. Metal caught the sun's rays. Guide tapped Antonio's arm and pointed. Someone was out there. With a gun. Did an enemy track us?

In Promise, I'd known little about airships. Mountain foothills probably weren't easy places for such craft to patrol. But now I was in British South California. Would the enemy approach from the sky once I reached the flat lowland?

•

Guide and I unloaded rope, cable, tools and canisters, then hauled them into Tunnel Ten. The tracks looked pretty good in the dim light from miner's hats, despite the premature blast in the lower bore. Still, the ceiling or floor might cave. And railway constables, if they arrived while I dangled on a rope, would open fire. Even if authorities didn't show up soon, the gunman on the next hillside could start shooting. A mystic died when the Shadow World decreed. But what about Guide? What about the rest of my mission?

I studied a wooden beam above Guide. Several drops of water dripped onto my nose. He shot a hand harpoon. The shaft's tip penetrated a ceiling beam and held fast. I whistled with approval and slapped his back. Guide could do anything.

I grasped the rope with my gravel-scraped palms and pulled myself upward, a loop of cable and clasps dangling around my neck. Once, I'd hung in terror over a chasm and reached for a goat's lead rope. I took a deep breath and inched higher, but didn't look down.

I rigged the pulley, banging my knuckles against the beam. My arms ached like I carried a sack of stones. Guide hoisted a canister. I maneuvered the cylinder into place and strapped it. Blood trickled from the backs of my hands. Here came the second canister.

At last, I slid with a wobble down the hoist line to the track, landing with a thump. Guide looped and gathered the rope. Antonio, on sentry, greeted us outside, his color somewhere between that of brandy and beer. He looked almost normal again. A canteen rested beside him in the gravel.

"Is our traveling companion still out there?" Guide said. "Can't be a U.S. Fed or a British constable. He would have interrupted our work."

"He's a Mendoza," Antonio said. "I can feel it. Problem is, I can't read his mind."

"Maybe it's time you learned how to run a train." Guide set down the coiled cable. "Start by watching us."

A wise back-up plan. I picked up the canteen to rinse my bloodied hands. As long as Guide did the teaching.

The routines in the remaining tunnels were roughly identical. Guide and Antonio deposited explosives in each bore. The men knew what they were doing. Stuff would blow up when it should. I minded the engine and prayed for their speedy return. As Guide slid shut the door of the ammo car for the last time, he whistled to Antonio.

"There's a charge and Clockman tucked in the corner," Guide called.

"Leave them where they are." Antonio climbed the engine cab's ladder.

"I'll move them to the stable," Guide said. "Nothing in the end car from here on."

I wound my pocket watch. I had worries enough. Let the men decide where to put the canister and the wind-up person. As long as they kept him and his staring amber eyes out of the engine cab.

•

The train made the sixth crossing over Tehachapi Creek at four-ten in the afternoon and headed down straight track. A series of muffled booms interrupted the rhythm of running noise. Antonio grinned. The rest of the tunnels had exploded. I could have danced atop the tender.

Guide's expression remained somber, but he was odd that way.

I leaned back in my seat and lit a cigar. Billy would have done likewise. I stretched my right leg along the length of the window and laughed. The tunnels were down, the train was working, and nobody had shot at me. I puffed on the cigar. The taste and smell of the tobacco weren't half-bad. The locomotive rolled over a bridge. Antonio's earlier comment slipped into my mind. This was the seventh and final crossing of Tehachapi Creek, a good omen, after all.

Crossings over water... For years the bridge on the way to the Cave of Light near Promise had been my stopping point. Yet I'd have no reason to turn back at this creek. A ghostly light shone ahead. I sat up straight and stubbed out my cigar. The whistle rope glowed plaid, but without an extra flash of green or red. What was going on?

"Trouble's coming," I said. I pulled the rope and generated a long wail on the whistle. "Ethan's gone tartan."

"The Brits must have gathered at Tehachapi Station," Guide said. "Or our friends with the bombs. Or both."

"And you're announcing our arrival," Antonio said to me, "with a signal to stop?" He readied his eighty-niner, steadying himself as the locomotive swayed.

"Bastards'll know something's wrong if I don't." I hadn't remembered the significance of a long whistle blast. I yanked the whistle rope a second time. "Rail book procedure," I added, figuring I was right.

"Then whistle but keep going," Antonio said.

I nodded and grasped the throttle. A red ball of light danced above the tracks ahead. I blinked. The light vanished. Had I seen Ethan's signal to stop or just imagined it? I whistled off again. The red light must have been for real, the Shadow World's reminder to add water to the tender.

"We can't just whiz past two full towers," I said. "The Brits will hit us now or later, after our tanks go dry."

Tehachapi loomed closer, a sprawling collection of low wood-frame and adobe buildings against a mountain backdrop. A tumbleweed rolled across a sandy road. The station appeared deserted. What I could see of the town looked quiet, too.

My eighty-niner rested against the front window. I slid it closer and applied the train brakes. What if I needed to fire the gun and couldn't remember how? The train crawled past the stationhouse. I overshot the first water tower and had to use reverse gear. A second tower lay ahead.

Guide looked in all directions before leaving the cab, his eighty-niner off the safety setting. With a rifle slung over my shoulder, I scaled the tender, then lifted open the nearest hatch. I balanced on the edge of the car, holding my long pole, unable to reach the rope on the waterspout. The wind whipped at my shirt and locks of loose hair.

Guide climbed up the crisscrossed two-by-fours beneath the nearest water tower. He tossed me the spout rope. I clutched the frayed line and maneuvered the pipe into position. As water gushed from the metal spout, I looked for movement in or around the stationhouse, which was forty or fifty feet to the rear of our end car. No sign of danger there. The far water tower appeared clear, too.

Guide's feet touched the ground again. He disappeared from view between the two remaining boxcars. Maybe he planned to use them for cover. But I, standing on top of the tender, would be an inviting target for a gunman. If only the tank would fill faster.

A light—tartan and taller than Galen—shimmered between the train and the stationhouse. Ethan's signal. Enemies must be out there. I needed to warn Guide and Antonio but couldn't see them.

"Ambush!" My heart thudded.

Gunfire ripped through the air. I crashed flat against the tender. Antonio returned fire from atop the engine cab, peppering the side of the stationhouse. Bullets tore overhead. I needed to help fight back. I pushed the butt end of my eighty-niner against my shoulder. Where the heck should I aim?

The next volley of bullets spewed from ahead of the locomotive. The spout near me floundered in the air and spurted cold water in every direction. Pelted by the cascade, I clutched my rifle. I couldn't see or shoot. Couldn't do anything.

Tobacco. I smelled tobacco—wonderful, stinky tobacco. Billy would help me. My brain screamed *Scotch whisky*. Billy's strength surged through my being. I wasn't him, though.

Ethan's tartan narrowed to a tight circle and zigzagged in the spurting waterfall. I could see the base of the far tower. I tracked Ethan's plaid light and opened fire. I kept firing, my ears unable to shut out human screams.

Screams. A sleeping baby in an asylum couldn't cry out as a worker smothered it. I would have been murdered if Great-Grandma hadn't rescued me. To defend myself, I had to focus on that thought. My gun stopped firing, must have run out of ammunition. No one else was shooting either.

I stood on wobbly legs, drenched yet unharmed. Billy was gone again. My palm pressed the golden pendant against my chest. The jewelry must have protected me, as it had on the night of the train. I heaved the waterspout clear of the tender, by then awash. Several bodies slumped near the stationhouse and three more by the far tower, their railway-constable blues oozing red. How could I have been part of this, even to save infants? I knelt on the opposite side of the tender and vomited.

"Billy!" Antonio said. "The old man's hit."

Shot? Guide had been shot? I scrambled to the iron grips and fumbled my way off the tender. Ethan couldn't have wanted us to stop. I must have misread that signal.

Guide was wedged underneath the end boxcar, his pistol aimed at a station guard. Thank God he was alive. A geyser of blood gushed from the guard's half-severed arm and spattered the ground. Twenty feet of gentle incline separated the boxcar from the train. Guide had uncoupled the box. The guard writhed where the railcar had struck him, his pleas for mercy countered by the trumpeting of the horses in the stable and the pounding of their hooves against wooden planks.

Antonio raised his eighty-niner, his face devoid of emotion. But no gunfire came, no bullets. Instead, a thread of blue light pulsed with a crackling hum, not from Antonio's gun, but from somewhere behind me. The beam hit the guard's forehead, directly above the nose. Smoke rose from his temples. His head burst into flames. *Lord of Earth and Heaven.* I dropped down, flattened my body against the coarse gravel, then twisted to look behind me.

"Unholy shit of Satan!" Antonio had already wheeled around. The air carried the stink of seared flesh.

"You should choose your water stops with more care," a man's voice shouted.

The length of several boxcars away, a man in a dark suit and top hat sat astride a black horse. He waved an odd-looking gun above his head. Longer than a regular pistol, shorter than a rifle, it had a polished brass barrel the shape of a narrow vase with a bulbous base. I'd seen this weapon in the Cave of Light. Replace the owner's suit with old-fashion breeches and a scarlet sash, shave off those muttonchops, and he'd look like Red Sash Man, the mysterious ghost I'd met two-and-a-half years ago. He spurred his mount and rode away in a cloud of dust. If I'd not noticed this friend arrive, what about an enemy?

"Block the engine's wheels," I said to Antonio, who still stared toward the receding rider. "Then comb that station."

Guide—I'd almost forgotten about him, about his wound. I faced him. Tears stung the corners of my eyes.

"Are you pinned?" I said.

"No," Guide said. "Caught a ricochet, I think, just after I cut the car free. Hid under here once it stopped rolling." He winced. "Anything leaking?"

"They got the forward tanker," I said. "It's losing water. The rest doesn't look too bad. They were aiming high, at me."

294

Guide inched out from under the car, his breathing labored, the lower left leg of his striped coveralls soggy with blood. I slit away the stained denim with my knife, exposing the wound in his muscular calf. This was my fault. All my fault. I'd read that signal wrong.

Antonio emerged from the stationhouse, the edges of his mouth turned down. He spat at the nearest corpse.

"There's a boy in there," he said as he approached. "Maybe eight years old. Bloody thunder, letting a kid tag along. To this sort of party? Sonofabitch!"

I clenched my abdominal muscles tight. Had my stupidity caused a child's death? Antonio rested a hand on my shoulder. My face must have expressed my inner turmoil.

"I didn't hurt the kid," he said. "He won't bother us. He's pretty scared." Antonio crouched and studied Guide's wound, his expression sullen. "You won't be pleased when I dig out the bullet."

"I'm sure I won't," Guide said.

Antonio stood and wiped his hands with a shop rag. I fetched two medicine satchels and a small blanket. I remembered the novice on the pilgrimage and knew what Antonio would need. I spread the blanket on a section of flat hardpan, weighted down the corners, then unpacked supplies.

Antonio removed his shirt. He splashed alcohol into two clean quart jars and added water, the veins in his arms prominent. Dried blood and scraped skin on his back marked the aftermath of my earlier error. I soaked cloth strips in one jar and waved them to dry. Antonio rubbed down his hands and lower arms with alcohol from the second container, followed by iodine. He blocked the rising wind with his own body and cleaned around Guide's wound.

He inspected a fine-tipped scalpel. I dug out the match tin with one hand, still clutching a rippling rag in the other. Antonio plunged the knife into alcohol and flamed the blade.

I clasped Guide's hand and braced for the bite of his fingernails. Antonio slid the tip of the scalpel into the wound. Guide's grip tightened. His free hand dug into the dirt.

"How you doing?" Antonio said.

"Hurt more that—that first time," Guide said through clenched teeth. "In your bedroom."

"You swore you liked it." Antonio pressed deeper, squinting.

"You kept a butterfly knife." Guide grimaced. "I would have sworn the moon was made of frijoles." His eyes closed. "You knew that."

How could the men talk about such matters in my presence, even if they thought I were Billy?

Antonio slid the tip of his scalpel under the bullet. Guide scraped the ground with his fingernails, but didn't dig into my skin. If only he'd hurt me. I deserved the pain.

"You once wanted to kill me," Antonio said to Guide. "Sorry you didn't?" He grasped the bullet with forceps and plucked it from Guide's calf.

I rinsed the wound with salted water, then applied the iodine solution. Best to remain silent. The men had to resolve past differences in their own way. I pinched shut the flesh and bandaged Guide's leg with the strips of clean cloth. The wound was more than superficial, and corruption a real possibility. Maybe the effect of the elixir from years past would help him heal. I closed my eyes to pray but blue light pulsed into my memory.

The stranger with the light-beam gun. He'd killed the railway guard and must be a Mendoza. My fingertips brushed my magic pendant. The manifestation in the Cave of Light must have been a prophecy.

Who else killed people with light instead of lead? Did only an occasional Mendoza possess such weapons, or did the South California constables, as well?

37. Shadrach, Meshach and Abednego

ANTONIO BOARDED THE train on the fireman's side of the engine cab. How could I run an engine with him? He crouched, stretched, and otherwise contorted to familiarize himself with the modest maze of pipes and valves. What were they called? The manifold. My mind repeated those two words a dozen times. To continue with my pretense, I'd have to remember the correct names for mechanical things.

A valve with a slow leak spat onto the hot steel rim of the firebox door, a solemn reminder of the deadly heat and pressure within the boiler. Repetitive huffs evoked a jumble of memories left by Billy. When the steam throttle was shut, the engine didn't chug. A blowing device had to push the smoke up the stack. The blower produced that noise.

Guide sat on the floor, one foot or so to Antonio's left and below the window, his back supported by the boxy base of a seat, his lame leg straight. The smell of fuel oil and grease permeated my mouth and nose, almost overpowering those of sweat and blood. *Poor, dear Guide.*

"All right," Antonio said to Guide, "the water glass is at the one-third mark. What's next?"

"Try not to step on me." Guide shifted position, his lips and jaws set in a tight grimace. "After that, be sure your reading's true."

Antonio rested his gloved hand on a lever. Guide grunted a warning, then hacked phlegm into a dirty red rag and motioned to me. He wanted me to do the demonstration.

I nodded, even as panic surged within. Earlier, I'd paid little attention to most of Guide's mechanical manipulations. Which gauge cock should I open? Something terrible might happen if I chose the wrong one.

I glanced at the nearest water glass, shaped like a handle on an urn. A thin halo of light formed around a gauge cock below the glass and sparkled. A secret message for me from the spirits. I pulled then pushed a little lever. The light reappeared on a stirrup-shaped handle attached to a short rod. My hand eased the control. A mushy whooshing sound followed. When I finished, the level of water in the boiler glass had resettled at the one-half mark. My brain had resettled, too. The air contained no hint of tobacco, but a member of my family was near.

"That's all there is to it," I said to Antonio with a shrug.

Wait. Billy would have done an actual explanation using railroad jargon. Had I just used the injector or the feed pump? And what did those three letters on the steam gauge mean?

"Push that thing over there," I said, "to keep water in the boiler when we're underway and working steam. And whatever else happens, hold this son of a gun at a half-glass and no more than 230 psi."

•

The western sky reddened. I pulled the train onto a sidetrack at Mojave. The golden-hued panorama looked surreal against the flat, dusty landscape of the railroad yard, with its many rows of tracks. I fixed the magnificence of the Sunday sunset to memory, a morsel of color worth savoring in case tomorrow's destination became a darkened Shadow World home.

Antonio hustled to inventory the water remaining in the damaged tanker. I dipped the stick to take a reading on the tender's fuel oil. We could stock up on tower water here but would have to transfer oil from our tank car. I didn't know how to accomplish such a job in full daylight, let alone in the dark. Maybe there was a way to move one of the fuel cars onto a parallel branch of track. I prayed for Ethan's advice.

"Time to switch some stuff around," I called to Antonio. Another challenge to recall railroad talk. "We'll cut a—an oil can to the siding. I want you to handle the hoses."

298

Antonio lowered his head, his knuckles pressed between his temples. Ethan's red glow shimmered beside him. Hopefully, Ethan delivered another talk inside Antonio's mind.

"Let's go," Antonio called. He wedged his hands into a pair of canvas gloves. "We're going to back up the train fifty feet."

At least he seemed to know what he was doing.

•

I limped beside the waiting train, a two-foot-long grease gun in my left hand. Every muscle in my body ached. Antonio patted my back, as if we were old comrades. He had shouldered most of the physical burden of refueling and switching cars during the past two hours. How thoughtful he'd behaved since that confrontation atop the tender at Caliente's water tower. Knowing Antonio, the respite wouldn't last.

He smiled and asked for the greaser. The lamp on his helmet lit up the wheel area he wanted to lube. He slipped the tip of a grease stick into the side portal of the gun. I held the bar in place.

"Billy," he said, "you know this run well?"

"Used to." What might he plan to ask next?

Antonio lined up the nozzle to reach some sort of mechanical part above a main wheel. The greaser hissed and delivered slugs of ooze. The stick was shorter then.

"How far to where the track splits to the south?"

The question caught me off guard. Guide's maps had mileage scales. I'd rarely paid much attention to them. How many miles did every inch on his rail map represent?

"It's about two hundred miles from here to the split," I said.

"Do we have enough fuel and water to get there?"

I'd no idea how long supplies would last. The locomotive had been using far more water than fuel.

"Water's going to be the problem."

Antonio faced me, his head tilted to one side. "Ever run a boiler down to the—what did you call it—the crown sheet?"

"Blazes, no." The name for the separator between the firebox and the boiler was one term I remembered. "A man would have to be crazy to—"

The corners of Antonio's mouth shifted into a half-smile. Why, he wanted to run the train to that crossing, even if the boiler ran dry and exploded.

"There's a lynch party fixing to head out of Yuma by now," he said. "If we block the east-south crossing, we've got a clear stab at the Colorado River. Unless an airship shows up. That last canister of nitro back there—we can detonate it inside our cab at the crossing. Between the shrapnel and destruction of tracks, it'll be days—even weeks—before another engine can pass in any direction."

"You're nuts," I said, doing my best to respond as Billy would. "Besides, Brits won't need a train to follow. They'll have horses and a..." What was the name of that raft-like platform on wheels, the one that rolled down the tracks when the riders pumped a handle? "And a handcar."

"They'll need half the horses to lug supplies," Antonio said. "There won't be more than eight or ten men sniffing our trail."

He wrapped the end of the grease stick in an oily rag. I walked beside him around the rear of the train. Antonio had been on the pursuing end of more than one manhunt. I'd have to rely on his expertise to escape the authorities.

"We'll have a long haul on horseback to the Colorado." I gestured toward the cab where Guide dozed. "His leg'll swell up like rice in a hot bath."

"Could we pick up a handcar at the next station?" Antonio lined up the nozzle of the grease gun with one of the remaining parts to be lubricated.

"You'll sooner shit gold," I said, gleaning bits of information left in my memory by Billy. "Everything valuable in that part of the desert gets stolen or melts."

"Graham's tough," Antonio said. "You know that."

The hisses of the greaser blended with those from the locomotive. Guide's wound. The constables. The boiler. The Colorado. I couldn't deal with so many problems at once. And I was growing dependent on Antonio. Sooner or later he'd use that to his advantage.

"So, how you plan to get downriver?" I said. "Do the backstroke?"

"There'll be a rubber raft." He wiped his hands on a grimy red rag. "And a man to ferry it."

I pictured churning white water roaring through rugged, isolated land. I couldn't question Antonio about the rapids or terrain we would encounter. He'd expect Billy to be familiar with the route.

"This guide," I said, "can we trust him?"

"Ramon's a bastard, but a good one." Antonio grinned, his left arm bent and palm turned up. His thick fingers clutched at the air with obvious pride. "He's my son."

Antonio had a son? Guide had mentioned the existence of a mistress but nothing about children. Antonio didn't seem the sort to be a decent father. But then, he was more responsible than my own father had been.

"Do you see him much?" I said.

"We write. He knows the Colorado like it flows in his veins. Can make a man vanish mid-river and reappear safe God only knows where." He smiled. "My son's the best."

My glance met Antonio's. His eyes held an odd expression, one I couldn't identify. I turned away and fumbled for my pocket watch. We should board the train and get rolling. He touched my shoulder.

"My woman had another baby, too," Antonio said. "Not mine, or one she wanted." He squinted. "She wrote and told me the infant died at birth. A shame. My barren cook woman had offered to raise the child."

Guide's story of rape surfaced from my pool of memories. The baby's father must have been the man Antonio had hunted and murdered. The point of Antonio's personal disclosure, intended for Billy, eluded me. Maybe his statements represented another proposition—an unwelcome verbal puff into my ear. I turned to avoid him. I reached for the ladder to the engine cab.

"Where's your woman now?" I said.

"Don't you keep track of your own family, Billy? Pneumonia got her eight winters back."

"Oh, yeah," I said. "Don't know why I forgot."

I climbed into the cab, my ears pounding with my heartbeats. Antonio followed. God, he'd almost guessed my secret. I eased open the throttle. The driving wheels slipped against the sanded rails before gaining traction. The slips of my tongue concerned me far more.

Guide dozed on the floor, hunched against the rear left of the engine cab. Antonio knelt beside him and checked his pulse. If only Guide were well. I turned away, longing to rock him in my arms and cry. The engine chugged louder. How good to hear the cacophony from the stack, flash wall and rolling steel.

"We'll be crossing the border at the Gila River," Antonio called. "Didn't you head down there with my father once?"

I searched the memories Billy had left in my head. Nothing about the Gila remained. Guide's topographical charts of South California and Arizona depicted many desert areas. I needed to pry more information out of Antonio to even discuss the subject.

"Stuff your idea," I said. "That place is a piece of Hell."

"You've lost your sense of adventure." Antonio laughed, his tone more amused than cynical. "Death's made you soft."

I mumbled an unintelligible reply. This conversation was over. The controls blurred. I leaned back in the engineer's seat and rubbed my forehead. So sleepy. The train swayed. My eyelids lowered. I jabbed my fingernails against my palm. I needed to stay awake and hold the speed to thirty.

•

I helped Antonio siphon the last of the tanker cars dry two stops and five hours later. Ten feet from the locomotive, he lifted his oil lantern, illuminating the painted numbers on a milepost. The east-south fork couldn't be more than fifty to seventy-five miles away. The tender wasn't full, though. We'd never get that far.

My eyes burned from lack of sleep. The rest of my body ached, throbbed, or did both. If only I could rest. I lifted my right foot to reach the lowest rung on the boarding ladder, then stretched my arms upward to grasp two iron grips. My mind told my arms to pull, but they couldn't part my left foot from the ground. Antonio gripped my hips from behind. He boosted me upward. I crawled into the engine cab like a dying lizard, then sat on the floor, my back pressed against the base of the seat. Guide slumbered on the opposite side of the cab, his shirt and red bandanna damp with sweat.

Antonio unscrewed the lid of a canteen and steadied the opening against my lips. His reddened eyes and hunched shoulders betrayed his own exhaustion. I gulped down a mouthful of water, then gestured toward Guide. Antonio roused him and offered the canteen. Guide managed a few lame swallows.

I knelt beside Guide and clasped his hot, limp hand. His precarious condition was my fault. The memory of Mama's final moments washed through me, leaving a deep, searing ache. Mama hadn't drunk much water that day.

Antonio touched my shoulder. His strong arms guided me to my feet. How kind his touch felt—not what I expected. The emotion radiating from his eyes mirrored that within my soul. He feared for Guide's life, too.

Oh, to weep, to shout my own name and confess I was no longer Billy. These two flawed men would forgive my lie. My hand trembled as I reached up to ease open the throttle of the locomotive. To Guide and Antonio, I was a vulnerable young woman who needed protection. Billy, on the other hand, could take care of himself. The men had enough concerns on their minds. I couldn't admit the truth yet.

•

The train traversed the darkened desert on Monday morning. Was this still the Mojave? The engine cab rocked from side-to-side, like a cradle in the wind. The water pump hammered with a steady rhythm. Each beat marked the pace at which the tender drained. No lapses to sleep happened then.

Antonio broke out portions of jerky. I chewed the dry, salty meat. The pump would suck air and sound different once the cistern in the tender ran dry. If only I knew how close we were to the fork in the tracks. I leaned out the window, looking for a milepost. A rush of cool air slammed my face. The straight tracks ahead of the locomotive's beam doubled and twisted, like snakes writhing in a pit. I blinked and pulled back inside the cab. Maybe more food would help my eyes focus.

Antonio's glance darted between the boiler water glass and the brass plate demarcating the crown sheet of the firebox. I could almost hear worries churn within his brain. According to Billy, plugs in a crown sheet usually melted before a boiler ran completely dry. When they did, steam and residual water poured through the plug holes into the firebox and quenched the flames, preventing an explosion. I, as Billy, hadn't found the inspection records for this boiler. The plugs in this crown sheet might be coated with accumulated minerals and not melt in time.

As soon as the pump sucked air, we would have to jump clear of the moving train. That wouldn't solve our other problem—the surrounding desert. We might survive an explosion, but wouldn't get far without horses and supplies. I stuffed a stub of dried meat into my mouth.

A light blazed in the darkness ahead. I jerked to full attention. Ethan's lamp flashed red followed by plaid. A warning. Constables couldn't have reached us so soon. Only one explanation for the display made sense. The water level in the tender dropped very low. Spirits knew such things.

Maybe I should rouse Guide and ask for advice. No, he was unresponsive, and every minute mattered. Antonio needed to get him clear of the train. Ethan's lamp sent another warning. Antonio's plan to run the tender dry was crazy. I'd order him to cut the fire.

I turned toward Antonio. His tall frame clothed in scuffed leather and rough burlap. His set jaw and determined expression. The sweat-soaked bandanna on his head. This man was as formidable as ever. He wouldn't let me halt the train. Only one course of action might work. I had to put distance between the locomotive and the boxcars that held our horses and supplies.

"Tank's nearly empty," I shouted to Antonio. "Get ready to ditch and help the old man roll clear."

Antonio stripped off his burlap shirt and wound the cloth around Guide's bandaged leg. Guide opened his eyes and squinted. Antonio's bare chest heaved in and out with every breath. He extracted his leather jacket from behind the toolbox.

"You better wear this," he said to me.

"Keep it," I said. Even if I were to jump, he needed to wear the jacket to protect Guide. Besides, I shouldn't let Antonio scrape his own hide to shreds for me. "I'm staying to uncouple the engine from the train."

Antonio just stood there, grasping the dusty jacket by the collar. His face contorted, as if he'd been kicked in the groin. I wiggled my hands into a pair of canvas gloves. He was wasting valuable time. Why didn't he move?

"Get on your frigging leather." The command spilled from my mouth, as if I were Billy. "Haul ass!"

Antonio snapped out of his daze and stuffed his arm down the sleeve of his jacket. I leaned in front of him, surprised by the force of my words. I notched down the control for the fire, then turned and slammed shut the throttle. Antonio clasped Guide against him. The two men clung to the boarding ladder, the sleeves of Guide's shirt whipped by wind. I'd better brake. Air hissed like a coiled snake, and the train slowed, wheels grinding against the rails.

"Jump," I shouted.

The men rolled off the ladder into the night like some four-legged tumbleweed in leather. I counted to twelve and jerked open the throttle. Fifteen seconds...twenty... What was that gurgling sound? The pump sucked both water and air. The train was running for nonexistent water and an unreachable crossing. I faced a race with death.

I scrambled up the front end of the tender in the dark, my hands grasping iron grips, ladder rungs—anything I could find. A rush of wind pelted the back and side of my head. Strands of unbraided hair veiled one eye. Grit lodged in the other. I pulled myself atop the rocking car, scooted on my hands and knees across a rounded metal surface.

The far end of the tender was only a foot away. I clung to iron handholds and edged down the rear face of that railcar. A mystic dies when the Shadow World decrees, and my turn might come within minutes. If so, may another woman's love comfort Galen. I prayed for Guide's healing and the safety of all my three men. Yes, even Antonio. I'd an asylum to build. Carla deserved a home. Alive or dead, I would need Tony's help. Besides, I needed to purify my heart with forgiveness to face the Guardians of the Portals for the last time.

A lurch of the tender slammed me against a wall of steel. My shoulders and arms throbbed with pain. My eyes still stung. I groped for footing. The tip of one boot touched something flat and hard. Ethan's crimson glow lit the darkness. There it was, the coupling between the tender and the first boxcar. Near my feet the connection stretched out tight.

Billy's railroad memories, the ones he'd left me, tumbled through my mind. Parting the coupling in this taut configuration would activate the brakes on both the locomotive and the train's cars. If there was any hope of the locomotive pushing onward, I needed slack. If only I could see the surrounding terrain. A slope might lie ahead, a dip. The cars might tip toward each other. There might be a chance, then, particularly if the throttle were closed.

"Walk the earth," I called to Ethan, "like Billy did. Like Jesus." I lurched from side to side. "Shut the throttle."

Ethan's glow tightened into a scarlet ball and didn't vanish. He couldn't help me. Death knells of stack exhaust pounded at my ears. Then the chugs halted. The outline of the tender drifted closer. We were in a sag, and someone or something had closed the throttle. Ethan blazed green on the end of a bent iron rod—the lever that would cut the cars free of the engine. I faced the boxcar, straddling the coupling and air. I reached for the lever and missed.

The car pitched to the side. My left foot slipped on the coupling. I teetered downward. The shifting metal would crush me if I fell. Green and tartan signals flashed in the blackness. I regained my footing. I stretched my hand toward the lever. Then something changed, felt different. The train was pulling out of the sag. The coupling would turn taut soon. Only one chance remained.

I lunged toward the cut lever. My gloved palm slipped against my only handhold on the tender. I yanked the lever with all the strength I had. A rush of air came, a hiss. The brake hoses had parted.

Both my hands reached out and clutched a grab iron on the boxcar. One of my feet dangled free in the air, then the other. I thudded against the wooden face of the boxcar. There was no way I could hang on.

My feet—a hard surface lay beneath them. I'd found the boxcar end of the coupling. My chest heaved in and out. My lungs couldn't get enough air. I turned my head and looked over my shoulder. The outline of the engine receded in waning night. My plan to keep the engine running had worked. Then a flash of unleashed steam hissed like Hell's gatekeepers and billowed from the locomotive in all directions. I scrunched my eyes shut and braced for the explosion and shock wave.

A brilliant light surrounded me. A fire. But my eyes were closed. How could I see fire? Four figures, three clothed in hooded brown robes and one in radiant white, walked amidst the flames, unharmed. I recognized the vision, a scene from a Bible story Mama had loved. An angel of God had delivered Shadrach, Meshach, and Abednego from the fiery furnace of King Nebuchadnezzar.

Two of the figures in brown pushed back their hoods, their faces those of Guide and Antonio. The third face should be my own, unless death poised to take me. I wanted to live, to marry and have children. To see that asylum built. To take care of Carla. Life was so precious. Was I the third figure?

The remaining brown hood fell away, revealing Clockman's stern leather face. He raised his arm. His hand clutched something I couldn't see. I tensed my muscles. This was it for me—the end. Then I beheld the face of the angel. My own face. What did the vision mean?

"Billy," a voice called, as if from a dream.

Did the sound emanate from the world of death or life? A cool breeze brushed my skin. I could feel my fingers, stabs of pain.

"We're both all right," the voice said. Antonio. "Where are you?"

At some point in time, Antonio peeled my hands loose from the grab iron and eased me down from the coupling bar. He lifted me into his arms. I nestled against his scuffed leathers, one part of my spirit within me and another somewhere else. In my strange dream of dreams, Antonio's sweat smelled so sweet. A floral scent grew strong. Lilacs.

Who was I? Whom did I love? Where was I going?

Journal of Desert, River and Wind, Year 1896

38. A Very Special Gift

THE PLEASANT AROMA of mint, where had it come from? I shifted my sore body and opened my eyes. Antonio crouched on one knee beside me, a metal cup in his hands. Aromatic vapor wisped from the cup toward his face and mine. Mint tea!

Scruffy whiskers covered Antonio's cheeks and chin. Dried blood streaked his temples below the edge of his bandanna. He tilted his head, the expression in his reddened eyes as warm as the fire behind him.

"Take a sip, Billy," he said. "Guide still sleeps. We need to eat breakfast and talk."

What did he want to talk about? I yawned and glanced at the sun, still low in the sky. I pushed back my blanket and sat up, then took a sip of the warm, tasty tea.

"Thank you," I said.

The morning chill had not yet dissipated. The time must have been about eight o'clock. Monday. Guide snored at the edge of the fire circle, the bandages on his wound fresh and white. Antonio had changed them already. I stretched my arms. More sleep would have been nice. Still, three hours were better than nothing. Antonio managed on less.

Antonio stood, stirred the coals of the fire, then added more brush. The black hair on his calves poked through the rips in his leather pants. His scraped jacket looked like the victim of a wildcat's claws. My overalls were filthy but intact.

Thirty feet beyond the railbed, the saddled horses nickered and foraged under creosote for dry grass. Sparse and stubby vegetation yielded a landscape of pimpled sand.

The locomotive sat at the crossing, a half-mile away. A miracle in itself. The engine had released billows of steam last night but hadn't exploded. And I'd found Clockman in the engine cab, its leather hand on the throttle. Its arm had been raised, as I'd seen in my vision. Only the Shadow World's power could have moved the mechanical person from the stock car to the cab.

Antonio filled a second cup with boiling water. He added a skimpy wad of leaves, then stared into the distance where a blue haze garbed rugged peaks. Something ate at him. Antonio still thought I was Billy, and Billy had known when to mind his own business. I'd let him start the conversation when he was ready.

"You rode with my father," Antonio finally said. "He was a cruel man, no?"

"Yeah, sometimes," I said, remembering what Guide had told me.

"My father took what pleased him, Billy," Antonio said. "I'm sure you found that out." He peered straight into my eyes. "The morning I turned twelve, I found out, too. You understand?"

Antonio turned away and downed the rest of his tea as if he drank a slug of Scotch. I responded with a sympathetic grunt, the way Billy might have done. With luck, Antonio would skip the ugsome details.

"What sort of man does that to his son?" He moved closer to the fire, his right fist clenched. "I cowered in my room afterwards, staring at a spider on the ceiling. Shame and fear gradually subsided. Anger didn't. The spider crawled down the wall. I squashed it. Then I feigned illness."

Antonio unscrewed the lid on one of the canteens and poured cloudy water into the blackened pot. He set the pot atop the hot coals. Moisture on the vessel's bottom sizzled.

"After the household retired for the evening, Guide came to my room with a slice of the chocolate cake my mother had baked. He coaxed me to eat. Then he sat on the floor by my bed and kept watch. Bad dreams came. Each time I cried out, he clasped my hand."

310

Why was Antonio confessing this? His choice of words didn't match his character. Perhaps he schemed to gain my sympathy and physical favors.

"I've never taken my son," Antonio said, "but I've abused the friend who's treated me like one." He straightened the bandanna on his head. "I've become what I hated most."

I rose, stepped over to the fire and stood beside Antonio. I wasn't sure why. This man wasn't trustworthy. The water heated in the pot. Little bubbles formed. The milky fluid cleared. Antonio turned toward me, slipped his hand under my chin and tilted my face upward. His bloodshot eyes, pupils dark and intense, expressed wisdom rather than desire. His lips brushed my forehead.

"My son's mother lied to me," Antonio said. "Her other baby, the one I told you about, didn't die at birth. My woman abandoned you on the government's doorstep, Juanita. One year later, I murdered your father."

I stiffened. What a preposterous idea. It couldn't be true. My own natural father had given me a family heirloom to wear—the blue-and-white gown. That other kid's father had committed rape and run away to hide. I couldn't possibly be that child.

I opened my mouth to deliver a rebuttal, then gasped. Antonio had called me Juanita. He'd guessed I wasn't Billy. I pulled away from him, my eyes wide. How long had he known?

Antonio clasped me against his chest. I could hear the thumps of his racing heart. The discovery of my pretense should have unleashed his anger, not his affection. Antonio actually believed I was his woman's daughter. Why?

When Antonio had confronted me as Billy at the water tower, he'd backed off instead of harming me. He'd looked at me in such an odd way. His obnoxious behavior had subsided after that. He'd carried me from the tunnel and saved my life. I grasped for straws of memories, anything to sort fact from fiction.

Perhaps he'd noticed a resemblance between me and his mistress in recent days. No, that didn't make sense. The similarity would have come to his attention when we first met. Maybe not, though. Early on, Antonio had guessed I was a Mendoza like his mistress. Hundreds of Mendozas lived in South California. Could his claim be true?

"I have a gift for you, my little rose," Antonio said, his voice soft. "A very special gift—my life. No man can offer more."

What did he mean? I tried to speak but couldn't find words. He stepped back and rested his finger against my lips.

"This afternoon I'll be waiting when the pursuit train arrives. That last canister of nitro will buy you and Guide some time."

I couldn't let him do this, not after all that had happened during the past two days. Enough violence weighed on my conscience. Besides, I needed his help to care for Guide, and his influence to construct a new asylum. There also was the matter of Carla.

"We're all staying together," I said.

Antonio shook his head. He removed his onyx ring and pressed it into my palm. The corners of his eyes misted.

"Give this to your half-brother when you and Guide reach the Colorado River. Tell Ramon that a man has the right to decide when and where to die, to the extent Heaven allows."

In the Cave of Light, flames had blackened and become a ring on my finger. My breath faltered in mid-inhalation. The ghost man's eyes—his hero's eyes—had been a combination of Antonio's and Guide's.

Tears spilled down the curves of Antonio's whiskered cheeks. This man was no hero, despite his eyes. He might be trying to trick me. What should I believe? Maybe it no longer mattered. I wept with Antonio, the tragedies of our lives and Guide's so overwhelming.

"I've made such a mess of things," I said. "I should have told you both when Billy left me."

"We guessed you weren't him right away," Antonio said. "Billy never would have panicked in the tunnel. We knew we faced an ambush, too. If not at Tehachapi, later. Guide wasn't wounded because of you. It just happened."

The men should have confronted me about the pretense. They must have laughed behind my back. If I were in the Shadow World, I would have glowed embarrassment pink.

"You handled the train fine," Antonio said. "We saw no reason to interrupt your game."

He motioned toward the horses. The animals were ready for travel. Railroad constables—even an airship—could arrive within a few hours. They might have light-beam guns. I had to take Guide to safety.

•

Antonio lowered the back of Clockman's overalls, moved several small levers, then wound a key. With jerky movements, the mechanical person mounted King Solomon. Somehow, we managed to seat Guide in front. He teetered in the saddle. In fact, Clockman didn't look too steady, either. Would they even be able to ride? I reached up and adjusted another control. Clockman wrapped its arms around Guide and held him in place. That looked much better.

Ibn Sina nickered. Great-Grandpa was ready to get going. Little time remained. But I wanted to know my mother's name. About Carla. So many things. For the past half hour, I'd either been too upset or busy to inquire. Antonio touched my shoulder. I turned and asked my first question.

"Your mother's name was Anita," he said.

"What makes you sure your woman was my mother?"

"Her ghost appeared behind you at the water tower, when you were Billy. Angry as blazes." He smiled. "She hovered beside you this morning, too. While you slept."

So it was true. I lowered my eyelids.

"Did you ever have a chance to write that letter to the asylum—to insist my friend's niece be protected?"

"Ah, yes, the letter. I meant to tell you. I delivered it in person to the man in charge." He shook his head. "It appears the girl was adopted recently. The trail ended there."

"Oh," I said. Another dream evaporated. Another loss gnawed at my stomach. Fresh tears stung my eyes. "Thank you for trying."

Antonio rocked me against him, the way Papa had comforted me years ago. In a few minutes I'd leave with Guide. Cross another river of life. Not turn back. I inhaled the odors of sweat, dirt and leather, embedding the smells in my memory forever.

39. The Price

FOLLOWING THE TRACKS led me east, past creosote, dry wash, branching cholla cacti and dunes. The warm autumn air smelled clean. Guide swayed in the saddle. Thank God for Clockman. King Solomon, still possessed by Great-Uncle Raúl, stepped with wisdom, as if transporting a newborn baby.

Antonio should have detonated the nitro with a timer, then traveled with us. The events of recent days had mellowed him. I would have tolerated his company and welcomed his help. The horses' shod hooves clomped with a mournful rhythm on the uneven dirt trail. Only the dead or Ramon, if I found him, could tell me about Anita, my natural mother. And that new asylum would remain a dream until I recruited another Mendoza to my cause. Life was little more than a chain of losses.

Distant rumbles marked the fourth hour of our travel. Ragged clouds gathered in the darkening midday sky. Had I heard thunder or an explosion? Guide's eyes remained closed. A gentle rain sprinkled. The heavens cried. Spirits whispered in my ears while Ibn Sina nickered. Antonio was gone.

I kissed the hawk's head on my ring, repeating my action each half hour. Seven kisses brought me to an eroded section of railbed, its flat base and vertical slope nearly devoid of gravel. Rusty rails and gray, splintered ties ran along the top of the bed, six feet or so from the base. These tracks weren't often used. A good place to camp for the night.

Clockman waited. I adjusted dials and levers on his back, then wound him with his key. He helped Guide dismount and sit against the slope of the railbed. Dark circles hung below Guide's eyes. The past few days had aged him a hundred years. I coaxed him to drink water, then changed the dressing on his wound. The redness and swelling had grown worse. If only I had better medicine than alcohol and iodine.

I set a fire of sticks and dry brush. Clumps of papery cheatgrass made good tinder. Guide shivered in the firelight, coughed and spat up phlegm. I wrapped blankets around him. Clouds shrouded sections of the star-studded sky. The healers on the pilgrimage to the River of Tears had discussed treating wound corruption. I should have memorized every word.

"Go to him," voices whispered as I sought more fuel. "You're a mystic. His ancestors can only heal him through your offering of love."

I glanced around, blinking. No ghostly lights, but those must have been spirit voices. I already loved Guide. What were the spirits talking about? My hand reached for a tangle of dry brush, then stopped. Could they possibly have meant—

"I can't go to him like that," I exclaimed. "He'd have nothing of it. I'm pledged to Galen."

"Obey," the spirits said, "or watch Guide die."

Wei, the old mystic man of Promise, had never mentioned spiritual healing through lovemaking. This crazy directive had to be another one of Magdalena's half-baked schemes. Magdalena was as twisted as strands of snarled hair.

My skin burned, as if seared by a red-hot poker. I recoiled and groaned. The pain subsided. Spirits had delivered their own graphic message. Mendoza style. And they expected me to do as told.

I dragged a tumbleweed to the fire circle. My lower lip rolled in a fat pout. Billy materialized. His railroader overalls matched mine.

"It's not like you're a frigging virgin." Billy lit a cigar. "Excuse the oxymoron."

"I'm filthy," I said. "And I'm supposed to act like I've just stepped out of the bath and Guide gives a drat about having a woman?"

"Don't you love him?" Billy said.

"Yes, but...but I love Galen, too. I've not made my choice." Tears slid down my cheeks. Guide practically had gangrene. So much was at stake. "Please don't leave. I'm sorry. Scared."

But Billy faded in a cloud of mustard yellow smoke. I couldn't let Guide die. I fumbled with my clothes and undressed. Firelight bathed my naked skin. Smithers of stones hurt my bare feet. I'd have to put on my boots. Riding boots and my bare skin—what a ridiculous combination. I unbraided my hair and combed out the tangles with my fingers. The night grew cold, even for the desert. The fire needed more brush.

I approached Guide and whispered his name. He didn't stir. I touched his shoulder and called again. He twitched, awakening. His glazed eyes stared at me. I smiled, a small, closed-mouth smile, my arms by my sides.

"Your rose has not forgotten you," I said.

"No," he said. "You, us...no."

I straddled his frame. He smelled sour, like rancid butter. Mama had smelled foul on her deathbed. Would Guide join Mama soon? He closed his eyes. I needed to arouse him, but he craved only sleep. So overpowering, my urge to cry grew. No, I must pray for wisdom and courage, think my way to a solution.

Moonlight illuminated my onyx ring, the one Antonio had placed on my forefinger when I'd been Billy. Antonio had liked to kiss me in embarrassing places. Maybe that sort of thing might please Guide, too.

I pressed the side of Guide's face against my abdomen. The stubble on his chin scraped the top of my thigh. I wasn't really being unfaithful to Galen. I could still be his bride someday if the physical love I gave Guide was selfless. Guide didn't move. Perhaps he was too weak to pull away.

"This love is from the spirits," I said.

"I'm an old sick man." Guide's shoulders shivered.

"A mystic heals." I listened to his uneven breathing.

My fingers stroked his damp, matted hair. A distant coyote howled, as if the eternal trickster voiced approval. Then Guide's lips brushed a private place between the tops of my parted thighs. I tingled. His tongue explored. Pleasure washed through me in ripples, then in waves.

The tip of Guide's tongue stroked my sensitive spot. The tempo of his rhythm quickened. My leg muscles tensed and weakened. My secret places throbbed. I shouldn't let the pleasure overpower me. My duty was to heal him, not to be his mistress. His warm hands, stronger now, gripped my hips. The gentle suction of his mouth destroyed the last remnants of my resolve. My gift to him tonight wouldn't—couldn't—remain selfless. My future relationship with Galen was doomed.

The voices of Guide's ancestors whispered in my ears. Whispers became echoes, then pulsing chants. I closed my eyes, dizzy. Rapture welled within my womb and breasts, building, cresting, a wave in a burning sea. A shudder plunged me through a sweet and sensual darkness. My remaining strength spilled away like falling sand.

He guided my hips downward, as carefully as he might have led me along a mountain path. His hardness waited. I reached back and touched the thigh of his injured leg, a spiritual energy flowing from my fingertips.

Our bodies and souls joined as one, then, our love as timeless as rivers and wind.

•

I dressed before dawn. I stirred the ashes of the fire and added fresh sticks. Guide slumbered on, illuminated by the moonlight and glow of the fire. I knelt beside him. No swelling remained in his injured leg. The Shadow World had cured his wound corruption.

Our lovemaking had been so beautiful. Sensual. My cheeks flushed with warmth. And how handsome he was, even with ragged whiskers and uncombed white hair.

My eighty-niner rested upright by the sloped railbed. I should keep watch for strangers. I sat near the fire, my left knee raised and tilted, the side of the gun pressed against my right thigh.

Guide would ache to touch me again. The invitation in his eyes would draw me to him, like a moth to a candle's flame. Still, I wanted a reputable relationship. We ought to marry.

He mumbled words. Not something he usually did in his sleep.

"Will you?" Guide called.

"Will I what?" I said.

"Me." He rolled on his back. "Will you?" He snored.

I leaned forward. Did he propose to me in a dream? Antonio had never married my mother. Guide was different, though. He would do the honorable thing.

Marriage. What would I say to Galen when we finally met again? We'd promised to share our lives with each other, raise a family. Somewhere, Galen waited for me in a safe place the Shadow World had chosen, perhaps just across the Mexican border. I couldn't hurt Galen. Maybe I shouldn't marry Guide.

"Old," Guide called. He thrashed one arm and turned on his side.

Did he dream about his age? The elixir had made Guide different from other men. And he was a hundred. But he wasn't too old to love. Yet I wanted children. Carla was no longer a possibility. Could Guide even father a child or live to help raise one?

"Clothes," he said. "The ring."

I glanced at the pants of my overalls, then into the darkness beyond the railbed. Men's clothing, a tattoo, an eighty-niner and onyx ring. I wasn't the innocent girl Galen had left by the fire. And Guide, unwashed and unshaven, could pass for one of Antonio's hired thugs. The fact that Guide and I had journeyed together would do more than arouse Galen's suspicion. I might lie about my love for Guide, but Galen would perceive the truth. Galen would be hurt no matter whom I married.

The firelight dimmed. I added more brush. Guide slept without talking. Perhaps his dream had ended with our mutual pledge of love. He understood and respected my feelings for Galen. Marriage to Guide would be the wiser choice.

A halo of dawn rimmed the desert horizon. Guide stirred and stretched, releasing a lazy yawn. He sat and wiped sleep from his eyes. His finger scratched the end of his beak nose, crusty and dry.

"Who are you this morning?" he said to me.

"Juanita Elise Jame-Navarro-Mendoza," I replied, tempted to include Locke, Guide's last name.

"No matter," Guide said. He winked. "You're one helluva good locomotive engineer."

Guide returned to a reclining position. Several minutes later, he snored. Where were his words of love? His proposal of marriage? I'd healed him, given everything. My shoulders shivered. Guide, like Antonio, might not want the confinement of a legally binding relationship.

I cupped my hand against the desert soil. I turned up my palm. Sand slipped through my fingers.

40. Colorado River Run

A MAN FOUND me and Guide beside a rugged dry wash the morning our food was gone. He rode a chestnut stallion and wore an eighty-niner. His spare horse was a roan. I tensed my hands around Ibn Sina's reins. Guide, astride King Solomon, waved and called Ramon's name. The man, clad in a sombrero and denims, dismounted.

"What kept you?" Ramon said.

This was Antonio's son and my half-brother. A long jagged scar wound beneath stubby whiskers on the right side of his face. His nose jutted from between heavy cheekbones like a slab of weathered basalt. Ramon was more angular and darker skinned than his father had been, but of equal stature. He resembled me only in his large earlobes and broad mouth.

He offered me a canteen but didn't smile. The cool water left a metallic taste in my mouth. I tried to read Ramon's eyes. He'd expected his father.

"The desert makes its own schedule." Guide took the next swig of water, then cast his glance toward the ground. "Antonio Mendoza did, too."

Ramon raised his chin, like he searched for a mystical sign in the pale blue sky. A hawk circled. I touched my ring. Ramon removed his sombrero and closed his eyes.

"I'm sorry," Guide said. He screwed shut the canteen and returned the vessel to Ramon.

We all rode for several hours, with Clockman slung across the back of the roan. We climbed a grade where trees and bushes thrived. Finally, I and the other two dismounted and led our horses to the edge of a wide and sluggish section of tuled river, almost like a little lake. A welcome sight. Ramon kindled a trench fire on a small beach. Guide and I bathed among reeds, washed clothes, and battled mosquitoes.

I draped myself with a coarse wool blanket and sat by the smoky fire. Oh, how the fabric made my skin itch. Drying denims and roasting raccoon produced an unpleasant odor. Ramon shared his buckskin bota of red wine while the food cooked. I glanced at the pocket watch Antonio had given me. Nearly five o'clock.

Hands served as utensils at dinner. The blackened raccoon meat was dry and tough as hemp rope. Better than no food. I washed down the most disgusting parts with wine, licking my fingers clean when I finished.

Ramon told stories about the Colorado River. He sounded less pensive now. His deep brown eyes appeared kind. How did he feel about Antonio's death? Perhaps he grieved on the inside in order to maintain a facade of strength.

Guide had no idea I was Anita's daughter. Ramon probably believed his half-sister had died at birth. I wanted to tell them the truth but didn't know where to begin.

I swatted a mosquito and walked to an improvised rack near the opposite side of the fire. My shirt and overalls were stiff but damp. My underwear fared better. I tightened my grip on the gray blanket wrapped around me. A dozen mosquitoes landed on my bare legs. I batted them as fast as I could. More landed.

"I declare my clothes dry," I said.

"Dress over here in the smoke," Ramon said. He sat cross-legged on the ground and chewed a piece of meat. "I won't devour you. They will."

I detected his suggestive undertone. Guide must have, too. A discreet hand signal would let Guide know I could manage the situation. A minute later, I plopped my damp shirt and overalls on top of Ramon's head. He yanked those garments off, his face scrunched and eyes squinted.

"You'd better not devour me," I said, my underwear dangling from my fingers. "I'm your half-sister, the one our mother gave away."

The crinkled skin on his forehead projected surprise and disbelief. I ought to say or do something more. I fingered the gold chain and onyx ring around my neck. Warmth from the fire spread across my back.

"Anita, our mother, dressed me in a little blue-and-white gown," I said, "an heirloom of my father's family." I waved my camisole and drawers. "I need less help with such things now. Close your eyes."

Ramon did as told. I put on my underwear, snapped my fingers, then motioned for my outer clothing when his eyes opened. I slipped into my denim shirt and overalls. He followed my every movement. Did he believe me? Guide's face bore a pained smile. He controlled his emotions well.

"I put that little gown on you," Ramon whispered. He turned away. "Our mother didn't want to look at you."

Ramon had done that? A rush of sadness flowed through me like an inner river of tears. Yet I couldn't hate him or our mother, or even be angry. Too much had happened. I unclasped the gold chain around my neck and removed Antonio's ring. He had asked me to deliver it. The onyx ring slid with ease onto Ramon's forefinger. Now he wore the signature piece of the Mendozas on both his broad hands. Poor Ramon, poor me...everyone.

"What was she like?" I said.

"Sometimes Mama was very brave," Ramon said.

I twisted a lock of my hair around my finger. Our mother hadn't been brave enough to keep me, or even give me to Antonio's cook woman. Had Anita ever regretted her action? In the Shadow World, had our spirits met?

"Did she have a favorite perfume or flower?" I said.

"Lilacs." Ramon tilted his head, as if puzzled.

I closed my eyes and recalled the sweet and mysterious scent of lilacs from the Shadow World at the River of Tears. When I'd faced pain and fear, Anita had offered the only comfort she could. Had life mellowed Anita, or had death?

"Her soul has brushed my own," I said.

Ramon clutched me to him and cried. His chest heaved against mine with each sob, as if he'd bottled up his grief for years. He must have carried me by wagon all the way to the adoption clinic near Hawk Valley and Great-

Grandma's home. He might have learned my father's identity and informed Antonio. I wrapped my arms around Ramon. Burning wood crackled.

•

Ramon scattered his horses at dawn. This man knew how to prepare for a raft trip. He planned to round up his animals after winter. I whispered into the ears of King Solomon and Ibn Sina. The spirits of my great-uncle and great-grandfather must direct my two horses south, along the river. With faith, this would happen.

The men stowed supplies in ammo cans and rubberized packs. My gaze probed Ramon's. I touched my onyx ring. Ramon pinched his lips together. He wasn't in the mood to discuss the past. I buried the fire. If only I could hide my sorrows with such ease.

I helped the men push an air-filled raft, large enough to hold several bathtubs, from the shore into the water. Guide tapped the toe of his boot against the bow and pulled the lifeline. The rope, slipped through a series of grommets around the upper rim of the raft, held fast. The line looked like a long running stitch around the soon-to-be-gathered waistline of a skirt.

"Impressive," Guide said. "How did you get your hands on this?"

"There are ways to get most everything," Ramon said. He produced a crafty half-smile, the way Antonio might have done. "I needed a good vessel to handle white water. The worst of the natural rapids are upstream, but the dam downstream failed last winter and left some jagged remains."

"Can't we carry our gear around the broken dam?" I rubbed the middle of my spine. "I mean, on land?"

"Not without encountering the U.S. Feds," Ramon said. "I'll take my chances with the river."

Ramon took his place at the stern to row, his bare chestnut arms muscular. Guide and I sat toward the middle, one on either side, a couple of feet from supplies and Clockman lashed in the bow. The glide was languid, serene silence interrupted by little more than morning calls of birds and soft splashes of oars dipping into the silty water.

A north wind arose by noon, and arid brown mountains enclosed the river passage. Two hours later, I heard a distant rumble. As the sound loudened, the raft gained speed. Ramon pointed downriver toward battlements of earth and concrete.

"That's what's left of the dam," Ramon said. "Those funnels'll give us a helluva ride."

I shut my eyes and practiced finding the nearest section of line, the wet rope smooth against my skin. Did the line have weak points that might magnify my own?

"Are you planning to scout the drops?" Guide said.

"Not this time."

Guide twisted his earring. I could feel his fear. I eyed the scattered concrete, one remnant over fifty feet high.

"Do you have a spare oar?" Guide said.

"A few miles downriver."

Ramon steered the craft left, toward the widest of three gaps between concrete—the funnels. I stiffened. The rapids roared louder than I'd anticipated. He should have tucked a spare oar in the raft. Maybe two. Monoliths ahead spewed foam. The brink was coming up too fast. I wasn't ready.

Arms stretched, I grasped the wet lifeline. Sunlight—or was it?—shimmered on the rope. My hands twined the line tighter. How far would the raft drop? I tasted tobacco, a warning from Billy. My muscles braced.

Guide clutched the lifeline, jerking as the raft slid down a tongue of water. A maw of churning foam engulfed us. I screamed. A lateral wave slammed the craft full force. I gasped for air and gulped water. The raft spun and broadsided the next drop. It crash-landed with a spine-jarring thud. Cold spray pelted me. I needed air.

The bow heaved upward. The raft leaped toward the sky. The force of the thrust wrenched my left hand free of the lifeline. Our boat was going to flip. I clutched the rope with my other hand, dangling between the raft and oblivion.

Clockman fell overboard. My lungs coughed out water. Spray blinded me. I couldn't find another section of line to hold. We'd all drown.

Then I smelled leather. Was Antonio here?

Sharp puffs of warm air blew into my ear and against my left hand. The wall of spray ahead shimmered tobacco-smoke yellow. My left arm shot into the glow and found the line. The raft pounded the water and leveled out. Precious air filled my lungs. Yet now, the vessel catapulted right-side-up toward jagged concrete. This was it! My eyes snapped shut. The rest of me braced or clung on for my life.

A sickening crunch heralded a wild neck-wrenching twist. One or both oars must have gone. The craft careened and plummeted down the gouged spillway. My lungs ached. Pain stabbed my shoulders, neck and arms. The lifeline bit into my palms. I had to hang on.

The raft slowed, and I sucked in fresh air. Wonderful air. I sat, hair dripping, in a pool of water. Ramon steered the half-swamped vessel with a single oar.

"You all right, little Sis?" Ramon said, sopping wet and breathing hard. His denims clung like a second skin. He unlashed the bailing bucket and tossed it to Guide. "The rest of the trip could rock a baby."

Ramon shot an apologetic glance in my direction. I'd already forgiven him for his choice of words. The blue-and-white gown symbolized my origins and past. I alone would choose the symbol for my future.

I scanned the river's edge for King Solomon and Ibn Sina. Had the horses found a safe path? Or drowned?

•

Ramon beached the raft at the portal of the Sonoran Desert. King Solomon and Ibn Sina nickered from the bank, sagging with each step. Saints and ancestors be praised. The horses appeared uninjured, although exhausted. Ramon stroked the animals' necks and

326

whispered in their ears, as if he'd followed their progress during the entire ten-day river run.

"Hey, Sis," Ramon said. "Go look in the barn."

Two bay mares, four pack mules and supplies awaited inside the weathered structure. Clockman sat in a pile of hay, his metal and leather head streaked with rust. Ibn Sina or King Solomon must have carried him here. I tingled. The rapids should have pounded the mechanical man to pieces.

I turned away and inspected the waterskins and sacks of grain, all in good condition. The brass spyglass looked almost new. And here were two new pairs of tan overalls, one my size, and two palm-leaf sombreros. Ramon certainly knew how to commandeer what was needed. Antonio's praise of him had been well deserved.

An odd feeling brought a shiver. Then came a metallic creak. Startled, I jumped and faced the opposite direction. Clockman's eyes of amber stared right at me. And he'd moved closer. I was sure.

If a spirit possessed Clockman, it ought to reveal an identifying odor. I smelled mostly hay. Something was wrong. I touched the magic pendant around my neck and walked to the barn's doorway.

A balmy wind outside rustled through the gray-green leaves of shrubby trees. Tumorous growths of mistletoe burdened the branches. I searched the memories Billy had left in my mind. This was desert ironwood. I surveyed the arid landscape. Yuma must lay to the south, maybe a two-day ride. Ramon approached with Guide. It would be best not to mention what had happened with Clockman in the barn.

"We separate here," Ramon said.

"I know," Guide said.

I was just getting to know Ramon. And he'd mentioned so little about our mother. We should continue to travel together. Besides, I could use his expertise to complete the final part of my mission: gaining Mendoza support to construct a new asylum in North California.

"Come with us to Mexico," I said, "at least for a while."

"The Colorado is my home," Ramon replied. "And your supplies will last longer without me." He turned and embraced Guide. "Follow the dry routes to avoid the Yankee Feds. Even the remaining Apaches stay clear of those roads this time of year."

"No Indians?" I said. Promise and our Yokut neighbors had shared cultural sensitivities, the ability to hear spirit voices and help each other in need.

"Go with God and ancestors," Ramon said, "to survive."

Ramon clasped my hands. Did he truly believe in God or ancestors? Antonio had, at least during the final months of his life.

"I go with your father, as well," I whispered. "His spirit saved me in the rapids. He's proud of you. I am, too."

Ramon boarded the raft and continued down river, looking behind only once. I glanced at Guide. Ramon had crossed his latest river in life. Somewhere a river awaited me with a choice I feared to make—the choice between Galen and Guide.

•

The trail divided a sandy plain in the shadow of low but rugged mountains. I shifted in Ibn Sina's saddle, my new overalls stiff and uncomfortable. Such harsh, barren land. If only we could have followed the river longer.

I eyed the clear, bright sky. Not even a hint of a dark cloud in view. I could wrestle cactus spines to obtain stored moisture. That wouldn't help the animals, though. Each of our horses would need fifteen to twenty gallons of water a day. The mules could survive with less.

"Does it ever rain out here?" I said.

"Occasionally, this time of year." Guide adjusted his sombrero. "By mistake."

Guide's chart had depicted where water might be found. Those marks had seemed so close on the chart, but not close enough. I straightened my back and noticed the fan of spindly stems on an ocotillo. Bunches of little green leaves sprouted around the plant's formidable thorns. A recent storm must have occurred. Storm water might have collected in the mountains.

"Sure we'll locate enough water?" I said.

"Supposed to be a couple uncharted wells," Guide said. He rubbed his whiskered cheek. "Trick's in the finding."

We rode awhile. My mouth turned dry. My eighty-niner grew so heavy against my back. Oh, to have a canteen full of snowmelt. A puff of air brushed against my ear and I smelled leather. Antonio was back. I mumbled a greeting. Without a doubt, the Shadow World had assigned him to work with Billy and protect me. If so, the Mendozas really did have a bizarre sense of humor. Billy's murderous deeds in life must have earned him a ten-thousand-year sentence of penance. Based on that assumption, Antonio would serve time until the Shadow World dissolved.

A series of puffs, almost frantic, tickled the side of my neck. The skin on my throat tingled, as if layered with gnats. Maybe Antonio tried to tell me something.

"Did Ramon learn about this place from his father?" I said.

"Probably," Guide said. King Solomon stopped and swished his black tail. He nibbled shoots of a young plant. "Tony once crossed it on a vendetta."

I gripped the reins tighter, listening to the plods of shod hooves. His quarry could have been my natural father. I didn't want to hear the gruesome details.

"The poor bastard traveled in July," Guide said, "with a day's supply of water and no map."

My father would have suffered a more brutal death, according to Guide's earlier story in the Mendoza safe house. The man in question must have been someone else. I should have demanded some answers from Ramon about my parents. Too late, now. Why did I always put off talking about important things?

A rush of cool air flowed down my shirt. Antonio again. I was almost his stepdaughter. How dare he do that? Wisps of air tickled my left ear over and over. They stopped, then resumed. The puffing had a pattern, like some sort of code. The numbers in each series might be important. I counted the spirit breaths. Always nine.

"You know," I said, "I've a feeling we'll get lucky in finding water."

Guide arched his eyebrows, then squinted until they thickened. He obviously questioned my opinion. I wouldn't mention what Antonio's ghost had just done.

"Look for water in about nine miles," I said.

"Nothing on my chart that close."

"Believe me." I smiled. "A mystic knows."

"Which side of the trail?" He glanced toward the left of the trail, then the right.

I scanned a dry wash for any unusual concentration of green shoots or leaves. Brush lined a nearby shallow sandy slope, mostly squat thorny mesquite with gray-green bark and spiny green or yellow palo verde. The spreading palo verde had no leaves at all. The corrugated ridges of a gaunt, forty-foot saguaro with twisted arms appeared tightly pleated. Everything looked thirsty.

Several wafts of air tickled the left side of my bosom, as if a disgusting desert creature crawled down my shirt. I couldn't bear to face Galen, Guide didn't want to marry me, someone else had adopted Carla, and I'd lost the opportunity in life to learn more about my natural mother. Now came Antonio's impolite sense of humor. And my mystic's calling obligated me to treat all ghosts with respect or risk facing ghastly consequences.

"We'll find water on the left side of the road," I said to Guide. "And watch out for scorpions."

41. Desert Prison and Freedom's Path

I STOOD STRAIGHT, stretched out my arm and pulled the trigger. The bullet from my pistol penetrated the bay mare's skull. The downed horse jerked once and bled between her eyes. Scarlet liquid from a fleeting life stained sands of time. Turkey vultures circled, as they had since the mare had dropped from thirst in the rugged desert. How many days had passed since Ramon had left us by the Colorado River? Possibly fifteen.

Guide peeled off his overalls and stripped to the waist, his baked skin darker than unblanched almonds. He unsheathed his bowie knife. The inevitable would happen next. I needed to fight the urge to vomit. I tightened my stomach muscles and closed my eyes. All I had to do was salt and roast the meat. He wouldn't carve the whole animal. Finding water today was more important than preparing food. Besides, winged scavengers would move in fast, and ammunition was too precious to waste on scattering them.

"I would have shot her," Guide said.

"You shot the other one." I opened my eyes to harsh daylight and reality. "I can do my share."

I tried to concentrate on the crackling sound of the mesquite fire, on its pungent aroma. Yet the sun-bleached bones of so many animals littered this desert. At least King Solomon and Ibn Sina were still all right. What if they dropped, too? I eyed the hazy rim of a distant mountain and prayed for rain, another flash flood, for any gift of water at all. God, even Magdalena's husband Cole couldn't have found water around here.

Guide rubbed the spattered blood of butchery from his arms and chest with sand. A wave of nausea coursed through me. I'd spotted vaginal blood since yesterday.

Maybe my period was finally going to come. I also had constipation, another reason for an unsettled stomach. Inadequate intake of food and water had disrupted my whole body.

I approached a forty-foot saguaro, its dull gray-green arms raised as if in prayer. The accordion ridges of the stately cactus were folded tight, a marker of dry weather. I sat down in the narrow shadow of the plant and drew my bent knees toward my chest. A few cotton-puff clouds dotted the otherwise clear sky.

I dug the pit out of a crusty date and slipped the desiccated fruit into my mouth. The sweetness triggered no desire to savor the food or chew. My tongue pressed the date against my inner cheek. I ought to get up and salt the horse meat. Guide touched my shoulder.

"I'll take care of the meat," he said. "You rest."

"Thank you." He so often knew what troubled me.

My eyes ached in this meager shade, even with the sun behind me. I lowered the brim of my sombrero. Warm wind rippled the loose sleeves of my denim shirt and evaporated sweat. A rock wren picked for a meal under the spindly branches of a low-growing creosote bush. When the supplies of food were gone, I'd pick for bugs, too. I chewed the date.

Guide arranged strips of horse meat in the glowing mesquite coals, generating sizzles and the odor of seared flesh. He unscrewed the dented cap on a metal cylinder, extracted a chart the length of his arm, then unrolled the parchment. A free edge rustled in the breeze.

"We should reach the Arizona-Mexico crossing in a couple days." He walked over to me, then crouched and set the chart on the ground. "We mustn't overburden the animals. From now on, Clockman will have to walk on his own or stay behind."

An uncomfortable feeling told me Clockman would manage just fine.

I shifted onto my hands and knees and studied the map. The bed of the Gila River marked the Mexican border. Guide pointed to our probable location. The Gila wasn't too far away, and rainwater might have collected in the riverbed.

The wind shifted, heavy with the stink of mules, roasting horse meat, mesquite and unwashed man. Time to stand and move upwind. My baggy denims fluttered against my sticky skin. Two weeks ago, these bib-overalls had fit. I'd lost weight. Mexican terrain would prove equally harsh, providing Guide and I weren't shot by U.S. federalmen prior to the crossing. Too bad we couldn't have made a coastal crossing from British South California.

Guide packed the chart, then lashed the cylinder to one of the mules, his beak nose and the outline of his backbone more prominent than ever. The past month had thinned him, too. In Promise, my people had accepted hunger and thirst as part of life. Survival was a matter of faith, luck and determination.

"The border is a long stretch to patrol," Guide said. "At least there won't be too many Feds in one spot."

"Even one is too many." Especially if that one carried a light-beam weapon. I tucked my pistol into Ibn Sina's saddlebag.

I grasped a long-handled fork and turned the roasting horse meat in the coals. The strips would be jerky in a while. Dead mare for dinner.

The sound of wings. A feathery cloud of vultures descended to feast on the carcass of the mare. Another wave of nausea hit me. If I ever got to Mexico alive, I'd eat fruits and vegetables until I sprouted.

The surviving horses whinnied. King Solomon reared. His hooves sliced through the air. The dun gelding pounded the dry ground as he landed, then bucked and lashed out with his hind legs. Solomon hadn't spooked since Great-Uncle Raúl had possessed him. Something was wrong.

"Fly get you, old fellow? Or do you worry you'll be next on the menu?" Guide checked over his skittish mount. He turned toward me, his eyes squinted. "Do you remember the story of Moses in the wilderness?"

"Who doesn't?"

That had been an odd question. Guide tightened the woven girth strap on King Solomon, then stroked the animal's nose. The gelding edged away with a nervous side step, leaving a gap between man and horse.

"Is this still your great-uncle?" Guide said. "He's different this morning. Jumpy."

I sniffed Solomon's muzzle and peered into his brown eyes. The gelding didn't shy away from me, yet there was no sign of Great-Uncle Raúl. The queasy feeling tumbling through my stomach strengthened.

"I don't understand," I said. "After all these miles, why would he leave now, before we're safe?" Ibn Sina's breath remained pungent with beer. "Great-Grandpa's still here."

Guide fingered his onyx ring. The wind blew the ends of his unbraided white hair. He slipped into his denim shirt, the faded blue fabric stained with sweat and dirt.

"God didn't permit Moses to cross to the Promised Land," he said. "Moses lost favor."

What was he talking about? The Shadow World had healed Guide. He wasn't like Moses.

"I won't listen to such nonsense." I pressed my palms to my ears. Guide grasped my wrists. I just stood there.

"Federalmen will be waiting for us at the Gila," he said. "I'll cover your back."

"No!"

My hands found his upper arms. He stood adamant, framed against barren ground and blue sky, as immovable as the monolithic ruins of the dam on the Colorado. Would it help if I shook him, yelled at him? Magdalena whispered to me. Only the words within my heart might change Guide's mind.

"The train," I said, "took me from a father who didn't want me. The desert brought me Papa. When the train got him, the desert gave me you. You're like a father, grandfather, friend. Husband."

"Galen's to be your husband."

"I won't leave you behind to die in this wretched place. Even if Galen waits on bended knee beside a fifty-foot tank of drinking water."

"It can't be." He stepped away from me, then put on his overalls.

Guide's face appeared so unemotional. He couldn't possibly feel calm inside. I wrapped my arms around him, clung to him as both woman and child, the coarse texture of his soiled shirt and overalls against the side of my face.

"We cross the Gila together," I said, "or not at all."

He kissed my closed eyelids, his dry lips warm. His gentle hand wiped away my tears.

"Tony had his assignment," Guide said. "I have mine."

"Antonio was evil for most of his days. You've been decent for twenty-six years. That man you were is dead. Don't you see?"

"I think not."

He tilted my chin upward. His hazel eyes held no more warmth than frozen marble. My heart could have dropped to my toes. On a night months ago he'd looked at me this way and slapped my face, but that hadn't been the real Guide. I had to make him understand.

"Graham Locke is dead," I said.

He turned and gazed southward. Distant ramparts of massive rock paneled both a spiny desert prison and freedom's path. That path was meant for two.

"Time to ride, little rose." Guide pointed toward our eighty-niners on the ground. "Time to ready ourselves and ride."

I stood with my legs braced, the wind pushing against my face and bosom. I wouldn't let Guide stay behind when we reached the Gila. That was my new mission. Thoughts about building an asylum in North California would have to wait.

Guide needed a chest-to-chest talk. My fingertips touched my pendant of magic, its power beyond my control.

42. Dust Blow and Defiance

GUIDE, RIDING IN front of me, reined Solomon to a standstill. He looked through his brass spyglass, then pointed toward a distant sea of squat trees and bushes on the arid plain. Ibn Sina halted, his gray-and-white ears pricked. I leaned forward in my horse's saddle and squinted. What was out there? Water?

He passed the spyglass to me. The circular lenses revealed the twisted green arms and tips of several prominent saguaros. The plants had to be fifty feet tall. They were poised, as if locked in position during a ritual dance for moisture. No way to tell from here if water swelled them.

I'd no desire to navigate another collection of velvet mesquite and cacti unless full canteens were my reward. The rawhide panels on my chaps already looked clawed by bears. Wearing a heavy rifle didn't make dodging thorns any easier. Ibn Sina snorted and pawed a shallow layer of yellow-beige sand. Great-Grandpa grew tired of spiny plants, too.

"That's the Gila," Guide said.

He returned the spyglass to its case, then removed his sombrero. Looking southward, he used his hand to deflect sunlight.

"Yes, the Gila," he added. "I'm sure."

"Will the riverbed be dry?" My mouth felt pasty, although the heat of the November afternoon was mild.

"Unless water flashed through in the last storm."

I gave silent thanks to Antonio for directing me to the mountain cache of rainwater the previous day. How inappropriate to pray to someone who had assaulted and humiliated me in life. But I'd need his help again. And again after that.

We rode for a while, Guide's jaws set tight. He didn't twist his earring, though. Maybe he was too tense to even do that. He raised his hand, a signal to stop. The spiny oasis lay a mile or so ahead.

"There are U.S. federalmen out there." Guide dismounted. "Maybe Brits, too." He relieved the lead mule of the ammunition box, then transferred several cartridge clips to a satchel strung off Solomon's pommel. "Most likely hiding where the river's cut a gorge."

Memories of checkpoint guards flooded my mind. Rape. Ambush. Guide's bloody leg. Plus some new vulnerability probably lay in wait. I shifted in the saddle. I could face another confrontation, if necessary, but would rather not.

"How can you be certain about the authorities?" I said.

"The Mendozas owned me, remember?" He gestured with his mouth, like he spat into the sand without bothering to waste saliva. "Ask the spirits how many and where."

I clutched Ibn Sina's reins, my head bowed and eyes closed. I concentrated. *Scotch whisky.* Billy didn't talk inside my mind. My thoughts focused on leather, then chocolate, men, cactus flowers, lilacs and bagpipes. Nothing worked. I scrunched my eyelids tighter and tried again.

Ibn Sina whinnied. My eyes popped open. My stallion shied to the left, jerking me in the opposite direction. What made him skittish? Great-Grandpa wasn't paying attention. The horse tossed his head and reared low. I clutched the saddle horn and braced my legs, slipping backward.

"Great-Grandpa!" I said.

An eerie amber glow shimmered near Ibn Sina's head, then vanished. Were horse and ghost no longer one? The animal steadied.

"Look south," Guide said with alarm. "A dust blow."

The sky darkened yellow-brown and ugly beyond the Mexican side of the Gila. A rising wind whipped sand.

Minutes ago, there'd been no evidence of a storm. Now one advanced northward with astonishing speed.

King Solomon bolted forward, away from Guide. A jumpy mule kicked and brayed. Sand swirled in mysterious curls off the nearby ground. The wind's moan intensified. This was no ordinary blow.

Guide put on goggles, tied a red bandanna over his mouth and nose, then pulled gauze sheets from a mule's pack. He blindfolded Solomon. My face would need protection. I dug in my pocket, knees tense against Ibn Sina's sides. Where were my scarf and goggles?

Guide moved toward the mules. Grit lodged in my left eye. Had I buried my things in one of the saddlebags? My eye stung and watered. I dropped Ibn Sina's reins and fumbled for one of the pouches. My horse must be uncomfortable, too.

"I need gauze for both of us," I called. "Hurry."

Guide approached. Ibn Sina trumpeted and skittered sideways. He was going to throw me. I slid down from the saddle as fast as I could, then stumbled clear. The stallion reared high and boxed the air. Guide ducked, leaping backward. Ibn Sina charged toward the border and the core of the storm.

A sharp boom, different from the sound of thunder, echoed in the distance. Gunfire? Solomon reared. A mule bucked and lashed out its hind legs. Guide and I dodged a flurry of hooves.

He grabbed my hand and pulled me to the ground. I flattened, face down, against the sand. Mules brayed. Hooves thudded earth. The boom repeated. That wasn't regular gunfire. Did someone have a cannon? I glanced toward the border. Ibn Sina galloped southward, his mane and arched tail billowing like flags carried to battle.

"I've never seen a blow like this one," Guide said, his tone edged with fear.

Flying sand forced my eyes shut, stung the lids like miniature wasps. The wind's deafening pitch stabbed my eardrums. The next boom threatened to rip my whole head into shards. I blinked over and over, searching the screen of dust and sand. Nothing. What produced that horrible din?

Then something dark in the blow spread like charcoal-blackened fog, maybe three or four hundred feet away. The cloud grew larger, closer, with each passing second, as if angels of death cast their shadows upon the ground. No funnel, though. Not a tornado.

My horizontal position might keep me safe. Guide's flattened form, ten feet away, appeared braced, too. Still, sand could bury us both alive if we let the storm sweep across our backs.

A high-pitched wail and a low, droning hum penetrated the storm's howl. I knew that sound. Bagpipes. Ethan must be near, had come to tell me what to do. I blinked and scanned the dust clouds for his tartan glow. Instead, shadows stretched as tall as giants, encased in shrouds of raging sand. An army. It was an army in human, yet quite nonhuman form. Hundreds, maybe thousands, marched in my direction. The reek of rotting flesh putrefied the air. I gagged.

Not British constables. Not Federalmen. The dead walked the earth.

"This is no storm," a voice—Magdalena's—screamed. "The Guardians of the Portals, the judgers of souls—Guide's name is on their list."

The Guardians of the Portals? I'd faced them on that trip to the Shadow World. Billy had helped protect me. He wasn't here now. And who would protect Guide?

"Graham Locke," a deep voice thundered.

Dear God, the dead closed in and chanted Guide's real name. I could feel the vibrations in my teeth.

Guide had committed murder but had changed. I was a mystic. If I shielded him, the judges might not condemn his soul to the place for the unworthy. But these spirits were angry, and I'd killed people, too. I might make things worse.

I searched for Guide's prone form and found him standing. I scrambled to my feet. He edged clear of me, his shoulders hunched. What was he doing? Didn't he understand?

"Stay by me," I shouted.

Guide faced the advancing onslaught, his head bowed, his eighty-niner still across his back. A cloud of grit blinded me. I had to reach him. Defend him. I lurched forward, stumbled and crashed to the ground. I'd have to crawl. My eighty-niner slipped to one side. Crawling didn't work right. I shed the bulky rifle and its straps.

Sand abraded my hands and knees, rasped at my nostrils and closed eyelids. Was Guide nearby? I might have headed in the wrong direction. The stench of rotting meat sickened my stomach. I could taste death. The Guardians of the Portals weren't far away. Even Billy and Magdalena couldn't help me then. I, only eighteen, neither prophet nor saint, would have to plead on Guide's behalf.

I pulled myself to my knees and forced open my eyes. Grit whirled around me. Not a single grain invaded my mouth, eyes or nose. The spirits granted me a chance to speak. Dear God, what should I say? I stood and raised my arms.

Biblical sounding words about Moses and a thief throbbed within me. Great-Grandma had written such things aboard that train the night she'd saved my life. When Moses had visited me by Promise's creek two-and-one-half years ago, had the Voice of the Creek—The Virgin of Guadalupe—told me about Great-Grandma's message to prepare me for this terrible day?

"God bless Graham Locke," I shouted. "Who will be saved on the Day of Judgment. Sit on the right hand of Barabbas, the thief. He who would have pissed on the babe in the bulrushes has parted the Red Sea. And—"

Merciful ancestors, what words came next? I'd have to use my own.

"And I defy any one of you—any single one of you—to show how the shit this man I love has failed to earn redemption."

The cloud of sand parted. Spirits of the dead marched and surrounded me. The earth shook. Cacophony from drums and bagpipes hammered my ears. I couldn't see Guide. Had he been spared?

Pain seared through me. Air turned to blood. I'd defied and angered the Shadow World.

Guide, Galen, life—all were lost. I was unworthy. Shame and agony awaited me, separation from my ancestors and beloved people of Promise. Apology was my only hope. No! I couldn't—wouldn't—desert Guide to save myself.

"God bless Graham Locke," I hollered.

A figure grabbed me. Gritty, leather-skin hands held me in place. Clockman! A force pulled my spirit toward a blue-green light.

43. The Airship

MY OUTSTRETCHED HANDS grasped the sides of a lantern. Not warm to the touch, this lamp, yet its twin deep-blue beams illuminated the bank of windows in front of me. Was the Virgin of Guadalupe inside the lantern? And where was I? What had happened to Guide and the Guardians of the Portals?

Speaking of my hands, I could see right through them. My body had again exhaled my soul. Odd, how my released spirit didn't take the usual shapeless form.

The lantern I held moaned, as if in reply to my thoughts. Ivory. The lamp was ivory in color. I blinked my ethereal eyes. Oh, dear ancestors. I held the shaman's skull from the Cave of Light. The skull I'd dropped down that chasm over two years ago.

"Do not," the skull said, "drop me again. Ever."

"I never meant to—"

"Juanita," the familiar voice of Red Sash Man said, "better let me hold the Yokut's skull. You take the helm of this ship."

Ship? Red Sash man claimed I was aboard a ship. I turned toward him. His flesh-and-blood hands rested on a free-floating brass wheel. Connected to nothing. How could I use the wheel to steer anything but air? A metal control rod, longer than my arm, was anchored in the vessel's floor. Like in Billy's magic tobacco tin.

"We modified Billy's tin," Red Sash Man said. "*Un poquito*. Just a little."

"We probably changed it too much." The light from the Yokut's skull shimmered. "Billy Mendoza, he is not happy with us right now. If I were you, Juanita, I would not ask him for help for the next ten-dozen moons. Or more."

342

"The airship picture on the top of his box gave us inspiration." Red Sash Man took the skull from my hands. "So did the Lady of the Light in the cave."

"When the Guardians of the Portals move on to their next targets," the skull added, "we'll bring you back to the Mexican border."

I grasped the helm wheel, or whatever it was called. All right, I'd escaped, but that didn't help Guide.

"Who's protecting the man I love?" The airship wobbled. "And what direction are we headed?"

"To the Cave of Light," Red Sash Man said, "using passageways between life and death."

"The Guardians of the Portals have no power in the cave." The skull's light surged. "Much magic resides in my bones."

"Much magic resides in the Lady of the Light," Red Sash Man said. "At Tehachapi station, she favored me with the blue beam to power my gun. Me! One of the gold war *bandidos*."

"Well, much magic resides in my love." I could still visualize the bullet buried in Guide's leg that day. "We're going back for Guide. Now!"

I turned the wheel hard. If I could run a real locomotive, I could run this ghostly airship tobacco tin. My free hand reached for the throttle. The vessel bucked like an unbroken horse, then rolled upside down. The top of the box flew off with a grinding metallic groan.

Wind thrust sand through my spirit. The echoing din of drums and bagpipes shook every bit of my soul. At least I headed in the correct direction.

"Hang on, Guide," I shouted. "I'm on my way."

44. The Crossing

I HEARD SOBBING. Grit coated my tongue. My knees ached and burned. This couldn't be the Shadow World. Was I still in the passageway between life and death? I opened my eyes to a sand-coated sleeve. Denim. The side of my face pressed against something—Guide's chest. The two of us were kneeling, together. Safe! Clutching me, Guide wept as if he'd saved all of his unshed tears since birth.

Sand hung in the air, although the storm of spirits must have passed. I shifted position. A low, dark shadow faded in the distance. The Guardians of the Portals had moved on toward the north. By now they would have swept away any nearby federalmen or constables in their path. As for the living Mendozas, they'd better start building that new asylum. Fast. Spirits far worse than Antonio's prepared chest-to-chest talks.

I stretched my arms around Guide and whispered a prayer of thanks to my ancestors, the saints and God. Guide just kept crying, even when I kissed his face. One hundred years had caught up with him all at once.

I pulled away from him and took a handkerchief from my pocket. Sand spilled from the fabric's folds. The blow had coated us with the stuff. My gritty underwear chafed my skin as I moved. I sat on the ground and laughed. I blew my nose, then poured sand from my boots. Guide had been spared and could cry freely, if only for now. Sand didn't matter.

Guide stood and faced northward. He didn't even brush off his clothes. The black shadow of the eternal judges vanished on the horizon.

"How many will they take," Guide said, "if not me?"

"Enough to make this world a better place." I stood, then threaded my arm around his. "At least for a while."

How strange. People had been doing ugsome things to each other for thousands of years. Why had the Shadow World chosen this day, even this century, to vent its fury? Might I be part of the reason? Despite the fact I'd offended a number of spirits today, something about who I was remained special.

Months ago, Billy had claimed I was like a piece of the Shadow World on loan to the living. The night before the train wreck near Promise, the spirits had visited my people in dreams. Had I served as a bridge between the dead and my community? Billy's ghost had walked the earth in human form to help me. Ethan had, too. And the train, the miraculous way the locomotive had stopped on the crossing. The appearance of the holy blue light. Yes, even though my defiance had angered the Guardians of the Portals, I was important, some sort of focal point.

My body tensed. In the Cave of Light, a voice had prophesied the birth of an important child. Might I be the predicted child from the houses of Navarro and Jame?

How far-fetched. I was only Juanita, a half-Mendoza abandoned in a blue-and-white gown at birth.

Guide kissed my forehead, his rough, chapped lips like scales on a lizard. No matter who I was, we needed to locate water. He rounded up King Solomon and the mules, while I gathered the scattered remains of thrown packs. I lashed our eighty-niners to our baggage. We'd carried weapons on our backs far too long.

Clockman, though, was nowhere to be found. Not even a mechanical finger remained, as if one of the Guardians of the Portals had taken him in Guide's place.

A sweet and beautiful sound drew my attention: the music of rushing water. Guide's smile and tilted head told me he heard, too. We led the animals through a maze of spiny brush and cacti. The whoosh of flowing water grew louder. The northern bank of the Gila riverbed lay nearby. A mountain dam must have burst. Surely a dangerous churn of flood debris and ugly foam would greet us. I edged around the mesquite and glimpsed water. The Gila babbled, like angels danced upon its surface. How?

"Someone has been expecting us," Guide said.

He nudged my shoulder and pointed toward the sky beyond the river. A craft floated through air below the clouds—some sort of river raft or giant basket dangling by ropes from a huge sausage-shaped object. This was an airship, and not Billy's.

The ship grew larger and larger, was descending. Looked like it prepared to land on the river's south side. On the ground below the craft, a dust cloud swirled. Fifteen or twenty riders on horseback approached. A riderless horse led the procession. Ibn Sina.

The riders waved shirts and bandannas as their party neared. They tossed sombreros and top hats into the air and cheered. Who were they? An old plump man stood in the basket of the airship. He waved. Perhaps he was Billy's lover—Great-Uncle Juan.

The man turned and hugged someone sitting behind him. Two arms with rolled-up white shirtsleeves and ebony skin hugged back.

Black arms. Strong. Arms of my betrothed, my first love. My hands covered my mouth. The old man, dressed in faded overalls, stepped aside. Galen, wearing a scarlet vest, dark trousers and a top hat—standing as straight and tall as he had the night of the train—reached out in my direction. He lifted a child into his arms, a toddler in a white dress.

"That's Carla," Magdalena's voice whispered. "Safe. I wanted to surprise you."

An ache clawed at the pit of my stomach. A ready-made family waited for me. The time had come to choose between Galen and Guide, and, right or wrong, live with my decision.

To return to Galen, all I'd have to do was cut through an opening in the spiny brush, skid down the north slope of the shallow gorge and wade or swim across the river. He would land and accept me, no questions asked. Time would mend the rifts in our relationship.

But I couldn't go to him as a Mendoza. The people of Promise had feared and despised that family. Galen's opinion probably hadn't changed.

I glanced at the hawk ring on my forefinger. The jewelry from Antonio, shiny and dark, symbolized my self-awakening and loss of innocence—everything good or evil I'd experienced during the past two and one-half years. If I cast off the ring, I'd rebuke my own identity, the Red Sash ghost in the Cave of Light, and half of my family.

I searched Guide's eyes. I'd braved the anger of the spirits on his behalf. If he wanted me, I couldn't leave him now. Yet I wanted marriage and children. He was old.

"You're free to go where you belong," Guide said.

He gestured for me to cross the river, his beak nose coated with sand and his jaw tight. He understood my dilemma. He would forgive me. Then I noticed a look of wisdom in his eyes I'd forgotten—the embers of an old hero's fire. My heart felt wrenched in two pieces.

I prayed in silence to Galen's ancestors, then to Guide's. They must provide solace and strength, ready one man's heart for a different woman. I twisted the onyx ring on my finger and took a deep breath. I removed the ring—that symbol of myself—and held it in my left palm.

"Without honor," I said, "a woman has nothing."

Guide nodded and took the ring. I turned my left hand over and waited. He tucked the ring into the bib pocket of his overalls and closed his eyes. I'd made my decision. What was he doing?

"A proper suitor," I said, "would know where to put that thing."

Guide's eyelids flew open. He tilted his head. His mouth spread into a toothy smile. He pulled a spare bandanna from his pocket and tore off a frayed corner. The scrap was soon wrapped around the band. He slid the jewelry onto my ring finger. The fit was perfect.

"I do," I said, "for better or for worse. Let the spirits be my witnesses."

"I do, too," Guide whispered.

I mounted King Solomon, my mind brimming with mixed joy and sadness. What would I say to Galen? The right words would come. And surely little Carla adored him. He had that.

Guide climbed on behind me. We cut through an opening in the thorny mesquite. The mules had already reached the water. An odd light sparkled in my peripheral vision. I turned to discover the source.

Beyond a budding cactus, Billy, Magdalena, Antonio, Wei and Moses hovered, their translucent grins broader than the brims of their sombreros. Great-Grandma Zetta joined them, wearing the same outfit she'd worn on the train when she'd rescued me, her silvery-white hair woven into a single braid. The aroma of chocolate grew strong. Great-Grandma rocked her cradled arms back and forth. Magdalena did the same. The men all raised their right hands—first and middle fingers together—as if giving a blessing. The graphic message raced to my brain. I was pregnant?

I'd spotted blood for days. I couldn't be pregnant. Magdalena laughed and rocked her arms again. Great-Grandma waved. For just a moment, the specters of all the people of Promise who'd died the night of the train shimmered in the sunlight.

"God Bless Graham Locke," Great-Grandma said.

The vision of visiting ghosts vanished.

King Solomon lifted his head and nickered. Great-Uncle Raúl had returned. I touched my flat stomach. A baby! I didn't know whether to laugh, shout, or cry, or try to do all three at once. Did Guide realize my condition? He'd displayed no manifestation of surprise. The vision must have been for me. I'd tell him the good news tonight. No, I must tell him sooner.

Or, was a baby good news? We would need a way to earn money and get food, might have to depend on Juan for help. Even on Galen. And I'd lost weight. A miscarriage could occur. The child could be born sickly or deformed.

Miscarriage. Bleeding. My knees gripped King Solomon's sides. An abbreviated period had occurred the week after my rape. If one partial period didn't end pregnancy, what about two? The baby growing inside of me might not be Guide's.

The Shadow World had ordered me to make love with him. Guide must have fathered my child. Unless our ancestors had plotted to obligate him, had sent the Guardians of the Portals to show they meant business.

No! Today the Virgin of Guadalupe's light had glowed through the Yokut shaman's skull for my sake. Great-Grandma had blessed Graham Locke. This baby would be beautiful and healthy. Juan would welcome us into his home. I'd earned that much. And Guide could be—probably was—the father. Even if he wasn't, the infant developing inside me was my new mission. This child of the houses Navarro, Jame, and Mendoza must be born.

King Solomon picked his way down the shallow gorge leading to the Gila. I teetered and gripped the pommel of the saddle, Guide's chest against my back. Whatever else happened, I mustn't fall. This mystic traveler girl prepared to live, not to die.

Guide wrapped one arm around my waist. I inhaled the aroma of his man sweat and smiled. Let new vulnerability happen. Guide would never want me to give away a baby, make the same mistake my own natural mother had. Wisdom, courage, and determination—all three dwelled within me. I pressed Guide's palm against my belly.

"You're one helluva good locomotive fireman," I said.

And we crossed the river together.

About the Author

Laurel Anne Hill grew up in San Francisco, California, with more dreams of adventure than good sense or money. Her close brushes with death, love of family, respect for honor and belief in a higher power continue to influence her writing and her life. Laurel is the author of the award-winning novel, *Heroes Arise*. Her published short stories and nonfiction pieces total forty. She continues to serve as a participant at many science fiction/fantasy conventions. She's the Literary Stage Manager for the annual San Mateo County Fair in California, a writing contest judge, and an editor for *Fault Zone*. Visit http://www.laurelannehill.com for more information.

If you enjoyed this book won't you please tell other readers about it on sites like Amazon, GoodReads and other places where readers and authors mingle?

SHRP
Sand Hill Review Press